I SPY

JACEY FORD

BERKLEY SENSATION, NEW YORK

THE BERKLEY PUBLISHING GROUP
Published by the Penguin Group
Penguin Group (USA) Inc.
375 Hudson Street, New York, New York 10014, USA
Penguin Group (Canada), 10 Alcorn Avenue, Toronto, Ontario M4V 3B2, Canada
(a division of Pearson Penguin Canada Inc.)
Penguin Books Ltd., 80 Strand, London WC2R 0RL, England
Penguin Group Ireland, 25 St. Stephen's Green, Dublin 2, Ireland (a division of Penguin Books Ltd.)
Penguin Group (Australia), 250 Camberwell Road, Camberwell, Victoria 3124, Australia
(a division of Pearson Australia Group Pty. Ltd.)
Penguin Books India Pvt. Ltd., 11 Community Centre, Panchsheel Park, New Delhi—110 017, India
Penguin Group (NZ), Cnr. Airborne and Rosedale Roads, Albany, Auckland 1310, New Zealand
(a division of Pearson New Zealand Ltd.)
Penguin Books (South Africa) (Pty.) Ltd., 24 Sturdee Avenue, Rosebank, Johannesburg 2196, South Africa

Penguin Books Ltd., Registered Offices: 80 Strand, London WC2R 0RL, England

This is a work of fiction. Names, characters, places, and incidents either are the product of the author's imagination or are used fictitiously, and any resemblance to actual persons, living or dead, business establishments, events, or locales is entirely coincidental.

I SPY

A Berkley Sensation Book / published by arrangement with the author

PRINTING HISTORY
Berkley Sensation edition / February 2005

Copyright © 2005 by Beverly Brandt.
Excerpt from *Dead Heat* copyright © 2005 by Beverly Brandt.
Excerpt from *Carved in Stone* copyright © 2005 by Vickie Spears.
Cover art by Mark Douet and Tony Stone/Getty Images.
Cover design by Erica Tricarico.
Interior text design by Kristin del Rosario.

All rights reserved.
No part of this book may be reproduced, scanned, or distributed in any printed or electronic form without permission. Please do not participate in or encourage electronic piracy of copyrighted materials in violation of the author's rights. Purchase only authorized editions.
For information address: The Berkley Publishing Group,
a division of Penguin Group (USA) Inc.,
375 Hudson Street, New York, New York 10014.

ISBN: 0-425-20112-0

BERKLEY® SENSATION
Berkley Sensation Books are published by The Berkley Publishing Group,
a division of Penguin Group (USA) Inc.,
375 Hudson Street, New York, New York 10014.
BERKLEY SENSATION and the "B" design are trademarks belonging to Penguin Group (USA) Inc.

PRINTED IN THE UNITED STATES OF AMERICA

10 9 8 7 6 5 4 3 2 1

If you purchased this book without a cover, you should be aware that this book is stolen property. It was reported as "unsold and destroyed" to the publisher, and neither the author nor the publisher has received any payment for this "stripped book."

To my wonderful editor, Cindy Hwang.
Here's to taking risks!
Next, let's try skydiving. It's much safer.

With special thanks to

Everyone at Berkley who works behind the scenes to transform our books from rough manuscripts to lovely paperbacks on the bookshelves—Susan McCarty, the copyeditor who so meticulously goes through every word I write, the production department, art, sales, marketing, and on and on. Thank you all!

Alesia Holliday, for all your insights . . . and your friendship.

Rocket scientist Dieter Zube (okay, that's not his official title, but it sure does sound cool, doesn't it?), for all the information about adjustable engine inlet geometry and high altitude cruise phase for reduced fuel consumption. In the end, I decided to make my missile a little less complicated than all that, and any errors are my own.

Fellow writer Diana Peterfreund, for sharing what you know about Australia. Again, any mistakes can be dropped at my door!

My sister, Kelley Price, for always seeming to know somebody who can answer my bizarre questions.

My father, Richard Price, for aerospace industry jargon. Guess those thirty-five years with Boeing really paid off, huh, Dad?

And while I'm at it, to my brother, Brian Price, who wanted me to say that without him I would never have become a writer so I owe him everything, but for starters I'll buy him a house. Yeah. Dream on, Hubey Baby.

Finally, to my husband, Wes. For funding this little adventure of mine . . . and for loving me. Talk about taking risks.

ONE

[As our] spies we must recruit men who are intelligent but appear stupid; who seem to be dull but are strong in heart; men who are agile, vigorous, hardy, and brave; well versed in lowly matters and able to endure hunger, cold, filth, and humiliation.

—SUN TZU, *The Art of War*

"WE'VE had a breakthrough on the propulsion system for the MC-19 fighter jet. Engineering is hopeful that we'll be able to step up production and get the aircraft to market a year before we anticipated. I don't think I have to tell you all that this could mean billions of dollars in increased revenue. The defense department's already told us that they'll buy as many MC-19s as we can produce. If we win this race to the market, we just might be able to put Rockton Aeronautical out of business."

Aimee Devlin sat in a corner of McConnell Aerospace's boardroom in San Antonio and transcribed the speech Joe McConnell was giving to his executive team. As her fingers moved almost silently across the keyboard of her laptop, she studied the six men and two women seated around the well-polished table. Her employer was convinced that one of these eight people was a spy, and he was paying Aimee a hefty sum to ferret out the traitor.

As the tiny clock at the bottom right hand of her screen rolled over to one o'clock, Aimee stifled a smile. Damn, but she loved billable hours. Getting out of the FBI—where she figured her hourly rate was about half of minimum wage, given the long hours she put in—was the best thing she'd ever done.

"I'm going to need details of the production process and what's involved in stepping up the rollout in order to make sure we have proper financing in place," Horace Gardner, McConnell's new chief financial officer, said.

Without turning her head, Aimee typed what the CFO had said into her Word document, then sent an instant message to her boss: *Too eager for information?*

She saw Joe's gaze flutter to the computer beside him before he looked back up and nodded almost imperceptibly. He was paying her to be suspicious, to note anything that struck her as odd. And their new CFO, who had joined McConnell just before Joe began to suspect that someone within his organization was engaged in corporate espionage, was number one on Aimee's watch list. Something about the man seemed off, though Aimee couldn't put her finger on exactly what it was that bothered her about him. There was just something that made the tiny hairs on the back of her neck prickle whenever he was in the same room.

Her background check hadn't turned up anything out of the ordinary, which Aimee thought must be the perfect word to describe Race Gardner: ordinary. He had medium-length brown hair, gray eyes hidden behind thick, wire-rimmed glasses, and an unremarkable physique concealed by the equally unremarkable blue suits he wore nearly every day. His résumé showed a steady rise in job responsibilities, from controller to VP of finance, and then to CFO. He hadn't job-hopped, but hadn't remained stagnant in one position for too long, either. He'd ranked in the top 20 percent of his class at Duke and had just-above-average SAT scores, but nothing that really made him stand out.

Aimee wondered if it was this utter blandness that had tempted him to sell McConnell's secrets to their top competitor. Perhaps he'd been wooed by the excitement of it—an element of danger in his otherwise dull life.

"Janine, give Race everything he needs," Joe said, waving a hand in the direction of his chief operating officer, who bobbed her head in agreement. Then Joe stood up, signaling an end to the meeting.

Aimee remained seated in the shadows as the executive

team filed out of the room. Joe made small talk with several people as they left, then stopped Race at the door and asked if he'd wait for a minute so they could talk. Aimee stayed motionless against the wall. Fading into the woodwork was her particular specialty, a skill she'd honed over the years to the point that even she was sometimes surprised by her ability to make herself invisible.

"How are this quarter's financials looking?" Joe asked when he and Race were seemingly alone.

Race sat back down at the mahogany table and set his yellow notepad in front of him. "Not so good," he replied. "Without the low-interest government loans that were available to us last year, our cost of borrowing has increased significantly at a time when our needs for funding are on the rise. Do you have a sense of whether Congress is going to approve another round of loans for the aerospace industry? Because, if not, we may be overreaching by trying to step up production of the MC-19. I know you don't want to hear this, but we may have to slow down this project."

"We can't do that. Getting our jet to the marketplace first is the only way we can beat Rockton and recoup our research and development costs on the MC-19. If we wait, that gives them more time to catch up."

"I understand that," Race said, his voice as bland and unemotional as the rest of him.

A vein in Joe's forehead began to throb as he slammed a fist down on the table, making Race's pad of paper jump. "You may understand, but do you care? I built McConnell Aerospace from nothing forty years ago. I'm not about to watch it self-destruct because you think it's bad timing. Now, it's your job to figure out how to keep us adequately funded. If you can't do that, I'll find somebody who will."

Race straightened his pad of paper until the bottom was perfectly aligned with the edge of the table. "I didn't say that I couldn't find creative, low-cost funding opportunities. I simply asked if you had any idea if Congress was going to come through with an aid package as they have in the past."

Watching him from the corner where she sat, Aimee had to admit that she was impressed by Race's ability to remain calm in the face of Joe's anger. Of course, if he *were* the spy, Joe's belligerent behavior would probably help Race to justify selling classified information to Rockton. Aimee was constantly amazed at how criminals managed to convince themselves that what they were doing was somehow warranted, as if the world owed them something for every slight.

"I don't know what Congress is going to do," Joe said with a frustrated sigh as he pulled out a chair and sat down across from the CFO. "Our lobbyists are doing the best they can, but with the economy being what it is, the Democrats are screaming for an end to corporate aid so that money can be diverted into welfare and day-care assistance programs and the like. I think we have to move ahead with the assumption that there will be no low-interest loans available to us from the government."

Race made a note on his pad of paper and nodded, then stood up to leave. "I'll put some ideas together so we can go over them at our meeting on Friday."

"All right," Joe said, not getting up as Race left.

When the door closed behind the CFO, Aimee felt a strange emptiness, as if all of the energy had left the room. *How odd.*

She set her laptop on the floor beside her and stood up to stretch. Remaining unnoticed for long periods of time often demanded that Aimee stay completely still, which wasn't as easy as one might think and caused her muscles to ache.

Joe swiveled in his chair, looking surprised. "Oh, Aimee, I forgot you were still here."

Aimee laughed. "Good. That means I'm doing my job."

Joe chuckled and stood up as Aimee bent to retrieve her computer. "Well," he said. "The trap's been set."

"Yes," Aimee agreed. "Now we just have to wait and see if our rat takes the bait."

"WE'RE going to have to step up our operation. They've had a major breakthrough on the propulsion system," Race said into his cell phone, looking around the sunny courtyard outside McConnell Aerospace headquarters to make certain no one was close enough to overhear his conversation. "Did you get a chance to check out the documents I sent on McConnell's new assistant?"

"Yes, and I found something you might be interested in," Jake Haven, Race's partner on this operation, said. "That diploma you sent is a fake, although it was a fairly good reproduction. Rogers University changed the design of their diplomas in 1992, the year after Ms. Devlin supposedly graduated. The diploma you gave me, with a 1991 graduation date, is the new design, which means that whoever forged the document was working off the wrong version."

Race rubbed his jaw and frowned. So it looked like his hunch about Aimee Devlin was correct. She was not who she appeared to be. "Did you find out anything else?"

"I still have more research to do, but the social security number you got from her personnel file is fake. It doesn't match the number I got after running her prints through the computer. I traced her real SSN to a bank account opened in Atlanta a year ago. She's made two five-figure deposits into that account in the past month. In cash."

"What kind of five figures are we talking about? Ten thousand?" It was difficult to believe that an executive assistant at a Fortune 100 company could make that kind of money, but Race had to admit that he wasn't exactly up on the latest pay scales for secretaries.

"No," Jake said. "More like thirty thousand. Man, if that's the going wage for support staff these days, we're in the wrong line of business."

"Yeah, being a spy ain't what it used to be," Race agreed dryly.

"So, did you get the surveillance equipment I left at the dead drop?" Jake asked.

"Yes." Their dead drop—a place where Jake could leave, or "drop" something at one time, only to have Race pick it up later, so the men never had to meet face-to-face and risk blowing their cover—was a hollowed-out tree trunk in the park where Race jogged every morning before work. "I'm going to plant a camera in Ms. Devlin's office tonight. As McConnell's assistant, she has access to classified information about the propulsion system—information I intend to uncover."

* * *

DURING her years at the Bureau, Aimee had learned to leave nothing to chance. She couldn't shadow Race Gardner twenty-four hours a day, so she was going to have to rely on technology to give her investigation an edge. She'd seen the lights go out in his office about an hour ago and had patiently waited to give him plenty of time to make a final trip to the men's room or stop to chat with one of his subordinates before leaving for the evening.

Clicking off the lights in her own office, Aimee set her briefcase down on the floor in the hall and turned to close and lock her door. Then she pulled a credit card out of her wallet and folded a small piece of Scotch tape over the edge, being careful to leave the ends loose. She slid the card through the crack between the door and its frame and quickly pulled it back out again. The tape stuck to the door and frame on the inside. If the door was opened, the tape would either break or would not adhere back to the door, and she'd be alerted that someone had broken in.

Satisfied with her handiwork, Aimee picked up her briefcase and headed down the hall to the deserted finance department. She checked all the cubicles surrounding Race's office to be certain that there were no other employees lurking about. Finding no one, she hauled a chair over from one of the cubes, withdrew a small round flashlight from her purse, got up on the chair, and shined the light into the crack between the door and the frame. She moved slowly, checking for a "trap" similar to the one she herself had just set. Even so, she nearly missed it.

There, just above the lock, was—of all things—a piece of Scotch tape stretched across the crack.

Aimee shook her head and chuckled wryly. She had thought her tape idea was so clever, but it seemed she wasn't the only one to have thought of using a standard office supply to booby-trap a door. She shrugged. Well, at least he'd chosen something she knew how to re-rig.

She dragged the chair back to its cubicle, smoothing out the telltale tracks in the carpet on her way back. Then she got out her key ring and used the master key Joe McConnell had given her to open Race's office door. The tape came free from the doorframe, and Aimee made a mental note of where Race had positioned it so she could put it back in exactly the same spot.

Taking a moment to let her eyes adjust to the darkness, Aimee looked around Race's office. It looked exactly the same as always—boring and impersonal. His bookshelf was stocked with such thrilling titles as *Fundamentals of Corporate Taxation, Strategies in Corporate Finance,* and *Investing Essentials Vol. 10*. There were no pictures of a wife and kids anywhere to be seen. He'd listed a woman as his emergency contact in the application that personnel made every employee fill out, but Aimee didn't know if she was a sister, a girlfriend, an ex-wife, or just a friend.

And it didn't really matter. She wasn't interested in dating the guy, she was interested in nailing him ... in the criminal justice sense, that is. Aimee certainly didn't think of drab, dull Horace Gardner in *that* way. Though only her closest friends knew it, Aimee possessed a wild streak and was attracted to guys who promised fun and excitement—preferably *wealthy* guys who promised fun and excitement. Her own ambition to make a fortune had led her to learn what she could from the FBI and then take that knowledge out to the business world, where companies were willing to pay dearly to stop illegal activities that impacted their bottom lines.

Her eyes now adjusted to the darkness, Aimee swiftly took a dime-sized listening device out of the pocket of her suit jacket and planted it in the one personal item in Race's office—a Zen garden complete with a minirake and several smooth stones. Aimee pushed the bug deep into the sand and smoothed the surface with her thumb. Then she pulled a piece of tape from his dispenser, removed the old piece from the door, and left his office, shutting the door behind her. She did her credit card trick again, leaving the tape right where she'd found it.

As she headed back toward the elevators that would take her down to the parking lot, Aimee felt a conflicting array of emotions. On the one hand, she was pleased to have discovered the source of McConnell's security leak so quickly. That would only reflect well on Partners In Crime, Inc., the corporate services firm she and her friends Daphne Donovan and

Raine Robey had started seven months ago. Still, it would have been nice to have the steady income that came with this job for a while longer. While Aimee didn't mind scouring the streets for new business, making cold calls didn't exactly pay well.

"Aimee, what a surprise. I didn't expect you to be working so late."

Startled, Aimee gasped. What the hell was Race Gardner doing here? And, even more importantly, had he just seen her come out of his office?

Aimee put a hand to her heart as if that would help slow her racing pulse. "You scared me," she said, eyeing the man across from her.

He smiled benignly, but for the first time Aimee noticed something in the gray eyes he hid behind those thick glasses. Something different. Something . . . dangerous.

A shiver ran through her body. "Someone walking over your grave," as her mother would say.

"Well, I'm going to call it a night," Aimee said, suddenly aware that she and Race were alone in the deserted building. Not that she wasn't confident in her ability to protect herself in most situations, but she wasn't foolish enough to dismiss the slight prickle of fear that raised goose bumps along her arms.

"Why don't you wait a second and I'll walk you to your car? I just need to get something out of my office." Race paused for a second, then added, "It's dangerous to be wandering around alone at this time of night."

Aimee forced herself not to shiver again at the slightly menacing tone of Race's voice. She swallowed, reminding herself that the guy was a harmless accountant. Even if he were stealing corporate secrets, it wasn't as if that made him capable of violence.

Did it?

"Oh, don't worry about me. I work late all the time. And I have pepper spray on my key chain," she bluffed. "Besides, it's not that late. It's only eight thirty."

Race studied her for a moment and Aimee was struck again by the niggling sense that she was missing something crucial in her analysis of Race Gardner. Finally, after what seemed like a long time but was probably only seconds, Race shrugged and started down the hall toward his office.

"Okay, then. I'll see you tomorrow," he said, tossing the words over his shoulder.

As she headed to the bank of elevators and pressed the call button, Aimee let out the breath she'd unconsciously been holding. It was only as the elevator doors slid closed that Aimee realized what was nagging at the back of her mind. When Race had startled her out in the hallway, he hadn't just emerged from the elevators. He'd been coming from the direction of her office.

TWO

"SHE'S accessing the plans for the propulsion system right now." Jake's words reverberated in Race's ear.

Damn it, he was going to be too late. He should have waited to sweep his office for bugs until the morning. Instead, after discovering Aimee heading toward him from the wrong direction, he'd used his surveillance detector to scan for listening devices or cameras. He couldn't believe she'd left a bug buried in the sand of his Zen garden. He had clearly underestimated the nondescript brunette who always seemed to be lurking in the shadows.

But what he really wanted to know was if she had figured out that he wasn't who he said he was.

His cover legend had been meticulously assembled, from college transcripts to SAT scores, a work history that could be verified by the IRS, and bank accounts under a false social security number. Still, it was possible that she had discovered his story wasn't true.

Race pulled the tan Honda he'd leased for the duration of this job into a space on the street about half a block from the front entrance to Aimee's apartment building. She was renting a third-floor walk-up in a redbrick building that looked as if it had once housed a wealthy family, but had since been chopped up into several small apartments. Race could see a light on in one of the rooms in the front of the top-floor apartment and guessed that it must be Aimee's living room or kitchen, since her bedroom would most likely be located in the back, away from the busy street.

She passed in front of the window just then, her body backlit by the lights from the room behind her. She had removed her suit jacket, but it looked as if she still had on the blouse she'd been wearing at the office that day. Her hair, which had been up in one of those twisty hairdos women were wearing nowadays, was down around her shoulders. Race didn't think he'd ever seen her with her hair down and was surprised to see that it was longer than he'd imagined.

"All right, I've got a visual on her, and it appears that she's alone. Are you monitoring her data transmissions?" Race asked.

"Yep, I've got her. If she attempts to e-mail the propulsion system plans to anyone, we'll put an immediate trace on the recipient," Jake said.

"What I want to know is why she has clearance to access those plans. She's a damn secretary, for chrissakes."

"And why is she looking at them now?" Jake added, voicing his own concerns.

"My guess is that she set up a meeting with her contact when she found out that McConnell's engineering team had a breakthrough. Why else would she take the chance of being discovered now?" Race said.

"Maybe she's just getting cocky," Jake suggested.

"Could be," Race agreed, then turned his head when he heard a car door slam. "Wait a second, something's happening. A pizza deliveryman just parked on the street and is heading toward the apartment building. This could be our buyer."

"I don't have audio yet. Can you tell if he's trying to gain access to her apartment?"

Race pulled a set of high-powered binoculars out from under the passenger seat and trained them on the pizza deliveryman, who was wearing a baseball cap, blue jeans, and a short-sleeved white shirt with "Papa Ralph's Pizza" stenciled on the back. The guy juggled a cardboard box in one hand while reaching out with the other to press one of the buzzers set into the brick front of the building.

"Move out of the way," Race muttered, cursing the man for blocking his view with the pizza box he was carrying.

A movement from the third-floor window caught his eye and Race jerked the binoculars up to see what was going on. The binoculars were so powerful that he could almost count the eyelashes surrounding Aimee's suddenly exotic-looking brown eyes. He supposed he'd never looked at her this closely before. Frankly, prior to today, he had hardly even noticed her, much less taken the time to really study her. Now, as she came to the window and looked down at the street—most likely to check out her visitor before buzzing him in—Race vowed not to underestimate her again.

If the deliveryman was her buyer, his cover was perfect. The money for the top-secret plans was most likely already hidden in the pizza box, and he could smuggle the plans back out of the apartment building in the thermal bag supposedly keeping the pizza warm on its way from his car to Aimee's apartment.

"I'm going in. Maintain radio silence until I give the word," Race said into the tiny microphone planted on his lapel. The earpiece in his ear hummed directly into his brain, the faint buzzing interrupted only when Jake said, "Got you."

Race waited until Aimee had stepped back from the window before quietly popping open the door of the Honda and slipping out of the car. As he crept stealthily toward the side of the building, he saw the pizza deliveryman pull open the front door leading into the lobby. Race had already determined that there was no elevator in the building, so he figured he had the advantage of his own athletic ability on his side. He wasn't even breathing hard after climbing up the fire escape to reach Aimee's apartment. The rubber soles of his boots barely made a sound on the metal grate as he pulled himself up onto her balcony and crouched down below what he presumed to be her bedroom window.

A quick survey of the room verified his guess. Now, if only he could be so lucky as to find the window unlocked . . .

Race put his thumbs under the wooden slat that divided the window in half horizontally and pushed upward, but it didn't budge. He saw a shadow cross the hallway and ducked down below the window again, pressing his back to the warm bricks just in case she'd caught a glimpse of movement.

He concentrated on keeping his breathing slow and even while his mind raced. He had to hurry. It was imperative that they find out whom Aimee was selling McConnell's secret plans to.

Hoping that the window was merely stuck, Race stood up and pushed on it again, but it wouldn't move. He looked for another means of entry and saw a smaller window higher up and to the left. Most likely it was a bathroom window, slid partway open to let in some fresh air. He'd have to stand up on the metal railing of the balcony to squeeze through, but it looked to be his only chance.

Balancing on the rail like a gymnast on a balance beam, Race put his palms on the bathroom windowsill and peered in. She had all sorts of girly stuff on the windowsill—shampoo and creams and a disposable razor. Race couldn't just shove it all into the bathtub because the noise would alert Aimee to an intruder. Carefully and quietly, he gathered up the tubes and bottles and set them on the balcony. As he hopped back up on the railing, the razor fell through the grate, noisily clattering down the fire escape, and finally hitting the concrete three stories below.

Race cocked his head and listened intently to see if Aimee had noticed the noise. He heard muffled voices inside the apartment, but couldn't make out any words. After several seconds, when the voices didn't get any louder, Race knew he had to go in.

Pulling himself through the window was easy. It was landing on the other side without making any noise that was hard.

The bathtub below him was one of those old porcelain models with the claw feet that some people—women mostly—seemed to think were charming. Race much preferred modern Jacuzzi tubs that could easily accommodate two people on a cold night. He slid down until he was hanging by just the tips of his boots, clinging to the windowsill outside. Putting his hands on either side of the tub, Race braced himself and slowly inched forward, hand over hand, letting his feet come forward until he was literally walking down the wall.

Finally, his feet were on solid ground again and he straightened up before stealing out of the bathroom and into the darkened bedroom beyond. He made certain he wasn't casting a shadow out into the other room as he inched along the hallway to better hear what was being said . . . and to get a look at the man who very well could be the elusive buyer he and Jake were hunting.

"Twenty-four ninety-nine?" he heard Aimee say, and wondered if she were naming her price for the latest top-secret information she had stolen. She was obviously new to this game. Twenty-five thousand dollars was cheap for the plans for an innovative new propulsion system that made it possible for a jet to circle the globe in less than ninety minutes. On the open market, something like that would go for millions.

"Yeah. Tip's not included," the pizza deliveryman said.

Race craned his neck to see beyond the wall blocking his view, then jerked back when he realized that Aimee was walking toward him. Shit. Two more seconds and she'd be staring straight at him. He stumbled back into the bedroom and dove into the walk-in closet beside her bed, cursing himself for cutting off his own escape route since the bathroom was on the other side of the room.

Aimee walked into the bedroom and Race flattened himself against the row of neatly hung clothes behind him. Plastic hangers dug into his shoulder blades as he burrowed even deeper into the closet. He heard Aimee rummaging around, heard the clink of coins, and then the sound of her retreating feet. When he looked through the opened closet doors, she and the deliveryman were framed in the hallway. Race saw Aimee hand the guy some bills and then watched as the kid—who couldn't have been more than sixteen years old—left the apartment.

So . . . it looked like his hunch was wrong. She really was just ordering a pizza for a late-night supper.

Race pressed himself back again when Aimee spun around and headed back toward the bedroom. Damn. Now what was he going to do? She'd see him for sure if he tried to make it to the bathroom, and she was blocking his way to the front door.

For now, it looked like he was trapped.

Aimee came into the room, raised her arms above her

head, and stretched, her movements graceful and catlike. Race closed his eyes, but then opened them again when he heard the sound of something landing on the bed. She was close enough that Race could see everything as she slipped off her panty hose and tossed them beside the gray skirt lying on top of her red-and-gold patterned bedspread.

Race blinked. Wow. How could he have missed noticing that she had such incredible legs?

He swallowed as her hands went to the front of her blouse. The silky fabric parted, revealing two shapely breasts held in check by a dove gray bra. When she shucked off her blouse and turned away from him, Race felt as if someone were tightening his hands around his neck, choking off his oxygen supply.

She had a tattoo of the Tasmanian Devil right at the spot where her lower back met her buttocks, easily visible above the lacy gray panties she wore. Jeez, he had not been expecting that. Of course, he hadn't expected this mousy wallflower to be engaged in corporate espionage, either.

To his dismay, she started toward the closet. If she saw him, his cover would be blown.

Silently, Race slipped a dark T-shirt off one of the hangers near his right hand. He waited until she was so close that he could smell the last faint traces of the perfume she'd put on that morning. And then he struck.

Holding the T-shirt up to hide his face, he leaped out of the closet. Aimee let out a startled gasp as he covered her head with the shirt, holding the ends together tightly with one fist. All he wanted to do was to put her out of action long enough for him to escape the apartment. Race figured it would only take a few seconds to push her in the bathroom and rig the door. After all, she was a secretary, not a trained fighter like he was.

When she slammed her heel down on the instep of his left foot, Race realized that he had once again underestimated her. She obviously knew a thing or two about self-defense.

Although he suspected that she was a spy, he really wasn't into beating up women, so he did his best to subdue her without hurting her. Besides, at this point she was just a suspect. If it turned out she wasn't a traitor . . . Well, he didn't have time to think about that now, not with her busy trying to gouge out his eyes.

He grabbed one of her wrists with his free hand in an attempt to get her to stop clawing at him, then shoved her hastily away when he saw her raise her leg to knee him in the groin. Since he had to keep one hand clutching the shirt around her head, he was at somewhat of a disadvantage here. He pushed her backward toward the bathroom door, and accidentally ran her into the sharp corner of her dresser.

"Ow," she yelped.

Despite himself, he felt guilty for hurting her, and for just a second, Race loosened his grasp of her wrist.

Aimee felt her attacker's grip on her arm go slack and lashed out with her clenched fist.

"Oof," he gasped when her blow connected with his solar plexus.

He pushed her back again, and she knocked over several bottles and knickknacks on her dresser, her fingers busily searching for the gun she kept hidden under a brightly colored scarf.

She felt the cool barrel under the thin fabric and her fingers closed over the handle. In one smooth movement, she pulled it up and pressed the barrel to her attacker's chest. But before she could squeeze the trigger, he slammed her back against the wall. Her head felt like a basketball that had just hit the backboard and dropped in for a two-pointer. For the first time in her life, Aimee knew what was meant by the term "seeing stars." She did her best to not lose her grip on the gun, but it wasn't easy with her attacker tightening his hold on her wrist until she was sure he would snap it right off.

Damn, he was strong.

She writhed against him, pushing with her hips to get him to back away. He kept her pinned to the wall, his heavy thighs trapping her and making it difficult to move. It took her a moment to realize that he had gone still, his chest heaving against hers. She could hear the faint sound of someone talking, like a radio that had been left on in another room.

"What do you mean she's FBI?" she heard her attacker say, and suddenly, she recognized his voice.

"Gardner? Get off me," she ordered, starting to struggle against him again.

He dropped the T-shirt from around her face and Aimee found herself staring at his Adam's apple. He didn't step back, though, keeping her pinned to the wall with his body. Aimee pushed against him, but he seemed distracted and didn't move. She couldn't see his face since he was looking to the right, toward the open door of her bedroom and the hallway beyond, muttering an occasional "Hmm" or "Uh-huh," seemingly to no one.

Finally, he turned back to face her. "You're FBI," he said, not asking a question.

"No, but I used to be," Aimee answered. "So what? I was the assistant to the assistant of the guy who ran the Miami office. I decided that being an executive secretary would pay better."

"You're not an executive assistant, and you weren't just some clerk in the typing pool. You were a special agent. You got out of the Bureau a year ago, and now you're a partner in a corporate services firm called Partners In Crime, headquartered in Atlanta. You've been hired by Joe McConnell to find out which of his employees is selling classified information to his chief competitor."

"That's crazy. I'm just a secretary." Aimee pressed her chest against Race's, trying to get him to step back. He still held her left wrist above her head, the gun clutched in her hand.

Race brought his free hand up and slammed his palm against the wall next to her ear, making her flinch. It occurred to her then that if Race Gardner was the spy she was pursuing, she was in big trouble. He would have to kill her. There was no way he could explain away his presence in her apartment. He'd be fired and his source of additional income would dry up, not to mention the fact that he'd be lucky to escape without charges being filed against him.

No, he had no reason *not* to kill her.

Aimee took a deep breath, her breasts brushing against the polo shirt he wore over his hard, muscled chest. She had never suspected he was hiding such a powerful body underneath those shapeless blue suits.

Putting all of her weight on the balls of her feet, she shoved with all her might.

Race stumbled just a bit and Aimee felt the first stirring of hope that she could get herself free. That is, until he stopped her with a hand around her throat.

Aimee closed her eyes, trying to come up with an escape plan.

"I'm with the CIA," Race announced. "I've been sent here because we believe a McConnell Aerospace employee is selling top-secret information—not to Rockton Aeronautical, but to hostile interests abroad. My job is to find not only the mole inside McConnell, but the buyer as well. This isn't just a case of unfair competition, it could well be a matter of national security."

Aimee opened her eyes again, blinking rapidly as she tried to take in Race's story. "And you thought I was the spy?" she asked.

Race nodded, contemplating her coolly, that hint of danger back in the depths of his eyes.

Aimee shivered and chewed on her bottom lip. "I'm not," she said, her voice quiet in the still bedroom.

Race's fingertips brushed the side of her neck as he withdrew his hand. "Yes. I know that now."

She was finding it difficult to breathe with him so close. Aimee raised her head, their gazes locked as they stood there, toe to toe and hip to hip. Her lips parted and she saw his eyes darken.

"Good," she said, trying to keep her voice even. "Then would you mind letting me go? Your hard-on is jabbing me in the stomach, and I think it would be better if we continued this discussion once I'm dressed."

THREE

NICKY Rodriguez huddled silently behind a sodden cardboard box that had once been used to transport lettuce. Nicky knew this because just moments before, he'd spotted a limp leaf clinging to the box and headed toward it. Fresh—or simply not rotten—vegetables were a delicacy not often seen where Nicky lived, and he was determined to have the prize for himself. Only, as he neared the box, he heard the telltale scritching of another bent on stealing his prize from him. Nicky was not going to let it go without a fight.

He never let anything go without a fight, which was most likely how he'd managed to survive to the age of twelve.

Rubbing the pad of his thumb over the dull blade in his hand, Nicky shifted his weight onto the balls of his bare feet and prepared to make his move. With one swift movement, he tugged the cardboard toward him and plunged his knife into the squirming body that had fallen off balance in the bottom of the box. Had it been another child, his blade would have most likely severed the jugular. Instead, it pinned the head of a well-fed rat to the box. The animal's tail lashed out violently, as if by doing so, it could free itself from Nicky's hold. Its two front teeth, yellowed and sharp, protruded over its bottom lip, and

Nicky knew that if he let it up before it died, it would delight in sinking those teeth into his flesh. But Nicky had no intention of letting the rat live. He was hungry, and tired of eating food that had been left out too long in the hot Caracas sunshine. By the time the garbage of the city's wealthy made it to the trash heap where Nicky made his home, it was half-rotted and mixed with dirty diapers, poisonous household cleansers, broken glass, and the ever-present cockroaches that made their way into people's trash. To Nicky, this rat was a welcome treat.

The animal's tensed muscles relaxed as it took its last breath, but Nicky left his knife embedded in its brain as he reached out to pluck the lettuce leaf from the side of the box. Greedily, he stuffed it into his mouth and chewed. Even wilted, it tasted like heaven, with a slight crunch at the base of the leaf where some moisture still remained.

Nicky closed his eyes and continued chewing, trying to get every second of satisfaction he could out of the unaccustomed treat. When he opened his eyes again, he spotted two of the older boys who also lived at the trash heap heading toward him. If he didn't move quickly, they'd discover his kill and try to take it from him.

Nicky snorted. *Try, hell.* They *would* take it from him. He could tackle them individually, but when José and Manuel ganged up on him, there was no way he could beat them.

Dislodging his knife from the rat's head, Nicky grabbed the animal by its hind legs. Without pausing to reflect on how life at the trash heap was a constant battle for survival, Nicky turned and ran. The rat's tail thumped against his side as he bounded over an upturned chair, one of its legs ending in a jagged break. He could hear José and Manuel behind him, their bare feet slipping as his own did on slimy waste and slippery trash bags that had been ripped open by scavengers— crows, rats, and the children who eked out their existence here.

Uncaring about his tattered clothing, which already smelled like the trash heap, Nicky lowered his rear to the garbage and slid down the side of the giant pile. He had burrowed into one of the smaller, lesser-used heaps and made a home of sorts. It beat sleeping out in the open, leaving yourself vulnerable to attack. Nicky had known several boys who died because they were too afraid of being smothered to tunnel into the trash piles. He thought they were stupid. Better to take your chances with the garbage than with boys like José and Manuel, who used the smaller children as human targets to hone their fighting skills. Or worse.

Nicky kept a tight hold on his dinner as his feet hit the hot earth. He headed toward the maze of smaller trash piles, where, in seconds, he'd be safely tucked away in his tunnel. He'd rigged it so that he could quickly fill the entrance of his makeshift home, making it so that he could hide himself whenever the need arose.

Rounding one of the trash heaps that littered the dump, Nicky dove headfirst into what appeared to be a solid stack of garbage. The scrap of brightly colored fabric he'd used to mark the entrance of his tunnel rippled a little in the breeze. Nicky scooted farther into the tunnel, ignoring the smell and oppressive heat that crushed in on his chest, threatening to suffocate him. When he'd built his first tunnel, it had taken him months to burrow deeper than a few feet into the stinking pile of garbage. The fear of being crushed alive, of being smothered to death, was too great. It had taken the murder of his best friend, Jorge, to make Nicky conquer his fear. Jorge, too, was afraid to dig too far into the trash heaps. Only, one night, a gang of boys a few years older than Nicky and Jorge had found a case of discarded tequila in the load of garbage brought in that day. The boys had gotten louder and meaner as the liquor ran through them. Nicky had urged Jorge to hide, to dig a new tunnel where the other boys wouldn't find him, and to dig it deep so that they would be afraid to come in after him. But Jorge couldn't do it, couldn't stand going in so far that he couldn't smell the relatively fresh air from the outside.

Nicky had burrowed as deep into the pile as he could stand. He remembered lying there, the sweat dripping off him as he tried to control his panic, the humidity so heavy it took all his energy to draw air into his lungs. Outside, he could hear the other boys screaming and howling like wild animals. When the panic got so bad he could hardly stand it, he crept up to the opening of his tunnel, pushed aside a thin sheet of tin he'd used to cover the entrance, and sucked in huge gulps of air. Then he crept back again, afraid to remain where the other boys could reach him.

After hours of this, Nicky finally fell into a light sleep, his dark hair matted to his scalp and his breathing shallow. He awoke suddenly, wondering what it was that had jerked him into consciousness. When he heard a boy scream, he thought at first that it was one of the older boys again, acting crazy from all the tequila he had drunk. He heard the scream again, only this time he knew it was not the drunken cry of one of the revelers.

Cautiously, Nicky inched his way toward the entrance of his tunnel, telling himself that no matter what was happening out there, he had to stay there, where he was safe. Too often, he'd seen one of the children attempt to save another, only to be killed. Out here on the trash pile, the only person you could save was yourself.

Nicky stopped well back from the tunnel's entrance and closed his eyes, taking a deep breath. He heard a low voice, pleading for help, begging the other boys to stop. It was Jorge. They must have pulled him out of his hole. Nicky didn't need to see outside to know what was being done to his friend. First, the boys would rape him, laughing as they tore Jorge's tender skin, uncaring about his pain. Then they would beat him, their fists and heels crushing the younger boy's fingers, breaking his ribs. If Jorge was lucky, they would tire of their fun or pass out before too long. If not, they'd keep at it until they killed him.

In the trash pile, one more dead child made no difference. Nobody cared.

Nicky felt the tears well up in his eyes and swiped them away viciously with the back of his hand. Stupid fucking Jorge. This was what he got for being such a girl, such a chicken. And Nicky was a fool for befriending someone so weak. He would not make that mistake again.

If Jorge died . . . well, it was no less than he deserved.

Nicky squeezed his eyes shut and clamped his hands over his ears to drown out the sound of Jorge's pleas. As he scooted away, as far from the violence outside as he could get, Jorge's voice grew fainter and fainter. Long after the night had become silent, Nicky stayed where he was, huddled deep inside the safety of his tunnel. It was only as the first pink rays of dawn touched the garbage dump that he crept outside to see what had become of his friend.

One of the older boys muttered something and grunted as Nicky emerged into the weak morning sunlight. Nicky stopped, frozen, waiting for a hand to clamp around his ankle. When the boy just rolled over onto his side, Nicky tiptoed past.

Jorge had been easy to find. Nicky simply followed the trail of blood to find his friend's naked body dumped among the discarded bottles of Dos Equis, rotted banana peels, and dirty diapers. Jorge's eyes stared at him accusingly, the whites surrounding the dark irises turned red from burst blood vessels. His friend's neck was twisted at an impossible angle and there was blood between his legs. Nicky felt the urge to do something, as if by cleaning him up or putting his clothes back on, he could bring Jorge back to life.

He felt that pressure behind his eyes again and dug his fists into his eye sockets. He should have known better than to care for someone else. He'd seen enough death in his short life to have learned his lesson—caring about another person just opened you up to more pain.

Nicky turned away then, turning his back on the only friend he'd ever known. He'd never feared the close confines of his tunnel ever again. Instead of feeling oppressive, the walls closed around him like a mother's arms, trying to keep her child safe.

Now, as Nicky heard José and Manuel outside, cursing him, frustrated that he had seemingly disappeared into thin air, Nicky burrowed deeper into the trash pile, sliding the rat in front of him as he went.

He remembered the satisfaction he'd felt later that night, knowing he had outsmarted his enemies. As he plunged his knife into the heart of his trophy, he had smiled. And as he took his first bite of the untainted meat, he'd savored it. Tonight, he would go to sleep with a full stomach because of his own strength and cunning.

It was a lesson Nicky Rodriquez would never forget.

"UGH, Daddy. That's gross. How can you eat your meat so rare?"

Nic Sabre lowered his fork and knife to the white linen tablecloth and smiled at the look on his daughter's face, her small, upturned nose crinkled with distaste. Nic knew he was biased, but he thought that Josie was the most beautiful girl he had ever seen. Her skin was a light brown, the color of the richest, softest lambskin. Her hair was a deep mahogany tinged with auburn highlights that caught the fire from the sun. She had inherited her father's dark, nearly black eyes. Whenever people commented on their heritage, Nic smoothly lied that his parents were natives of French Polynesia. Claiming to be Polynesian was much more glamorous than the truth—that Nic and his daughter were 100 percent Venezuelan.

When Nic had left South America twelve years ago, he had abandoned Nicky Rodriquez. In his place, Nic Sabre had been born. Nic had taken the gun-running skills Nicky Rodriguez had learned and expanded into global arms dealing when his transformation was complete.

If it were up to him—and it was—Josie would never know the truth about her father's heritage. She would also never know anything about her mother except for what Nic had told her—none of which was true.

"I like my meat rare, Josie. Most connoisseurs of exceptional food do. This is something you're going to have to learn. We wouldn't want potential suitors to think you are crass because you like your filet mignon well done, now do we?"

Josie rolled her eyes heavenward. "Gross, Dad. I don't even like boys. Why should I care what they think about what I eat?"

Nic smiled indulgently at his daughter, who, at nearly thirteen, wouldn't admit to even the most minor of crushes. Which was just fine with Nic. He would keep Josie with him for the rest of his life if he could. He had never thought it would be possible to love anyone with the fierceness that he felt for his daughter. Someone once likened having children to watching your heart walk around outside of your body. Nic thought that was a fairly accurate description of how he felt about his daughter.

He took another bite of his steak—rare, just as he liked it. "I have a business meeting tomorrow evening. Will you be spending the night with Giselle?"

Josie crinkled her nose again and forked a bite of the strawberry-stuffed French toast the chef made especially for her into her mouth. "No. Gi and I are not speaking."

"Again?" Nic raised his eyebrows and smothered a laugh. Josie and her best friend, Giselle, fought like two alley cats, but always made up within hours. Nic often wondered if this was what it would be like to have siblings, but he'd never had any interest in giving Josie a little brother or sister to find out. He wasn't certain he could love another child the way he loved Josie and didn't feel it would be fair to test out his theory on a child.

Having been unwanted and unloved himself, this was not something he'd ever put another child through.

"Why can't I just stay here?" Josie asked, a tinge of whiny preteen in her voice.

Nic frowned as he set his silverware down again and wiped his lips with a monogrammed napkin. "Josephine, I will not tolerate temper tantrums. You know when I do business it requires my full concentration. I can't work while you're upstairs playing your music so loud that the chandeliers rattle. If you don't wish to stay at Giselle's house, then I will arrange for Mrs. Jacobs to take you tomorrow evening."

It was Josie's turn to frown, though she hid it quickly, looking down at her plate of half-eaten food as she did. She sighed loudly, dramatically, as only a twelve-year-old could do. "Okay, Daddy. I understand. I'll call Giselle after breakfast."

Nic nodded approvingly. "That's my girl," he said. Then, suddenly feeling as if Josie needed his reassurance, he reached out and lightly squeezed her arm. "You know you always come first with me, don't you?"

Josie pushed a strawberry around her plate with a fork. "Yes, Daddy."

Sliding his hand under his daughter's chin, Nic nudged her face up so he could see into her dark eyes. It was like looking into a mirror, her eyes so black that nothing, no emotion, could be read in them. Nic was glad for that. Letting your enemies see what was in your heart made one vulnerable.

"I mean it. My business, my money, it's all for you. I am going to make it so that you never want for anything. Not money, not love. Nothing."

Josie lowered her thick, dark eyelashes. When she looked at him again, a smile was tugging at the corners of her mouth. "Daddy, you're crazy."

Nic smiled, too, at the game they'd played since Josie had been old enough to talk. "Yes. Crazy about you," he said, giving her chin one last squeeze before picking up his fork once more and tearing in to the bloody, still-warm meat on his plate.

FOUR

"SO, what blew my cover?" Aimee asked, dragging a slice of lukewarm pizza from the cardboard box onto one of the paper plates she'd bought at the grocery store the other day. She hadn't expected to do any entertaining here in San Antonio, so paper plates and plastic utensils were all she had to work with in the culinary department. No use wasting money making this apartment feel like home when she'd be back in Atlanta in a month or two, at the latest.

Race eyed the leftover pizza as if debating whether to have another piece, but in the end, he turned and walked over to the couch that Aimee had rented for the duration of her stay in Texas. The furnished apartments she had looked at before deciding on this unfurnished one all seemed to have a strange smell, as if each renter before her had left his unique odor buried deep within the fabric of the place. This rental furniture didn't exactly suit her taste, but at least it had arrived thoroughly cleaned and odor-free.

"Your diploma," Race answered as he sat down on the sturdy green couch that dominated the small apartment's living room. "Rogers University changed the layout the year after you supposedly graduated, but yours used the new design."

Aimee grimaced and mentally berated herself for making such a stupid mistake. As she well knew, an error like this could cost her her life. Building an impeccable cover legend—including all the necessary documentation—was the key to running a smooth undercover operation. "It's always the little things that trip you up," she said aloud, tossing her paper plate and half-eaten slice of pizza into the trash with disgust.

"Admittedly, though, I would never have been able to discover your true identity without having access to the FBI's classified personnel records," Race said, as if that would placate her.

Aimee stalked over to the black leather chair she'd positioned at a right angle to the couch and plopped down in it, drumming her fingers impatiently on the arms. "I have to assume that our traitor has the same resources at his fingertips as you do. It was a foolish mistake on my part, one I intend to rectify first thing tomorrow. I can't give anyone reason to question my story. If they look past the surface or dig deeper into my background, my cover will be blown."

She drummed her fingers one last time on the cool black leather, then stopped. It was no use beating herself up about this anymore. There was only so much she could do to cover her tracks. Unless she could somehow convince the government to erase her fingerprints from their database, she was always going to have to take extra precautions to ensure that her documentation was flawless. Another mistake like the one she'd made with her diploma and she could wind up dead.

"So, why is the CIA involved in this case?" Aimee asked, crossing her legs and watching Race watch her. "Corporate espionage isn't usually you guys' sort of thing."

Race cleared his throat and deliberately looked away from her bare legs—a move that Aimee found amusing. After he'd discovered that she was a former FBI agent and was working for Joe McConnell, he'd released her, but not before Aimee discovered that their struggle had affected him in more ways than one. He'd left her alone in her bedroom, where she'd changed into a pair of black shorts and an oversized gray T-shirt. Aimee was still finding it hard to believe that the hunky guy in worn blue jeans sitting across from her was the same man she had thought was a bland geek less than two hours before. She imagined that Race was feeling pretty much the same way about her.

"We don't think McConnell's spy is selling secrets to Rockton. We suspect his buyer is someone else entirely."

"Oh?" Aimee asked, leaning forward and clasping her hands between her knees.

"Yes. We're afraid the plans for the new propulsion system might end up in the hands of a foreign government—one directly in opposition with the interests of the United States. Just think of what might happen if any rogue nation in the world could launch fighter jets that are able to travel around the globe in an hour and a half."

Aimee reached up and twisted her hair into a makeshift ponytail as she studied the tan carpet beneath her feet. "That would be terrible."

"Exactly," Race agreed. "By the time we realized they were heading into our airspace, we'd be scrambling to mount our defense. Right now, we'd know hours in advance if an attack was on the way. But if we only had minutes to prepare . . ." Race shrugged as he let his voice trail off.

The thought of what could happen under such circumstances was so chilling that Aimee shivered. She could imagine the widespread terror and chaos a scenario such as the one Race had just described would create. What if every petty dictator or terrorist with an ax to grind had such power at his fingertips? No country would be safe from sudden, unprovoked attack. As melodramatic as it sounded, life as they knew it would be over.

Aimee swallowed and raised her gaze to Race's. Like her, he now sat, leaning forward, with his hands clasped between his knees. "What makes you think the plans aren't staying within the U.S. aerospace industry?" she asked, hoping he'd say this investigation was just a precaution.

Race studied her silently for a moment, then looked away again. With a shrug, he said, "We've heard rumors," and Aimee knew that meant someone somewhere had talked, and the CIA felt that whoever that someone was, he or she was credible enough to take seriously.

She closed her eyes, then took a deep breath and let it out

again. This was it, the exact root of her problem. Her "I can save the world" attitude was what had prompted her to go to work for the FBI and, if she let it, was going to lead her down the path to self-destruction now, too. She could *not* save the world. Her decade-plus career in the Bureau had taught her that. Yes, she might have stopped a few crimes here and there, but it had come at great personal sacrifice. Here she was, on the downward slope to forty, with nothing to show for all her years of hard work aside from a small house in Atlanta, a modest stock portfolio, and dreams of bigger things on the horizon. She was not going to let Race Gardner and his farfetched tales of global destruction suck her back into a life she didn't want.

The leather beneath her creaked as she leaned back and rested her head on the chair. "I was only hired by McConnell to discover the identity of the mole within their organization. I'm happy to cooperate with the CIA, but my job ends when I find out who the traitor is."

"Don't you care that if these plans fall into the wrong hands, it could threaten the safety of our country?" Race asked, disapproval deepening his voice.

Aimee watched him, her gaze even and steady. "I care about what I get paid to care about. In this case, I'm being compensated to stop McConnell's secrets from being leaked to a competitor. If the U.S. government wants my help beyond that, I'm happy to do so." She paused, not taking her eyes off of Race as she added, "For a price."

A muscle in his jaw tightened, indicating that her answer had annoyed him.

So what if he's annoyed, Aimee thought. She had given over ten years of her life to U.S. government service for very little reward. She'd done her time. Now was her chance to get rich, and she planned to make the most of it. Working for the CIA—for free—didn't exactly fit in with her new financial plan.

Race's eyes narrowed on her but Aimee refused to look away. Let him try to save the world if he wanted to. That was his choice. She was done playing Superman.

Finally, he sat back and shrugged, as if to say she wasn't worth the aggravation. "All right. But I expect—"

A loud bell went off, interrupting whatever it was he was about to say. Aimee grabbed her laptop from the coffee table and opened the lid. A string of what looked at first to be gibberish rolled across her screen, much like the ticker tape that ran at the top of CNN's programming listing up-to-the-minute news or New York Stock Exchange data.

"What's going on?" Race asked, just before the wire in his ear buzzed to life.

"Mmm," Aimee answered, intently studying the information scrolling across her computer.

"Gardner?" Jake Haven's voice sounded in his ear. "You there?"

"Yes. What's up?" Race asked, getting up off the couch and moving into the kitchen.

"The tracer we installed on the propulsion system file just went off. Someone's accessing the plans."

Race glanced briefly at Aimee, hunched over her now-silent laptop. Not being one to believe in coincidences, he had to assume that Aimee had installed her own trace on the plan file and that she was, at this moment, accessing the same information Race himself was about to receive.

"Do you know who it is?" he asked, turning to look out the kitchen window at the still-busy street in front of Aimee's building.

"User name says ronjeff. You know who that is or should I go look it up?" his partner asked.

"No need. That's Ron Jefferson, the head of IT."

"He has access to the entire network, as well as the expertise to crack the passwords of files that are password-protected by specific users," Aimee said from behind him.

Race turned to see her leaning against the door frame, her arms wrapped around her waist, making the fabric of her tent-sized T-shirt bunch up under her breasts. He nodded, then spoke loudly enough for both her and Jake to hear him. "Yes, and there's no legitimate business reason that he should be accessing those plans."

"Hold on, I'm looking up his address right now," Jake said.

But before Race could answer, Aimee had unfolded herself from the door frame and reached out to grab her car keys off the kitchen counter. "Come on," she said, tossing the words over her shoulder as she headed toward the front door. "We've got a traitor to catch."

"NICE car," Race remarked as they sped down highway 281 toward Ron Jefferson's house in the suburbs north of San Antonio.

With the top down on her new BMW convertible and the air conditioner set at seventy, the early July heat was bearable. Of course, it helped that it was nearing midnight and the relentless sun had set hours ago. During midday, even her air conditioner blowing at full blast wasn't enough to keep her cool with the top down so she was sometimes forced to put it up. Fortunately, Atlanta wasn't quite as hot in the summer as San Antonio, so her convertible wasn't as impractical at home as it was here.

Besides, there were some areas in life where practical was the wrong answer. In Aimee's opinion, personal transportation was one of those areas. She could put up with boxy gray suits and wearing her hair tucked neatly into an impeccable twist, but one thing she'd decided she'd never do again would be to drive a boring car.

It was almost obscene how much she loved her baby—a mystic blue 330 ci convertible with soft gray leather seats and a dark blue top. Even better than how it looked, though, was how it performed. The engine slipped into its rhythm at eighty-five and glided on air at a hundred.

Aimee slid her hands down the steering wheel and did her best to stifle a self-satisfied grin. God, she loved this car. If only there were someplace she could really open it up and see what it could do.

That's the problem, she thought. *America needs Autobahns.*

She exited the highway and accelerated into a curve and felt the solid weight of the car take the turn like a cheetah doubling back for its prey. The wind picked up her hair and tossed it across her face and Aimee grinned as she pulled it back and gathered it in one fist, keeping her other hand on the wheel. If she were planning to drive for a long time on the highway, she'd put her hair up in a ponytail. If she didn't, it ended up hopelessly matted, as if each strand had been braided to the next. But she loved leaving her hair down, letting it whip around her in a wild frenzy. There was something so freeing about it, something that made her want to toss both hands up in the air and yell to the world, "I'm alive!"

She'd be willing to bet no minivan ever inspired that feeling.

"Should I leave you two alone?" Race asked, the corner of his mouth twisted up in a half-smile.

Aimee laughed and put both hands back on the wheel. "Sorry. This is the first cool car I've ever owned and I can't seem to get over it."

"That's understandable. I have an M3, myself—333 horses, and all of them fast," Race said with a grin.

Aimee's gaze swept the man in her passenger seat for a moment, then went back to the road in front of them. "It just occurred to me that I know nothing about you. At least, I assume that all the information on your résumé is phony. God, your name really is Race, isn't it?" Her head swiveled toward him as that thought hit her.

He put his hands up, presumably to stop her barrage of questions. "Yes, my name is really Race Gardner. Or, rather, *Horace* Gardner, thanks to my parents, who felt some strange obligation to a long-dead relative to hand down the name to me."

Aimee winced. "Ouch," she said.

"Yeah, it was quite an unfortunate name to have in grade school, as you might imagine. Didn't help that I was also about twenty pounds overweight until the day after my high school graduation. Once I got that diploma, the extra weight just melted off. Go figure."

"That sort of thing happened to a lot of us," Aimee said wryly. "That's why high school reunions are so popular. The urge to go back and prove you aren't as dreadful as you were back then is nearly too strong to resist."

Race laughed without a trace of humor. "I've never been to one of mine."

"Neither have I." Grinning over at him, Aimee turned into one of those new self-important housing developments with a sign out front announcing its name. She had no idea why they did that. With what seemed like fourteen billion new developments springing up every year, did the developers really think people would recognize the names? Plus, they all sounded the same: Whispering Oaks, Autumn Wind, Serenity Trails. Yuck. They all sounded like cemeteries, which perhaps was closer to the truth than anyone who lived there might want to admit.

No, she'd take city living over this any day of the week.

Aimee turned left onto a street with large, two-story houses set on quarter-acre lots. You could tell when you were in an upscale housing development by the number of different models on each block. Aimee figured this was one of the nicer ones, because there were several different styles here. In the cheapest neighborhoods, every other house was the mirror image of the one next to it—meaning there was really only one floor plan. She wondered how often someone stumbled into the wrong house after a long day at work or one too many beers at the local sports bar. In this neighborhood, you'd have to be really drunk to get it wrong.

"Ron's house is on the next block," Aimee said, turning into the driveway of a two-story faux-Tudor with a For Sale sign stuck into the neatly trimmed yard.

"I take it you've been here before," Race said, raising his eyebrows at her before he opened his door and stepped out into the quiet night.

Aimee shrugged and got out of the car. "I've done some background work on all my top suspects."

"So have I, but I haven't had the chance to pay them personal visits yet."

"My day job's not as demanding as yours," Aimee said nonchalantly as she headed down the driveway toward the street. The rubber soles of her tennis shoes squeaked slightly and she wished she'd worn an older, more broken-in pair. "I wonder if we should walk on the grass," she said.

"We'll look less suspicious if we stick to the street." Race surprised her then by grabbing her hand, intertwining their fingers together. What surprised her even more than the gesture itself was the sudden jolt of awareness that shot up her arm and made her shiver despite the warm night air.

"Just two lovers taking a moonlit stroll," Race said, squeezing her fingers.

Great. Like she wanted him putting *that* thought into her

head. Before tonight, she had not thought about Race Gardner—or anyone at McConnell Aerospace, for that matter—in a sexual way. Having his erection prodding her in the stomach as they'd struggled had changed all that, however. And now it seemed as if that particular genie wasn't going back into its bottle. She couldn't look at Race and not think about how his body had felt pressing her up against the wall in her bedroom.

Funny, she'd completely forgotten the fear she'd felt before he'd found out that she was working for McConnell. Instead, all she was left with was arousal.

They reached the end of the street and Aimee leaned into Race, her forearm brushing his. "Ron Jefferson lives in the fourth house on the right. The brown one with the river rock facade," she said quietly.

Race nodded and assessed the area. There was no easy way to access Jefferson's house. His backyard abutted his neighbor's and was surrounded by a six-foot-high wooden fence. All the neighbors had similar fences, making Race wonder why people chose to live so close to one another and then went to such lengths to shut one another out.

"That's not his car in the driveway. He could be meeting with the buyer," Aimee said.

"Does he have a dog?" Race asked.

Aimee shook her head. "His neighbor to the west does, though. It's a little one with one of those electronic collars that lets it go outside and back in as it pleases." She looked up at the house for a moment, then pulled Race back into the shadows where they couldn't be seen from Ron Jefferson's house. "Okay, here's what I think we should do. In order to avoid rousing the neighbor's dog, we go in from the east. There's a gate on the side fence—the kind where you have to reach around the top to undo the latch. Jefferson's got a pool with a spillover spa in the backyard. If the filter's running, the sound of the water will help mask any noise we might make. There are two sets of sliders that lead onto the patio, one from the family room and the other from the master suite. There's also an entrance to a pool bath that leads through a utility room and into the house. When I was here last, the door to that bathroom was unlocked."

"Are you telling me you searched his house? Without a warrant? Or even probable cause?" Race asked.

Race imagined that his questions earned him a roll of her eyes, but it was too dark for him to confirm his suspicions. "Of course I did. How are most corporate spies discovered?"

"By following the money trail," Race answered.

"Exactly. So I'd already checked out the official bank records of my top suspects and didn't turn up anything suspicious. I figured the next order of business was to search their homes, to see if I could find expensive cars stashed in the garage or top-of-the-line stereo equipment sitting around. It's not like I planned to steal anything. I just wanted to have a look around."

"Must be nice not having to worry about little things . . . like the law," Race said, his voice dripping with sarcasm.

"Yeah, like the CIA is known for its strict adherence to the justice system and its rules," Aimee responded, and Race guessed he was on the receiving end of another eye roll. "Besides, do you think the traitor selling McConnell's secrets cares about the law? I'm just leveling the playing field."

Race went to put a finger against one pounding temple and realized he was still holding Aimee's hand. With a gesture of surrender, he let her go. "All right. Just don't tell me about any more of your criminal exploits. I wouldn't want to have to arrest you."

"Yeah, right. Like what we're about to do is perfectly on the up-and-up."

"I think we could justify checking out this lead without waiting on a search warrant. Although to be honest, I really don't care about building an airtight case against McConnell's spy. The buyer is the one I'm after."

Aimee dipped her chin in consent. "And I figure we can build a case against the traitor once we know who he is."

"Then it's a win-win," Race said.

"Right. You ready?" Aimee asked.

Race nodded. "I'll take care of the gate. Give me a thirty-second lead," he said. Then, without another word, he vanished.

Aimee stood in the darkness, blinking. It was as if he had disappeared into thin air. She looked to her left and then to her right, unable to see where he'd gone. When she glanced back at the gate on the east side of Ron Jefferson's house, it was hanging open, about a two-inch gap showing between the gate itself and the rest of the fence.

Aimee blinked again. Geez, that was the spookiest thing she'd ever seen.

She backtracked about thirty feet before dashing across the street, well out of sight of all but one of the second-story windows of Ron Jefferson's house. Keeping to the shadows, she stole across the lawns of the quiet suburban neighborhood, hoping the occasional barking dog wouldn't arouse anyone's suspicions. She slipped through the crack in the gate and pushed it until it was nearly closed, but not latched shut. Undoing the latch would cost them precious seconds if they had to make a hurried exit.

"Been a while since you've had to sneak up on someone, huh?" Race whispered in her ear, simultaneously sliding a hand across her mouth to stifle her surprised gasp.

She turned to scowl at him and whispered back, "Sorry, I must have been sick the day they taught skulking at Quantico."

Race grinned at her then, and she suddenly realized that he was enjoying this. Even more surprising, she was, too. Yes, the stakes were high. But that just seemed to make the adrenaline rush that much more intense.

He stepped in front of her, put a finger to his lips, and motioned for her to follow him. Aimee did her best to mimic his motions and quickly discovered that he excelled at moving silently. The focus of their training at the Bureau had been on the proper use of firearms and proper investigative techniques, not clandestine operations. It was one thing to remain still and unnoticed in a crowded boardroom and quite another to move stealthily around someplace you didn't belong.

Race crouched down behind a hedge that had been trimmed to about waist-high, and then moved slowly toward the corner of the house. Around the corner was the master bedroom, which overlooked the patio with several floor-to-ceiling windows flanking a wide sliding glass door. The houses in this development were all oriented toward their backyards. Most had swimming pools or, at the least, hot tubs and built-in barbecue grills. Ron Jefferson's house had all three.

Aimee stopped at the corner of the house and peered around the hedge. At least one light was on in the master suite, which connected the bedroom to an enormous, marble-tiled bath and a smallish home office that faced the street.

The faint sound of voices seemed to be coming from the living room, but Aimee couldn't identify who was speaking. Race tapped her on the shoulder and motioned with two fingers toward some low-lying shrubbery that surrounded the pool. The pool deck itself was made up of large sand-colored tiles, dotted with terra cotta pots overflowing with a profusion of flowers. The pots, unfortunately, were useless as cover. The closest they could get to the house would be the shrubs Race had indicated.

Aimee nodded and watched Race drop down to the ground and creep silently toward the patio. When he was situated among the shrubbery, she followed his lead, hastily scurrying the last few feet when she heard the unmistakable sound of voices headed their way. Race pulled her down beside him on the ground and Aimee rolled to her side so she was facing the house.

Someone switched on a floodlight and Aimee and Race both froze, knowing that if someone looked in their direction, they'd see the bushes still rustling.

There was the soft sound of someone murmuring and the harsh light was doused. Behind her, Aimee felt Race's warm breath on her neck as he exhaled. Another light went on, this one glowing with the soft bluish green of an underwater pool light. Aimee watched as a dark-haired woman emerged from the shadows surrounding the house, a glass of red wine in her hand. Close behind her was Ron Jefferson, McConnell's vice president of information technology, a midforties, slightly overweight man who had always been so nice to Aimee that she'd hoped he wasn't her man.

It looked like her hopes were about to be dashed, though. The only reason that Ron Jefferson would access the propulsion system plans, especially at midnight on a Wednesday night, would be if he were planning to meet with the man—or woman—who was paying him to steal his employer's secrets. Only, when the woman set her wineglass on a nearby patio table, turned toward the pool, and began unbuttoning her blouse, Aimee began to wonder if McConnell's secrets were all that Ron Jefferson was compromising.

"Please tell me we're not going to have to lie here and watch these two having sex," Race nearly groaned in her ear.

Aimee stared fixedly through the leaves of the shrubs in front of her as the brunette shot Ron a smoldering look and stepped out of her skirt, leaving her standing in front of him wearing her bra and panties and a pair of red high heels. The head of IT swallowed half his drink in one gulp and set his glass down beside the woman's before reaching out to squeeze one of her breasts.

The woman moaned and, watching her, Aimee's eyes narrowed. The couple was perhaps twenty feet away, close enough that Aimee could clearly read the expression on the other woman's face as she leaned into Ron's groping hands. She was faking it. The small, panting noises she made were at odds with the sharp look in her eyes. But Ron was too busy with his hands already at the woman's crotch to notice that his partner wasn't as enthralled with his hasty dash toward the finish line as she pretended to be.

"Aren't you going to take your clothes off?" Aimee heard the woman suggest, her voice low and breathy.

Ron immediately began fumbling with the snap at his waist, missing the disgusted look the brunette aimed at his chest. Instead of telling him to slow down or putting her clothes back on, however, she kicked off her shoes and tossed her underwear onto a patio chair. Then, doing nothing to shield her nakedness, she confidently strode across the warm tile and slipped into the pool, wearing nothing but a gold chain around her neck.

The head of IT didn't seem to share the woman's total disregard for his neighbors, as he looked nervously around the darkened yard before shucking his briefs, leaving them lying in a pile on the patio as he hurried over to join his waiting lover in the swimming pool. Their lovemaking reminded Aimee of a scene in the movie *Bridget Jones's Diary,* where Bridget is watching a show on the mating habits of lions.

"The mating is perfunctory . . . brief," the announcer says in a complete monotone as the male lion has his way with the bored-looking lioness. Aimee had to admit, in terms of sex shows, Ron's performance left a lot to be desired. Of course, none of this was apparently evident to Ron—not surprising, since the brunette gave an Oscar-worthy performance of hair tossing and neck rolling and moaning as if she were truly enjoying herself.

The woman made a big show of coming at the same time Ron did, a feat Aimee knew from experience was damn near impossible. The couple clung to each other for a moment at the side of the pool, Ron facing the house, his face shadowed so Aimee couldn't see his expression. The brunette, on the other hand, was turned toward the backyard, her eyes focused about ten feet to the right of where Aimee and Race were lying. She raked her hands up and down Ron's back and muttered soft gibberish in his ear, but her eyes were cold and hard.

Aimee lay still, afraid to move for fear that the woman's gaze would shift. If she glanced their way, Aimee wasn't certain how well the darkness would hide them. She could feel Race's chest rising and falling behind her, but he was as silent as if he'd been turned to stone.

Ron finally raised his head, dropping a light kiss on the woman's forehead before pushing himself away from the edge of the pool. "I'm gonna take a shower," he said, loud enough for Aimee to hear him clearly.

The woman followed him out of the pool, gliding up the steps with a grace and complete lack of self-consciousness that Aimee envied. She was as confident as the next woman with her clothes on, but standing around naked with every flaw exposed for the world (or even one man) to see was another matter entirely. This woman obviously didn't have the same body-image issues that Aimee did.

"Why don't you use the pool bath?" the woman suggested, reaching for her glass of wine and leaving her clothes untouched. "That way, you won't have to worry about mopping up the master bath when you're done."

Aimee frowned. What the hell was that all about? Who cared about having to wipe the floor with a towel when you were done with a shower?

Apparently, Ron's brain was too dulled by the aftereffects of sex to question the woman's reasoning, because he nodded, finished off his drink, and obediently headed toward the white-tiled bathroom that Aimee had found unlocked on her reconnaissance mission earlier that week.

As soon as the door closed, the woman's mask dropped. Her features hardened, her mouth drawing into a tight pink line. "Insensitive clod," she muttered, turning toward the bedroom. Still without a stitch of clothes on, she hurried through the open sliders and into the house.

Behind her, Race relaxed, his chest touching Aimee's spine as he inhaled a deep breath of air. "Well, that was quite a show," he said quietly.

"Yes. Most interesting," Aimee agreed.

"I'm going to try to see what she's doing," Race said, flexing his feet to get the circulation back in his legs before attempting to stand up.

"I'll go around the front." Aimee started to push herself into a sitting position, but stopped when she felt Race's hand on her cheek. Startled, she turned her head to see him point toward the adjoining neighbor's backyard, where something was moving in the darkness. She felt a rumbling behind her and looked back to Race, wondering what was going on. It took her a moment to realize he was laughing silently.

"Looks like we weren't the only ones watching tonight's performance," he whispered.

Aimee glanced back up at the neighbor's yard to see what looked to be a young man crossing the patio toward the house. In seconds, he disappeared.

"Do you think he saw us?" she asked.

"I don't know. I didn't see him when we first entered the yard, so either he came out after we got in place or . . ."

"Or he was already there when we arrived."

Race nodded and they both remained silent for several seconds.

"It's possible he's just some neighbor kid who likes Ron Jefferson's live porn shows," Aimee said.

"Yeah." Race paused, then voiced the fear that had occurred to them both. "Or he's also following Ron Jefferson. In which case, he was probably already here and saw us come in."

"Well, we'll just have to watch our backs," Aimee said, knowing there was nothing else they could do.

"All right, I'm going to see what our exhibitionist is up to."

"Okay. I'll meet you back at the car when you're done."

With that, Aimee glanced back at the neighbor's house, hoped like hell the person who had been watching them was just some teen out to get his jollies, and silently stole out of the backyard.

FIVE

JOSIE Sabre's day had started off with yet another argument with her so-called best friend and had only gotten worse from there. It seemed that all she and Giselle ever did anymore was fight and then tearfully make up. Josie didn't know what was wrong, but every little thing she said or did lately sent Gi into a tantrum. Unaccustomed to dealing with such melodrama, Josie only ended up feeling bewildered about how to deal with her friend and wondering what she was doing that was so wrong. She wasn't used to questioning every word that came out of her mouth. Her father was so loving and encouraging that she felt she could tell him anything and he wouldn't get mad.

She used to feel the same way about Giselle, too, but not anymore. She found she had to guard everything she said lately so that her friend wouldn't go on the attack.

Driven by her father's insistence that she make up with Gi after the previous night's argument, Josie had gone outside right after breakfast and walked down the beach to Gi's house. Gi's dad worked for Josie's father, but Josie didn't really know what he did. She didn't think Gi knew, either.

Gi's mom worked for the company, too, and she traveled a

lot, which seemed to make Giselle's father angry. There seemed to be a lot of anger lately in the Simondses' household, a constant tension that made Josie nervous whenever she visited. She figured it had something to do with Gi's parents, and thought that maybe their fighting was having an effect on her best friend. Maybe that was why Gi was so upset all the time. Josie couldn't imagine what it would be like to have your parents fighting all the time. All she had was Daddy, and he almost never got angry.

Vowing to try to be a little bit more understanding about Gi's moodiness, Josie had climbed up onto the wraparound porch of the house that was similar to her own home, only about a third the size. There was no crime on the island, so it didn't occur to her that anyone would lock the doors leading from the rooms of the house out onto the porch. She supposed the island was so crime-free because everyone here worked for her father and everyone knew everyone else.

Besides, there was nothing here on the island except for about a dozen houses. To get anything—even groceries—you had to boat across to Longport, though most of the time they just called in an order for whatever they wanted and waited for it to arrive in the delivery from Mel's Air Service.

Josie tugged on one of the French doors outside Gi's bedroom, figuring she'd find her best friend still sleeping. That was another thing that had changed lately. Where before she and Gi used to get up early and go wandering around the island, pretending to be shipwrecked actresses like Ginger on *Gilligan's Island,* now Gi would sleep in past noon if somebody didn't come wake her up. They had classes today, but they weren't supposed to start for another hour, so Josie expected that Giselle would still be asleep.

But this morning, Gi wasn't lying buried in the mound of covers on her bed, so Josie wandered out into the hallway in search of her friend. When she heard raised voices coming from the direction of Gi's parents' room, Josie warily took a step in the other direction. Maybe Gi had done something and was getting yelled at. If that were the case, Josie didn't want to witness it. Only, before she could back her way out of the house, Giselle came stomping out of her parents' room and spotted Josie in the hall.

"What are you doing here?" Giselle asked, spearing Josie with the same look she got right before she popped the head off one of Josie's Barbies and speared it with a Popsicle stick, pretending that Barbie had been captured and killed by a tribe of hungry cannibals.

"Uh, nothing," Josie said, backing toward Gi's bedroom. "I was just taking a walk and thought I'd come see what you were doing."

"What, you think that because your father owns this whole stupid island that you can just walk into my house whenever you feel like it?" Giselle asked belligerently.

Josie shook her head, bewildered. She and Giselle had always come and gone in each other's houses without knocking. What was the big deal about it now? "Why are you mad at me?" she asked, blinking rapidly to keep from crying.

Giselle turned her head to look at the wall, her teeth clenched together. Then, suddenly, her lower lip began to tremble. A sob escaped her as she threw herself facedown into the tangle of covers on her bed.

Josie stood near the set of French doors she'd left open earlier, the bright blue waters of the South Pacific lapping soothingly at the white sand beyond the thin tangle of palm trees and beach grasses that sprang up just beyond the porch steps. The temptation to escape, to walk out the doors and into the sea until she could no longer hear Giselle's sobbing, was strong. But Josie resisted, taking a tentative step toward her friend instead.

She crept closer, her heart aching for Giselle, who was crying as if the world were about to come to an end. Josie sat down on the edge of the bed and awkwardly folded her hands in her lap, not knowing what else to do with them. Two months ago, she would have patted Giselle's back comfortingly, but now she wasn't certain whether or not the gesture would be welcomed.

"What's the matter, Gi?" she asked when her friend's sobs finally subsided.

Giselle sniffed loudly and swiped at her face with the back of one hand before turning toward Josie, her normally bright blue eyes red-rimmed and swollen. "Your father is ruining our lives," she said, her voice accusing.

Josie's head flew back as if she had been slapped. Frowning, she got up off the bed. "What are you talking about?" she asked, stepping backward until she was leaning against the wall. She crossed her arms protectively around herself and watched Giselle sit up on her bed and pull her legs under her.

Giselle wiped both her cheeks with her palms and took a hiccupping breath. Then, in one smooth movement, she pulled her long blond hair into a ponytail and secured it with a black band from off her nightstand. "My mom wants to quit because she has to travel too much, but your father won't let her," she announced, still eyeing Josie as if this were all her fault.

"Why would he stop her?"

"How should I know? I just know that every time my parents talk about Mom's job, she and my dad end up fighting. Just this morning, I overheard them talking on the phone and Daddy said that your father would never let her quit. She's in America and she hasn't been home for weeks and I miss her. It's not fair that your dad won't let her come home." With that, Giselle started to cry again, fat teardrops that dripped down her face and dropped onto her bare thighs below the short nightgown she had obviously slept in the night before.

Josie lowered her gaze to the hardwood floor beneath her feet. She didn't know what to say. Her father never left her for more than a week at a time. She was certain she'd miss him terribly if he were gone longer than that. Still, it wasn't as if Giselle was stuck with only her housekeeper like Josie was when Daddy was gone. Gi at least had her father around when her mother was gone. Anyway, all this nonsense about Daddy not letting Gi's mother leave her job couldn't be true. What was he going to do, chain her to a desk to make her stay?

Swallowing a disbelieving snort, Josie looked back up at her friend. Even if it were true that her father didn't want Mrs. Simonds to leave her job, that didn't mean that Giselle had the right to take it out on *her*. She had nothing to do with it.

Some days, being friends with Giselle was more trouble than it was worth.

So, even knowing that this meant she was going to be stuck watching old black-and-white movies with Mrs. Jacobs all night, Josie defiantly stuck her chin in the air and crossed the room, stopping in the doorway with the soft sea breeze at her back. "I'm sorry, Giselle," she said with a dramatic whoosh of her hand in the air, as if to help make her point, "but sometimes, life is just not fair."

Then, without waiting for Gi to respond, she stomped across the porch and down the stairs, heading back to her house, where at least nobody would try to make her believe mean things about her daddy.

RACE made certain there was more than one means of escape from Jefferson's bedroom before he slipped inside the room. He'd already been trapped once this evening and didn't plan to make the same mistake twice. As he stepped silently from the patio onto the carpeted floor of the bedroom, he checked to see that the lights were still on in the pool bath, indicating that the head of IT hadn't yet finished his shower.

Seconds earlier, Race had watched Jefferson's lover come into the bedroom and grab a purple silk robe off the bed, cinching the belt tightly around her waist as she moved deeper into the shadows. Staying close to the wall—and the exit to the main part of the house—Race followed the woman as she headed toward a wide doorway on the other side of the bedroom. Through it, Race could see the dark outline of a desk and a high-backed office chair.

The woman was muttering to herself, her voice a low hum in the otherwise quiet house. Race carefully placed each booted foot one in front of the other, making certain the floor didn't creak beneath his feet as he walked. When he got to the door leading out to the living room, he stopped, unwilling to close off his only exit, even though it meant he couldn't quite hear what Jefferson's lover was murmuring under her breath. The occasional word reached his ears—"stupid," "password," "fucking plans"—but nothing that made any real sense.

Race saw her pull back the chair and slide into it, her back to him for the moment. She moved her right hand and the unmistakable glow of a computer screen lit up the room. From ten feet away, Race heard her typing something on a keyboard, and then came the whirring sound of a printer coming to life.

Was it the propulsion system plans she was printing, or

something else entirely? Race had no way of knowing, and he couldn't risk moving closer to find out.

"Come on, hurry up," he heard the woman say, her voice louder than it had been before.

She was standing now, her silhouette lit by the bluish light coming off the computer. If she turned her head a fraction of an inch, she would have been able to see him, so Race took a step backward, out the door and into the hallway leading to the rest of the house. The printer seemed to take a long time to spit out each page, and with each one, Race felt the woman's tension rise.

Finally, when it seemed that she was on the verge of ripping the pages out of the machine, it stopped. Race peeked into the room and saw her turn back toward the computer screen just as Ron Jefferson stepped into the bedroom and said, "Rita? Where are you?"

Race flattened himself against the wall beside the door as the other man started toward the office. There was the shuffle of papers and the click of a laptop being closed, then the woman—Rita, Race assumed—called out, "I'm back here. Thought I'd check my e-mail while you were taking a shower." Her voice held none of the irritation it had before, when she thought she'd been alone.

"What's that?" he heard Jefferson ask.

"Oh, nothing. Just the agenda for tomorrow's conference and directions to the convention center," Rita answered.

Race squinted at the wallpaper. If the papers Rita held really were nothing but innocuous documents, why had she been so uptight about making sure they were printed before Ron returned?

"Ah. Well, I'm going to hit the hay," Ron said with a yawn, his voice growing fainter, as if he had changed directions and was walking back toward the bed. Good, that meant the couple would soon be asleep and Race could get the hell out of here.

He began to relax, his muscles tense from having remained still for so long.

"I'll be there in a minute. I need to get a glass of water," Rita said, coming through the door before Race had time to think, much less react.

He kept his breathing calm and even as she walked past, glad that he wasn't in the habit of using cologne or other scented personal hygiene products that could give away his position. Rita disappeared down the hallway, and Race swallowed with relief. Damn, that had been close.

Hearing the bedsheets rustling, Race didn't waste any time following Rita. He had to know what she was going to do with those papers. If it was the plans, as he suspected, it was possible that Rita had planned a drop, perhaps telling the buyer she'd leave the plans outside behind a potted plant or under the front welcome mat in exchange for a wad of cash. If that were the case, Race was determined to intercept the drop. It wasn't enough for him to stop the flow of information. He had to know who was paying for McConnell's secrets.

Race stepped out into the living room and crouched down behind a chair as Rita flipped on the kitchen light. He heard the clink of glass on glass, then water running. Balancing on the balls of his feet, Race pushed himself up so that he could see over the back of the chair and into the kitchen. Rita's head was tilted back, her long dark hair brushing the robe at her waist as she drank from the glass in her left hand. Her right hand was resting atop a manila file folder that she'd set on the granite countertop.

She lowered the glass and glanced back toward the bedroom, apparently making certain that Ron had not followed her. Satisfied that she was alone, Rita hurried over to a large black handbag that was propped up against the side of a couch. Race watched as she hurriedly stuffed the folder inside and zipped the purse shut. She stood over it for a moment, frowning. Then, to Race's surprise, she pulled a lock of hair across her forehead, separated out one strand, and tugged. She draped the single strand of hair across the opening of her purse, then stepped back with a nod, obviously pleased at her ingenious trap.

Race rolled his eyes heavenward. She'd obviously seen one too many spy movies.

With one more self-satisfied nod, Rita turned off the kitchen light and headed back toward the bedroom with her glass of water. Race waited for thirty long minutes, crouched behind the chair, until he was certain that both Rita and her lover were asleep. Then he quietly crept from his hiding place toward the woman's purse.

His eyes had had plenty of time to adjust to the moonlit night, and Race took care to note the exact position of Rita's booby trap before placing the strand of hair under the heel of his boot, where it would be safe. With painstaking care, he released the zipper, tooth by tooth. He had to know what Rita had printed. They didn't have the manpower to tail her if she wasn't their spy, but if she was . . . Race would stick closer to her than her own shadow.

When the handbag was finally open, he paused to listen and assure himself that nothing was amiss. Then, convinced that no one had been roused, he slipped a thumb and index finger inside the manila folder and slowly drew out the pages Rita had printed.

It only took one glance to discover that his suspicions had been well founded. The McConnell Aerospace logo was in the upper left-hand corner of each of the pages.

Clearly, they had found their spy.

Race replaced the pages in the folder and, as silently as he had unzipped Rita's handbag, he closed it again. Then he lifted his heel and felt around for the hair he'd tucked there. Finding it, he took great pains to put it back exactly as she'd left it.

With that part of his mission complete, Race now had to get out of the house and make plans for the next phase—including setting a trap for Rita's buyer. Race stood up and looked around the room. The sliding glass doors leading to the patio were closed and presumably locked. He hadn't heard the telltale beep of a security system being enabled, but wasn't about to take anything for granted. Escaping out a window would be his safest bet, since it was less likely that all of Jefferson's windows were wired to the security system than the doors.

Race left the kitchen and walked to the far end of the house, away from the master bedroom where Ron and his lover were still fast asleep. He found three bedrooms down the hall, one an obviously well-used guest room complete with its own private bath. The other two had the stale smell of rooms left closed just a bit too long. Race chose the more cluttered of the two. Sliding a set of skis out of the way, Race checked the bottom and sides of a large window for the telltale signs of security sensors.

Not finding anything other than a regular lock, Race took a moment to plan his exit strategy. It was possible that Jefferson had a state-of-the-art security system that worked without sensors. If so, he'd—

"Ron left the pool bath unlocked again," someone whispered from behind him, making Race spin around, his right hand reaching for the gun he usually kept at his waist.

Aimee raised her eyebrows, but didn't say anything more, gesturing instead toward the hall. Then she turned and disappeared. Race quickly followed. No use playing 007 and leaping out of windows when there was a perfectly good door at one's disposal.

They both remained silent until they were half a block from Jefferson's house. Then Aimee turned to him and asked, "So, what did you find out? Is Ron our spy? Or is his lover just using him? Come on, spill. I've been waiting nearly an hour to hear what happened in there."

Her cheeks were flushed with excitement, her eyes bright, and Race realized that she was enjoying the thrill of the hunt. He found himself smiling. Well, there was nothing wrong with that. He'd never have lasted a year in the Agency if he didn't also get a kick out of chasing the bad guys.

He stopped in the shadows of a house on the corner, still within sight of Jefferson's house, but out of view of anyone who might be watching them. "I'm not one hundred percent certain, but I believe our gal's in this alone. While Jefferson was in the shower, she printed the propulsion system plans. When he caught her with the documents, she lied and told him they were directions to some conference she's attending."

"I knew it," Aimee said, punching the air gleefully with one fist. "I could tell by the way she looked at Ron while they were having sex that she was just using him."

"You noticed that, too?" Race asked.

Aimee sniffed disdainfully. "Her orgasm was as fake as the boobs on a beauty queen."

Race grinned for just a moment, then sobered up. "Did you happen to see our peeping Tom again?"

"I don't think we need to worry about him," she said, her gaze shifting to her tennis-shoe-clad feet as a flush crept up her neck.

Puzzled, Race rocked back on his heels. "Why do you say that?"

Aimee cleared her throat. "Well, because I went to check him out. I figured we'd be safer if we knew whether this guy was just your average voyeur or if he was after the plans, too."

"And?" Race asked when it seemed that Aimee wasn't going to continue without prompting.

"He's just some kid who gets his rocks off by spying on his neighbors," Aimee answered.

Race watched the blush creep up her face until even the roots of her hair seemed to turn red. "You caught him jerking off, huh?" he asked.

She looked up at him, then closed her eyes and shook her head. "Yeah," she mumbled.

"Seems everyone's getting some tonight," Race said dryly.

"Seems like it," Aimee agreed, opening her eyes again.

"Anyway, it's good news about the neighbor kid. At least we know he wasn't interested in us."

"And if he did see us, it's not likely he'll go to Ron and tell him. If he did, he'd have to explain what he was doing out there in the first place."

Race nodded. "Okay. So it looks like we both won here tonight. You've discovered the identity of McConnell's traitor, inadvertent as the man's defection might be. McConnell can do whatever he wants to plug his security holes, all I ask is that you wait until after Jefferson's lover leads me to her buyer before you close the net around him."

Aimee chewed thoughtfully on her bottom lip for a moment. "Can you guarantee those plans won't end up at Rockton Aeronautical?"

"I'll do my best," Race said, his gaze unwavering on hers, knowing there wasn't a hell of a lot he could do to keep her from recommending to Joe McConnell that they fire Jefferson on the spot . . . and blow Race's entire operation by tipping off the buyer that his source of information was about to dry up.

"How certain are you that this goes beyond simple corporate espionage?" Aimee asked, her head tilted to one side as she looked up at him.

Race raised his hands out at his sides, palms up. "I'm here, aren't I?"

She studied him silently for a long moment as the warm South Texas wind teased tendrils of her hair into dancing to its soft tune. Finally, she started to nod. "All right. I'm certain I can convince Joe that his secrets are as safe as they can be for the time being. I assume you have some sort of plan?"

"Yes. First, I'm going to have my partner run a trace on the lover's car to see if we can find out who she is. And then . . ." Race paused, rubbing his forehead with one hand before beginning again. "And then I'm going to do whatever it takes to keep those plans from falling into the wrong hands."

SIX

"I'VE paid the contractor his final installment for completing the manufacturing plant," Luke Simonds said, tapping the end of his pen on the pad of paper on his lap. "With no more income expected until the LoRS missile demonstration in a month, Sabre is dangerously short of funds."

Nic contemplated the man who had been his finance manager for the last thirteen years, ever since he'd accumulated enough wealth to need someone like Luke, who knew more about getting dirty money into legitimate banking channels than Nic would ever know. A few months after hiring Luke, Nic had bought this island off the eastern coast of Australia and then moved his newly formed "corporation" here when he'd left Venezuela to begin his new life. Two years ago, Nic realized how valuable an asset Luke truly was when he decided to branch out into weapons manufacturing instead of simply brokering arms deals. Soon, he would be in control of supply, where the margins were much higher. And then, men would come to him. He would no longer have to put himself in danger, traveling to war-ravaged countries to meet with terrorists, guerilla, and despots in order to make a living.

He would be safe. Josie would be safe. Nic would finally be at peace.

But that couldn't happen if the long-range stealth missile Nic's engineers were working on wasn't completed on schedule. If the prototype wasn't ready in one month as he'd assured his customer it would be, the organizations that Nic depended on to place orders would hold on to their multi-million-dollar checks until they could see for themselves what a powerful weapon it could be. And Nic needed those checks to keep Sabre afloat. If he failed, Nic would forever be at the mercy of the arms trade and buried under the crushing worry of what would happen to Josie if he were killed. There was no one Nic trusted enough to raise his daughter.

Frowning, Nic pushed back his chair and folded his hands on the top of his desk. "Have you talked to Diana? Is she on schedule to obtain the propulsion system plans and return to the island tomorrow?" he asked. Those plans were the key to developing the LoRS bomb prototype. Without them, Nic would be ruined.

Luke looked down at his pad of paper before answering. "Yes, everything is going according to schedule."

Nic nodded shortly. "Good." He turned his head slightly to look out the open French doors that led to the wraparound veranda and the ocean beyond. The sound of the waves seldom failed to calm him, but today, he had to force himself to listen to the soothing sound. "How much is left after we pay the contractor?" he asked.

"Two hundred thousand, but that will need to be used to fund payroll at the end of this week. We'll need more to pay the engineers to continue working on the LoRS project through the end of the month. If we don't, we'll have nothing to show at the unveiling."

"And with nothing to show, we'll have no orders—" Nic began.

"And no money to push the bombs into production," Luke finished for him.

"All right. Then it appears I need to put some pressure on al-Zwahiri this evening to come up with some cash as a show of faith."

"Yes, and we'd better pray that Diana is successful in procuring those plans for the propulsion system. If not . . ." Luke's voice trailed off as he left the remainder of his thought unsaid.

Nic turned his dark gaze on his financial manager. "I don't believe in praying. Your wife must successfully complete her mission. God willing or not."

"SORRY, guys. I was hoping this job would last a bit longer," Aimee said as she accelerated past a law-abiding citizen barely doing thirty in a thirty-five zone on her way to the Mc-Connell Aerospace plant. Simultaneously, she stifled a yawn with the back of one hand, inched up the volume on her cell phone, and sped through a questionably yellow light. Man, she needed another Americano.

Her partners—Raine Robey and Daphne Donovan, former FBI special agents like herself—were both an hour ahead in the Eastern time zone and, hopefully, had more sleep last night than Aimee had. After leaving Race at Ron Jefferson's house to continue his surveillance, Aimee had gone back to her apartment and fallen into bed, exhausted. It took another two hours for sleep to come, however, her brain still buzzing over the evening's events.

"I've almost closed the deal with American Trust Bank's chief information officer," Raine said, sounding as sleepy as Aimee felt. Raine wasn't exactly what one would consider a morning person.

"The jobs coming my way have been laughably easy," Daff said. "I'm lucky to get a couple hours' worth of work out of any of them."

While Aimee's specialty was investigating claims of corporate espionage, Raine was Partners In Crime's network security specialist and Daphne's prime talent was her ability to find out anything about anyone, a skill that came in handy for corporations investigating employees who'd absconded with company funds or doing thorough background checks before making critical hires.

Aimee found herself missing her friends. In the six months they'd all been in Atlanta together before they'd each taken their first cases, they'd become even closer than before. With her assignment to San Antonio expected to last no more than a few months, Aimee had made no effort to meet new people and she hadn't realized until this morning how lonely she was.

Well, with McConnell's traitor identified, it looked like she'd be back in Atlanta shortly, so there was no need to feel sorry for herself about her current lack of a social life.

"By the way, you guys wouldn't believe the CIA hunk who's masquerading as a CPA," Aimee said, remembering her astonishment at the body Race Gardner was hiding from womankind.

"Do tell," Raine said, seeming to perk up a bit with the change in topics.

"Yeah, you got him ready to pop the question already?" Daphne added, alluding to Aimee's nearly legendary success rate with men.

Aimee laughed as she turned into McConnell's parking lot, waving her security card across the reader and waiting for the arm to swing up. "Hardly. I thought last night that he was trying to kill me. Plus, I'm fairly certain he's bugged my office."

"So what's a little espionage between friends?" Raine asked, making Aimee laugh again as she pulled her car into an empty space on the already hot pavement outside the building that housed McConnell's administrative offices.

"If I had more time, I'd make Race Gardner more than a friend," Aimee said wryly. "He's got this whole Clark Kent thing going on that's sexy as hell."

"He probably thinks the same thing about you," Daphne said.

Recalling the unmistakable erection that had been jabbing her in the stomach last night after their struggle, Aimee had to agree. "You may have something there," she said into the microphone connected to the headset she was wearing. Of course, it didn't really matter if she and Race shared a mutual attraction since they'd be going their separate ways before either of them had a chance to act on it. Aimee admonished herself for even thinking about it. She didn't even know where Race lived.

Another thought struck her then. God, he could even be married. With four or five kids. Ugh. Not that she didn't like children, but Aimee was the pragmatic sort who believed it was just as easy to fall for a guy without a wife and kids than one with a lot of baggage. And a healthy financial portfolio wouldn't hurt, either.

She hung up after promising to give her partners a full report later, then reached over and grabbed her purse and briefcase from the floor on the passenger side of the car. As she straightened up, her headset beeped to indicate an incoming call. Thinking it was Raine or Daff calling her back, Aimee pressed the talk button and said, "What's up?"

"Uh, Aimee? It's Race."

"Oh, sorry. I thought you were—" Aimee shook her head, interrupting herself. "Doesn't matter. What's going on? Is Rita on the move?"

"Yes. And unfortunately, I need to ask for your help," Race said.

Aimee blinked and pushed her sunglasses back up the bridge of her nose to cut the light from the sun glaring at her from overhead. "What is it?"

"You know that conference our subject's attending today?"

"Um-hmm."

"It's for women in IT."

Aimee slipped off the jacket of her navy blue suit. It was way too hot out here for a jacket. "Yeah? So?"

"So, in case you hadn't noticed, I'm a man," Race said, his voice tinged with amusement.

"Yes, I believe that fact became painfully obvious last night," Aimee reminded him, tucking a loose tendril of hair back into the twist at the nape of her neck.

Race ignored her comment and continued, "There's not enough time to get a female agent out here before the conference begins. And once Rita goes into the workshops, anything can happen. The buyer could be anyone here."

Aimee's eyes narrowed on the hood of her car. "Let me check with Joe McConnell to see if he'll authorize paying me to tail your subject. It's in his best interests to make sure Rita's buyer isn't someone from Rockton—"

"Rita's with Rockton," Race interrupted. "She's their head of IT."

"Then Rockton's already got the plans."

"No, I'm telling you, she isn't handing the plans over to

her own company. If she were, she would have headed straight to the office this morning. There's no way she'd sit around at a conference all day with those papers in her purse. She wouldn't take the chance."

Aimee was already shaking her head. "Then there's no way I can ask McConnell to pay me to tail her. I'm sorry, I can't do it."

"To hell with the money. We need your help," Race said.

"And I need to get paid for my time. You wouldn't expect McConnell to turn a fighter jet over to the U.S. government for free, so why would you expect me to perform services for you for free?"

"Because I don't have time to get the authorization to pay you. You know how the government works. There are forms I have to fill out, approvals I have to get."

Aimee could hear the frustration in Race's voice when he answered and steeled herself not to give in. It wasn't easy—she knew what was at stake here—but she also knew that the CIA could afford to pay her if they really needed her help. If she allowed them to use her without paying her, they'd take advantage of her for as long as she remained in San Antonio. When she'd quit the FBI, she'd vowed never to devalue her services again. Now here it was, just seven months later, and she was tempted to give in.

Hmm. But maybe they could work a compromise . . .

"All right, listen, I'll do it," Aimee said, twisting the key in her convertible's ignition. "But I want you to promise me something in exchange."

Race heaved an audible sigh of relief. "Yes, whatever you want."

Aimee sped out of the parking lot and turned toward the conference center. "I want my FBI records eliminated so that I can no longer be traced back to the U.S. government."

"What?" Race asked, incredulous. Aimee could almost picture him holding the phone away from his ear and frowning at it.

"You guys make people disappear all the time. Now I want you to do the same with Aimee Devlin, former FBI special agent. That shouldn't be so hard to do."

There was nothing but silence on the other end of the line

for a long time, so long that Aimee was only a few blocks from the convention center when Race finally answered. "All right. Fine. Consider your records erased."

With a self-satisfied grin, Aimee pulled into the parking garage at the corner of Bowie and Market and pushed the button for a ticket. "Great. I'm in the garage. Where should we meet?"

"There's a coffee shop next to the convention center where Rita's having breakfast alone. I'm sitting three tables behind her and to the right."

"See you in a few," Aimee said just before ending the call. She resisted the temptation to roll her eyes as she pulled into a parking spot on the third floor and killed the engine. Did Race not think she'd recognize him?

She hopped out of the car, deciding as she did that on the off chance one of McConnell's IT staff was at the conference, she'd better do a little disguising of her own. Pressing a button on her key chain to open the trunk, she leaned over and grabbed her suit jacket from the passenger seat. As she walked to the back of the car, she pulled the pins out of her hair, put her head down, and shook out her hair. *God, that felt good.* She fluffed her hair a little more, going for a sexy, just-got-out-of-bed look. Laying her suit jacket out neatly in the trunk, she unbuttoned her white blouse until a fair amount of cleavage was visible. She pulled a red leather jacket out of the trunk and put it on, then exchanged her plain navy pumps for a pair of high-heeled red leather boots that zipped up to the knee. She grabbed the emergency makeup kit she always kept in the trunk and slid back into the driver's seat. Looking in the rearview mirror, she applied violet eye shadow, dark eyeliner, and mascara with an expert hand. She finished it off with blush that highlighted her high cheekbones and a swath of red lipstick in place of the beige-tinted gloss she typically wore.

Satisfied that her transformation from mouse to mink was complete, Aimee stepped out of the car, tossed her makeup bag back in the trunk, pointed her key chain at the convertible, and gave a nod as the locks clicked closed with a beep.

Aimee held back a grin as she imagined Race's surprise upon seeing the changes she'd wrought in her appearance.

Not for nothing had she absorbed hair, makeup, and clothing tips from her two supermodel sisters.

The heels of her boots echoed loudly off the concrete as she made her way to the elevators that would take her down to street level. On her way, she made a quick call to Joe McConnell to tell him she'd had a break in the case and would be in later to discuss her progress with him.

The elevator doors swung open and Aimee sashayed over the threshold while the current occupants hurried to make room for her. One thing Aimee had discovered was that the world was different for beautiful people. For them, there was always an empty seat on the subway, or a free drink, or a convenient job offer . . . or room on a crowded elevator. As the plain Jane big sister to two gorgeous younger siblings who had practically come out of the womb charming the hospital staff, Aimee had learned all of this at an early age. All of that bullshit about "pretty is as pretty does" and beauty being skin deep was just that: bullshit. Not that Aimee didn't love her sisters—she did. It was just that a lifetime of seeing the advantages good bone structure and silky hair got a person had made her a bit jaded.

As a gawky, awkward teen, she'd never imagined that one day she might grow up to be the type of woman who would turn men's heads. Compared to her sisters, she was still a bit of an ugly duckling, but hell, sometimes even *they* were ugly ducklings compared to themselves.

"What floor?" a tall man wearing khakis and a dark blue polo shirt asked, appreciatively taking in her appearance.

"One, please," Aimee answered. She could easily have reached over and punched the button herself, but having someone wait on her was so much more satisfying.

By the time the doors slid open at street level, Aimee was fairly certain the man beside her was about to ask her for a date. Without giving him a chance, she stepped off the elevator, not looking back. He was cute in an off-duty banker sort of way, but she really wasn't interested.

She hurried to the coffee shop without stopping at the deserted hostess station and immediately spotted Ron Jefferson's lover nibbling on a piece of toast. Aimee hurried past her, pausing when she reached the table where Race said he'd be. In his place sat a young man wearing worn jeans, a T-shirt claiming he was FBI—Female Body Inspector—and a San Antonio Spurs baseball cap. The man didn't look up from his paper as Aimee walked past, certain she'd misheard Race's instructions. So as not to look suspicious, she headed toward the ladies' room at the back of the restaurant.

She took a few minutes to re-fluff her hair and wash her hands before slowly emerging from the bathroom to try to find Race again. As she stepped out into the darkened hallway that led to the restrooms, the men's room door opened and the young man who had been sitting at Race's table stepped out.

"Have you got her?" the man asked in a hushed tone.

"Pardon me?" Aimee asked.

"Rita. Can you see her?"

Blinking with surprise, Aimee realized that the scruffy young man who had been sitting at Race's table *was* Race. Amazing.

"Great disguise," she muttered.

"Thanks. You, too," Race said, eyeing her approvingly.

"I've got it from here. It looks like our target is finished with breakfast and is getting ready to leave," Aimee said.

Race squeezed her shoulder. "All right. My partner and I will be at the convention center all day. If you need backup, you've got my number."

Aimee took a deep, calming breath. "Yep. I'm ready."

Letting his hand fall to his side, Race smiled at her, looking far younger than Aimee had assumed he was. "Great. Let's go catch ourselves a spy," he said, sounding as if this were all just a game.

Race disappeared back into the men's room and Aimee remained in the shadows for a moment, waiting for Rita to get far enough ahead of her that the other woman wouldn't suspect she was being tailed. Then Aimee went to work.

She followed Rita into the convention center and up the escalator, staying focused on the other woman's cap of shiny brown hair as she made her way across the crowded convention center. Aimee hung back for a moment as Rita stopped at a long, low table, presumably the registration desk for the conference she was attending. Cursing under her breath,

Aimee watched as Rita gave her name to one of the women manning the desk. The woman rummaged through a box containing registration packets and pulled one out, handing it to Rita along with a three-ring binder. Had the packets been lying loose, Aimee could have looked over someone's shoulder to find a name that she could use, since most all packets of these types had labels affixed to them telling registration desk volunteers who got which packet.

Well, no use grousing about it. There were other ways to overcome this hurdle.

Keeping watch over Rita, Aimee squinted at the name badge of a woman standing several feet away, deep in conversation. *Ah, perfect.* She moved away from the registration desk, where a woman who had just received her conference materials was juggling a purse, briefcase, registration packet, and a Starbucks cup while trying to pin on her name tag. With a frustrated "ugh" the woman turned and set her coffee and conference materials on the edge of a round tray that had been set out to collect used mugs and glasses before attendees went in to sit down in the auditorium.

Aimee breezed past the table and slid the woman's three-ring binder off the tray, then circled back to the registration desk. Pasting a friendly smile on her face, she approached the same woman who had given Rita her materials.

"Hi," she said, setting the three-ring binder down on the desk. "My name is Joan Richards from *Glam* magazine. I'm afraid I've lost my name badge. Can you believe it, ten minutes into the conference and the darn thing has already disappeared."

The volunteer smiled back, completely unsuspicious. Of course, it wasn't like crashing an information technology conference was high on Homeland Security's priority list.

"Oh, that happens all the time. We always print an extra set, just in case." The woman obligingly pulled out a second set of printed name tags and searched for the name Aimee had given her. In seconds, she'd slid the card into a name badge and handed it to Aimee.

"Thank you," Aimee said, clipping the badge to her blouse and covering it up with her jacket.

"You'll need to show that at the door. That's how the room attendants know who to let in," the woman said, apparently not realizing the complete ineffectiveness of this system given the fact that the registration desk volunteers didn't even ask for identification when giving out name tags.

"Thanks," Aimee said again. She didn't have much time to consider this conference's security—or lack thereof—since Rita was headed toward the entry doors of the auditorium. Aimee hurried after her, flashing her name tag at the uniformed guard standing outside the doors. He waved her in and Aimee fought a moment of panic when she realized she had lost track of her subject.

Aimee guessed that the auditorium was large enough to seat at least five hundred and the seats near the middle were filling up fast. She shivered under her jacket. As usual at such events, the room was cooled to near-Arctic temperatures, apparently in the hopes that the struggle to keep warm would keep participants from falling asleep.

She scanned the room, searching for the spy in her midst.

Damn, where was she?

Aimee stepped to one side as a group of women entered the auditorium and headed down the shallow steps toward the stage. Finally, she looked back to the last row of seats and found Rita settling in and placing her purse on the seat next to her so that it wouldn't be taken by another participant.

Breathing a sigh of relief, Aimee decided to take a more direct approach with Rockton's spy. Walking quickly, she headed toward the last row of seats.

"Excuse me," she said, drawing up next to Rita and smiling as she gestured down the row, indicating that Rita should move her toes or risk getting stepped on by Aimee's four-inch high heels.

Rita scowled and looked as if she wanted to tell Aimee to go sit somewhere else, but in the end, manners prevailed. With an inelegant grunt, she stood up to let Aimee pass.

Aimee made a big show out of taking off her jacket and rummaging around in her purse for a pen before taking a seat. Unwilling to drag an innocent person into this charade, she surreptitiously unclipped the name tag from her blouse and dropped it into her pocketbook. With an innocent smile still pasted on her face, she turned to Rita and held out her hand. "Aimee Richards. *Glam* magazine," she said.

After a slight hesitation, Rita took her hand. "Rita Romano."

Aimee noted that the other woman omitted her place of employment, but didn't press the issue. "It should be a great conference, huh? I'm especially looking forward to the session on image. You wouldn't believe how many people think I'm kidding when I tell them that I work in IT. It's like they expect us all to be walking around wearing pointy Spock ears or something." Or at least that's what she'd heard from her partner Raine, who, aside from being a top computer network security guru, was also a hacker extraordinaire.

"Mmm," Rita said, glancing away as if hoping that Aimee would get the hint that she didn't want to be pals.

"I work in fashion and there's no way I could go to work dressed like a slob every day. In my industry, image is everything, you know?" Aimee crossed her legs, dangling one high-heeled boot in Rita's direction as if to make her point.

Rita was spared from having to make a comment by the appearance of a middle-aged woman on the stage. The woman walked to the podium that was set up center stage and leaned in to the microphone.

"Good morning, ladies and . . . well, ladies," the woman said, pausing for a round of expected laughter. "Welcome to the third annual 'Women in Information Technology' conference." As the woman went on about the particular challenges and rewards of being a female in a male-dominated field, Aimee couldn't help but think back to her days in the Bureau, when she, Raine, and Daphne had been three of just a handful of women in their class at Quantico. Talk about being outmanned.

On the bright side, being thrown together as the only females among so many males had caused the three women to form a strong bond that even now, more than ten years later, had not been broken. Smiling, Aimee absently rubbed the tattoo at the base of her spine with one hand. The Tasmanian Devil inked there was her reminder of the friendship and experiences she and her friends shared.

During their special-agent training in Virginia, Aimee had learned that, for whatever reason, guys liked nicknames. Or maybe it was just law enforcement guys who loved to think up creative names for one another. In any event, Aimee had quickly been dubbed "Dev" because of her last name. Daphne became

"Daff" and, as logic would have it, Raine, by association, became "Bugsy"—fortunately not Porky or Petunia after the Looney Tunes pigs, Raine often remarked.

One night, after Raine had been framed for murder, drummed out of the FBI, and dumped by the love of her life, all within a few weeks, the women had gotten together to commiserate over an endless supply of alcohol. Aimee wasn't exactly certain whose idea it had been to get tattoos, but she was sure it had seemed like a good idea at the time. The next morning, hungover and laid out in various states of repose in Aimee's living room, they'd compared their artists' handiwork. Raine had Bugs Bunny tattooed on the inside of her left ankle, Daphne had Daffy Duck wearing green tights and a Superman cape on her right butt cheek, and Aimee, who was glad she'd had so much to drink the night before that she'd barely felt the pain, sported the Tasmanian Devil right at the spot where her lower back met her buttocks. Apparently, the pain of getting a tattoo there was supposed to be excruciating, but Aimee barely remembered it. She was so pleased with the result that she'd do it again if she had it to do over, even without the liquor-induced haze she'd been in the first time.

The woman in the front finished her opening remarks, and Aimee came back to the present with the sound of the audience's applause. As the next speaker came onstage, Aimee sighed inwardly and settled in for what she expected to be a fairly dull few hours. She opened her binder and pretended to make notes, instead working up a revised budget now that she knew her job with McConnell would soon be over. She didn't mind prospecting for new business—as a matter of fact, she actually enjoyed it—but the sales cycle in their business was fairly long. It had taken each of the partners six months to sign their first clients, and none of their jobs had yet lasted over six weeks. While they each had resources they could draw on if the need for cash became too desperate, they were loath to go outside the partnership to ask for help.

Aimee sighed. Nothing like having to ask one's family for money at thirty-five years old.

She'd just finished figuring out how to rearrange Partners In Crime's debt structure, when out of the corner of her eye, she noticed Rita checking her watch for what had to be the fifth time in half as many minutes.

Something was about to happen.

Aimee continued writing in her notebook, but the figures changed from actual numbers to nonsensical doodles as she focused all of her attention on the woman to her left. In less than thirty seconds, Rita checked her watch again. Then slowly, as if trying not to attract any attention, she slid her binder onto the floor beneath her feet and inched her purse onto her lap. Crouching like someone at a movie theater who is attempting to leave without anyone noticing, Rita got up out of her seat and backed toward the exit.

Damn. What was Aimee supposed to do now?

She narrowed her eyes on the back of the head of the woman seated in front of her. If Rita had left the plans in the binder under her seat for the buyer to pick up later, Aimee should remain with the notebook. However, if Rita had simply not wanted to take the bulky item with her when she met with the buyer, Aimee would be stuck sitting here babysitting the handouts for this stupid conference.

As she waited to hear the auditorium door whoosh closed, Aimee could feel the seconds ticking by in the pulse of each heartbeat. She wiped her upper lip, perspiring despite the icebox-like temperature in the room. After looking around to see if anyone was watching, Aimee casually gathered her things and slid over into Rita's seat. Grateful that she hadn't written anything in her notes that could be traced back to her or Partners In Crime, she bent down to swap Rita's binder with her own. Then, without wasting the time to check and see if the notebook she had grabbed contained the plans, she hurried out of the auditorium to regain visual contact with her target, knowing she might already be too late. It would have only taken Rita a moment to leave the plans at a prearranged dead drop or to hand them over to her buyer in a split-second exchange as they passed each other in a hallway.

Once outside the auditorium, Aimee scanned the now-empty floor. Had Rita had time to make it to the escalator? Or used the elevator to go to another floor? If so, Aimee knew she'd get away.

Barely pausing on her way toward the escalator to see if Rita was on her way down to the floor below, Aimee pressed the speed dial number on her cell phone to call Race. He answered on the first ring and Aimee didn't waste any time. "I've lost her," she said. "The escalator's clear but she could be in an elevator or going down the stairs."

"We're on it," Race said.

"I'm going to check the ladies' room on this floor. If she's not there, she's gone."

Race grunted before hanging up. They both knew that if Rita wasn't in the bathroom, their chances of finding her again before she made contact with her buyer were slim.

"Damn, damn, damn," Aimee muttered as she hurried toward the ladies' room, wishing these high heels didn't make it so difficult to run.

She hit the door to the bathroom with the open palm of one hand, clutching Rita's binder to her chest with the other. Her stomach nearly crawled up her throat as her gaze took in the scene in the ladies' room. Rita had just emerged from a stall, its door swinging halfway shut on well-oiled hinges. The other woman looked surprised, that emotion lasting for just an instant before being replaced with suspicion. Aimee knew she had to do something immediately, something drastic and unexpected that would make Rita dismiss her as a potential problem.

"I feel awful," she said, slurring her words as she dashed to the stall Rita had just vacated. Then, throwing her stuff down on the floor, she turned toward the back wall, stuck her finger down her throat, and started to gag.

That was one thing about growing up around models. You certainly learned a lot about your various eating disorders.

Knowing she had to make this as realistic as possible, Aimee forced herself to throw up. Coming back up, the coffee she'd drunk that morning burned her throat and she choked on the acidic bile. Aimee spat and swallowed, then coughed and spat into the toilet again. Then she shuddered and leaned against the stall.

God, she was glad she'd never gotten over her aversion to throwing up. The temptation to eat all she wanted and still lose weight by throwing up had been strong at one time. She supposed she could blame it on her sisters—or rather, on the way people would look at her when they asked, "*You're* Lauren and Kaylee's sister?" The implication, of course, being that poor Aimee had been gypped in the looks department. But, of course, lots of girls without gorgeous sisters became bulimic, so Aimee let Lauren and Kaylee off the hook for that one.

Aimee coughed again and flushed, then reached out to grab some toilet paper off the roll to wipe her mouth. As she did, a flash of something out of place caught her attention. There, wedged behind the toilet, was a manila file folder.

She turned around and sat down on the toilet seat, tilting her head to see through the narrow gap between the stall door and the wall. Rita was still at the sink, her back turned toward Aimee as if she were washing her hands. If she were, she'd win the prize for least bacteria remaining after using a public restroom.

Taking advantage of the noise made by the running water, Aimee quickly pulled the file folder out from behind the toilet. Then, reaching forward, she grabbed her purse off the floor and made noisy work of rummaging around in it, as if searching for something to settle her stomach. She pulled out a pen and looked for something to write on, but didn't have anything except a few loose one-dollar bills. Without dropping her purse back on the floor, she opened the file folder, holding back a gasp when she discovered that the plans were, indeed, there.

They were too big to fit in her purse without being folded, so Aimee rolled them into a tube, not even trying to mask the sound of paper crinkling. She dropped the plans into her purse, set her purse on the floor, and, empty-handed, pushed open the stainless steel trash receptacle that was to be used for the disposal of feminine hygiene products. The trash bin banged closed as Aimee hastily scribbled a message on the inside of the file folder and then slid it back into place. Then, pulling off a length of toilet paper, Aimee swiped it across her face, taking care to smudge the mascara under her eyes for good measure.

Finally, she stood, flushed the toilet again, and gathered her things up off the floor. With her purse tucked under her arm, she unlatched the lock on the stall door and stepped out into the ladies' room, where Rita was now making a show out of drying her hands on a brown paper towel.

"Wow, I didn't realize I'd had that much to drink last night," Aimee muttered as if the comment wasn't directed to anyone in particular. She set Rita's binder on the counter and covered it with her red leather jacket before leaning in and studying her reflection in the mirror. As intended, she looked ghastly, her face splotchy, mascara melting under her eyes.

"Mmm," Rita said. In the mirror, Aimee saw the other woman glance back toward the stall Aimee had just vacated. A corner of the manila file folder peeked out from behind the porcelain toilet. Reassured that the plans were right where she'd left them, Rita turned and headed toward the door.

"Have a great conference," Aimee called to the other woman's retreating back.

Rita didn't bother to answer as she pushed open the lavatory door.

Aimee closed her eyes and let out a relieved breath. Now that she had the plans, McConnell's secrets were safe. Rummaging around in her purse, she found a tin of mints and quickly popped one into her mouth to erase the sour taste of vomit. Then she, too, headed out the door, nearly hitting another woman who was pulling open the ladies' room door from the other side.

"Excuse me," Aimee muttered.

"No problem," the other woman said, her voice tinged with an accent Aimee couldn't immediately place.

The woman stepped back to let Aimee pass and, as she walked past, their eyes met for the briefest of seconds. And, although she had no evidence of it, Aimee suddenly knew that she was looking into the eyes of a killer.

SEVEN

"I can assure you, we're on schedule with the LoRS bomb and expect the weapons to start shipping in less than six months. As you'll see at the demonstration next month, this missile will exceed your organization's every expectation," Nic said, keeping his gaze steady and focused on the man sitting across from him. If his client suspected that Nic was lying, the man would kill him without giving it a second thought. In this case, however, it was easy to remain calm. For one of the few times in his life, Nic was actually telling the truth.

Ahmed al-Zwahiri studied him silently, assessingly. As the second-in-command of a well-funded terrorist group, al-Zwahiri was accustomed to dealing with all manner of people—from wealthy oil sheiks sympathetic to his cause to suspected traitors within his organization to arms dealers like Nic himself. Only, with the LoRS bomb, Nic planned to shift the focus of his company from merely brokering deals to the actual manufacture of weapons. He had banked everything on the success of this new mission, sinking virtually every cent he had on the manufacturing plant that, after two long years, was finally nearing completion. With his finances on the verge of collapse, Nic desperately needed al-Zwahiri's order for a significant number of LoRS bombs—as well as his prompt down payment. If al-Zwahiri was convinced that the bombs had a chance of being delivered before New Year's Eve, he might be inclined to make a large enough order to keep Nic's operation from going under.

Nic supposed that was the downside to being an arms dealer. It wasn't like he could just walk into his local bank and ask for a loan.

"Let me—" al-Zwahiri began, just as the door to Nic's office was flung open.

Narrowing his eyes, Nic stood up. He was going to kill whoever it was who had the nerve to interrupt him. His staff knew better than to—

Josie poked her head inside his office, her dark eyes watery and red-rimmed. "Daddy, I need to talk to you," she wailed, wiping her tears away with the back of one hand.

Nic clenched his teeth. God damn it! What was she doing here? She was supposed to be spending the night at Mrs. Jacobs's house. He had one rule about mixing his business and personal lives, and that was that he didn't. None of his clients had ever seen Josie and vice versa. And Nic intended to keep it that way.

"Josephine, go up to your room this instant," he ordered.

"But Daddy—"

"Now! I will be up when I'm finished."

Josie's eyes filled with more tears and the look she shot him was full of hurt. He never talked to her this way, but she had to understand that she was not to interrupt him when he was doing business. Damn his housekeeper anyway! Why hadn't she kept Josie at her house as she was supposed to? If nothing else, she should have called him before letting Josie come back home.

Josie sniffled loudly but did as she was told, retreating from the room and closing the door behind her with just a bit more force than was necessary.

"Ah, daughters. They can be a trial, no?" al-Zwahiri said, his tone surprisingly tinged with amusement.

Who would have thought a man who had no compunction about murdering thousands of innocents would have a soft spot for little girls?

Nic managed a wry smile, even though he was fuming inside. Of course he could not hide the fact that he had a daughter from those who might want to know such things, but he was furious that this man had seen her, had put a face to the statistic. Nic wasn't certain why the thought of this upset him so much, he only knew that it did. For some reason, it threatened the notion that he could keep his daughter safe despite the type of people he did business with.

But he revealed none of this inner dread, instead favoring al-Zwahiri with a nonchalant shrug and saying only, "She's twelve," as if that were explanation enough for Josie's emotional outburst.

"Ah," the terrorist said. "A difficult age. Not yet a woman, but no longer a little girl, either."

Nic nodded, then turned the conversation back to business, hoping al-Zwahiri wouldn't find his abruptness rude. "Yes. Now, about the LoRS bomb? I should think your organization would find a weapon such as this incredibly effective."

Ahmed al-Zwahiri finally turned his gaze from the now-closed door back to Nic, who had taken his seat again behind a massive mahogany desk that took four men to lift. Nic forced himself to breathe evenly as the man stroked his dark beard for one long minute that turned into two, and then three. To stay calm, Nic focused his attention on the warm breeze blowing in from the open French doors that led out to the wraparound porch of his home. Beyond the porch was a white sand beach and the turquoise blue waters of the South Pacific. This ten-thousand-square-foot beachfront home was just one of the advantages of his line of work.

"Yes," al-Zwahiri said finally, breaking the silence. "I believe my organization will find your new bomb very useful. We already have plans in the works for a—shall we say, festive?—New Year's Eve celebration, plans I may need to rethink now. Can you absolutely assure me that this new weapon will be in my hands prior to December 31?"

Without hesitating, Nic nodded. "Yes. I give you my promise. The LoRS bomb will be delivered before the end of the year."

"Good. I'll make arrangements to wire you the down payment when I arrive back in Damascus next week." The terrorist stood then, his body lean from many years spent in barren training camps. He held out one deeply tanned hand. Nic stood and reached across his desk, taking al-Zwahiri's hand in his own and shaking it firmly.

As he looked into the man's dark eyes, he thought to himself, *Here's to making yet another deal with the devil.*

"WHAT makes you think the blonde you ran into was Rita's buyer?" Race asked after stepping into Aimee's office at McConnell Aerospace and closing the door behind him.

Like her, he had changed back into his mild-mannered office drone disguise, a shapeless blue suit hiding his muscular frame and thick glasses obscuring the sharpness in his gray eyes. He sat down in the chair across from her desk and crossed one ankle over his knee, his brown leather shoes polished to a high shine.

"It was just... I don't know. The look in her eyes, I guess," Aimee said with a shrug. "Plus, I held the bathroom door open just long enough to see her enter the stall where Rita had stashed the plans."

"Could be a coincidence," Race suggested, pushing his glasses farther up the bridge of his nose.

"I'm not a big believer in coincidence." Aimee pushed back her chair and stood up. She felt restless being cooped up in this ten-foot-by-ten-foot box after the morning's excitement. "If it was her, it will only take one call to Rita for her to confirm that I was the only one who was in that stall between her and the buyer."

Aimee leaned back against the air-conditioning vent that ran under the windows facing the McConnell parking lot below and crossed her arms in front of her chest. She *knew* the blonde was the buyer as surely as if the woman's name tag had proclaimed it so. Even worse, she knew that meant the CIA was going to ask her to meet with the buyer instead of—as she'd planned when she'd hastily scribbled her note on the file folder that morning—sending an agent in instead.

This was a whole level of danger she had not anticipated—or charged for—on this job. When Joe McConnell had first contacted her to ask if she could ferret out the employee in his organization who was guilty of corporate espionage, she had figured it would be a fairly easy case of identifying those with access to top-secret files and then following the money trail that would lead to their spy. Her hourly fee was adequate compensation for investigation and surveillance, but wasn't nearly enough to make up for risking her life.

"We really need you to meet with the buyer," Race said, leaning forward with his elbows on her desk, his fingers laced tightly together. "If she was the woman coming in as you were leaving, she'll know something is wrong if we send in another agent."

"I know," Aimee admitted glumly, dropping her gaze to the bland beige carpet beneath her feet. "But then what? So I hand you the buyer and you take her into custody. She's not likely to tell you anything—she has to know her boss would kill her if she does."

"She might cooperate."

Aimee looked back up at him and saw that he looked as doubtful as she felt. "Right. So that's all you want me to do? Meet with the buyer, set her up so you guys can arrest her?"

Race kept his gaze steady on her, at least having the decency not to look away as he answered. "No. What I'd really like is for you to tell her you're not going to hand over the plans to anyone but her boss. Would you be willing to do that?"

She could not believe the gall of this guy, thinking she'd just throw away everything she'd worked so hard for over the last seven months—her company, her new life . . . her future. He had to be nuts if he thought she'd do it. Aimee shook her head and pushed away from the window to sit back down in her chair. Race was so close she could have reached out and took his hands in hers. But she didn't. Instead, she steepled her fingers together over the top of her desk, looked him straight in the eye, and said, "Sure, I'll do it. For twice my usual hourly rate."

Race didn't even blink as he stood up and walked to the door. Then, with his hand on the doorknob, he nodded once and said, "Done."

EIGHT

JOSIE burrowed deep under the covers of her bed, clutching the well-worn brown and once-white stuffed dog to her chest as tears dripped off the bridge of her nose and onto the clean sheets beneath her. It seemed as if everyone had turned against her today: first Giselle, then God, and then her own father.

Although she probably shouldn't blame God for what had happened to her earlier that evening at Mrs. Jacobs's house. Getting her period for the first time was really Mother Nature's fault.

Josie put a hand on her stomach and groaned as another cramp seized her, making her draw her knees up to her chest as if that would make the pain stop. It didn't, of course, and two more fat tears dripped down onto the lavender sheets one of the housekeeper's assistants had put on her bed that morning.

She had felt a little sick to her stomach and tearful all day, but she'd blamed that on her fight with Giselle. She hadn't been looking forward to spending the night with Mrs. Jacobs. She hadn't been looking forward to spending the night with Mrs. Jacobs, not because the woman who ran their household didn't treat her well, but because she was so . . . Well, Josie wasn't quite sure what the word was. It was just that whenever she went to spend the night with Mrs. Jacobs, she felt like she was in the way. Mrs. Jacobs politely answered her questions, but she seemed to prefer it when Josie watched DVDs in the TV room and didn't say anything at all.

Unfortunately, with the argument she and Giselle had had that morning, Josie had no choice. Daddy refused to let her stay in the house when he had his business parties—even if she promised to stay in her room and not sneak downstairs for anything, not even a Coke. So after an early supper of grilled shrimp and rice, she'd packed an overnight bag with pajamas and Puppy and her toothbrush and headed off down the beach to the small bungalow where Mrs. Jacobs lived with a Siamese cat that always looked at Josie as if she were a bug he'd like to smash under one of his delicate silver paws. Josie didn't much like that cat, and she suspected the cat felt the same way about her.

Resigned to a dull night of watching the same old Doris Day/Rock Hudson movies Mrs. Jacobs always played when Josie came over, she'd curled up on the white sofa in the TV room, clutching one of the sky blue and white striped pillows in her lap as her stomach continued to ache as it had on and off all day. She hated fighting with Giselle. It made her feel awful.

Only, when Josie got up to go to the bathroom after *Pillow Talk* ended, she realized with a mounting sense of horror that it wasn't her argument with Giselle that was making her stomach clench. The couch where she'd been sitting was spotted with blood.

With a gasp, Josie threw the pillow she'd been clutching over the stains. As she backed out of the TV room, her mind raced. She couldn't let Mrs. Jacobs see what she'd done. She'd rather walk out into the ocean and have a shark eat her than to have to face the housekeeper and tell her she'd bled all over the woman's couch.

God, this was horrible.

Josie raced down the hall and into the bathroom, locking the door behind her. She leaned against the door and squeezed her eyes tightly shut to stop the tears that threatened to spill down her cheeks.

If only Gi were here. She'd know what to do. Gi had gotten her period almost a year ago, and, with a mother around, it had never seemed like a big deal to her. But this humiliating accident was a big deal to Josie.

Another cramp squeezed her insides and Josie wrapped her arms around her middle. What was she going to do?

With a shuddering breath, Josie told herself to stop being such a baby. First, she had to do something about the blood. She could deal with everything else once that was taken care of.

Quietly, so as not to make Mrs. Jacobs think she was snooping around in her things, Josie went through the cupboards below the sink, hoping she'd find an old box of Kotex or something. Giselle had explained to her how those worked. Josie should have thought to ask her best friend for a few extra just for this type of emergency.

Not finding anything in the cupboards, Josie opened the medicine cabinet, wincing when it squeaked loudly enough to be heard all the way down the hall. Her fingers skimmed over tubes of Neosporin, Ben-Gay, Vicks cough medicine, Q-tips . . . but not even one old forgotten tampon. Not that she'd really know what to do with that. It wasn't like she and Gi got into that much detail about what went where.

Desperate, Josie sat down on the toilet and put her head in her hands. She had to get home. Daddy would know what to do. And even though it was the coward's way out, she knew that he would take care of what Josie had done to Mrs. Jacobs's couch. Josie was too mortified to tell the housekeeper what had happened.

Her decision made, Josie flung open the door of the bathroom and raced back to the guest bedroom Mrs. Jacobs had made up for her. She grabbed her bag off the bed and snuck back down the hall. As she shuffled past the TV room, she saw that Mrs. Jacobs had gone over to straighten the pillows on the couch. Her back was to Josie and she was muttering and shaking her head, the blue and white pillow Josie had clutched in her lap during the movie dangling from one hand.

"I'm going home, Mrs. Jacobs," Josie called as she fled down the hallway with her overnight bag bumping her thigh as she ran. She heard Mrs. Jacobs's voice as she pushed open the front door, but she didn't stop. She was too embarrassed to face the woman right now.

Josie started to cry as she slipped inside her house through the unlocked back door. She knew Daddy would be angry with her at first for coming home during one of his meetings, but after she told him what was wrong, he would make everything all right again.

Only, when she'd interrupted him, everything hadn't been all right. Daddy had been furious with her, not even giving her the chance to explain what was wrong. And it wasn't like she disobeyed him all the time. He had no right to get mad at her like that and order her up to her room like a naughty child.

Josie's breath caught in her throat as another sob choked her. She rubbed her chin across the top of Puppy's head, feeling as if the stuffed animal she'd had for as long as she could remember was her only friend in the whole wide world.

"I love you, Puppy," she said, clutching the dog tightly to her chest.

Then she heard the sound of her bedroom door opening and curled herself up into an even tighter ball in the middle of her big bed. For the first time in her life, today Josie had gotten a taste of what it was like to be totally alone.

"Josie? Come out, honey. We need to talk," her father said, his voice much nicer than it had been half an hour before.

Josie felt the side of her bed sag under her father's weight as he sat down, but she stayed huddled under the covers, even the sound of the waves on the beach outside her open windows muffled by the thick comforter enfolding her. She wished she could hide here forever, just her and Puppy. Safe and sound in their little cocoon.

"Mrs. Jacobs called me," her father said hesitantly.

Josie closed her eyes, feeling the heat of embarrassment creeping up her cheeks.

"I told her I'd . . . uh, take care of her couch. This is not the sort of thing that's never happened before, you know."

Yes, but it's never happened to me *before,* Josie wailed silently.

"I had one of the staff, uh, gather up some things you might need. I'll just leave them here. Unless you, uh, need some help or . . . er, anything?"

Josie remained silent under the covers, half-wanting to come out and put her arms around her father's neck and sit in his lap and have him tell her everything was going to be all right, and half-wanting to just remain where she was, alone with her misery.

In the end, misery won out.

The bed creaked ever so slightly as her father stood up. He hesitated for a moment, then Josie felt the warmth of his big, strong hand on her head. He squeezed gently for just a second. And then he was gone, leaving Josie caught in a world between stuffed animals and sanitary pads.

"HE agreed to pay you how much?" Daphne Donovan, Aimee's housemate and one of the three founders of Partners In Crime, sounded impressed.

"Twice our regular rate," Aimee repeated into her headset, swiveling around in her chair to look at the bookshelf in her office and frowning when she realized she had forgotten to remove the diploma that had caused Race to question her true identity. "I at least expected him to try to bargain me down or tell me that he had to get approval. Instead he just said 'done' and walked out of my office as if I'd just asked for a fifty-cent raise."

"He obviously expected something like this."

"Obviously," Aimee agreed as she stood up to take the diploma off her shelf and tuck it into her briefcase. She'd have to get a new one made before taking her next case. "I suppose that's not surprising. I've made my motives pretty clear. I'm in this to make money. If I do some good along the way, that's just icing on the cake."

"Speaking of making money," Daff said over the hum of what sounded like coffee beans being ground. "Your sister Lauren dropped by today. Didn't you tell your family you were going to be in San Antonio?"

Aimee grimaced at the microphone of her headset. "No. I didn't want anyone to be able to track me here. I've been in touch by e-mail, but Lauren never mentioned that she planned to stop by."

"She said she had just gotten back from somewhere and felt like a visit. She was in one of those B places—Bermuda, Barbados, Bahamas. I can't remember exactly what she said."

Aimee sat back down and stared at her computer screen.

She was still more than a little stunned that Race—and the government—had agreed to pay her exorbitant hourly fee. If they'd paid her that much as an agent, she never would have left the FBI. "Bermuda," she said. "Lauren was in Bermuda doing a shoot for *Sports Illustrated*. It's Kaylee who's in the Bahamas."

"Photo shoot?"

"Bra commercial."

"Rough life," Daff said.

"It's not as glamorous as it seems," Aimee said, having heard her supermodel sisters say it over and over again throughout the years.

"Yeah, I'll bet." Daphne didn't sound convinced.

Aimee wasn't certain she was convinced, either, although she'd gone on a few shoots with her sisters and seen the long hours the models put in. Not to mention the brutal way they were discussed by photographers, makeup artists, wardrobe people, and everyone else involved. The models were often treated as if they had no feelings, as if having a photographer say to a five-foot-nine woman who weighed one hundred and ten pounds that her stomach was so fat it looked as if she'd just eaten two dozen donuts, and couldn't she just go and throw up like everyone else wasn't hurtful. And, of course, most models didn't make the type of livings her sisters did, either. Still, when you considered that most law enforcement officers made less than $50,000 a year and were expected to put their lives on the line, it was difficult to feel too sorry for someone netting close to three million whose biggest worry was a little premenstrual bloating.

"I'll give Lauren a call and let her know I'm sorry I missed her," Aimee said, absently clicking on the e-mail message Joe McConnell had just sent her. She, Race, and Joe had met after Aimee returned from the conference. He was stunned to discover that Race was with the CIA, and eagerly agreed to let them remain in their current positions so as not to arouse anyone's suspicions. Joe had been equally stunned to learn that Ron Jefferson was the man responsible for the information leak. Ron's father had been with McConnell back when Joe had first started the company. He was the last person Joe had suspected, although it seemed to make him feel better when he found out that Ron's part in the plot was unintentional.

"All right. Well, you'll let us know if you need our help, right?" Daphne asked, sounding unconcerned.

Aimee closed her eyes for a moment and pinched the bridge of her nose. Of the three partners, Daphne had been the most affected by her time in the FBI. She'd been tracking one of the 9/11 hijackers but had been unable to stop him before he successfully led a team of terrorists to fly their plane into one of the World Trade Center towers. She had lived with the deaths of the people killed that day on her conscience ever since. Both Aimee and Raine feared that Daff would never forgive herself.

Every day she seemed to grow more and more disconnected to the world around her, and less concerned about her own safety and the welfare of those who cared about her. Aimee had suggested counseling, but Daphne refused to talk about her guilt with anyone. Aimee often wondered if it was because Daff didn't want to heal.

Aimee sighed and opened her eyes. "Yeah, I'll let you know if I need you," she said, then hung up after Daphne said her good-byes.

She pulled the headset from around her neck and tossed it down on her desk. Rubbing the back of her neck with one hand, Aimee rolled her head around to loosen her taut muscles. Despite the nonchalant, I'll-do-anything-for-a-buck attitude she wore along with her mousy disguise, this whole situation scared the hell out of her. She'd be a fool if it didn't.

It was one thing to perform a nice quiet investigation on someone and his bank records—or even to break into his house when she knew nobody was home—and quite another altogether to be playing mind games with the representative of a suspected arms dealer.

Geez, what had she been thinking when she took those plans?

She sighed again, knowing the answer to that question lay so deeply ingrained within her value system that she'd never be able to eradicate it. What she'd been thinking when she took those plans was that she would do anything, *anything,* in her power to keep them from falling into the wrong hands.

Aimee nearly jumped when someone tapped on her office door. Looking up, she saw that it was Race and motioned for him to come in.

He looked different today, having discarded his jacket and tie and unbuttoned the top two buttons of his starched white shirt. He'd also lost the thick glasses he usually wore around the office. That alone made an enormous difference in his appearance.

"Do you need the glasses, or are they just a prop?" she asked as Race sat down across from her.

One corner of his mouth quirked upward. "Unfortunately, I need them. I usually wear contacts, though. The glasses are part of the disguise."

"Ah. They work really well."

"Yes, don't they? You know, growing up, I never thought I'd need a disguise to downplay my looks."

Surprised, Aimee leaned over to pick up a pen lying on her desk. "So you weren't always the gorgeous hunk you are now?" she asked with a grin and a bat of her eyelashes.

A hint of color stained Race's cheeks and Aimee was amused to realize that she'd embarrassed him. He cleared his throat before answering. "Let's just say that when your parents give you a name like Horace and it turns out that you're really good at math, it's almost inevitable that you're going to wind up fat and pimply."

Aimee laughed and sat back. "Okay, I don't get the correlation."

"When you don't have any friends, it's easier to stay inside and eat than go outside and try to play with kids who just make fun of you."

Aimee winced, remembering how mean kids could be. She, herself, had been hurt enough times to know that. The whispered remarks behind her back about "Aimee the ugly duckling" had certainly found their mark a time or two. "I'm sorry," she said.

Race waved a hand in the air, as if waving away childhood pain was that easy. "It's all right. Crap like that builds character."

"So they say," Aimee agreed. They eyed each other in silence for a moment, lost in the remembrance of those so-called character-building moments. "Anyway, what brings you here? I'm sure you didn't come to discuss your childhood."

"No, I didn't. I wanted to let you know what was going on in the case." Race straightened his shoulders and leaned forward, slipping into no-nonsense mode. "We were able to get a warrant to tap Rita's phones. She got a call from the buyer but we were unable to trace the number or pinpoint the woman's location."

"Did the buyer tell Rita the plans were gone?"

"Yes. And she told Rita she'd better deliver another set. The buyer didn't specifically threaten Rita's life, but I think they both knew that was implied."

Aimee grimaced. She had no doubt the woman they were dealing with would kill to get what she wanted, which meant Rita's life was in real danger. "She won't be able to get another set of plans. Joe talked to Ron Jefferson this afternoon. Ron was horrified to learn that he was the key to McConnell's information leak. Joe granted him an immediate leave of absence and I think they both realize that Ron won't be coming back to McConnell. It's sad, really. Ron had no idea he was duped. He thought Rita loved him."

"I hope Joe plans to revamp McConnell's network security. If this sort of thing happened once, it could easily happen again."

"He blocked out several hours tomorrow morning to meet with Ron's second-in-command to discuss that very issue."

"Good. We've got a man on Rita to keep her out of danger, but we don't want to roll her up just yet. If she disappears, the buyer might balk at meeting with you. We're hopeful that once she realizes Rita can't get another set of the plans, she'll arrange to meet with you before attempting to go after Rita."

"Have your people checked the Hotmail account I gave to the buyer as a way to contact me?" Aimee asked.

Race nodded his head. "Yes, but there's been nothing yet. I figure the buyer will ignore you until she realizes you're her only other option."

"I agree. She'll try to stick with the devil she knows until it becomes clear that Rita can't deliver."

"We've done all we can do for now. We've got a guy staked

out at Ron Jefferson's house in case Rita shows up and there's trouble. Now it looks like all we can do is sit around and wait."

Aimee sat back in her chair, lacing her fingers together on top of her desk. "Well, now you've found the one thing that I am definitely good at."

"What's that?" Race asked.

"Playing the waiting game," Aimee answered with a smile.

NINE

"I'M sorry to interrupt you, Mr. Sabre, but Josephine hasn't come out of her room all day. Miss Simonds has come calling twice, but Josephine refuses to come down to see her. I thought you might like to know."

Nic looked up from his computer screen, where he was researching the current head of a group in Haiti that was trying to overthrow a rival drug lord. It was never difficult to find a spot in the world where one group of people was attempting to annihilate another, but Nic was only interested in the well-funded groups. It was no use offering weapons to people who couldn't afford to buy them.

He cleared his throat. "Ah, thank you, Mrs. Jacobs. I'll go up and talk to her."

After the housekeeper discreetly closed the door behind her, Nic neatly stacked the files scattered across his desk, closed the lid of his laptop, and unplugged it from the power supply. Then, as he always did upon leaving his office—even for just a few moments—he placed it all in the walk-in safe hidden behind a set of shuttered folding doors. The heavy door to the safe swung shut without a sound and Nic spun the tumbler to lock it securely. Unconsciously, he tugged at the door, making certain it was firmly shut before he closed the folding doors and left his office, locking the door behind him.

Nic had come into this business with a distrust of others that was so firmly rooted in his soul that he trusted no one, not even his most loyal employees, with access to his personal files. Of everyone who worked for Nic, Luke knew the most about all of Nic's various business ventures. At some point, it had simply become too much for Nic to handle on his own. He knew the implication of this; that Luke, being the closest to him, was also the one most likely to betray him. Which is why, when Nic had been searching for a financial manager, he had chosen a man who was married and wanted children. If Luke ever turned on him, Nic would hunt down Luke's family and would kill them all while Luke watched.

He sincerely hoped that just knowing Nic was capable of such a thing would keep Luke quiet. That and the handsome salary he paid the man, who, like Nic, had never earned a high school diploma but was brilliant at what he did.

Nic heard Giselle Simonds's laughter as he turned toward the front entrance of his home. Giselle was a bright child, if somewhat moody and unpredictable at times. Still, she was good company for Josie, who was sometimes too serious for Nic's liking.

"Hello, Giselle," he called. "How are you today?"

"I'm fine, Mr. Sabre. I came to see if Josie wanted to play, and Mrs. Jacobs told me to wait here. This is Bob from Mel's Air Service," she said in a rush.

Nic nodded to the young man who looked to be about twice Giselle's age. Their age difference didn't stop the man from eyeing the young girl dressed in a pair of denim shorts and a mint green T-shirt that clearly outlined her budding breasts.

After he managed to get Josie out of her room, he would make a call to Mel himself. If that young man came to the island again, Nic would arrange for another service to make their deliveries.

"I'll go up and see what's keeping Josie. I assume you have work to do?" he said, addressing the question to Bob. Only an idiot would have missed the warning in his tone, and Bob apparently was no idiot.

"Yes, sir. Giselle, it was nice to meet you." With that, the young man hurried off.

"I'm sure Mrs. Jacobs would be happy to pack you girls some sodas for the boat ride," Nic suggested.

Giselle seemed bewildered by the ease at which he had dispatched her new friend, but she nodded her head, her curly mop of blond hair dancing around her face as she did so. "Uh, thanks," she said, before heading off in the direction of the kitchen.

Nic allowed himself a small smile as he headed up the stairs. Let Giselle test out her fledgling feminine wiles on a boy closer to her own age.

When he arrived in front of Josie's door, he found it closed, which was unusual. Josie almost never closed her door, even while dressing. He supposed she was still young enough to feel unself-conscious about her body. Although, he was beginning to think that was about to change.

It was odd, he had never felt inadequate as a parent until the night before. As a man who'd had a fair number of lovers, he wasn't unfamiliar with the process of menstruation. But, as a man, he also had no idea what it was like for his daughter to go through it for the first time and, last night, he had been at a loss for what to do to comfort Josie or to ease her embarrassment about something that was as natural—and as inevitable—as the tides.

"Josie?" he called, rapping softly at her bedroom door.

There was a long pause before she answered, as if she had spent some time considering whether to ignore his summons or not. "Yes?" she said finally, her voice faint.

"May I come in?" He wasn't sure why he had asked . . . or what he would do if she said no.

Again, she paused for a long moment before answering, "All right."

Nic pushed open the door to the first room he'd had decorated after building this house. The floors were wide planks of Brazilian teak, the wood a rich red color that made the room warm and inviting. A light-colored silk carpet woven with deep greens, reds, and blues lay on the floor under Josie's bed. She had told him once that she loved burying her bare toes in the carpet every morning after getting out of bed. The bed itself was a simple sleigh bed carved from the same teak as the floors. For her bedding, Nic had insisted on Egyptian cotton and a light-colored duvet. The room reminded him of a picture of a fancy beach cottage he had once seen in a discarded magazine from the trash pile where Nic had grown up.

He loved the room and all it represented.

Curled up on the padded window seat that overlooked the upstairs balcony and the beach beyond, Josie watched him silently, waiting for him to make the first move. Nic walked across the room and sat down near her bare feet. Her toenails were painted a garish blue—Nic had long given up trying to convince her that red and pink were the only appropriate colors for a young woman's nails—and the nails were ragged and uneven. He supposed that was how pedicures turned out when they were given by another child.

"Honey, I know you aren't feeling your best, but I think you'd feel better if you got out of your room and did something. Giselle's downstairs. She thought you might like to go outside and play."

Josie put her thumb in the book she had been reading and rested it on her drawn-up knees. "I'd like to keep reading, if that's all right," she said, her voice sounding painfully grown-up to Nic's ears. Her dark eyes were so full of sadness that Nic felt the muscles around his heart constrict. The pain was so sudden and so intense that he unconsciously raised a hand to rub his chest. This seemed to be more than just the hurt of cramps or the embarrassment of facing Mrs. Jacobs again after what had happened last night.

Nic reached out and squeezed one of Josie's knees comfortingly. "Is there something you'd like to talk about?"

Josie looked down at the book in her lap, her dark hair shielding her face from him. When Nic saw two teardrops splash onto the pages of her book, the ache in his chest became nearly overwhelming.

"I miss having a mom," Josie said as another set of tears dripped down her cheeks to blur the pages of her book.

Nic opened his mouth to say something consoling, but stopped himself before the words slipped out. There was nothing he could say that wouldn't sound trite. Of course she missed having a mother. And despite how much he loved her, being her father was not the same. He had no idea what it felt like to grow from a girl to a woman, had no advice to offer her on the things she would need to know.

"I'm sorry," he said simply.

As inadequate as those words were, they seemed to be enough. Pushing her book off her lap, Josie threw her arms around her father and sobbed as if she were going through the heartbreak of losing her mother for the first time. In some sense, she was, Nic thought as he rubbed Josie's back as he had done when she was a baby. Before now, it was almost as though she hadn't realized what she was missing by going through life without a mother. Before now, her father had been enough.

But suddenly, he wasn't enough anymore.

Nic squeezed his eyes shut as he pushed that thought away. He had no choice but to be enough. He was all Josie had.

He opened his eyes again when the cell phone he'd slipped into his pocket before coming upstairs rang. Wishing he could just ignore its insistent summons, Nic kept one arm around his daughter as he fished the phone out of his pocket and looked at the display. Unknown number, unknown name. Nic sighed. Nearly everyone he did business with had untraceable phones. This could be anyone, including Ahmed al-Zwahiri, calling to perhaps get more information about the LoRS bomb before authorizing a wire transfer for the down payment on his order.

Nic gave Josie one last pat on her back before pulling out of her embrace. "I'm sorry, honey," he said. "I have to take this call. I think it would be good for you to go play with Giselle. You girls need to stop fighting. She was mature enough to make the first move, now it's your turn to act like an adult."

Josie sniffled one last time and wiped her eyes with the heels of her hands. As Nic flipped open his phone and said, "Hello," she was already off the window seat and was heading toward the bathroom that adjoined her room. Nic nodded approvingly, impressed as always at Josie's willingness to do the right thing, even when it was difficult for her.

"Nic, it's Diana," Giselle's mother—and one of Nic's key employees—said, her voice sounding odd to Nic's ears.

Nic looked to the bathroom door, which Josie had closed.

He could hear water running, but didn't want to chance that she could overhear his conversation, so he walked across her room and out into the hall before responding. "Yes? Where are you?"

"Not where I'm supposed to be," Diana Simonds said shortly.

"You're *supposed* to be on a plane back to the island," Nic said, then added, "With the propulsion system plans."

"Well, I'm still in San Antonio, stuck in this miserable dry heat. We've been double-crossed. Our target left the plans at the drop site, but she was stupid enough to let herself get tailed. Someone else took the plans and insists I contact her to discuss new terms."

Nic clenched his teeth and stared unseeingly down the hall. This couldn't be happening. Not now. They had to have those plans to go forward with the LoRS bomb production. They couldn't afford a delay of even a few days—if al-Zwahiri found out that the demonstration had to be postponed, he would likewise postpone his down payment . . . if he didn't back out of the sale entirely.

"How did you let this happen?" Nic asked, attempting to remain calm despite his rage.

Diana had been with him long enough to know better than to attempt to deflect the blame, knew that Nic would hold her 100 percent accountable for the success—or failure—of her part of this mission. "I saw our target being followed to the drop site but I underestimated the woman. I heard her in the restroom being ill, and fell for it. I should have known, should have suspected."

Nic closed his eyes, telling himself to think. They needed those plans. Now. "Have you contacted the target, told her to go back in and get another set of the plans?"

"Of course," Diana said. "Unfortunately, she will not be able to procure them through her regular channel. The man she was using to get to the information refused to see her. I believe he's been told that he was being duped, although he simply informed our target that he no longer desires her company."

"Have you taken care of her? I don't want her loose. She may be able to give the authorities something that might lead them back to us. Now that we have no use for her . . ." Nic left the remainder of his thought unsaid. They both knew what he meant.

"She's being watched, but I'll deal with it later this evening. You can rest assured, in this I will not fail."

"I know you won't. The risks are too great. Your family . . . your daughter . . . they depend on you to succeed, Diana."

"I understand," Diana said. "I wasn't calling you to admit defeat, merely to let you know that there's been a delay. But I will take care of it. This upstart who dared to interfere with me—"

"With us," Nic interrupted.

"Yes, of course. With us," Diana conceded. "She will give me the plans. And then . . ." She paused for the space of a heartbeat, then added softly, "And then she will die."

"See to it, then," Nic said sharply, ending the call. It was only as he turned to go back down the stairs that he noticed a shadow moving behind his daughter's door.

WHEN Race ran his tongue lightly over the instep of her left foot, Aimee nearly died from the sheer pleasure of the sensation. She threw her head back and moaned as he moved up, slowly licking and kissing his way up her calves to the sensitive skin behind her knees to her firm inner thighs. Her hips arched, waiting, wanting him to touch the part of her body that was now throbbing with need.

"Please," she whispered, opening herself to him.

"Aimee." His breath was warm in her ear, tickling her and making her shiver.

"Yes," she said.

"Aimee, wake up," he said.

Aimee's eyes slid half-open to see Race crouched, fully clothed, beside her bed. He was not naked and sweaty, nor was he doing any of the delicious things she had imagined him doing in what suddenly became clear was only a dream. She groaned again, this time in frustration. Then, from that part of her brain that told her to go ahead and have that triple fudge brownie ice-cream cone even though she was on a diet, a thought popped out. Why deny herself? She was single. Race was single . . . or, at least, she thought he was.

Aimee rolled onto her side, her face now just inches from Race's. "Are you married?" she whispered.

Race shot her a look that told her he was concerned that she had lost her mind. "No."

"Not attached? No girlfriend waiting back home for you or anything?"

His brow furrowed, his dark eyebrows drawing together over those dangerous gray eyes. "No," he repeated. "Why do you ask?"

"Because if you were, I wouldn't do this," Aimee said, then reached one hand up and slid her fingers into his thick hair as she closed the gap between their lips.

He succumbed easily enough, Aimee thought with no small measure of satisfaction. Their lips met, mouths open, and tongues eagerly exploring. It was even better than she had imagined it would be, his lips firm and warm, his touch smooth and knowing.

Race was the first to pull back, a smile playing about his mouth. "That must have been some dream, huh?" he said.

"Yeah, right up until the end," Aimee answered wryly, knowing that no matter how tempting it was for them to have sex, the timing wasn't exactly right.

Race planted a soft kiss on her forehead before standing up, the bulge in his jeans unmistakable. "Believe me, I'd like nothing better than to make love right now. But—"

Aimee laughed and sat up, the sheet she'd covered herself with pooling around her waist. "But we're too busy saving the world to take time out for sex," she said before he could finish.

Race grinned back. "Exactly. Although, if you don't put on some clothes soon, I may have to rethink my position."

Aimee looked down at the low-cut green silk nightie she'd bought for herself last month at Victoria's Secret. While it wasn't exactly risqué, it wasn't flannel jammies, either. That same devil that had taunted her to kiss Race in the first place teased her again. Blinking up at Race, she slid out of bed and walked toward him. Then, leaning out, her breasts brushing his chest, she pulled a matching robe from her closet.

She saw him cringe as he turned and walked out of her room and into the living room. Aimee tried not to gloat as she followed him out into the living room—after all, she was just as aroused as he was.

"What are you doing here anyway? And how did you get in?" she asked, curling her feet under her on the couch as she watched Race sit down on the far end of the sofa.

Race gave her one of those "That's classified, ma'am" looks and said, "They did teach us a thing or two at spook school."

"As a taxpayer, I'm glad to hear it," Aimee said.

"I'm here because we've received a message from the buyer. I didn't use the front door because I didn't want to alert anyone that I was here. Just in case you're being watched."

Aimee pulled her robe tighter around her. The thought that someone might be watching her every move was more than a little disturbing. She'd never been on the receiving end of a surveillance before. She looked up to make certain the kitchen blinds were closed, and vowed to keep them that way from now on.

"The buyer wants to meet and is going to send details of the rendezvous spot later," Race said, interrupting her thoughts.

"Later? Why not send them now?" Aimee asked.

"My guess is she doesn't trust you. If you're planning a trap, she doesn't want to give you the opportunity to get a team in place at the meeting point. When she does send instructions, I'll bet she gives you just enough time to get there."

"Ah. But then why contact me now? Why not just wait until she's ready to meet?"

"She wants you to know she's interested, so you don't destroy the plans or misplace them or think they're nothing, after all. I think she's desperate. If not, she'd take her time, try to find another mole inside McConnell. Meeting with you . . ." Race paused, shook his head. "It's risky. There's got to be a lot at stake for her to take this sort of chance."

"How does she know I'm not setting a trap?"

"She doesn't, not really. She asked for some personal information about you—your social security number, where you were born, that sort of thing. I'm sure she's doing a background check on you right now. If there's anything that makes her suspicious, we won't hear from her again."

Aimee set her feet down on the floor with a thunk. "What about my fingerprints? In the FBI files? Surely, she'll—"

"We took care of that," Race interrupted.

Aimee raised her eyebrows. "Wow, you guys are fast."

"We've had some experience making people disappear," Race deadpanned.

"Okay, so what's next? We sit around and wait some more?"

Race sighed and nodded at the same time. "I'm afraid so. But that doesn't mean we don't prepare. That's actually the main reason I came by tonight. We weren't certain when the buyer would want to meet and we want to make sure that you're ready."

"What do you mean?" Aimee asked.

"I mean, we're going to do everything we can to protect you, but there may be times when you're only going to have yourself to rely on."

Aimee thoughtfully chewed on the inside of her cheek for a moment. She wasn't foolish enough to think that Race was questioning her abilities. The truth was, what she was about to do was going to be dangerous. And because she'd gone undercover without backup before, she knew how risky it could be. Stomping her foot and saying, "I don't need help, I can take care of myself," was only something a complete idiot would do.

Aimee would take all the help she could get.

"So, what have you got for me?" she asked. "Should I start calling you Q?"

Race turned a thousand-watt smile on her, a smile that killed her mocking sarcasm where it stood. Damn, but he was handsome when he smiled like that.

"No," he said, his words seeming to take an inordinate amount of time to make it from his lips to her ears. "I can't take credit for inventing any of this stuff. But you'd better not start calling me Miss Moneypenny, either."

Aimee cleared her throat to restart her brain. "Uh, no, I don't think that fits at all," she said, then muttered under her breath, "Clark might be more fitting."

"I'm not Superman," Race said, his grin widening as he caught her mumbled words.

Aimee grimaced. "Well, neither am I, so I hope like hell that whatever gadgets you brought for me are going to do the trick."

Race leaned over and squeezed her shoulder. Aimee looked up at him, and saw that his eyes had gone serious. "I won't let you down," he said.

"I know you won't," Aimee said, equally serious. It was odd that she felt such trust in a man that, a few days ago, she had suspected might be a traitor. If was as if in seeing him out of disguise, she had seen him for the man he really was.

Either that or she had been duped by a cute guy with a nice ass. She certainly wouldn't be the first woman to fall for that.

"What are you smiling about?" Race asked.

Aimee blinked and shook her head, breaking the spell between them. "Nothing. So, are you going to show me your toys?"

Race shot her a strange look before he, too, shook his head and got up off the couch. He picked up a canvas bag that Aimee hadn't noticed sitting behind the sofa. Setting the bag on her dining room table, he motioned for her to join him.

"This is a transmitter that can tell us, to within two feet, your exact location," Race said, holding up a black and silver disk that was smaller than a dime. "Because of the risk that the buyer may sweep you or your belongings for bugs, this transmitter only works when you activate it by pressing this button continuously for three seconds."

Aimee took the transmitter and studied it for a moment, making certain she understood how it worked.

"Obviously, if you don't activate the transmitter, we won't know where you are," Race added, studying her face for a reaction.

Aimee's gaze met his. "I understand," she said. And she did. If she couldn't find a safe place to transmit her location, she was all alone in this. The CIA couldn't help her if they didn't know where to find her.

Next, Race handed her a thick gold pen. "We've engraved this with your initials, to give you a cover story about it. You can say it's something special—a gift from a now-deceased relative or something. It's fourteen-karat gold. If you unscrew it, it appears to be nothing more than a regular pen."

Aimee unscrewed it from the middle and looked at both pieces in her hands. As Race said, it appeared to be nothing more than an ordinary writing instrument. She screwed the two halves together again and handed it back to Race. He pressed the clip at the end of the pen while twisting the bottom half. This time, the outer casing of the pen slid apart. Race moved to stand next to her, so close that the denim of his jeans rubbed against her bare thigh. Aimee reminded her libido that her life could be at stake here, which sent it crawling back to its hiding place, at least temporarily.

"It's a digital camera. It can only store sixteen pictures at a time, but it's the best we've got right now. To take a picture, you look through the lens like this," Race said, holding it out so she could see through the tiny viewfinder. "Then you store the picture by clicking the clip."

"How can I get the pictures off of it?" Aimee asked.

"Unfortunately, you have to have a special reader. The memory chips are hardwired into the pen itself, so there are no replacements. You have to bring the pen in, download the pictures from it, and then you can start over again. As I said, it's not perfect, but it's the best we have right now."

Aimee took the pen and slid it back together again. Then she tested out making it come apart several times before nodding and saying, "Okay, what else have you got?"

Race held up an ordinary-looking compact and slid it open, slipping a thumbnail under what looked to be a bed of pressed translucent powder. "This is enabled with a surveillance detector that can tell you if a room is bugged for either audio or video surveillance and also indicates if you're in an area where GPS tracking signals are being monitored." Race tilted the compact so that she could see the three indicator lights, all green at the moment. "The lights will flash red if surveillance equipment is detected."

"Amazing," Aimee said. She took the compact and turned it over a few times. It was light—no more than a few ounces—and gave no indication that it was not exactly what it seemed to be.

"That's all I've got," Race said, while Aimee looked appreciatively at her new gadgets.

"This stuff is great. I never got toys like these in the Bureau," Aimee said, running her hand over the smooth surface of the compact. When Race yawned, she realized that they both needed to go back to bed. Alone, unfortunately. "Will I see you in the office tomorrow?" she asked, stifling her own yawn with the back of her hand.

Race reached down, gently pushing a strand of hair behind her ear before cupping her cheek in one large, strong hand. "I'm not leaving until this is over," he said gently.

Aimee leaned into him for a moment, closing her eyes. Then she turned her head slightly and pressed her lips into the palm of his hand. It felt so good to have someone in this that she could count on. Especially because she knew that once the buyer agreed to meet with her, this was going to cease seeming like just a game. Soon, it was going to turn deadly serious.

TEN

"DO you know where your mom is?" Josie asked, trying to act like the question had just occurred to her as she and Giselle sat on the bench outside of Mittman's ice cream shop.

The boat ride into the bustling port town of Longport had taken about forty-five minutes. Josie's father owned a forty-two-foot cruiser and hired a man Josie and Giselle called Captain Jack to take care of the boat and ferry people on and off the island at all hours of the day or night. Since her father hadn't needed the boat today, he'd told them that they could stay in Longport until four o'clock. He didn't like Josie to ride in the boat after dark, so he expected her back on the island before the sun went down. To be honest, Josie didn't much like being out in the boat at night, either. The water got so dark that her imagination seemed to spring to life, conjuring up monsters from the ocean's depths that didn't seem to frighten her at all when the sun was out.

It was two o'clock now. She and Gi had stopped in for pizza for lunch, then headed out to the arcade near the beach to pretend that they were Olympic skiers and race car drivers for a while.

Since yesterday when Giselle had come and forced her out

of her room, they had settled back into the easy friendship they'd shared before this last year, before things had suddenly been thrown off kilter. Now, sitting in the sunshine, watching tourists walk along the beach in their brightly colored swimsuits and eating double scoops of ice cream, it was easy to forget that they had ever fought at all.

Except for the phone call that Josie had overheard yesterday morning. She'd heard her father call the person on the other end of the line Diana, which most likely meant he'd been talking to Giselle's mom. And he had sounded angry. Josie loved her father and didn't want to believe that he had any part in making Giselle and her family unhappy, but if he had been talking to *her* like that, she would definitely be afraid of him. Was Mrs. Simonds afraid of her dad and that's why she couldn't quit?

"She's in America, closing some kind of deal for your father," Giselle answered, swirling her tongue around the bottom scoop of ice cream so it wouldn't melt and drip down the cone. "She was supposed to be home tonight but my dad said she called and told him she was going to have to stay another day or two. He didn't even let me talk to her."

Giselle's shoulders slumped forward and Josie instinctively reached out and patted her friend's back. "I'm sorry. I know you miss her."

Giselle shrugged and remained silent for a moment before turning to Josie. "I'm sorry for yelling at you before."

Josie struggled with what to say. She knew Gi wanted her to say it was okay, but it wasn't. She had really hurt Josie's feelings. "Um, let's just try not to fight anymore, okay?" she said finally, tossing her half-eaten ice-cream cone into the garbage can next to the bench.

"It's a deal," Giselle said, then threw her arms around Josie and hugged her.

Surprised, Josie accepted the embrace. She was even more surprised when she pulled away to find that Giselle was crying. "What's wrong?" she asked.

"Nothing. I just missed you," Giselle said, using the sleeve of her shirt to wipe her eyes.

Josie put her arm around her friend's shoulders and

squeezed as she swallowed the lump in her throat. "I missed you, too. Want to go look at makeup?"

Giselle laughed and nodded. "Yeah, let's do that."

As they got up off the bench, Josie began to think that maybe there was an explanation for all of this. Maybe the Diana her dad had been angry with yesterday morning wasn't Giselle's mom. After all, how many Dianas were there in the world? Millions probably. And all of this nonsense about Daddy making Giselle's mom work for him was silly, just like Josie had said yesterday. You couldn't force a grown-up to do anything.

She and Giselle crossed the street and headed toward the drugstore that sold everything from beach towels to souvenir ashtrays to shampoo, medicine, and makeup. Josie reached the door first and held it open for Giselle, then froze when her gaze lit on the row of newspapers sitting in their brightly colored dispensers outside the drugstore entrance. The headline of the one nearest the door proclaimed "Top Terrorist Caught" in big letters right above the picture of a dark-skinned man with even darker eyes.

Josie stared at the photo, not even blinking as her mind raced. *No,* she thought at first. *Why* came next. It just couldn't be. She kept trying to think of a good reason, of any reason at all, why this man was being called a terrorist. Because that man, the one on the front page, she had seen him before.

Two nights ago.

In her father's office.

Her father had been meeting with a terrorist.

"Josie? Are you coming?" Giselle asked, tapping her foot impatiently as she stared at her friend, obviously wondering why Josie was just standing there in the doorway, staring at the windows.

Josie blinked, then looked down at the sidewalk where multicolored blobs of chewing gum had baked onto the pavement. *No!* she wanted to scream. She didn't understand. It was as if her world, everything she believed to be right and true and good, had shattered in that one instant, making her incapable of thinking or moving or doing anything but standing here on the hot sidewalk, watching the colored spots of gum circle slowly around and around, moving faster and faster and faster, until they all ran together—yellow and blue and green and red, mixing and mixing together.

Until, suddenly, they turned to black and Josie felt herself falling, unable to stop her slow slide to the ground.

"AND this quarter's earnings before interest, taxes, depreciation, and amortization are down nearly 4 percent over the same quarter last year, due in large part to the increase in our workers' compensation costs year over year," Race said, pressing the button on his mouse to advance his PowerPoint presentation by one slide. The screen at the front of the room flashed as the next slide appeared, showing two columns of figures, with one line item—the one for work comp expenses—highlighted in bright yellow.

This was the sort of thing that had turned Race off from corporate accounting. Quarter after quarter, year after year, you went through the same process. Close the books, create the financial statements, compare this quarter's results to last quarter's results, compare this year to last year, compare all of it to the most recent budget, and explain why the numbers were better or worse than expected. Every three months, the same old thing.

It was enough to drive a person insane.

In the CIA, Race used his financial prowess to ferret out money-laundering schemes, track treasonous spies, and uncover funding going to terrorists overseas. While the skill sets might be the same for both jobs, Race found that what he did for a living was a lot more fulfilling than standing around telling stockholders and analysts why their insurance costs had gone up 3.6 percent from the previous year. Of course, the pay in the corporate world was much better. The CFO for a company like McConnell Aerospace had a base salary of nearly a quarter of a million dollars, and that didn't count the bonus or extra benefits like stock grants or thousand-dollar car allowances.

Still, Race's job paid him enough to own his own home and drive a kickass car—even if he *had* bought it used—and not worry about paying the next month's bills. And at the end of the day, he felt like he was really making a difference in the world.

He certainly didn't feel the same way about what he was doing here in front of McConnell's executive team.

Race clicked his mouse to move on to the next slide. "As you can see from this slide, our revenues from government contracts are increasing as a percent of total revenue, surpassing private sales for the first time since the first Gulf War . . ." As he droned on, Race began to wonder if it was possible to put *himself* to sleep with what he was saying.

Suddenly, the cell phone lying beside his laptop beeped, jerking Race out of his trance. He quickly turned the presentation over to the VP of finance and excused himself. As he walked out of the darkened conference room, he searched the gloom for Aimee, who was unobtrusively making notes in the back of the room. Their gazes locked.

This could the call they were waiting for.

They'd waited all day yesterday, but heard nothing. Nothing from the buyer. Nothing from Rita, who, according to her tail, had called in sick to work that morning and hadn't left her apartment since. Now it was nearing six o'clock on a Friday night. The presentation he had worked on all day with Aimee's help was supposed to be over in a few minutes, and Race had found himself wondering if she was going to be thinking about him over the weekend. They'd spent so much time together over the past three days that not seeing her until Monday seemed wrong somehow.

Geez, man, get a grip on yourself, he chided with a derisive snort. He and Aimee had only shared one kiss—it wasn't like they had become instant soul mates.

"Gardner," he answered, striding down the hall toward his office.

"We've received contact," Race's partner said. "She wants to meet at the Lone Star Brewery down at the Riverwalk in thirty minutes."

"Shit. That barely gives us enough time to get there," Race said, stopping in the hallway.

"I'm sure that was her plan," Jake agreed. "The buyer gave

the usual warnings. Come alone, don't let yourself be followed, etcetera, etcetera."

"People watch too many spy movies," Race said as he changed direction and headed back to the conference room to get Aimee.

"Yeah. Is our girl ready?"

"Yes. We spent some time last night going over the equipment."

"Sounds like fun," Jake said, then continued in a more serious tone when Race didn't laugh. "She knows this is going to be dangerous, right?"

Race swallowed a sigh. "She knows. Even worse, she seems to be looking forward to it."

Jake laughed. "That's my kind of woman."

Race found himself scowling into the phone. He couldn't imagine Aimee with his partner . . . or with any other man, for that matter. Or rather, he *could* imagine it, he just didn't want to. He pinched the bridge of his nose and shook his head. This was no time to be thinking about Aimee in any sort of romantic way. They had work to do.

"All right. She's to be at the bar in, ah"—Race glanced at his watch—"twenty-eight minutes. Any other instructions?"

Stopping in front of the glassed-in conference room, Race waved to catch Aimee's attention. She nodded, then tapped Joe McConnell on the arm to indicate that she had to go. Race watched as Joe squeezed her hand. When Joe looked up at Race, Race was surprised to see concern written in the older man's eyes. Apparently, McConnell also suspected that the next step in their plan was going to place Aimee's life at risk.

If Race could have thought of any other way to trap whoever it was who was funding these purchases—and he had gone over and over it in his head for hours—he would have taken Aimee out of the equation. But he hadn't been able to think of another way. Chances were, Rita's contact had seen Aimee walk out of the bathroom with the plans. If Race tried to send someone else to meet with the buyer in Aimee's place, the woman would walk and they'd have to start this case all over from scratch. And next time, they might not be so lucky. Next time, the buyer might find someone within McConnell to sell her those propulsion system plans before the CIA or anyone else found out.

No, the repercussions of having those plans fall into the wrong hands without bringing them closer to the ultimate buyer were simply too dire for Race to consider shutting down the op simply because he was concerned for Aimee's safety. He tried to comfort himself with the thought that Aimee knew the dangers and was being well compensated for them. Of course, no amount of money would be enough if she ended up dead.

"That's all the instructions she gave," Jake said, interrupting Race's thoughts just as Aimee stepped out into the hallway and closed the conference room door behind her.

"Okay. We're on our way," Race said, then flipped his phone closed and turned to Aimee. "You ready? We've got to be at the Riverwalk in twenty-five minutes."

Aimee nodded. "I'm ready. Just let me get my purse." She hurried into her office and quickly unlocked the bottom drawer of her desk, where she'd stashed her pocketbook. She was surprised to find herself tempted to stop in the doorway and look around because she had the feeling that this would be the last she'd see of the place.

Shaking off that maudlin sentiment, Aimee slipped the strap of her purse over her shoulder, switched off the light, and pushed the button to lock her office door. She didn't bother booby-trapping the door.

"All right. Let's go," she said, straightening her shoulders.

Race was quiet as they rode the elevator down to the lobby. As the doors slid open on the first floor, he waited for her to step out before following her. It wasn't until they were outside that he finally spoke. "I'll ride with you to Houston Street so we can go over the plan. You can let me out and I'll walk from there just in case she's got people watching for you to arrive."

Aimee nodded and pushed the button on her key chain to unlock her convertible. She laid her purse on the floor in the backseat and slid into the driver's seat, pulling her hair out of its twist as she did. The buyer would be expecting the "other" Aimee—the one with long, windblown hair and high-heeled, fuck-me-against-the-wall boots. Aimee didn't have time to get into the rest of her disguise, so simply letting her hair down, taking off her suit jacket, and unbuttoning several of the buttons of her blouse would have to do.

"You have everything, right?" Race asked as he buckled the seat belt across his chest.

Aimee turned the key in the ignition and gripped the steering wheel tight before pulling out of the McConnell parking lot. "Yes. After you left last night, I took care of hiding the transmitter in the top of a lipstick tube. I used a piece of clear plastic adhesive to make sure it doesn't come loose when the tube is opened. The pen is in my purse, along with the compact."

"What about the plans?"

"I uploaded them to a website that's password protected. The URL is something terribly convoluted, nothing that anyone would find if they were doing a random search."

"How are you going to remember what it is?" Race asked as they turned onto Broadway and headed toward the San Antonio River.

"I encoded both the URL and the password and stored the coded information in a Word document on a disk. Since I'm the only one who knows which encryption systems I used, just having the disk by itself wouldn't be enough."

"Brilliant," Race said.

"Thank you." Aimee glanced sideways at him and smiled, and Race once again had to remind himself that he had no choice but to let her meet with the buyer when what he'd rather do was to tell her they no longer needed her services.

Aimee's gaze slid back to the road in front of them. "Stop worrying about me," she said, her voice almost too low for Race to hear.

Race rested his arm on the door of the convertible and put his head in his hand as the warm wind rushed by. "I can't."

"You're not responsible for getting me into this. I could have said no," Aimee reminded him.

"Why didn't you?" Race asked.

Aimee shook her head as if attempting to deny something to him . . . or to herself. "The money was too good to pass up. My partners and I need it to keep our business afloat."

"Is that the only reason?"

"No-o-o," Aimee said, drawing the word out.

Race raised his eyebrows, waiting for her to say something about patriotic duty or saving the world from tragedy or something. Instead, she grinned, batted her eyelashes at him, and said, "I also get to spend time flirting with my favorite secret agent. What more could a girl want?"

Race sighed. Aimee Devlin was crazy.

ELEVEN

"HAVE you talked to Rabin about funding for the LoRS bomb? Has he released the down payment al-Zwahiri agreed upon?" Luke Simonds asked, pouring another two inches of Scotch into the Waterford crystal tumbler in his hand.

Nic craned his neck to make certain the door to the drawing room was closed. Giselle and Josie were supposedly sound asleep upstairs in Josie's room, but after yesterday morning, when he swore his daughter was listening in on his conversation with Diana, he wasn't going to take any chances. He would do anything to keep Josie from discovering exactly what it was he did for a living—at least for a little while longer. When she was older, she might be able to understand why he did what he did. For now, the moral ambiguities would be too much for her twelve-year-old mind to comprehend.

Satisfied that he and Luke were not being eavesdropped upon, Nic allowed himself another tumbler full of Scotch as well. He didn't drink often, and never allowed himself to become inebriated—life in the garbage dump had taught him well the dangers of allowing oneself to be overcome by the effects of drugs or alcohol—but he did enjoy the occasional taste of a well-aged whiskey.

"Yes. I put in a call to him as soon as I learned about al-Zwahiri's capture. He's afraid that he, too, will be captured. He was en route to a new location as we were speaking. He's told me he'll call to arrange a meeting when he feels that he's safe."

"This couldn't have happened at a worse time," Luke said, sitting down heavily on the chocolate-colored leather couch that dominated what Nic referred to as the drawing room. The room had been decorated like something out of an Ernest Hemingway novel—with heavy, masculine furniture and dark paneled wood. "We need funding *now*. And what if Rabin asks for a copy of the plans to prove that we are on schedule? What will we tell him? The plans are not complete without the information Diana is working to obtain."

Nic took a sip of Scotch and refrained from telling Luke that he was not telling Nic anything he didn't already know. This sort of frantic tail-chasing that Luke indulged in was what set him apart from Nic. Yes, Nic had the same concerns. He simply did not feel the same need to voice them again and again.

"We have no choice in the matter but to wait," Nic said. "Rabin's organization needs to purchase these missiles as much as we need to sell them. And if Rabin requires further convincing that we can deliver on our promises, then I will convince him. Now, why don't you finish your drink and head home? I'll send Giselle back tomorrow morning. I appreciate that she was able to stay with Josie this evening. After Josie's fainting scare, I'm grateful she's here, even though the doctor said Josie was fine."

Luke drained his glass of Scotch and set the empty tumbler on a coaster on the heavy mahogany table in front of him. "All right. I'll go. I know my worrying upsets you."

Nic smiled at the man who, under other circumstances, Nic might have considered a friend. Nic, however, chose not to have friends. That sort of sentiment toward others only led one to hesitate when it came time to do what was necessary for survival.

"We mustn't panic," Nic said. "If Rabin can't meet with me, I'll simply have to find another source of income. The LoRS bomb demonstration must remain on schedule in order for our other financiers to remain confident in our ability to deliver this weapon. I will find a way."

Luke stood then, studying Nic intently for a moment. Then, with a curt nod, he said, "Yes. You always do," before turning and striding from the room, leaving Nic alone.

CONTRARY to what Race believed, Aimee was not crazy. As a matter of fact, she was terrified. But she didn't think that meeting with the buyer with her knees knocking together with fright was the right approach. Instead, in order to get what she wanted, Aimee was going to have to convince the other woman that she had the upper hand, that none of this scared her at all.

So, as she always did when playing a part, Aimee slipped inside the head of the woman she wanted to be. Brash, unafraid, sexy, intelligent. That's what she needed to be to pull this off.

As she pushed open the door to the bar, she added a little more sway to her hips, stuck her chest out and her chin up. Now she was ready to conquer the world.

The place was packed with the after-six crowd, early thirty-something men and women openly eyeing one another, some looking for love, others just hoping for a weekend score. Aimee sashayed her way to the bar, taking in all the activity around her. This wasn't the type of place where people came for a drink or two before heading off to dinner. It was, instead, the sort of bar where people came after work to stay until they either hooked up with someone for the night or went home alone after watching all their coworkers pairing off. It was, in short, a meat market.

Aimee waited patiently at the five-person-deep line in front of the bar. She forced herself not to fidget or worry about what to do with her hands. *You fit in here,* she silently assured herself, adding a slight hair toss as if to prove her point.

"What can I get you?" the bartender asked loudly above the drone of voices.

"Cosmopolitan," Aimee answered. She spotted Race coming out of the back hallway, his usual blue suit replaced by jeans and an off-white polo shirt. As the bartender handed her the drink, Aimee wondered where Race had found clothes to change into. When she'd let him off four blocks from here, he'd been wearing a suit.

"Here, let me get that for you," a man said, making Aimee turn. Time to forget about Race and focus on her mission.

Aimee smiled. "Thank you," she said, stepping away from the bar with her drink in her hand. Until the buyer contacted her, she had no choice but to stay here and play the mating game.

The man traded the bartender a twenty-dollar bill for their drinks, then leaned toward Aimee with a hand outstretched. "I'm Bill."

"Aimee," she said, taking his hand.

Instead of simply shaking her hand, the man surprised Aimee by pulling her toward him, so close that the people around them would have found it impossible to hear what was being said over the din in the noisy bar. "You have sixty seconds to get down to the corner of Commerce and St. Mary's. A car will be waiting. If you stop anywhere along the way, the car will be gone. Understand?"

Aimee nodded and, without another word, set her drink on the bar. Bill released her immediately, then stood back, sweeping the room with his gaze. Aimee knew that if anyone tried to follow her out of the bar, the meet would be canceled.

Retracing her steps, Aimee left the bar, breezing past Race without so much as a sideways glance. He had to know she was being watched.

Once outside, Aimee turned to the left and hurried down Commerce Street toward the slow-moving San Antonio River. She passed relatively empty restaurants that would later fill up with locals and tourists alike and bars packed to overflowing with the Friday evening happy hour crowd. When she got to the corner of Commerce and St. Mary's, she saw a silver car sitting near the curb, its engine running. Without hesitating, she yanked open the back door and slid inside.

Before she had even managed to get completely inside the vehicle, she felt the cool barrel of a gun at her temples.

"Drive," a blond woman said.

As the driver punched the accelerator, Aimee smoothly tucked her right leg inside the cab and used the forward momentum of the vehicle to close the door. Then she turned her head, slowly so as not to alarm the woman sitting next to her on the backseat of the car.

The blonde from the conference center sat staring at her with those cool blue eyes that had marked her as a killer the first time she and Aimee had met. The Walther PPK was aimed right between Aimee's eyes, the woman's hand steady as if she had quite a bit of target practice.

"Is that really necessary?" Aimee asked coolly, fiercely quelling that part of her that was screaming for her to run as far and as fast away from this situation as she could. Contrary to popular belief, aided in large part by the television and movie industries, FBI agents did not often find themselves staring down the business end of a firearm. Aimee could count on one hand the number of times during her decade-plus-long career that she'd had a gun leveled at her. And never had the threat been quite so close.

But she had no choice but to act calm. If she panicked, she'd be dead for sure.

"Where are the plans?" the woman asked, not lowering her weapon.

Aimee raised her eyebrows. "What, we're not even going to exchange pleasantries first?"

"Where are the plans?" the woman repeated humorlessly.

Patting the purse on the seat next to her, Aimee leaned back, trying to ignore the fact that she had a gun to her head. "The key to the whereabouts of the plans are in here," she answered. "The plans have been stored somewhere safe. And don't even bother threatening to kill me. I am the only one who knows where they are or how to interpret the encoded instructions for accessing the plans. If you kill me, you'll have nothing."

The blonde narrowed her eyes, her cheeks flushing with rage. "I'm not playing games with you. Turn over the plans or I'll kill you."

Aimee sighed. "Didn't I just go over that? Look, I wouldn't be here if I wasn't willing to deal, right? Let's stop with the theatrics and talk business."

The woman looked as if she would like nothing more than to push Aimee out of the car and repeatedly run over her until she was a boneless, lifeless stain on the pavement. Aimee surreptitiously slid her hand out and clutched the edge of the seat just in case the blonde acted on that impulse.

The driver kept his gaze focused on the road ahead, apparently having been paid well enough to ignore what was going on in the back of his car. It had always amazed her how little money it took to pay for such things as a person's life. In one case she had worked, a man had killed a friend's girlfriend and her two children for $150 each. For less than what Aimee paid for a new pair of Kate Spade boots, three lives had been snuffed out. Aimee wondered what her life had been worth to this driver—a hundred dollars? A thousand?

"I'll offer you the same deal as the other woman and not a cent more. Half a million. Wire transferred to an untraceable account in the Cayman Islands."

Aimee looked out the window. How many lives were going to be lost for that? Five hundred thousand dollars for a countless number of murders. It would probably work out to less than ten cents a head.

How could Rita have done this?

"No deal," Aimee said.

The vinyl seat squeaked as the blonde shifted positions. "Five hundred thousand. Nonnegotiable."

Aimee turned back toward the woman. "It's not the money," she said. "You're asking me to sell out my employer. Most likely to sell out my country, too. I want to meet the devil I'm selling my soul to. That's my price. Five hundred thousand dollars, and you take me to meet your boss."

The blonde laughed an ugly laugh. "You must be joking."

"No," Aimee said, shaking her head. "I'm not."

"Then you're fucking insane. You will deal with me or with no one at all." The gun was back, aimed again at Aimee's head.

"I'm not turning down your deal," Aimee said, speaking around the lump in her throat. "All I'm doing is adding one small condition. I will turn over the plans as soon as I've met with your boss."

The woman was silent for a long moment. Then, suddenly, she tapped on the back of the seat in front of her. "Stop the car," she ordered. The driver did so without saying a word.

"Get out," the blonde said, waving her gun at Aimee.

Aimee looked around at the deserted industrial area the driver had driven to. She'd stand out here like a hooker at a nunnery. But it didn't seem that she had much choice, not with the other woman staring at her down the barrel of her pistol.

Aimee pushed open the door and backed out of the car. If she was going to be shot, she at least wanted to see it coming. She reached for her purse, but the other woman grabbed the strap and pulled it away from her.

"Go," the blonde ordered.

Aimee barely had time to step back before the vehicle sped away, narrowly missing running over her toes. She attempted to read the license plate, but it was obscured by dirt—intentionally, Aimee had to assume. As the car disappeared from sight, relief rushed through her. It was over. She had done everything she could to help the CIA find their culprit, but she had failed. And while it was troubling to think that someone was lurking out there, doing everything he could to get his hands on McConnell's top-secret plans, Aimee felt some satisfaction in knowing that, for now at least, he had been stopped.

She sagged against the side of a warm building for just a moment, letting the relief wash through her. Finally, she straightened. She had to call Race, to let him know that she was safe, but that their mission was unsuccessful.

Too bad she had nothing with her—no cell phone, no money, no car keys. Aimee closed her eyes for a moment as she gritted her teeth.

The blonde had left Aimee stranded here, out in the middle of nowhere, knowing it was miles back to town. Aimee looked down at her feet and grimaced. Her pumps weren't exactly uncomfortable, but they weren't designed for walking long distances.

Well, there was no use whining about it. She had no choice but to walk until she could find a pay phone, make a collect call to Daff or Raine—since she didn't have Race's cell number memorized—and have them send her a cab. There was *no* way she was walking all the way back into town.

As she started up the road, her feet already starting to ache in anticipation of the journey ahead, Aimee comforted herself by imagining just what sort of torture she'd inflict on the blonde if she ever had the misfortune of seeing her again.

TWELVE

"SO, I guess this means we're no longer working together," Aimee said as she and Race stepped out of the conference room where Race and his partner, Jake, had just finished debriefing her. She'd told them everything, including the amount of the blonde's offer. Jake had left a few minutes before, leaving Aimee and Race alone in the deserted building.

"True," Race agreed. "As far as the CIA is concerned, your involvement with this case is through."

Aimee looked down at the light blue carpeting beneath her feet. She was still wearing her navy pumps, which were a bit dusty but none the worse for her mile-long hike earlier that evening. She'd had the cab take her back to her apartment, where she found Race's cell number and called to tell him the blonde had taken her purse and disappeared. He'd told her to meet him here, at the temporary office Jake had rented for the duration of this case. Before hanging up, he'd added the unnecessary warning that she make certain she wasn't being followed. Aimee had already planned to make sure of that.

"Then let me ask you a question," she said, raising her head to look into his eyes.

"Shoot," Race said, sliding his hands into the front pockets of his jeans. Of all his disguises, Aimee liked this one the best, which surprised her since she was usually a suit-and-tie kind of gal.

"You remember the night you found out that I was with the FBI? The night at my apartment?"

Race cleared his throat and looked more than a little uncomfortable. "Uh, yeah. What about it?"

"I feel the same way about you," Aimee said, allowing herself a faint smile at his obvious discomfort.

"I don't follow."

Aimee stepped forward, stopping when their bodies were separated by just a fraction of an inch. She reached out then, putting her hands on his strongly muscled forearms, feeling the roughness of his hair on the pads of her fingers. "Really?" she teased. "You don't understand what I mean?"

Race lowered his head until their lips were nearly touching. "Oh," he said. "You mean this?"

Then their mouths met, their tongues searching.

Race ran his hands lightly up Aimee's back, his fingertips tickling her spine. He fisted his hands in her hair, tilting her head back so he could have access to her smooth neck. He trailed a line of moist kisses from just below her ear to her collarbone, which felt so good that Aimee nearly purred.

He pulled her back into the conference room, closing and locking the door behind them. With a twist of a wand, he closed the blinds on the interior windows, shutting them off from the outside world. He left the lights off, the faint glow of moonlight coming in through the windows providing enough light to see by.

Aimee came up behind him and wrapped her arms around his waist, leaning her head against his shoulder. Playfully, she untucked his shirt, making Race's stomach muscles twitch when her fingers dipped below his waistband.

Putting his hands over hers to still them, Race turned in her arms. He'd had enough of her teasing him, of thinking she was the one in control. He crowded her, pushing her backward until she was trapped against the wall, her breath coming in little gasps. Reaching out, he buried his hands in her hair again, cradling the back of her head in one strong hand. He planted one booted foot between her knees and slowly leaned into her, her skirt riding up as his jeans-clad thigh rubbed along the sensitive skin of her upper thighs.

Aimee closed her eyes and tilted her head back as Race gently nipped her bottom lip.

With one hand, he slowly unbuttoned her blouse, letting it fall open to reveal a white satiny bra. She shivered when he caressed the soft skin just below her breasts. Aching for more, she arched her back, and Race dropped his hands to unhook the front clasp of her bra. His fingers teased her, circling her nipples, but not touching them until Aimee was nearly writhing with the agony of waiting. When finally he let the roughened pads of his thumbs drag over her nipples, Aimee cried out from the pleasure.

Race's low laughter rumbled from his chest and Aimee's eyes opened to slits when she realized what he was doing.

"You're a tease," she accused, her voice husky.

Race lowered his mouth to her breasts, licking her nipples and then blowing warm air on the wetness, making Aimee squirm. "Do you want me to stop?" he asked, his voice filled with amusement.

"I'll kill you if you do," Aimee groaned.

Race laughed again, before covering her mouth with his. Aimee wasn't certain exactly how he had managed to get her panty hose off, but the feel of his jeans against her naked thighs made her moan. She pressed herself closer, rubbing against him.

"God, you feel good," Race nearly growled.

"Yes, I do, but not good enough, yet," Aimee agreed, almost desperate to feel Race inside her.

"Give me a minute," Race promised, then stepped back for just a second to divest himself of his clothes.

Aimee watched him strip, amazed at how he'd been able to hide that strongly muscled body from her for so long. His biceps were nearly as big around as her thighs, his chest and stomach muscles firm. When he turned away for just a second, Aimee couldn't help reaching out to see if his rear end was as tight as it looked.

It was.

"Just checking," she said when Race turned back to her, looking at her questioningly.

He was fully erect, obviously just as ready for her as she was for him. "My, my, is that all for me?" she teased, nodding toward his crotch.

Race got a serious look in his eyes as he stood, watching her. "It's all yours," he said, then added, "I don't like sharing."

Aimee shivered at the possessive tone of his voice. Okay, she'd admit it, she found this side of Race really sexy. "I'm clean and I'm wearing a birth control patch," she blurted as she heard the telltale crinkling of a foil packet.

"You sure I don't need to use this?" he asked.

"Not if you're disease-free," Aimee said.

Race tossed the condom over his shoulder without watching to see where it landed, his gaze intent on Aimee's. "Now that that's out of the way . . ." he began, an unholy light in his eyes that made goose bumbs rise on Aimee's skin.

Then he was pushing her against the wall, her back braced by the cool paneling. Aimee was about to tell him that it was impossible to have sex against a wall when she felt just the tip of his penis enter her, her legs stretched wide to accommodate Race's hips between them. The sensation was incredible and Aimee pushed herself forward, trying to capture more of him, but Race held back with a self-satisfied chuckle that nearly drove Aimee mad.

He pulled out and pushed back inside her again, just the tiniest motion that made her want to scream because it felt so good but wasn't *enough*. Throwing her head back, she braced herself against the wall as Race continued to taunt her. Finally, she couldn't take it anymore.

"Please," she whispered, almost sobbing with need.

"Please what?" Race asked, sliding one hand along the back of her neck.

"Please. More. I need more," Aimee panted.

"You mean, like this?" Race asked, lifting her with his hands beneath her buttocks, burying himself inside her as far as he could go.

Aimee screamed as she wrapped her legs around Race's waist and leveregred herself against the wall. In two seconds, she was done, having just had the most mind-blowing orgasm of her life. Race pumped into her one more time, then he, too, came, groaning out her name as he found his release.

They stood there like that, their bodies entwined, until Aimee felt the weight returning to her body. She unwound her legs from around Race's waist, saying, "Let me down, I'm too heavy."

Race stepped back and slowly let her slide to the floor, kissing her lightly on the forehead once her feet were buried once again in the carpet. "You're perfect," he murmured.

Aimee rolled her eyes but didn't protest.

"Why don't you come home with me? Spend the night at my place?" Race suggested, running his fingers up and down Aimee's spine and making her shiver.

"I don't think that's wise," Aimee said.

Race sighed, his breath stirring the hair at the nape of her neck. "You're probably right. It's possible that the buyer is staking out all of McConnell's top employees. If she sees the two of us together, she may think we're in on this together. There's still a chance that she may approach other employees in the company and see if we're willing to sell McConnell out."

"Hmm." Aimee nodded, letting Race believe that her reservations about staying with him were professional rather than personal. The truth was, she was feeling a little too vulnerable right now to spend the night in his arms. Feelings like this were what led women to beg men not to leave them—something Aimee had vowed she'd never do. No, she had a company back in Atlanta and Race had work to do here in Texas . . . and then wherever his job took him. There was no sense in trying to cling. It would just embarrass them both.

Aimee pulled back, breaking their embrace. She wasn't one for false modesty, but felt just a bit too exposed right then. She hurried to find her panties and bra, slipping them on and feeling a bit more guarded now with something on. Slipping on her blouse, she turned her back on Race and started buttoning it up. She heard the sound of his zipper sliding up, just before he asked, "What's wrong?"

She turned back to him, smiling brightly. "Nothing. I'm just tired, I guess. It's been a long day."

Race raised one eyebrow at her, something she had never managed to learn how to do. She wished she had. It was very effective at conveying disbelief.

She blew out a breath and sat down in one of the leather chairs flanking the conference table, the fabric cold beneath her bare thighs. "Okay, truth?"

Race sat down next to her and put one large, strong hand over hers. "And nothing but the truth," he said.

"You make me feel . . . scared."

"I scare you?" he asked, incredulous.

"Not physically. Emotionally, I guess," Aimee said with a shrug. "You're someone I could really get to like. Someone I respect. But we want different things out of life, so the more I let myself care about you, the more I know it's going to hurt when we go our separate ways."

Race squeezed her hand and leaned into her, their arms touching. "You don't think I could give you what you want?" he asked.

Aimee turned her hand over and squeezed him back. She closed her eyes tightly against the pain of what she knew she had to do. "No," she said. "Because I want the world."

Race didn't bother to argue. Instead, they both stood up and finished dressing in silence. Since her car keys had been in her purse and her spare was being overnighted from Atlanta, Race called her a cab and they waited in the darkened lobby until the yellow taxi pulled in front of the building, its lights illuminating the black road ahead.

Putting his hand beneath her elbow, Race led Aimee down the steps toward the waiting cab. He opened the door and stepped back to let her slide inside. When she was settled, he rested one arm on the door and leaned in, his eyes steady and surprisingly filled with warmth.

"I might not be able to give you the world, Aimee, but I could be a part of yours," he said.

She took a deep breath and let it out, then sadly shook her head. "How will I ever know if that's enough?" she asked.

Race was quiet for a moment. Then he stepped back onto the sidewalk, taking his steadiness and his warmth with him. "Only you can answer that," he said.

And then he turned, walking away from her until he disappeared into the darkness.

* * *

"YOU'RE certain that you're willing to take this risk?" Diana Simonds asked, the dark hair of the wig she was wearing ruffling slightly in the warm breeze. "If I kill her we have no other choice."

"Do it," Nic said, his voice clear from thousands of miles away. "And then get back here as soon as possible."

"All right. I'll be on the plane in two hours."

"Good." Nic paused, then said, "And, Diana?"

"Yes?" she answered, flicking the lighter and watching the flame while Nic remained silent.

"If you fail this time, you'll never see your daughter again," he said flatly, as if announcing that it was raining instead of threatening the person Diana loved most in the world.

She forced herself not to react. She knew that if she did, it would only give Nic the satisfaction of knowing he had the power to hurt her. "That is as I would expect," she said calmly instead. "I will be on that plane in two hours."

Then, without waiting for the man on the other end of the line to respond, she hung up. And as she touched the lighter to the trail of gasoline she'd already laid, Diana refused to allow herself even a second of remorse for the life she had chosen. It was much too late for that.

AIMEE woke from a troubled sleep with the sound of a buzzer going off in her ear. She bolted upright, thinking it was her alarm clock and that she was going to be late for work. Disoriented, she slapped the off button of her alarm, but the buzzing continued.

As she glared at the digital clock cheerily glowing the time of 2:13 A.M., she realized that the buzzing was not coming from the alarm clock. It was coming from the building's fire alarm.

She threw back the covers, her mind suddenly alert. Was there anything here worth risking her life to take with her? She thought briefly about running back into the living room to get her laptop, but discarded the thought almost immediately. Raine backed up their network nightly, so all she would lose was the laptop itself, which was covered under their insurance.

With no idea where the fire might be, it just wasn't worth the risk.

Aimee unlatched the locks of her bedroom window and pushed it up. Looking down, she saw that many of her neighbors were already milling around on the ground. The fire escape was clear, with no sign of danger. Aimee clambered out the window and hopped onto the cool metal grate of her balcony. She was glad now that her only choice of clean nightwear had been red silk tap pants and a matching camisole. She hadn't realized she was so far behind on her laundry, and all her other pajamas were in the wash. Some of her neighbors would have gotten quite an eyeful as she climbed down the fire escape if she'd had the choice of one of her favorite short nighties instead.

She hadn't made much of an effort to get to know anyone in the building and, with her case complete, this early-morning gathering didn't seem like the place to start. Instead, Aimee stood away from the crowd as the fire department arrived, one of their gaily colored trucks pulling into the alley followed by a white ambulance. Aimee stepped back as the vehicles approached, cutting a swath in the crowd.

"Hell of a time for a fire drill," a dark-haired young woman whom Aimee had never met said.

"Yeah," Aimee agreed, not really interested in conversation. She was too drained by the events of the last twelve hours, by doubting the decision she'd made to break it off with Race before they'd even had a chance. Rationally, she knew she'd done the right thing, but—

"Oh, God, I must have cut myself climbing down the fire escape," the young woman said, holding out one blood-soaked hand. She looked at Aimee with wide, saucer-round brown eyes.

Aimee instinctively grabbed the woman's arm. "Here, the ambulance driver should be able to help." She led the woman toward the ambulance, but the driver wasn't sitting in the front seat so she headed around the back, hoping the EMT would be there. She saw the legs of the white-uniformed man, his body hidden by the open back door of the ambulance.

"This woman is bleeding," she said.

The next seconds passed like a slow-motion movie being played out in Aimee's head. The woman at her side stepped away as the man came out from behind the ambulance door. She recognized him instantly from the bar. Bill, wasn't that his name?

What a coincidence, she thought. Then, *No.*

Aimee gasped when the hypodermic needle was stuck into her arm and the plunger depressed. One of her neighbors turned.

"Help," Aimee heard herself say, as if listening to the words from the end of a long tunnel.

Her neighbor started toward her, but the woman at Aimee's side grimaced and held up her hand. "It's okay. She cut herself on the way down the fire escape."

Aimee's head bobbed on her neck like one of those bobble-head dolls that were so popular a few years ago. She saw the blood on her own arm and had trouble figuring out how that had happened. She didn't remember cutting herself.

No. She wasn't hurt. The other woman was. But why was *she* bleeding if she wasn't injured?

Aimee tried to think but her brain just wouldn't seem to focus on any one thought long enough for it to make sense of anything. She needed Race. He would help her make sense of everything.

Race. Her CPA. With the CIA. Aimee fought the sudden urge to giggle. The letters echoed in her head. CPA . . . CIA . . . CFO . . . FBI. Aim . . . e . . . e . . . e.

And then, nothing.

THIRTEEN

"SHE'S dead," Race's partner said, leaning over the brunette who had been pulled from Ron Jefferson's swimming pool. Her dark hair, nearly black when it was wet, clung to her shoulders and cheeks, but didn't completely cover the bruises at her neck.

Crouching on the tile patio, Race looked up at a tall blond man who was studiously avoiding looking at the dead woman at Race's feet. The blond had soot on his face and on his clothes, with long dark smears along his arms.

"You were supposed to be watching her. Protecting her," Race said, censure clear in his voice.

"I was, but when the fire alarm went off, all hell broke loose. Smoke was everywhere. You couldn't even see two feet in front of your face. I only lost sight of her for a minute."

"Yeah, well, that's all the time the killer needed," Race said, dusting off the knees of his jeans as he stood up.

It was bad enough that the junior agent had lost sight of his subject; even worse was that he had waited nearly an hour before calling Race to alert him to the problem. Race was willing to cut the guy some slack—after all, he'd risked his life by going back into the burning building to try to find Rita when he couldn't find her milling about in the crowd. But the end result was that the woman he had been assigned to protect had shown up facedown in her ex-lover's pool. Race had already talked to the police officer in charge of the investigation and found out the 911 call had been placed from the neighbor's house. Although the caller had refused to give the operator his name, Race guessed that the teenaged voyeur had been the one to spot her, most likely hoping he was in for another late-night triple-X show, but getting quite a different sort of show instead.

He pinched the bridge of his nose and squinted down at the dead woman. He'd be willing to bet that whatever amount of money she'd been paid wasn't worth losing her life. *Why is it that people never think they'll be the ones to end up like this?* he wondered.

Race's cell phone chirped and he unclipped it from his belt. "Gardner," he said after flipping it open.

"It's Dobbins. There's been a fire."

Race frowned into the phone. "Yes, I know. We've found Rita. It was too late to save her."

"What does that have to do with Miss Devlin?" the other agent asked.

"I thought you were talking about the fire at the Chelsea Arms," Race said.

"No. There's been a fire at Miss Devlin's apartment. Or I guess I should say, there's been a fire *alarm* here. Someone pulled the alarm on the third floor and the entire building was evacuated."

Race was already on the move, motioning to Jake that he'd call later as he crossed the patio and headed toward the gate. "I'll be there in fifteen minutes," he said, pulling up short on the lawn when he heard Dobbins's next words.

"Don't bother hurrying," Dobbins said glumly. "She's already gone. She got into an ambulance with another woman and a man. My car was blocked in by the fire trucks. By the time I commandeered another vehicle, they were gone."

"You make it sound as if she went willingly," Race said.

"Once you see the footage from the security camera on the third floor, you'll understand why," the other agent explained.

* * *

RACE watched the woman on the tape reach up and pull the lever to activate the fire alarm. The red pajama shorts she wore rode up to show off a vast expanse of long, firm leg. Her hair hung down her back and Race's fingertips tingled, remembering the feel of those silky strands tickling his chest a few hours earlier. She kept her face turned away from the camera, but the hair and those long legs certainly resembled Aimee's.

"It could be our buyer, wearing a disguise," Race said, refusing to believe what the others so readily had—that Aimee had staged her own disappearance.

Jake tapped a button on the laptop on the conference table in front of him; the conference table in the same room Aimee and Race had made love in just a few short hours ago. Race wearily pushed a hand through his hair and forced himself to concentrate.

"This photo blows a dump-truck-sized hole in that theory," Jake said, pointing to the screen behind him without bothering to turn around to see the picture for himself.

Dobbins had made it outside before Aimee and had stood on the ground, snapping digital photos of Aimee as she climbed down the fire escape. The outfit she wore exactly matched the one being worn by the woman on the security tape. It did seem a little far-fetched to believe that the buyer had known which pajamas Aimee was planning to wear this evening, even if she'd suspected that there would be a man on the ground taking pictures and matching them with the security tape.

Race released a frustrated breath. "I just don't understand why she'd do this."

"Why do they all do it?" Jake asked dispassionately, then answered his own question. "Money."

"I don't buy that. This isn't something Aimee would do, no matter how much the buyer was offering."

"Come on. She wouldn't agree to help us until we paid her, even knowing what was at stake. Of course this is something she'd do. It's half a fucking million dollars. Most people would sell their own children for that."

Race shook his head. "You're wrong. I know it looks bad, but I don't think Aimee went willingly."

His partner leaned back in his chair, lacing his fingers

across his stomach and regarding Race coolly from across the table. The two men had worked together for years. Race would even have gone so far as to say that Jake Haven was a good friend. But it was clear they were on opposite sides of the fence on this issue. Race refused to believe that Aimee had duped them, pretending that the deal was dead only to hook up with the buyer later when she thought the Agency wouldn't be looking.

"It doesn't make sense," Race said. "Why would she leave with the buyer when she could have just handed over the plans last night? We would never have known."

"Maybe she made her own deal with the buyer. Maybe part of her plan was to get passage out of the country in addition to the cash, maybe that's what tonight was all about."

"Well, there's one way to find out if she's capable of doing something like this," Race said, staring fixedly at the screen in front of the room, showing the back of Aimee's tanned legs as she dropped down from the second floor onto the ground. Her arms were outstretched as she let go of the bottom rung of the ladder, her sleeveless nightshirt riding up past her waist. The top of her tattoo was visible above the waistband of her shorts, the Tasmanian Devil mocking the rest of the world with his wild grin. Was that what Aimee was doing, whirling around, making her own choices, not caring what destruction she left in her wake?

"And how is that?" Jake asked.

It took some effort, but Race pulled his gaze away from Aimee. His eyes were as cold as his partner's as he answered, "I'm going to Atlanta."

AIMEE came awake to the noise of someone tut-tutting near her head. She lay there—not exactly sure where *there* was—and let her mind come to full consciousness, trying to test out certain functions while remaining perfectly still. She had no idea if her limbs would move at her command. It was as if she were standing outside her own body, unable to feel anything at all.

"Come on, missy. You're going to need to wake up soon. You're going to get dehydrated if I don't get some water in you."

The woman sounded kind, a bit concerned but not overly so, as if she would like Aimee to wake up but wouldn't have any sleepless nights if she didn't. It wasn't Blondie's voice, for which Aimee was grateful. Aimee wasn't quite ready to deal with her yet.

"Well, that's that. I'll be back in an hour or so to check on you again. Right now, I've got to go see to Josie's lunch." It was obvious this wasn't the first time the woman had spoken to her, and Aimee wondered just how long she'd been out. The fire had happened on Friday night; no, make that early Saturday morning. And today was . . . hell, Aimee didn't know.

The lights dimmed and Aimee heard a door close softly. She waited, unmoving, listening to every creak and hum, until she was certain she was truly alone.

Then, slowly, she opened one eye, just à crack. After the complete darkness of being unconscious, even the dim light in the room made her eyes water. Blinking, Aimee opened both eyes but remained lying in the same position. She was on a bed, her head resting on a comfortable pillow. There was a nightstand next to the bed with a lamp and a pitcher sitting on top of it. The floor was a dark hardwood, the planks wide and seamlessly fitted together. Aimee could see a dresser across the room, with a mirror hung above it.

As certain as she could be that she was alone, Aimee opened her mouth and attempted to separate her tongue from the roof of her mouth. Her head pounded and her tongue felt swollen to three times its normal size. She knew this feeling. She last felt it the morning she woke up with a brand-new tattoo of the Tasmanian Devil at the base of her spine. The night before, she, Raine, and Daphne had gotten drunk. Not just one-too-many-martinis drunk. This was an I-can't-believe-we-drank-a-fifth-of-vodka drunk.

And, although she hadn't regretted Taz, she had vowed never to drink that much ever again. The way she felt right now was the reason why.

Aimee finally managed to loosen her tongue from the roof of her mouth and tried to moisten her lips. Ugh. She felt like crap.

She rolled onto her back and felt a tug on her right arm. She wiggled her feet, then moved her legs, taking a physical inventory. Her upper left arm was throbbing and it took Aimee a moment to realize why. That was where that asshole Bill had stabbed her with the hypodermic.

"Bastard," she muttered, her voice raspy from lack of use.

She smacked her lips again and, satisfied that she was substantially none the worse for wear, attempted to sit up. Only, as she pushed her head up off the pillow, she was jerked back down. For some reason, her right arm refused to cooperate.

Aimee turned her head to look at her arm. It was flung upward, toward the headboard, and when she mentally commanded it to move, it refused. She wiggled her fingers, her skin tingling to protest the lack of blood her body was sending to her right arm. It felt as if a thousand bees were simultaneously stinging her and Aimee grimaced. She hated it when her limbs went to sleep.

Finally, the stinging stopped and Aimee wiggled her fingers again, and this time she heard the rattle of metal against metal. She rolled over and reached up with her left hand to feel around her right wrist. As she had begun to suspect, she was handcuffed to the bed.

"This shows a decided lack of imagination," she grumbled, scooting toward the headboard so she could sit up.

Fortunately, the pitcher was on the right-hand side of the bed. Had her captors been masochists, they would have put it on the opposite nightstand, taunting her with the promise of a drink just beyond her reach. She picked up the pitcher and sniffed, although rationally she knew that if Blondie had wanted to kill her, she would have done so by now. Still, it didn't seem prudent not to at least take some precautions.

The liquid smelled like . . . nothing. And it was clear, so Aimee assumed it was water. Since getting caught using bad manners was the least of her worries, she didn't bother pouring it into one of the paper cups on the nightstand, choosing to gulp it straight from the pitcher instead.

She didn't lower the pitcher, even when she heard the door open. She had no idea how long it may be before she was able to drink again, and this tasted like heaven.

"Well, it appears that our guest is awake," Aimee heard a man say. She took one more giant swallow of water before finally lowering the pitcher.

She found herself looking at one of the most handsome men she had ever seen. He had thick dark hair and deep, chocolate-colored eyes. His shoulders were broad and his hips lean, with a flat stomach and long legs and the golden brown skin of someone who was born in the sun.

"You're quite handsome," Aimee said, after she'd had a chance to look her fill. "I wouldn't think you'd need to handcuff women to keep them in bed."

FOURTEEN

"DOESN'T it bother you knowing that the men who buy your weapons use them to wage war against innocent people?" Aimee asked, knowing her only hope of surviving this was to stay in character and not show her fear. The woman who had insisted on meeting the ultimate buyer of McConnell's plans was confident that she could think—or charm—her way out of any situation. Now Aimee must believe the same thing.

When he'd come into the room moments ago, Nic Sabre had allowed himself a small smile at her comment before he'd introduced himself and taken a seat on the cream-colored upholstered chair on the left side of the bed.

Aimee felt uncomfortable, propped up against the headboard wearing the same red pajamas she'd had on for who knew how many days, but she refused to hide under the covers. Instead, when she caught Nic studying her, she stretched out her bare legs and crossed them at the ankle, pointing her red-painted toenails directly at him.

"Morality is the luxury of the rich. I do what I must to survive," Nic said.

Aimee glanced around her, at the wide windows showcasing a vast expanse of white sand beach and rolling turquoise water beyond and at the obviously expensive furnishings of the room itself. "You appear to be fairly wealthy to me," she observed.

Nic shifted in his seat, raising one arm to rest it along the back of the heavy chair. "Not wealthy enough," he said.

Dipping her chin in acknowledgment, Aimee favored Nic with a smile. "It is difficult to know when one has reached that point, isn't it?" she asked.

"It would seem so," Nic agreed, then fell silent, continuing to watch her.

Aimee resisted the urge to squirm under his scrutiny. *Think calm. Think sexy. Give the man what he expects,* she told herself, pushing a length of hair back from her face with her free left hand. "Why are McConnell's propulsion system plans so important to you?" she asked after a while. Ostensibly, her reason for wanting to meet this man was to understand him better. If that were true, he would expect her to ask some questions.

"I'm building a new weapon that requires the technology developed by McConnell's engineers. The profit margin for the manufacturing segment of my business is much greater than that of simply brokering arms deals. I found I was unable to amass the wealth I desired simply by being a dealer, so I decided to invest in manufacturing instead."

"I'm surprised by your honesty," Aimee admitted, lying back against the headboard.

"You said you would provide me with the plans in exchange for—how did you put it? Meeting the devil to whom you were selling your soul? I am that devil. You want to know me, know why I do what I do, before handing over the plans?" Nic shrugged. "Fine. I will indulge you in that. The plans are too important for me to play games."

"So, then, it's all about the money?" Aimee asked, shivering a little in the chill air from the ceiling fan slowly turning overhead. She was surprised when Nic, obviously noticing her discomfort, got up from his chair, walked over to the switch on the wall, and turned off the fan.

"Yes," Nic said, seating himself once again. "I'm not one of those fools who think money does not buy happiness."

"Amen to that," Aimee muttered.

"So what else would you like to know? I'd like to get this over with as soon as possible. As you may have guessed from the haste at which we brought you here, I'm quite anxious to get my hands on those plans."

Aimee reached out and picked up the pitcher of water, glancing at Nic as a silent means of asking if he'd like a drink. He shook his head, so she filled one paper cup for herself and then set the pitcher back down.

"Once you have the plans, how long until you bring the new weapon to market?" she asked after taking a sip of water.

"I hope to begin shipment at the end of the year," Nic answered.

"Where are the weapons being manufactured?"

"Someplace secure."

"What exactly is this weapon going to do?" Aimee asked.

Nic smiled at her and shook his head. "You must realize there are some questions I cannot answer."

Aimee raised the cup to her lips, watching Nic over the rim as she took another drink. Their gazes remained locked as she swallowed. "Why?" she asked slowly, tilting her head. "We both know you have no intention of letting me leave here alive."

"COULD she have done it?" Race asked, studying the three women sitting in the living room of Aimee's house in Atlanta. Her partners, Raine Robey and Daphne Donovan, were there, along with Aimee's sister, Lauren, who had apparently dropped in unannounced a few days back and had decided to hang out in Atlanta for a few days before returning to her own home in Manhattan.

"No," Raine said with a decisive shake of her blond head.

"Absolutely not," Daphne agreed.

"Was there a lot of money involved?" Lauren asked dryly.

It was impossible to miss the quelling looks Raine and Daphne shot Aimee's sister. "Yes," he answered. "Half a million dollars was the number she was quoted."

"She wouldn't do it," Raine said with a sideways look at Lauren that clearly indicated the other woman should just keep quiet. "Aimee is determined to make a good living, but not that way. If she wanted to get rich doing something illegal, she'd go into something more profitable, like selling drugs. After our time in the FBI, we all made enough contacts to set up a drug network—and we know what to do to avoid getting caught. There's no way Aimee would take a measly five hundred thousand to give up those plans."

"So you're saying she'd do it for more? A million, perhaps?" Race asked.

Raine closed her eyes and rubbed her forehead. "No, that's not what I meant. I meant if money were so important to her that she was willing to do something illegal to get it, she would do something huge. She wouldn't waste her time on a one-shot deal like this."

"Besides, I was just kidding," Lauren said, looking contrite, as if only now realizing the seriousness of the situation. "Aimee is one of the good guys. She wouldn't sell out her employer, no matter how much money was involved."

Race leaned forward on the dining room chair he was seated on and rested his elbows on his knees. "Are you certain?" he asked.

This time, all three women nodded.

But as he studied them, Race only wished they looked more convinced.

"I believe you and Diana are about the same size. You should be able to find something here that will fit," Nic said, laying a pile of clothes down on the foot of Aimee's bed. He had been saved from responding to her comment about his intentions when his cell phone rang, a welcome call at a most opportune moment.

Rabin had surfaced safely in Iran and agreed to send representatives to Australia to discuss the LoRS bomb. Nic was more anxious than ever to get his hands on the propulsion system plans, but he was oddly conflicted about what to do with this woman once she delivered. It was true that before having met Aimee, he had no intention of letting her live. If he did, she would forever be one of those loose ends he would regret not tying up. There was something about her, however, that had him looking forward to seeing her again once his call was completed. It was that same something that had him hunting down proper clothing as well—he found it unsettling to converse with her while she was dressed so scantily. She, on the other hand, seemed perfectly at ease.

"I don't suppose you'd like to release me long enough for me to take a shower?" Aimee asked, remaining stretched out on the bed, her long legs crossed.

Nic shrugged nonchalantly and reached into the front pocket of his trousers for the key to the handcuffs. "Certainly. The alarm system is armed and there are sensors on all the doors and windows in this room. When you're finished, you can reach me on the house phone. Dial fifty-five for my office. Diana included some makeup and other toiletries as well as the clothing, but if you're in need of anything else, extra towels or personal items or the like, call the housekeeper, Mrs. Jacobs, at extension fourteen."

Nic reached out to unlock the handcuffs, his fingers brushing the soft skin at Aimee's wrist. She neither pulled away nor leaned into him and Nic found himself amazed once again at her sangfroid. He was tempted to ask her if she realized that he had no qualms about killing her, but he wasn't certain what he would do if she said that she already knew that about him. And most likely, she did.

When he released the lock, Aimee didn't rub her wrist as Nic had suspected she might. Instead, she yawned and stretched, catlike.

"All right, then. I'll give you a ring when I'm ready," she said.

Nic gave her a small smile as he nodded. "Very well," he said, allowing himself to be dismissed. He left the room and locked the door behind him, then checked the keypad next to the door to make sure the alarm was set properly. The security system in this house had been built both to keep intruders out and to keep guests in, if necessary. There were also security cameras mounted strategically around the grounds, plus armed guards who regularly patrolled the island. One did not remain alive long in Nic's line of business without a healthy dose of paranoia.

The room Aimee was being kept in was on the opposite end of the house from Nic's office and the bedrooms upstairs where he and Josie slept. To get to this part of the house, one had to first make it through a locked door that separated the guest wing from the rest of the house. The rooms all opened to the outside, which made it convenient for getting guests in and out of the house without them being seen by anyone else, but were shielded from prying eyes by tinted windows that allowed guests to see out, but not for anyone on the outside to see in.

Nic entered the code to open the door leading to the guest wing and stepped through the doorway into the main area of the house. He needed to make arrangements to fly to Sydney to meet with Rabin's representatives, but planned to check on Josie first. She had been quiet, moody almost, for nearly two days, ever since she and Giselle came back from Longport. Nic worried that she had been injured after fainting, but the doctor he'd brought over from the mainland had assured him that there was nothing physically wrong with his daughter. The doctor suggested that perhaps it was hormones that were making Josie act strangely and Nic conceded that this was possible. He only hoped this was not the beginning of years of such behavior.

He found Josie lying despondently on the couch in the media room, watching *The Princess Diaries* for what had to be the three thousandth time.

"How are you feeling?" Nic asked, resting one hand on the doorframe.

"Fine," Josie mumbled without raising her head off the pillow.

"Are you done with your studies?"

"Yes."

"Do you know what the word 'monosyllable' means?"

Josie turned her head and looked at him, then looked away again. "Yes," she answered, without so much as cracking a smile.

Nic sighed. For some reason, he had always thought Josie would escape the terrible changes that puberty wrought on so many other teens, most likely because Josie had always been such a model child. Nic hoped this sullen, uncommunicative state wouldn't last long.

"All right, I'll leave you alone. Enjoy your movie." Nic waited for a moment, wishing that Josie would reach out to him or say something more. But she didn't, keeping her gaze glued to the sixty-inch flat-screen television that Nic had installed last year.

He left the media room and strode down the hall to his office, which he had locked before setting off to the Simondses' home in search of clothes for Aimee. He keyed in the code to unlock the door and then pushed it open. His desk was just as he'd left it, with not so much as a Post-it note in sight.

After closing the door behind him, Nic unlocked the safe and removed his laptop and a pad of paper where he'd scribbled some notes to himself. Rabin had said his envoy would arrive in Sydney tomorrow around noon, which meant that Nic would need to leave the island at 8:00 A.M. He was glad, as always, that he did not have to rely on commercial airlines to get him from one place to another. With the long security lines and other delays, a meeting like this could take an entire day instead of just hours.

Nic called his pilot and told the man to have the plane ready to go by 7:45. Then he called a car service to arrange to have a car waiting for him at the airport when they landed. Rabin had said that if all went well, his representatives would call once they were in Australia to tell Nic where to meet them.

Nic spent the next several minutes downloading information about the LoRS bomb onto a special laptop that he used only for offsite demonstrations. Although his computer was backed up regularly, Nic refused to risk taking it off the island, both because of the increased chance of having it stolen, and also because there was too much sensitive information stored on it that could lead the authorities back to him. This other laptop held no such incriminating evidence. Nic had the hard drive completely erased after every time he used it.

He was nearly finished copying the information he would need, when the phone on top of his desk rang. He looked at the digital display and saw that the call was coming from the guest room next to the one where Aimee was ensconced. Nic frowned. That didn't make sense. None of the other guest rooms were occupied. Perhaps it was Mrs. Jacobs, although Nic had no idea why the housekeeper would need to call him.

"Yes," he said, lifting the receiver to his ear.

"Your security system needs work," Aimee said, sounding amused.

Nic pulled the receiver away from his ear and stared at it incredulously. He checked the display again just to make certain he was not mistaken.

She had escaped.

Where Nic should have felt anger, instead he was filled with a surprising sense of admiration for this woman, perhaps because he saw in her the same qualities he admired in himself.

"I'll be there in a moment," Nic said, hanging up the phone before tapping the keys to shut off his second laptop. He put it back in the safe along with the pad of paper he'd taken out, then pulled out the purse that Diana had brought back to the island with her. She'd had it screened for transmitters before putting it on the plane back in America, of course, and they'd both searched it thoroughly once she'd arrived on the island with an unconscious Aimee in tow. There was nothing unusual in the handbag, but Nic wasn't quite ready to hand it over just yet. Hell, he hadn't yet decided what to do with Aimee when this was all over. He supposed it really depended on what happened next.

He took the disk from Aimee's purse and replaced the handbag in his safe. Then he looked back toward his desk to make sure nothing else remained out before closing the door of the safe and twisting the tumbler. Then he tugged on the handle to test that it was locked and, when satisfied that it was, he took the disk and his laptop and left his office, once again locking the door behind him.

FIFTEEN

"NOTHING from the transmitter?" Race asked, pushing back his chair and stalking to the window of the office in the conference room where he and Aimee had made love the night before she disappeared.

Jake didn't look up from his computer. "Nothing," he answered, his fingers busy on the keyboard.

"Where the hell is she? She hasn't contacted anyone—not her partners, not her family, not me. I'm telling you, Aimee is in real danger." Race reached out and put a hand on the glass. Even though it was past midnight, the window was still warm from the air outside. Summer in San Antonio meant temperatures in the 80s during the day and only a few degrees cooler at night.

Jake looked up then and Race saw his partner's reflection in the glass, his eyebrows raised as if to say, "Give me a break." What he said instead was, "There's no evidence of that."

Race closed his eyes and wearily pinched the bridge of his nose. He hadn't slept since Aimee had disappeared, his mind going over every possibility, rejecting again and again that she had sold them out. There was something that he was missing, some clue that would prove Aimee's innocence... only he just couldn't figure out what it was. Instead, it hovered, just out of his grasp, taunting him like the keys dangling from the mouth of that damn dog in the *Pirates of the Caribbean* ride at Disneyland.

"Look, Race, I'm going to say this because we've known each other a long time. I've never seen you get personally involved with any of our cases like this, but it's obvious that you like this girl and it's clouding your judgment," Jake said, not unkindly. "We have Aimee Devlin on tape, wearing the same sexy little red pajamas as she pulls the fire alarm that she's wearing when she escapes from her apartment and loses her Agency tail. Now, I know that's not enough evidence to—"

"That's it!" Race interrupted suddenly, slamming his palm down on the conference table. "Where's that security tape?"

Jake looked at him as if he'd lost his mind, but pointed to a pile at the far end of the table. "It's in there, under a mountain of witness statements."

Race hurried over and unearthed the tape from where it had been buried. He took the tape over to the glassed-in media center that housed a VCR, DVD player, television, and a cabinet full of audio equipment. Flipping the VCR on, he slid the tape into the machine. An empty hallway flashed on the large screen behind Jake's head.

"We've seen this thing a dozen times," Jake protested, swiveling in his chair to look at Race and ignoring what was happening on the screen.

"Just watch," Race ordered as a woman came into the picture. She was careful to keep her face hidden behind a curtain of dark hair. She had come from the direction of Aimee's apartment, but the camera had not caught her exact point of origin. The camera was mounted so as to record people getting on and off the elevator, not to keep track of who came and went from each apartment. "Keeps the vandalism down," the landlord had said when they'd asked why he even bothered.

The woman on the tape reached out toward the fire alarm, the hem of her silky red nightshirt rising above her waist.

Race pushed the pause button on the VCR and stepped close to the screen, pointing to the woman's back. "There," he said excitedly. "That's it. I can't believe I missed it."

"Missed what?" Jake asked.

"Aimee has a tattoo right here. The Tasmanian Devil. You'd be able to see the top of his head in this shot. I don't know who this woman is, but she isn't Aimee Devlin."

AIMEE knew that handing over the plans was the equivalent of handing her life to Nic Sabre. Once he had the plans, he no longer had any need to keep her alive. So she stalled, trying to figure out how to convince him to let her live.

She hadn't been certain whether her trick of escaping from her room would intrigue Nic or piss him off, but she figured she had nothing to lose by giving him proof that she could have left the house but chose to stay. She'd refused to tell him how she got out, preferring to let him think that she was some sort of escape artist instead of revealing the truth—that she had slipped the mirror side of an eye shadow case under the door as Nic had punched in the key code to lock the door. Lying on the floor, she had watched his motions, then mimicked them when she was ready to change rooms. She had taken a shower first, however. No use going to the grave all sweaty.

It took her three tries to get the code right, but it hadn't been all that difficult since she'd only been trying to crack a four-digit code. To her delight, she'd discovered that all the doors used the same code, which seemed awfully lazy, but understandable. Trying to remember which code went with which room would be too much for anyone to handle. If Nic let her live, Aimee might suggest that he consider exchanging the keypads for magnetic card readers.

If he didn't . . . well, then he was on his own.

"So, tell me. What sort of things does an international arms dealer actually do? I mean, do you travel to all these war-torn countries and meet with despots or do they come to you?" Aimee asked after she finished decoding the next three digits in the link to the plans.

Nic was in his usual place, sitting in the chair across the room, his arm resting comfortably along the top. He acted as if they were not locked in a battle for her life, so Aimee took her cue from him and did the same. She was sitting in the middle of the large bed with her legs crossed yoga-style, the laptop he'd allowed her to use to descramble the encoded information on her lap. She was about halfway through and could have easily had it done by now if she hadn't been stalling. But as long as Nic remained patient, Aimee figured she might as well keep talking.

"It varies," Nic said, "although now that I have an established reputation, they come to me more often than not. I must admit, I much prefer it that way. Many war-torn countries, as you call them, do not have the best of accommodations."

"I can imagine," Aimee said.

"Is it my turn to ask something?" Nic said, favoring her with a look that told her he knew he had the upper hand here but was willing to pretend that he did not.

Aimee breezily waved her left hand and said, "Shoot." Then, because she couldn't seem to stop herself now that she'd slipped into this alternate, completely unafraid persona, she grinned and added, "Sorry, poor choice of words."

Nic didn't smile, just continued to watch her intently with those dark eyes of his. Aimee still hadn't quite gotten over the shock of how handsome he was, sort of like a larger, darker Pierce Brosnan. Too bad his soul was as black as his eyes.

Aimee forced herself to look away, hiding her sudden shiver of fear as she pretended to stretch out her arms.

"How is it that you came to be in possession of those plans?" Nic asked. "We did a background check on you before bringing you here and we know you were working for McConnell. How did you know that one of Rockton's employees was stealing the plans?"

Aimee drew in a slow, measured breath and prayed that Race had been right in assuring her that all traces of her former FBI career had been eliminated. If not, Nic would no doubt catch her in this lie. "Joe McConnell hired me about a month ago to be his executive assistant. I have a . . . a talent, shall we say, for blending into the woodwork. Over the years, I've found this talent to be very lucrative. I've been in meetings where the most classified, top-secret information is being discussed, only everyone seems to forget that I'm in the room."

"I find that hard to believe," Nic said, eyeing her in a disconcertingly dispassionate manner.

Aimee looked down at the computer and then back up at Nic. "Would you like a demonstration?" she asked.

Nic narrowed his eyes and remained silent for a long moment, as if coming to a decision of much more import than what was being discussed on the surface. "Yes, go ahead," he said finally.

Aimee nodded and set the laptop aside. She looked down at the flowing red pants and white tank top she'd chosen from the clothes Nic had brought for her. These would not do at all. She walked over to remaining clothes and pulled out a pair of khaki shorts and a white T-shirt.

"I'll be right back," she said, heading toward the bathroom. It took her less than three minutes to return and, when she stepped into the room, she had to hold back a laugh at the disbelieving look on Nic's face.

"My God. It's as if you're a completely different person."

Aimee didn't say anything. He had no idea how true that was.

"All right, so now I understand how you could manage to be overlooked, but that still doesn't answer my question. How did you find out about the plans?"

Here's where things got tricky. Did Nic know about the CIA? Or that a private firm had been hired to find the mole within McConnell? A private firm where Aimee was a principal? If he didn't know about Partners In Crime, Aimee would be a fool to lead him there. She figured it would be less risky to let him know that the CIA had been involved. He was probably accustomed to having his activities monitored by various governments and their agencies.

"Joe McConnell suspected someone in his organization was stealing secrets. The CIA became involved, and this is how I found out about the espionage. Joe asked me to bring in coffee for a meeting between himself and an agent, and I did . . . but I never left. Later, the agent assigned to the case called Joe to tell him that they'd found their spy. I was in Joe's office when he took the call and immediately afterward, he asked me to set up a meeting with his head of IT. I knew Ron Jefferson couldn't be the culprit, because if he was, Joe McConnell would have had the man removed from the premises that instant."

"How did you figure out who it was then?" Nic asked.

I don't know, Aimee was tempted to shout, trying to remain calm as she dug herself deeper into this trench of lies. She licked her dry lips and crossed the room, ostensibly to pour herself a glass of water. Then she sat down on the edge of the bed, crossing her legs and contemplating her painted toenails. "Um, I went back to my desk and accessed the phone bills for the past two months. As an executive assistant, I was responsible for analyzing things like phone usage and such. I found all the outgoing calls from Ron's extension and saw that there were a large number of them going to the same number. When I called that number, a woman from Rockton Aeronautical answered and I knew then that I had my culprit."

"Why didn't you just access the plans yourself? Why go to all the trouble to go to that conference and steal them?" Nic asked.

Aimee slowly let out her breath. This was much easier. "First, I had no idea how to get in touch with the buyer, so I had to follow Rita to find her. Second, if you had the plans that Rita left, why would you bother buying them from me? And, third, by the time I realized what was going on, it was too late for me to access the plans. I knew the CIA was monitoring who was accessing the plans and I had no plausible excuse for why I would do such a thing."

Nic nodded. "Very well then. That answers my question. Now, would you mind handing over those plans?"

Aimee looked down at Nic's computer, knowing it was time to stop stalling. "Yes," she answered. "I'll have them for you in five more minutes."

SIXTEEN

JOSIE slowly twisted the doorknob, half-expecting the door to be locked. Something was up. Her father had gone back and forth from his office to the guest wing at least three times since she'd been sitting in the TV room. Somebody was here, and Josie was determined to find out who it was and what Daddy was doing.

Seeing the picture of that terrorist the other day had shaken her badly, but she wasn't sure what to do about it. There was a part of her that wanted to ask her father what he'd been doing meeting with someone like that, but another part of her really didn't want to know. That latter part kept insisting that there had to be some explanation that made sense. Like maybe Daddy didn't know that man was a terrorist.

She didn't know what she expected to find out by snooping around now, but couldn't seem to stop herself from doing it. For some reason, she just *had* to know who Daddy was visiting in the guest wing.

The door opened easily and silently and Josie slipped down the darkened hallway. She seldom came here, was forbidden from doing so when Daddy had guests and had little reason to do so otherwise. But if she was quiet, maybe she'd be able to put her mind at rest without getting caught.

"This file now contains the decoded URL, user ID, and password to access the propulsion system plans," Josie suddenly heard a woman say.

She pressed her back against the wall. There were eight guest suites down this corridor, four on each side. The voice had come from the last room on the right side of the hallway. Doing her best to remain out of sight, Josie sidled farther down the hall, hoping to get a glance at her father's guest.

"You can access the plans from here. I have a wireless network," her father said.

Josie crept closer, glad her feet were bare so that her movements didn't make any noise on the hardwood floor. With her back pressed up against the wall, she turned her head slightly to see into the room, but her view was blocked by the half-closed door.

Quietly, she turned so that she was facing the doorway. She took one step sideways, and then another. Then she craned her neck and could finally see inside the room. Her father was sitting with his back to her, facing the bed that dominated the room. On the bed sat a woman hunched over a laptop. The woman's hair was pinned up in a twist at the back of her head. She wore a pair of tan shorts and a white T-shirt and, like Josie, her feet were bare.

Just before Josie pulled her head back, the woman glanced up and looked right into Josie's eyes.

Startled, the woman blinked.

Equally startled, Josie nearly choked on a gasp. With her heart pounding, she moved out of the doorway and clutched the wall, closing her eyes and silently praying that the woman wouldn't say anything.

"What's wrong?" she heard her father ask.

"Nothing," the woman answered. "The plans are taking a minute to— Really, there's nothing—"

"Josie, what are you doing here?" her father asked, sounding as if he were standing very close.

Josie was afraid to open her eyes, so she kept them closed.

"Uh. I heard voices, so I thought I'd come see who was here. I didn't know we had guests."

"*We* do not have guests, young lady, and you know you're not supposed to be here."

"I'm sorry. I didn't mean to blow your cover," the woman said, sounding amused.

Josie cracked open one eyelid. The woman had gotten off the bed and was leaning against the doorframe of the room with her arms folded across her chest. In contract to Josie's father, who was scowling, the woman was smiling in a friendly fashion. Josie decided immediately that she had found an ally.

"It wasn't your fault. I wasn't quick enough," Josie said.

"Nic, I must give you credit. You're very observant," the woman said, before extending a hand to Josie. "I'm Aimee Devlin. Nice to meet you."

Josie saw her father's face turn red, as if he were blushing. Josie guessed that he was more angry than embarrassed, but she took the woman's hand anyway, just to be polite. "Josie Sabre," she said.

Ms. Devlin raised her eyebrows as she shook Josie's hand. "So you're Nic's daughter, are you? Yes, I can certainly see the resemblance. You have lovely eyes."

Josie smiled shyly. "Thank you."

"You're welcome," the woman said, then turned to Josie's father, who seemed to be even angrier than before. "There's no harm done here, Nic. I'll be gone by—when? Tonight? Tomorrow?"

Josie knew that she should just keep quiet or, even better, apologize for intruding and get out of there as quickly as possible. But, instead, she couldn't seem to stop herself from asking, "You're leaving? Where are you going?"

Nic sent Aimee a quelling look before he turned to his daughter. "I have a meeting in Sydney tomorrow. Ms. Devlin will be coming with me and she will not be returning to the island."

"Oh," Josie said, disappointed. Then, suddenly, her face brightened. "Can she have dinner with us tonight? I'm sure Mrs. Jacobs wouldn't mind setting an extra place."

Nic stared at his daughter, stunned. Why was she behaving

this way? She had never taken any interest in his guests before today. Why was she so eager to get to know this particular one?

He narrowed his eyes and looked at Aimee. With her hair up and her makeup scrubbed off, she looked like an ordinary woman, not the sexy, brash woman he knew her to be. Was it possible that Josie was subconsciously looking for a mother figure? If so, he could see where Aimee might fit his daughter's vision. Unfortunately, Nic knew better. Aimee Devlin was not the kind, maternal type. She was only in this for the money.

Besides, by tomorrow evening, she would be dead.

"No," Nic said. "I'm afraid Ms. Devlin can't join us."

"Why? Is she going into town for dinner?" Josie asked. "Maybe we could all go."

Aimee's smile widened, as if enjoying his discomfort. "Yes, Nic, do tell. Am I going into town for dinner?"

Nic rubbed his throbbing left temple with an index finger. "No. No one's going into town."

"Then why can't Ms. Devlin eat with us?" Josie asked.

"Because I said so," Nic ground out between clenched teeth.

"Ah, the dreaded 'because I said so' defense," Aimee said, her eyes flashing amusement before she decided to take pity on him. Stepping out into the hallway, she put a hand on his daughter's shoulder. "Thank you for the invitation, Josie, but I'm afraid I have work to do this evening that forces me to decline your kind offer. Perhaps some other time?"

Disappointed, Josie nodded. She didn't know why it seemed so important that Ms. Devlin have dinner with them that evening, maybe because she felt that the woman could somehow redeem her father. Ms. Devlin seemed nice, not the sort of woman to have dinner with a man who met with terrorists. If she had agreed to have supper with them, it would almost be like all of Josie's doubts would be erased.

Josie turned toward the doorway that led out into the main house. "I'm sorry for interrupting," she mumbled.

Behind her, her father sighed.

Standing in the shadows of the hallway, Aimee looked

from father to daughter and back again. Discovering that Nic had a daughter had come as a complete shock, but Aimee had done what she could to use that to her advantage. As heartless as it sounded, she was not above using the child to get closer to the arms dealer . . . and to stay alive.

"All right, fine," she heard Nic say, and let out the breath she hadn't realized she'd been holding. "Ms. Devlin may have dinner with us tonight. She's leaving tomorrow, however. You do realize that?"

Nic looked at Aimee pointedly, and she guessed he meant that as a reminder more for her sake than for his daughter's.

Josie turned and a smile spread across her face, lighting up the dark eyes that were so like her father's. Aimee was struck by how beautiful Josie was and suddenly wondered where the girl's mother was. It didn't take a genius to figure out that Josie's mother would not be joining them for dinner, but that could mean the woman was simply out of town and her daughter was lonely.

"Josie, I need to talk to you. Let me just get my laptop and I'll be right with you," Nic said.

Aimee didn't envy the girl the lecture she figured was about to be delivered. She was about to turn and go back into the guest room, when a thought occurred to her. If, as she suspected, Nic planned to kill her tomorrow, the CIA would still have no clues as to Nic's whereabouts—and Nic would have the plans he needed to build his weapon. Somehow, she had to let the CIA know where she was. She'd already tried using the house phone but was unable to get an outside line. She'd briefly considered trying to escape, but that had seemed foolish with such limited information as she had. She had no idea where she was or how well guarded the house was. She'd heard Nic mention that they were on an island, which would only make her escape more difficult. So for now, it seemed that she was stuck here.

The only way she could think of to contact the CIA was to get her transmitter back and send them a signal. She had no doubt the house itself was being monitored for such transmissions, especially here in the guest wing. But maybe, if she could manage to get outside this evening, she could send a signal.

Nic came through the doorway, holding his laptop under his left arm. He glanced meaningfully behind him, silently signaling her to reenter the room, where he had since changed the security code.

Aimee took a step toward him and then said nonchalantly, as if his answer made no difference, one way or the other, "If you have my purse, I would appreciate getting it back. Not only is my favorite lipstick in there, but so are my eyeglasses and an extra set of contact lenses. I've had these in for several days now and they need to be replaced." She motioned toward her eyes as if to illustrate her point.

Nic studied her for a moment before giving an unconcerned shrug. She was certain he had gone through her purse and removed anything he thought was suspicious. "Fine. I'll have Mrs. Jacobs bring your things to you along with something to wear this evening. Unlike you Americans, we dress for dinner."

Aimee breezed past him with a decidedly wicked wink. "Ah, that's too bad. It's been a while since I ate in the nude," she said, too softly for Josie to hear.

Then she closed the guest room door behind her, leaving Nic coughing out in the hallway.

THERE were days that Race missed being an active-duty Army Ranger, days when he'd delight in attaching a bit of C-4 explosive to the brick walls he ran up against to just blast the shit out of them.

Today was one of those days.

Race stared at the receiver on the conference table in front of him, praying for the red indicator light to appear. Aimee had been gone for more than forty hours now and they'd had no contact from her. He was beginning to fear the worst.

"Damn it, I shouldn't have asked her to put herself in danger," he said, getting up from his chair to pace the conference room in frustration. There was nothing worse than this awful waiting, not knowing whether Aimee was being tortured or had already been killed. Proving that she wasn't the one who pulled the fire alarm had been both a blessing and a curse. The CIA was convinced that Aimee had not intentionally evaded her tail, but now it was certain that her life was in danger. And following the breadcrumb trails that might lead them to Aimee was slow and tedious work. Patience, Race had found, may be a virtue, but it sure as hell wasn't exciting or sexy.

He couldn't help but think that this was why most spy movies were so unrealistic. They showed agents always on the brink of danger, crashing cars and dodging bullets in exotic locales. The truth was, most of their cases were solved through sheer dogged determination. Not that they weren't trained to crash cars and dodge bullets and kick ass when the situation called for it, Race even more so than most agents courtesy of his eight-year stint with the U.S. Special Forces.

He didn't often miss those days—although, yeah, the blowing shit up part really was cool—because the day he'd been honorably discharged from the Army, his life expectancy had about doubled. Today, however, he longed for some physical activity to take his mind off of worrying about Aimee.

Forcing himself to sit back down at his computer, Race checked his e-mail and found that a report he'd been waiting on had come in from Research. He scanned it to find a listing of all of Rita's incoming calls in the past week. The analyst had done much of the legwork for him, cross-referencing the phone numbers with the names and addresses of the accountholders. Several calls had come from unknown accounts—prepaid calling cards, Race discovered after querying the analyst who had compiled the report.

Good. That at least gave him somewhere to start. Although many people assumed that these calling cards were untraceable, that wasn't exactly true. If they were bought with a credit card, they were as easily traced as any other purchase. First, he needed to find out where the card had been sold, so he put in another call to his research analyst, who told him she'd look up that information and put him on hold.

Race leaned back in his chair and looked out the windows, only to realize that the light dusk he'd noticed that last time he'd glanced outside had turned the dark of full night.

"How are you holding up?" Jake asked, breezing into the conference room with two tall paper cups. He handed one to

Race. "I had them make yours a double since it's obvious you're not going to sleep until we find this girl."

Race took the cup and ignored his partner's sarcasm. "I'm following up a lead on a phone card. How are you coming along on matching outbound airline passenger video to the picture of our buyer?"

Jake flopped down in his chair, appearing as relaxed as if they were trying to find a missing fifty dollars rather than attempting to save a woman's life. A woman that Race just happened to care about very much.

Over the years, Race had come to realize that he and his partner were nothing alike, at least not where women were concerned. In the pre-feminist days, Jake would have been considered a ladies' man—the original James Bond type before women got tired of seeing movies where females were all portrayed as complete bimbos and Bond got to sleep with every one of them. Race had overheard some of the women back in the office referring to Jake as a "bad boy." Race didn't figure anyone ever called him that.

It wasn't that he didn't enjoy women, because he did. It was just that he was always a bit suspicious of their motives, and that made him cautious. He supposed that came from spending his teen years as the slightly overweight math nerd who brought his Hi-Q team to victory but never got up the courage to ask a classmate out. What could he say? He'd learned all about mockery and rejection from the age of five. His first day of kindergarten and he'd had no idea the horror that awaited him.

He'd wondered what his parents were thinking when they saddled him with the name Horace. Yeah so, fine, it had been his maternal grandfather's name, but what sort of cruel joke was it to name your only child something that other kids were certain to mock him for? They could have named him Bob and stuck him with Horace as a middle name.

So, the unfortunate name, coupled with an equally unfortunate amount of body fat that refused to disappear until after Race's senior year in high school, hadn't exactly made him popular with the ladies. And when he had emerged from the cocoon at eighteen and suddenly (and, to him, inexplicably) become the object of positive female attention, Race couldn't understand what they saw in him now that they hadn't seen before. The answer, of course, stared back at him from the mirror every morning. And Race wasn't stupid, he'd used his newfound good looks to get laid throughout his college years. But it hadn't taken him long to realize how empty and meaningless those encounters really were—and how quickly they'd end if he suddenly found himself a chubby geek again.

The bottom line was, Race didn't often let women get close to him. When he slept with a woman, it was because she was someone he liked and wanted to have a relationship with. Whatever it was that had been happening between he and Aimee had been over too soon and he wasn't ready to let it end.

"You know, this could be a colossal waste of time," Jake said, bringing Race back to the subject at hand as he leaned forward and took a sip of his coffee. "The chances that the buyer and Aimee left town on a commercial flight are about as high as me getting it on with Devlin's supermodel sister."

Race raised one eyebrow at his partner. "Have you got any other ideas about how to find her?"

Jake took another drink of his coffee before setting it back on the table with a heavy sigh. "No," he said, turning to his own computer. "You know, some days I hate this fucking job."

Race clamped his mouth shut on his answer to that when the analyst came back on the line.

"Agent Gardner? I have that information for you," the analyst said.

"Go ahead." Race picked up a pen and scribbled some notes as the woman talked, then thanked the youthful-sounding analyst and hung up the phone. As he hit the button to send the report to a printer, he stood and shrugged into his suit jacket—an article of clothing worn more to conceal the weapon at his side than to keep up appearances—before addressing his partner again. "This may not be the exciting career we envisioned back when we were going through training at The Farm, but this 'fucking job,' as you called it, is what helps catch the bad guys. You want to drive hovercraft over landmines and go on car chases in ice hotels, then you're welcome to walk away from this op anytime. But you can rest assured, I will not give up, no matter how many dead-end leads I have to follow or how futile it may seem. I am not leaving Aimee out there alone."

SEVENTEEN

WITH two sisters in the beauty business, Aimee had learned a thing or two about hair and makeup and she used every trick she knew to make sure she looked fabulous this evening. Yes, it was true that she wanted to be valued for her brains more than her looks, but if tonight was going to be her last night on Earth, she wanted to go out knowing she'd given the world her best.

Nic's housekeeper had been amazingly cooperative, bringing Aimee everything on her list, including a curling iron, hair spray, eyeliner, and bobby pins.

Standing in front of the bathroom mirror, Aimee let the last curl fall, warm against her neck. She twisted her head to one side and then the other, then unplugged the curling iron, satisfied with her handiwork.

She glanced at her watch as she stepped into the bedroom. 8:15 P.M. Nic said he'd come to collect her at 8:30. She slid out of the thick terry cloth robe that had been hanging on the back of the bathroom door and looked over the items she'd laid out on the bed. Mrs. Jacobs had brought not only a dress for Aimee to wear this evening but a handful of lingerie with the tags still on, as well. Aimee didn't ask how the housekeeper had managed to guess the correct size; she was too grateful for clean underwear to question anything.

Aimee pulled the tag off a pair of black panties and checked the tag—100 percent silk. Nice. The matching bra was nearly sheer and completely impractical, but pushed her breasts together to give the illusion of cleavage. The housekeeper had also left a pair of sheer stockings—silk, not nylon, Aimee noticed as she slid the fabric first up one leg and then the other. These were not your typical sausage-casing-like nylons, designed to squash your ovaries into your stomach and make even the slimmest woman feel fat. Instead, they caressed her legs with every move, soft fingers of silk against her skin.

Of all the items Aimee was grateful for, however, it was her handbag that she had been the most happy to see. She'd already pulled her lipstick with the transmitter inside and the compact/surveillance detector out and, pretending to use the powder in the compact, had determined that, while there were no cameras in this room, it was bugged for audio surveillance and was being monitored for electronic transmissions—which meant that Aimee couldn't signal the CIA unless she was willing to blow her own cover. She'd slipped the lipstick into the tiny evening bag Mrs. Jacobs had brought, but found to her dismay that, because of the purse's oval shape, the compact would not fit. If she were to try to find a safe place to transmit a signal, she would need her detection device.

Aimee tried to think where she could stow it. The only place that came to mind was a bit risky . . . and more than a bit personal. But she had no other choice. She slipped the compact into the crotch of her panties, shuffling her feet a bit to make sure it would stay put. It would be impossible to explain it away if it somehow ended up falling out at some point in the evening. She wished then that Mrs. Jacobs had left her with regular panty hose instead of these sexy stockings. At least with panty hose, if the compact fell out, it would be trapped against her legs by the tight nylons.

Running her hands along her backside, Aimee turned and looked into the full-length mirror mounted on the back of the bathroom door to make sure she couldn't see any telltale bulges from behind. Then she turned to the dress Mrs. Jacobs had brought. It was gorgeous, the sort of thing worn by Hollywood stars at the Academy Awards or on opening night. The fabric was the color of the ocean on a sunny day, in a place with white sandy beaches where palm trees swayed. It was covered with sequins of the exact same color, which caught the light every time she moved. Aimee wasn't exactly the sequin type, but as she smoothed the dress down over her hips and turned to see the softly draping fabric, she had to admit that this was a heavenly dress.

"Would you like some help with the zipper?" Nic asked from the doorway.

Aimee resisted the urge to spin around. No use letting him know he had startled her. "Yes, thank you," she said, suspecting that he had expected her to refuse his help. She walked toward him slowly, her silk-clad feet sliding over the smooth hardwood floor.

Nic had changed from the lightweight linen slacks and short-sleeved shirt he'd been wearing earlier into a charcoal gray suit and crisply starched Oxford shirt with a burgundy and gray tie. His black shoes were highly polished, his dark hair freshly combed, and his eyes as deep and unreadable as always.

Aimee turned and presented Nic her back. The dress's zipper began a few inches below the spot where her lower back met her buttocks, and she knew her tattoo was easily visible, but Nic made no comment on it. She felt the edges of the fabric close as Nic slid the zipper up, ending at the base of her neck. His fingers were warm as they brushed her skin and Aimee shivered despite herself. He had quite a light touch for someone responsible for so many deaths around the globe.

"You look lovely," he said, resting his hands on her shoulders.

Aimee fought the chill inside her as she looked up and met his eyes in the mirror. The most she could manage was a wobbly smile, her reservoir of bravado running dangerously low. "Thank you," she said, hoping he would release her.

Instead, he lifted one hand and twisted one of her curls around his index finger. "Josie likes you," he said, sliding his thumb along the hair trapped around his finger.

"She doesn't know me," Aimee said softly.

"True. And she's often too trusting. So far, the world has been kind to her. Except for losing her mother as an infant, she's not had any tragedy in her life. She hasn't learned yet how dangerous people can be."

"She's just a child," Aimee protested. "She has years ahead of her to learn that lesson."

"I'm hoping she never will," Nic said, tugging on her hair so that Aimee was forced to tilt her chin up. Nic lowered his head and pressed his lips against the soft skin below her right ear, his eyes closing for just a moment. When he opened them again, their gazes locked together. "What's even more troubling to me is that *I* find myself drawn to you. The world has not been kind to me. I know better than to trust you."

Aimee didn't know what to say. She knew she ought to tell Nic that he could trust her, but she wasn't certain she could pull off the lie. Instead, she said, "You wouldn't believe me if I said you could trust me, so why don't we simply go on as we have been and leave it at that?"

He didn't move for a long moment and Aimee was scared that she had just flunked some test. When Nic smiled at her and laid another light kiss on her neck, however, she got the feeling the opposite was true. Indeed, his mood seemed considerably lightened when he released her and stepped back.

"Come along, then. Dinner awaits."

He offered an arm for her to take and Aimee held up one finger before walking to the bed to retrieve her small evening bag. Aimee slid the thin strap over her shoulder and then slipped her feet into the matching sandals she'd left at the foot of the bed, leaning on Nic's arm for support.

She straightened and smiled up at him. "All right. Let's go."

Nic held open the bedroom door and motioned for her to precede him. As they emerged from the guest wing, Aimee chewed on the inside of her lip and tried to take in the layout of the house without being too obvious about her surveillance. The house appeared to be built around a large central living room, with a wide hallway surrounding the living room and leading off into smaller rooms. Some of the living room walls were fixed, while others were mounted on a track and could be slid open or closed. Several of the panels were open this evening, giving Aimee glimpses of large white couches and heavy dark wood. As they walked down the hallway, they passed several smaller rooms on the left, including a billiards room, a TV room, and a spacious tiled bathroom.

"I asked Luke and Diana Simonds to join us," Nic said as they turned a corner and started down another hall.

"And they are?" Aimee asked.

"Uh, Diana is the one you met in America," Nic said, sounding a trifle embarrassed. "Luke works for me, as well. Their daughter, Giselle, is Josie's age."

"Ah. I'll try not to hold it against Diana that the last time we met, she helped someone stick a needle in my arm," Aimee said.

Nic pulled her to a stop on the hardwood floor. "Josie and Giselle know nothing about my business, and I intend to keep it that way. You will not mention any of this—not the plans, not what happened back in San Antonio, none of what we discussed about the weapons. Nothing, do you understand?"

His grip had tightened painfully on Aimee's upper arm, but she refused to do so much as flinch. "Of course," she said. "Your secret is safe with me."

Nic loosened his grasp, as if just now realizing what he was doing. "I'm sorry. I'm just . . . cautious around my daughter. By the time she's old enough to start being aware of what's going on around her, I hope to have made my fortune and be long out of this business."

Aimee recalled the way Josie Sabre had snuck into the guest wing, clearly aware that something was "going on around her," but she didn't point that out to Nic. If he wanted to believe that his daughter was oblivious to her surroundings, far be it from her to disillusion him.

"I understand," she said instead.

"Good. The others are waiting for us in the drawing room." They began walking again and, within a few strides, Aimee heard the sound of voices coming from a room near the end of the hall. They passed a dining room, its walls, like the living room, partially open to show the room inside. A massive table stood in the middle of the room, covered with a white linen tablecloth and set with white plates rimmed in gold and sparkling crystal glassware. A centerpiece of white candles and gardenias floating in a serene pool of water was flanked by ivy, the green foliage contrasting sharply with all the white surrounding it.

They passed the dining room and the voices grew louder. As they neared the next room, Nic moved his hand to the small of her back and guided her in front of him and through the doorway.

All conversation ceased when Aimee stepped over the threshold. The "drawing room," as Nic had called it, was decorated similarly to the living room, only with a more masculine flair. The chairs here were chocolate leather, the wet bar in the corner a dark mahogany. The man behind the bar was average height—no more than six feet tall—with curly brown hair and an unthreatening look about him. Aimee immediately recognized the blond woman seated in front of him on one of the barstools as the same woman she'd seen coming into the conference center ladies' room back in San Antonio. The woman was watching her with cool blue eyes that didn't seem quite as hard as they'd been the first time they'd met. The reason for that softening, Aimee guessed, was the miniature version of the woman seated on the barstool next to her. Diana's daughter was an exact replica of her mother, with the same long, golden hair, high cheekbones, and blue eyes.

Josie, who had also been sitting on a barstool sipping on a brightly colored drink, was the only one of the quartet who seemed happy to see her. She set her drink on the bar, hopped down off the barstool, and looked up at Aimee with her large, dark eyes full of awe.

"You look beautiful," she breathed.

Aimee smiled down at the child. She'd forgotten that the last time Josie had seen her, her clothes were drab and her face devoid of makeup. "Thank you. You look quite charming yourself."

And she did. Her hair was clipped up with a dozen blue glass butterflies and she wore a black dress spotted with butterflies that matched her hair clips. It was obvious that Josie was well cared for; it showed in the shine of her clean hair and the glow of her skin. This was a child that someone loved.

"This is my best friend, Giselle," Josie said, reaching out a hand to pull her friend out of her seat.

Like Josie, Giselle Simonds was clean and well dressed.

Unlike Josie, however, Giselle's eyes held a tinge of something . . . adult. Call it caution or suspicion, Giselle seemed more guarded than her friend. Still, she introduced herself politely enough, shaking Aimee's hand when it was offered.

"I believe you've met Diana," Nic said. "This is her husband, Luke."

"We've not met formally," Aimee said, doing her best to keep the sarcasm out of her voice as she extended her hand to Giselle's mother. "Aimee Devlin."

"Diana Simonds," Diana said, her voice equally flat.

Luke didn't offer his hand but merely nodded, then said, "I've been elected bartender this evening. Would you like a Shirley Temple like Josie and Giselle here, or do you prefer something stronger?"

"I believe I could do with something stronger," Aimee said. "How about a vodka and tonic with lime?"

"Coming right up. Scotch for you, boss?" Luke asked, turning to Nic.

"Please," Nic answered, resting one arm along the bar.

Aimee wracked her brain trying to think of some topic of conversation that would be neutral, but couldn't think of a thing. What exactly did weapons dealers discuss when they were off the clock? "So," she said to the room in general as the silence lengthened beyond what could be considered comfortable. "What are you girls' favorite subjects in school?"

"We don't go to school," Giselle answered with just a hint of that "you adults are so stupid" attitude that made parents want to lock their kids up from ages thirteen through about twenty-two.

"We have a tutor who comes every day," Josie added. "His name is Mr. Howe, but he lets us call him Colin."

"Is he a good teacher?" Aimee asked, taking the drink Luke handed her and carefully sitting down on the edge of one of the leather chairs, the hard plastic case of the compact digging in to the soft flesh of her inner thigh.

"He's okay," Giselle said with an indifferent shrug.

"I like him." Josie sounded defensive, as if she and Giselle had fought about this subject before. "This is our last year with Colin and I'm going to miss him. Next year, we're going to start attending classes over the Internet. Daddy says the subjects get more difficult and one teacher isn't enough." Josie plopped down on the couch across from Aimee, her expression a mixture of sadness and apprehension.

"He's right," Aimee said. "Try to think of it this way: Instead of one Colin, you'll have five or six." She took a sip of her drink, smothering a sigh of delight as the chilled alcohol slid down her throat. She could only allow herself one or two drinks this evening, but welcomed the instant calming effect the vodka had on her nerves.

"That's a brilliant way to look at the situation," Nic said, leaning one hip against the arm of Aimee's chair. He balanced his tumbler of Scotch on his knee, holding it there with one large tanned hand. He didn't wear any rings or jewelry except for the expensive-looking gold watch that peeked out at her from below the cuff of his white shirt.

Josie seemed to be considering the idea, while Giselle looked bored by the entire conversation. Aimee had to bite her bottom lip to keep from laughing. Only a teenager could pull off a look of such abject disdain.

"How long have you two been married?" Aimee asked, directing the question at Luke, who seemed by far the friendliest of the three Simondses.

"Sixteen years," Luke answered.

"Good for you. How did you . . . um, how did you meet?" Aimee asked, cringing when she realized the answer might be at a gun show or at some terrorist camp.

Diana was the one who fielded that question, saying, "We met at a bar in Boston. Luke was the bartender and I was attending college a few blocks away."

It sounded like a well-rehearsed lie, but Aimee nodded, relieved that she hadn't just introduced an off-limits topic of conversation. Fortunately, the conversation turned to the States, with Josie and Giselle, who had obviously never been, listening in. Aimee joined in when appropriate, but remained focused on trying to find an opportunity to suggest they go outside so she could attempt to use her transmitter away from the house. If that opportunity didn't arise, she was going to have to risk using it inside.

"Excuse me for interrupting, Mr. Sabre, but dinner is ready," Mrs. Jacobs said, poking her head into the doorway of the drawing room.

"Thank you," Nic said, without making any effort to stand up. It was clear that dinner would be served when Nic was ready, and not a second before.

The group took about ten more minutes to finish their cocktails and when Nic stood, so did everyone else. Nic reached out and took Aimee's empty glass from her, then held out a hand to help her up.

"Thank you," she murmured, smoothing her dress over her hips and shifting just a bit to make sure she could still feel the detection device between her legs.

Nic nodded appreciatively before herding everyone into the dining room. "You may sit on my right, with Josie to my left," he said, as if bestowing a great honor upon her.

Aimee sat where Nic indicated and tried to keep her nerves about her as dinner progressed. She sipped her wine slowly, but it seemed that every time she picked up her glass, it had been refilled. By the time dessert—amaretto bread pudding with crème anglaise accompanied by tiny crystal goblets of liqueur—arrived, Aimee was beginning to feel the slightest bit tipsy. She had alternated sips of wine with larger sips of water, but hadn't wanted to arouse anyone's suspicions by appearing to limit her alcohol intake.

She also felt that her bladder was about to rupture and, fearing this might be her only chance to transmit a signal to the CIA, she decided it was time to take a chance. If Nic planned to have her killed, she would not have her death be in vain. If nothing else, she would alert the CIA to Nic's whereabouts before he took her out.

"Excuse me," she said, laying a hand on Nic's arm as he reached out to take his glass of amaretto. "I need to use the ladies' room. Is the nearest one back that way?"

Nic stole a glance at Diana, which made Aimee curse silently. Surely he wasn't going to send the other woman into the bathroom with her?

"Here, I'll show you where the restroom is," Diana said, standing up and placing her napkin neatly next to her dessert plate.

Damn. She had no choice but to accept this escort. Aimee smiled at the other woman, pushed back her chair, and hooked a finger around the strap of her purse before following Diana out of the dining room. They went down the other leg of the U-shaped hallway, the sound of their high heels echoing on the hardwood floor.

Diana stopped in front of a door and pushed it open, revealing a multistall restroom. "There's both a men's and a women's," Diana explained. "They're perfect for when Nic throws large parties. No one ever has to wait."

Aimee attempted a smile but was certain it came out more like a grimace. "What a great idea," she said, trying to unclench her teeth.

Diana waited until Aimee had chosen a stall before picking the one right next to her—which was a giant faux pas in bathroom etiquette and confirmed to Aimee that she was, indeed, being tailed. Damn, damn, and double damn. Well, she'd just have to be careful and pray that Diana wouldn't go so far as to snoop beneath the stall door.

Aimee pulled up the hem of her dress and slid her hand inside her panties. She had to get the detection device out, otherwise it would fall into the toilet when she took down her underwear. When the unit had been safely extricated, Aimee relieved herself while at the same time silently opening the lid of the compact and using her thumbnail to dislodge the powder hiding the indicator lights.

Aimee waited for Diana to flush before turning on the power switch, just in case the other woman was listening as intently as Aimee suspected she was. She clamped her hand over her own mouth to smother a disappointed groan when the screen immediately showed several beeping red lights. Not only were her transmissions being monitored, there was a chance that she was being taped as well. If that were the case, she'd be dead by morning. There was no way she could explain why she'd stored a compact at her crotch.

She flushed and replaced the unit back in her panties, then smoothed her dress back down over her stockings. As she pushed open the stall door, she suddenly hoped that she'd live to be rewarded for the lengths she was willing to go to for her country.

"Nic's home is lovely," she said, running her hands under the water coming from an antique brass faucet.

Diana nodded, her gaze impassive.

Aimee took her time drying her hands, then reapplying her lipstick, wistfully eyeing the cap where she'd stashed the transmitter. Even if she were able to contact Race in the next hour, it would take nearly an entire day for him to get here—and by then it might very well be too late. She wasn't the type who normally looked to others to save her, but a little help out of this mess would be welcomed.

"How long have you worked for him?" she asked, mostly because she was annoyed at Diana's continued silence.

"A long time," the other woman answered cryptically.

Aimee twisted her lipstick back into its tube and started to put the cap back on, when Diana grabbed her left wrist, the one attached to the hand holding the cap . . . and the transmitter.

"You can cut the act," Diana all but growled. "I know what you're up to."

EIGHTEEN

WHEN the light at the intersection ahead turned yellow, Race forced himself to take a slow, deep breath in order to squelch the urge to shove his fist through the windshield of his leased Honda. If he'd been driving his own car, he'd have run the light, knowing that the engine would immediately respond to the added pressure on the accelerator. Not that the Honda was a bad car, but it wasn't exactly the performance machine his BMW was.

He tapped his fingers impatiently on the steering wheel as he waited for the light to turn green. This waiting game had been bad enough when his mind had been occupied with running down leads, but ever since leaving the office, all he'd had to think about was Aimee. Was she hurt? Was she frightened? Did she know that he wouldn't give up until he found her?

The light turned green and Race gunned the engine of his car and sped through the next block. He spied his target—the Alamo Street Quickie-Stop—up ahead on the right and eased his car into a parking spot. As he got out of the car, he looked around the well-lit street, almost wishing he'd run into a mugger or be just in time to stop a robbery at the convenience store or something. All of his pent-up frustration needed an outlet and he wouldn't mind a little crime stopping-related adrenaline rush to let off some steam.

Unfortunately, there were no obliging criminals lurking in any of the dark alleyways Race passed on his way to the minimart. The electronic eye mounted at the front entrance of the store beeped when he walked in, but the female clerk manning the counter didn't even look up from her *National Enquirer*. Race went over to the soda machine to get himself a large Coke and thought that with all the caffeine coursing through his system, he'd probably never sleep again.

The Quickie-Stop was a clone of the millions of other convenience stores in America, with several racks of snack foods and first aid supplies surrounded on all sides by chilled beer, wine, and soda, all watched over by a bored-looking clerk. Race waited until the market's lone customer had purchased a twelve-pack of beer and a bag of Fritos and exited the store before approaching the clerk. She was one of those curvy, overweight women who either couldn't afford new clothes and so had to continue trying to squeeze into things two sizes too small for her ever-expanding body or who thought rolls of fat peeking out from between her shirt and jeans were attractive.

The woman set her tabloid aside and looked him up and down as he pulled out the money to pay for his drink. He set a five-dollar bill on the counter and waited for her to give him back his change before he spoke.

"I'm Agent Gardner with the CIA. I wonder if I might ask you a few questions," he said politely, pulling his ID out of the breast pocket of his jacket and making certain to give the clerk a glimpse of his gun as he held his credentials out for her inspection.

The clerk's eyes narrowed and she began nodding, as if listening to music only she could hear. "Yeah, I had you pegged for a Fed the minute you walked in," she said.

Race hoped that she'd cooperate if he pandered to her intelligence. Not that he couldn't get a warrant and come back tomorrow morning and clean the place out, but it would save him several hours—not to mention the hassle of doing the paperwork—if she'd just hand over what he needed. "You look like a woman who knows what's what," he said and shot her an approving look.

"You got that right," she agreed, crossing her arms under her heavy breasts. She had a red smock on over her too-small white T-shirt, with the name Kathleen embroidered in yellow on the upper right shoulder.

"Good. Then I'll bet you'll be able to help me," Race said. He reached out and tapped one of the plastic phone cards that were clipped to a metal hanger on a pole near the cash register. "I'm trying to trace someone who bought one of these and used it for the first time five days ago. The distributor said that the card in question was shipped here, but they don't have any way to trace who may have purchased it. I wonder if you might be able to search your sales records, perhaps by UPC, to see if we can get to a credit card number or something I can use in my investigation." Race had already noticed—much to his delight—that the mini-mart had a scanner that read Universal Product Codes and tallied up the amount of each customer's purchase.

God, how his logical mind loved the twenty-first century's data collection devices.

Kathleen seemed to consider his request for a moment, then shrugged as if deciding that it wouldn't hurt to give out that information. "Sure. I can pull that up right here." She clicked several keys on the computerized cash register and then pulled one of the calling cards off the hanger and typed in the bar code from the back. A few seconds later, she twisted the screen toward him.

Race took a drink of his soda and tried not to get his hopes up. It would be a miracle if this lead took them all the way back to the buyer. Rarely would one small detail yield the solution to the entire puzzle. He could only pray that this would be the one time it did.

"Do you have the card number?" the clerk asked.

Race fished around in his jacket pocket for the report he'd printed before leaving the office. "I do, but I'm surprised you have that much detail. I figured the UPC would be all that was stored in your sales records." Which meant that he'd hoped the market would be able to separate out phone card purchases from the other products sold here, but he hadn't expected them to be able to find the one specific card he was looking for.

"We have the card numbers, too," the clerk said helpfully. "The way it works is that until somebody buys these cards, they're just useless pieces of plastic. That way, if they get stolen, it's no big deal. When you buy one of the cards, we run it through a machine that reads the magnetic stripe off the back of the card—"

"Just like a credit card?" Race interrupted, making sure he understood.

"Exactly," the clerk answered with a nod of her head. "It's kind of like processing a credit card refund, only we key in the amount of the air time purchased and the phone company records that card number such-and-such has x number of minutes on it. I don't think we've ever used the card numbers for anything, but since it's electronic, it's captured by our computers."

Race was having a difficult time believing his good fortune. As he read off the card number the analyst had provided, he couldn't help but hope that the buyer had purchased the calling card on credit. If she had made that mistake, he'd be one step closer to finding her . . . and rescuing Aimee.

"Okay, that card was purchased last Tuesday at 11:53 P.M. Looks like whoever bought it was thirsty, because she got a six-pack of Sprite along with her fifty-dollar phone card."

Shifting his weight impatiently onto the balls of his feet, Race leaned over the counter to look at the computer screen. He caught a movement out of the corner of his eyes and turned to see himself caught on a security camera. The screen changed at that instant, switching to a view of the back of the store, and Race turned his attention back to the computer.

"Was a credit card used for that purchase?" he asked eagerly.

Kathleen scrolled down a line or two, then shook her head. "Sorry," she said. "Looks like this was paid for in cash."

"Damn," Race swore softly, pinching the bridge of his nose. Now what? He thought for a moment. "Can you check purchases from the ten minutes before and ten minutes after the calling card was bought? It's possible that she used cash to pay for the calling card, just in case she knew we might try to trace it, but bought other items using credit."

"Sure." Kathleen went back to clicking keys. Race was not surprised at the woman's cooperation with his investigation.

He'd found that the majority of people were willing, if not eager, to do what they could to help solve crimes. Unless, of course, they were involved in those crimes. Then they tended to be a bit more reticent.

"Okay, here's a list of the transactions for thirty minutes on either side of the calling card purchase. I know you said ten minutes, but it was a slow night and there weren't very many," Kathleen explained, handing over a report she'd just printed.

Race looked it over thoughtfully. This was great. There was not much more he could do with the cash transactions, but he could start tracing the credit card purchases to see if that turned up anything suspicious. He knew his next request would be a real long shot, but he had to ask. Most companies recorded over their security videos every twenty-four hours or so. After all, if a robbery occurred, it was typically called in almost immediately, so there would be no need for surveillance tapes going back for days or even weeks. Still, he had to ask.

He leaned across the counter again and glanced briefly at the security camera, which appeared to be panning across a stockroom. "Do you know how many days' worth of security video is saved?"

If he hadn't been paying attention, Race might have missed it—that shifting of her gaze up and to the left that told him Kathleen was mentally preparing to lie.

Her lips parted briefly, then closed again before she grimaced and, lowering her voice, she confided, "It's not even taped. The cameras are just there for show. You know, to make shoplifters think they're being watched so they won't take anything."

"Hmm," Race said, nodding agreeably as if he had bought her story, all the while wondering why she had lied. "Well, thank you so much for all your help. Can I give you a call if I need anything else?"

Kathleen's smile turned hopeful at that, as if she thought that maybe he was fishing for a way to ask for her phone number. Race just kept a pleasant look on his face as she made a big show out of hunting around for one of the Quickie-Stop's business cards. She crossed through the name on the front and wrote her name and phone number in big loopy handwriting on the back. Then she handed the card to him, saying, "I work nights, Sunday through Wednesday. Feel free to call me anytime."

Race took the card and looked it over before sliding it into his breast pocket. He held out a hand and she took it, squeezing it longer than was necessarily polite. When she released him, Race gave her one final nod and started for the door. With his palm against the door, he stopped, as if a thought had just occurred to him. He turned back to find the clerk avidly eying his backside. Race cleared his throat and felt a bit guilty at seeing the eager expression on her face.

"It was nice meeting you, Kathleen," he said. The clerk's smile faded as the warning buzzer on the door bleated, and Race wondered if she knew that this would not be the last she'd seen of him.

JOSIE took a bite of her dessert and smiled, feeling as if the cloud that had been hovering over her head for the last few days had finally lifted. There was no way someone as nice as Aimee would like her father if he wasn't a good man, Josie just knew it. She must have been mistaken about that terrorist. After all, she'd been upset and crying. She hadn't even gotten a really good look at the man her father had been meeting with.

No, it was all Giselle and her suggestion that Josie's dad wasn't a very nice man—that he was forcing Mrs. Simonds to work for him when she didn't want to—that had Josie imagining all sorts of awful things.

"What are you smiling about?" her father asked, patting her hand with his own.

"Nothing," Josie said, but she couldn't stop. She was so relieved that it had only been her imagination. Maybe this was the sort of thing that happened when you got your period. She'd often heard Giselle's dad tell Mrs. Simonds she was being a bitch and asking if she was on her period. Maybe the hormones made you act crazy and believe strange things.

"Come on, share your secret with me." Her father leaned toward her, blocking out everyone else in the room and enclosing them in their own private world.

Josie felt the sudden urge to cry, and blinked back tears. She turned her hand over on the table and squeezed her dad's fingers. "I love you, Daddy."

Her father squeezed back. "I love you, too, baby."

"Oh, brother," she heard Giselle mutter from the seat next to her, but even her best friend's censure couldn't darken Josie's mood.

"I'm going to go see if Aimee wants to take a walk after dinner," Josie said, pushing back her chair.

Her father frowned and said, "She'll be back in a moment," but it was too late, Josie was already racing out of the room. Nic shoved back his chair and started after her, but by the time he reached the hallway, Josie had already pushed open the bathroom door.

"—what you're up to." Diana's voice, raised in anger, could easily be heard down the hall.

Josie stood in the bathroom doorway, staring at Mrs. Simonds and Aimee. She had never seen Gi's mother so angry, her pale skin a mottled red.

"Daddy?" Josie looked back at her father, uncertain what was going on here, but knowing it wasn't something good.

"Go up to your room. Right now," her father ordered.

Josie didn't argue. That sick feeling was back in her stomach again and she wanted nothing more than to get away from the people who kept causing it.

Nic watched his daughter disappear around the corner before stepping into the bathroom, where Diana and an ashen-faced Aimee stood facing each other. "What the hell is going on here?" he asked.

Aimee swallowed and shook her head. "I don't know. Ask her."

Nic turned his gaze on Diana and waited, without saying anything more.

"I know what she's up to," Diana said, more quietly this time.

"And what would that be?" Nic asked. He slid his hands into his pockets and leaned back against the door, as much to ensure no one came in as to block the exit.

Diana let out a disgusted breath and crossed her arms under her breasts, which served to increase the already healthy amount of cleavage spilling out over her low-cut black dress. "Can't you see it? She's trying to befriend Josie as a way to get to you."

Aimee blinked, obviously as surprised as Nic was by Diana's observation.

"I am?" Aimee asked.

Diana shot her a deadly look before turning her back on Aimee altogether in an obvious gesture of dismissal. "This is why she insisted on meeting you. She planned on getting her hands on more than just the half a million we were offering. She wants it all. She wants *you*."

Nic tried to absorb some of Diana's outrage, but was finding himself more amused than anything else. "And that would upset me how?" he asked, looking Aimee up and down assessingly.

"All she wants is your money," Diana protested.

"That's a motive I can understand. I believe you can, too," Nic said. He'd made Luke and Diana very wealthy over the years and he did not for one moment believe they had stuck around this long simply out of loyalty to him. Like him, they were in it for the money. So what if Aimee was, too?

Diana dropped her arms to her sides. "Fine, don't take me seriously. But when this goes bad, you can't say I didn't warn you."

Stifling a laugh, Nic nodded and stepped away from the door to let Diana pass.

"I'm not using Josie to get money from you," Aimee said when she and Nic were alone, her voice devoid of its customary teasing edge. "I'm the first to admit that I'm in this for the cash, but I wouldn't hurt an innocent child for any amount of money."

Nic studied her silently for a long moment, wondering how it was that she had managed to get under his skin in such a short amount of time. He knew he was probably a fool for believing her, but he did. He held out a hand and Aimee took it.

"Would you mind going up and saying good night to Josie? I think she would appreciate it."

It was Aimee's turn to study him for a moment, her brown eyes searching his. "Can I ask you a question?" she said finally, the words echoing off the tile.

"Yes."

"Do you really intend to take me with you to Sydney tomorrow?" she asked.

Nic knew what she was really asking: Now that he had the propulsion system plans, did he intend to kill her? The problem was, he didn't know. It should have been easy for him to say yes and mean, *Yes, I'm taking you to Sydney because I don't want your body to be found anywhere near my island. Yes, I'm going to kill you.* Instead, he asked a question of his own. "You said Joe McConnell hired you as his executive assistant, correct?"

Aimee frowned, tiny wrinkles appearing on her forehead. "Yes."

"Are you good at it?"

"Yes, very," Aimee said with a shrug.

"I might be able to use your help tomorrow managing the logistics of this meeting. Would you be willing to cooperate?"

"Of course." Aimee's frown slowly disappeared and, like the sun beginning to peer up over the horizon, she began to smile. "As a matter of fact," she said slowly, "I may have a way to prove to you just how valuable I can be."

WITH Nic walking silently beside her, Aimee made her way up the wide staircase leading to Josie's bedroom, her right hand trailing along the smooth wooden banister. Chances were that she was not going to return to the island tomorrow. Nic's hesitation had given her the answer she needed. In all likelihood, he had concocted the story about needing her assistance so that she would not upset his daughter when she came to say her good-byes. Frankly, she was surprised that he let her come up here at all. If he was going to kill her, why give her any more time with Josie than was necessary?

Aimee shivered at that thought. The truth was, she didn't want to die. If Nic was indeed taking her to Sydney with him tomorrow, she'd have a much better chance to get away from him in a city than here in an environment that he completely controlled.

But if Nic intended to take her off the island first thing tomorrow morning, how was she going to have a chance to transmit the location of the island to Race? Once she left this place, she'd have no idea how to get back. And, even if she did escape, she didn't think it would help the CIA to tell them they could find Nic "somewhere in Australia."

Aimee clutched her purse, frustrated that she had the necessary equipment to bring Race here, but couldn't use it for fear of detection. *There has to be a way. Think, think, think.*

Nic stopped in front of the first door on the right side of the landing and knocked softly. "Josie, can I come in?"

There was the muffled sound of a sniffle and a creak of a floorboard before Josie opened the door. It was obvious that she had been crying and was trying to hide it without much success. Aimee quashed a twinge of guilt because despite what she'd told Nic, Diana was right—Aimee was using Josie to get to Nic. Not for money, but to stay alive.

"Hey, what are the tears for? Diana was mad at me, not you," Aimee said.

"Why was she yelling?" Josie asked.

Nic seemed content to let Aimee speak, leaning against the door jamb as Aimee walked over to the bed in the middle of the room. The covers were disheveled as if Josie had recently been lying on top of them. "Do you mind if I sit here?" she asked, waving a hand to indicate a spot at the foot of Josie's bed.

Josie shook her head and climbed onto the bed herself, leaning back on the pillows she'd propped up against the headboard.

"Giselle's mom cares about you and your father. She was just making sure that I knew that," Aimee said, awarding herself the "spin of the year" medal as Nic dipped his chin in an almost imperceptible gesture of approval.

"That's all?" Josie asked suspiciously, wiping the last of her tears away with the back of one hand.

"That's it." Aimee smiled.

Josie pursed her lips and seemed to be considering whether or not to believe what Aimee had told her. When Josie smiled back at her, Aimee knew what her choice had been.

"Will you have dinner with us again tomorrow?" Josie asked, wrapping her arms around her legs. She had changed out of her dress and into a pair of mint green pajamas and her hair was loose around her shoulders.

"I'm not sure. It depends on what happens at your father's meeting. He may not need my help any longer," Aimee said, not chancing a look at Nic.

"Mmm. Well, I'd like for you to come back," Josie said as if she had a vote in the matter.

"I'd like that, too," Aimee said, knowing that Josie had no idea how true that was.

"Would you tell me a bedtime story?"

Nic's cell phone rang just then and he looked at the caller ID and then shot Aimee a glance full of warning before saying, "I'll just be out in the hall."

"I'm not sure I know any good bedtime stories," Aimee said once Nic had left them alone, but was then struck by an idea so horrible and yet so perfect at the same time that she found herself blinking rapidly, examining it from all angles in just a split second. She weighed the damage it might do to Josie against the lives that might be saved if Josie's father was stopped and decided she had no choice but to do it.

"Wait," she said, digging into her tiny cocktail purse for her lipstick. "I do know a story. It's a story about a magic lipstick."

Josie wrinkled her nose. "A magic lipstick?"

"Yes. Do you want to hear it?"

With a shrug, Josie said, "Okay," and settled back into the pillows.

Aimee's mind raced. She had to make this good, make Josie *believe* in this story. Otherwise, not only would she be signing her own death warrant, she'd be giving up her last chance to stop Nic.

She closed her eyes and took a breath to center herself. "Once upon a time," she began, opening her eyes again and completely clearing her mind of anything else, "there was a family. A mother, a father, and their beautiful daughter."

"What was the daughter's name?" Josie asked.

"Delphine. That means dolphin."

"That's pretty," Josie said, clearly approving Aimee's choice.

Aimee laughed. "Yes, it is. Delphine and her family were

very happy. Her mother loved pretty clothes and shoes and she and Delphine often played dress-up and held fancy tea ceremonies out in their garden. Delphine's favorite thing of all was when her mother let her wear lipstick. Her mom had hundreds of lipsticks, and wore a different color every day, but Delphine had her favorite and would only wear that one."

"What color was it?"

Aimee tilted the tube of lipstick in her hand and tried not to squint as she read the color off the bottom. "Plum Gorgeous. And whenever Delphine wore the lipstick, that's what her mother said—'Delphine, you look plumb gorgeous today.'"

"What happened next?"

"Well, one day, Delphine and her mother were playing dress-up, but instead of having tea in the garden, Delphine wanted to take a blanket and have their tea out by the ocean. Her mother said no. You see, there was an underwater city near where Delphine and her family lived and sometimes, if they got too close to the water, girls were snatched away to live forever under the sea. The legend was that there was a prince who lived in the underwater city and he would not be at peace until he found his one true love. The people of the underwater city loved their prince so much that they took girls from the land to try to make him fall in love, but they hadn't found the right one yet. But once the prince found his true love, no one else from above would be taken."

"Wow," Josie said, her eyes wide with a mixture of fear and delight.

Aimee nodded. "Yes, wow. So anyway, the next day Delphine's mother wasn't feeling very well and she stayed in bed all day. Since she didn't have any sisters or brothers to play with, Delphine was very, very bored. She decided to play dress-up all by herself, but it wasn't much fun, so she thought she'd go out to the beach and pretend that she was one of the sea people. She told herself she would not get too close to the shore, but when she got down to the beach, she saw the reflection of a handsome prince in the water and she stepped closer to get a better look.

"The prince was riding on a mighty seahorse and was dressed all in red with a shiny gold sword at his hip. He smiled at Delphine and waved and she took one more step closer, not realizing that the waves were lapping up against her feet. The prince was so handsome that Delphine fell instantly in love with him. Without thinking about how much she would miss her mother and her father, she dove into the water to catch the prince."

"She left her mom and dad for a guy?" Josie asked, incredulous.

Aimee shook her head and shrugged. "I know. Pretty stupid, huh?"

"Yeah."

"Well, Delphine wasn't as smart as you and me. At the same moment she jumped into the ocean, her mother looked out of her bedroom window and saw what was happening. She ran down to the beach, but it was too late. Delphine had been taken to the underwater city to live. Delphine's mother stood there on the beach for three days and three nights, waiting to catch a glimpse of her daughter. She wouldn't eat. She wouldn't sleep. She just stood there on the sand, crying because Delphine was gone."

"That's sad," Josie said.

"Delphine's mother even tried to swim out to her daughter, but the underwater city had disappeared."

"Is that because Delphine was the prince's one true love?" Josie asked.

"Yes. That's it exactly. Now, here's where the magic lipstick comes in."

Josie leaned forward, eager to hear the rest of the story.

"After three days, Delphine's mother realized that her daughter wasn't coming back. She didn't know if Delphine could see or hear her, but she knew she had to try to let her know how much she loved her. She went up to her room and got Delphine's favorite lipstick. She opened the tube and pasted a picture of her daughter in the top so that if one of the people in the underwater city found it, they'd know to take it to Delphine. Then she went back down to the beach. It was nighttime and the stars were sparkling like tiny diamonds on the water. She stood in the moonlight, her dark hair flowing down her back."

"Was she pretty?" Josie asked.

"Very. She looked like the woman in that picture," Aimee

said, pointing to the photo on Josie's nightstand, which Aimee prayed was of Josie's mom.

"That's my mother," Josie whispered.

Aimee had to turn her head so Josie wouldn't see her wince. She knew that she was manipulating Josie and hated having to do so, but this was her only hope. "She's beautiful," Aimee said. She remained quiet for a moment, letting Josie feel the sadness of a mother being separated from her daughter, a pain Aimee guessed Josie knew quite well.

"What did Delphine's mother do with the lipstick?" Josie whispered, blinking back tears.

"Well, she was standing on the beach, thinking about how much she missed Delphine. She took off the top of the lipstick and, pressing her thumb on her daughter's picture as hard as she could, she repeated, 'I love you,' five times."

"Why did she press on the picture?" Josie asked.

"Because she knew that the harder she pressed, the more Delphine would know how much she loved her," Aimee said, hoping that Josie wouldn't question her lame answer.

Josie let her head drop and nodded as if it all made perfect sense, and Aimee knew she had to hurry and finish her story before Josie asked anything more—and before Nic finished his call and returned.

"Then Delphine's mother put the cap back on the lipstick and raised her arm and threw the tube as hard as she could. It landed in the sea and slowly sank to the bottom. Delphine's mom watched as tiny bubbles rose to the surface as the lipstick disappeared. Then, finally, knowing her daughter was truly gone, Delphine's mother turned to leave." Aimee paused for effect. "But suddenly, something caught her eye."

"What? What was it?" Josie asked, her voice so hopeful that Aimee had to swallow around a lump in her throat.

"A dolphin had surfaced right where she had thrown the lipstick. The dolphin looked at Delphine's mother and smiled at her. And just before the dolphin went back under the surface of the ocean, Delphine's mother noticed that it had a spot on its cheek. And do you know what color the spot was?" Aimee asked.

Josie drew in a breath. "Plum Gorgeous?" she whispered.

Aimee nodded. "Yes, exactly. And from then on, whenever

Delphine's mother wanted to see her beloved daughter again, she brought a tube of Plum Gorgeous down to the beach, pressed her thumb on Delphine's picture while she said 'I love you' five times, and then she threw the tube into the water."

"Did it work?" Josie asked, then held her breath while waiting for Aimee to answer.

"Yes. Every time." Aimee had to force herself to go on. "And do you know what?"

"What?" Josie breathed.

Aimee leaned closer to Josie and said softly, "Can you keep a secret?"

Josie nodded, looking so serious that Aimee's guilt level rose another notch.

"Well, I don't tell a lot of people about this because they would think I was crazy, but every time I want to let someone I love know how much I miss them, I do what Delphine's mother did. And you know what? It always makes me feel better."

"Really?" Josie asked.

"Yes. I do it even when I don't have a picture of the person to put in there. I just close my eyes and think of them and press really hard to let them know how much I miss them. Then I throw the tube into the ocean."

Josie sighed with all the longing and sadness that was pent up in her twelve-year-old soul. Aimee had no idea what it would be like to grow up without a mother, but she thought of her own mom and how, even when she was at her most infuriating, Aimee still loved her. And vice versa. She hated knowing that she was using Josie's sadness to get her to do this, but she had no choice.

Aimee held out her hand, the silver tube of lipstick rolling on her open palm. "I have more of these at home. Would you like this one?"

Josie looked at her as if afraid that when she went to snatch up the lipstick, Aimee would close her fist and say, "Gotcha." Tentatively, she reached out. "Really? I can have this?" she asked.

Aimee tipped her hand, letting the tube roll down her fingers. "Yes. I want you to have it."

"What are you two up to?" Nic asked from the doorway.

Josie grasped the lipstick and put her hand behind her back, as if afraid her father might take it away from her if he saw it. Aimee took a deep breath and forced herself to relax. She winked at Josie, as if to seal their secret pact, then turned to Nic. "I was just telling Josie a bedtime story."

He came and sat down next to Aimee at the foot of Josie's bed, his jacket and tie discarded and his shirt open at his neck. "Oh, what about?" he asked.

Aimee tried to smile but was shaking so hard inside that it was difficult. What was she going to tell him? What if Josie blurted out the truth?

In the end, she needn't have worried. Josie removed the hand from behind her back, having safely stowed the lipstick behind a pillow. Her smile was easy, as if she kept secrets from her father every day. "It was just a story about a dolphin, Daddy. You wouldn't be interested."

Nic raised his eyebrows at his daughter's obvious dismissal. "Well, I suppose you're right," he said. "Now, you're going to have to let Ms. Devlin go. She and I have an early morning ahead of us."

Nic got up off the bed as Josie scooted under the covers. He planted a kiss on her forehead and said good night.

Aimee stood, then blinked with surprise when Josie reached out and grabbed her hand. With surprising strength, she pulled Aimee toward her. Aimee bent down and turned her cheek to accept the girl's kiss. Then Josie let her go, laying her head back down on the pillows.

Nic put a hand on Aimee's lower back and guided her from the room. He paused for a moment to turn off the light, and as they left the room, Josie's words followed them down the stairs. "Good night, Daddy. Good night, Aimee," she said. "I'll see you both tomorrow."

NINETEEN

RACE pressed his back to the wall as he turned to look around the corner at the deserted alley. He waited in the darkness, making certain that he was alone before stealing toward the door he'd noticed earlier when filling up on Coke. He tried the doorknob—locked, of course. But a little thing like that was not going to stop him.

He didn't know why the convenience store clerk had lied to him about the security tapes and he didn't much care. He had to see that video. Tonight. It might do nothing more than prove his hunch that the woman who was after McConnell's plans had been the one who purchased that calling card, but the thing was, you just never knew what would unravel the entire sweater unless you pulled at every loose thread.

Race recalled a case he'd worked that was solved by a spot on a check. They were investigating a possible terrorist plot to infiltrate the private security force that was contracted to protect several nuclear power plants in the United States. Race had obtained a warrant to search the security company's records and found that the training fee for several of the guards had been paid together on one check.

Since so often the solution to a crime could be found by following the money, Race had the check traced through a convoluted system of banking records that dead-ended in Switzerland. The Swiss were under no obligation to provide details about their client to the CIA, so it looked as if that lead was dead. Only, when Race had first seen the check, he'd found a tiny blood-colored spot down near the lower left-hand corner and had sent it in to the CIA laboratory for analysis. The results came back listing the composition of the paper used, its point of origin and date of production, as well as an breakdown of indentations and impressions found on the check (from which the lab determined the check writer was left-handed, was most likely a male, and wore a large ring on the pinky of his right hand). The report also included an analysis of the spot—a 1998 Delas Frères Côte-Rôtie, from the Seigneur de Maugiron region in France. Race had no idea what the hell all that meant except that it was some fancy red wine but, armed with this information, he was able to determine the wine's distributor, which led, in turn, to the specialty wine stores that carried it, and finally, to the man in upstate New York who had purchased two cases for his wine cellar a year before the check was written. They put the man under surveillance and soon had enough evidence to raid his home and confiscate his computer, which proved that he was the financial mastermind behind a number of sleeper cells in the U.S.

And all of this from one seemingly innocent drop of wine.

Which was why Race would not leave without the security tapes from this convenience store. Perhaps the buyer had purchased a medication that would lead them to discover an injury she had that they could trace back to the treating hospital. Or a certain snack food that could only be found locally. Or perhaps supplies for an infant.

That was the whole point of conducting such a thorough investigation. They sometimes didn't know what they were looking for until they found it.

Race saw a light in the back room of the mini-mart go on and hurried out of the alley and toward the street. He had hoped to be able to gain entry through the back door, but that was not to be.

No matter. As the old adage went, when one door closed, another one opened.

He approached the front entrance of the market and checked to make certain the sidewalk around him was clear. As he'd been leaving the store earlier, he'd paused in the doorway just long enough to assess the laughably simple warning system. It was similar to a standard garage door opener, with a laser beam on one side of the device directed into an "eye" on the other side. When the beam was interrupted, the garage door stopped moving—the assumption being that a child or pet was standing under the door. With the security system, an alarm sounded when someone walked through the beam. Of course, all it took to bypass the system was to step over the beam, thus not interrupting the flow of light as one entered the room. The mini-market could have made it a bit more difficult by mounting another eye a foot above the first, making it harder—though by no means impossible—for an intruder to evade the beam. But they hadn't, so Race waited outside until the security monitor mounted in the cashier's area behind the counter switched its view to the back of the store before slowly pulling open the glass door, sidestepping the warning system, and entering the market.

When he'd been chatting with the clerk earlier, he'd kept one eye on the security monitor, counting the number of seconds it remained on any one area of the store. He knew he had five seconds to make it across the front of the store and into a dead space near the soda machine that was not covered by any camera. He supposed there wasn't a dire need to police the free refill station.

As he walked toward the Coke machine, Race methodically began pulling off his suit jacket, tugging off his tie, and unholstering his gun as he counted to five. The monitor now would have switched to the stockroom. Race unbuttoned his shirtsleeves and rolled them up, then ran a hand through his hair to dishevel it. He wasn't certain a disguise would be needed, but wanted to be ready in case it was. He also wasn't sure that Kathleen had another security monitor in the back of the store that she was watching, but he was taking no chances. Until he had his hands on those security tapes, he would assume—and plan for—the worst.

When five more seconds had passed and the monitor had moved to the front of the store, Race crept toward the stockroom. Just as he got to the doorway, he felt a prickling sensation on the back of his neck, as if something in the atmosphere around him had shifted.

Race casually turned toward the soda machine as the convenience store's front door was flung open and a loud group of twenty-somethings came in. He didn't look up as the clerk came out of the back room, straightening her red apron as she hurried back behind the counter. He felt her gaze on him as he pushed a plastic cup under the icemaker and hunched his shoulders to make himself appear smaller.

"Hey, look. J. Lo's having an alien's baby," one of the twenty-somethings announced loudly with a snicker.

"Does that mean she's getting married again?" another of them joked.

Race didn't have to turn around to know that the clerk had turned her attention from him to the group of younger men scattered throughout the store. He sensed it, felt a sudden absence of energy or electricity or whatever it was that was no longer directed at him.

He finished his countdown. Three. Set the cup down on the counter.

Two. Cover it with a lid.

One. Turn to the wall. Take a step backward. Slip through the doorway and disappear.

Race cautiously picked his way around the boxes and stacks of bottled water littering the stockroom floor and hurried to the lighted office along the back wall. Kathleen had obligingly left the security videos—neatly burned to CDs and labeled with each day's date—stacked in a CD tower on top of the desk. One of the slots was empty, so Race stepped behind the desk to look at the computer screen that was glowing with a bluish light. Obviously, Kathleen had taken one of the CDs out to look at it after Race's visit and he was curious to know why.

The reason for her reluctance to share the tapes became apparent in four seconds. The computer screen panned on the deserted back of the convenience store. The time stamp on the video said 24:01:06. Military time for one minute and six seconds after midnight. Four seconds later, the view changed to the stockroom.

Race blinked.

Ah. Mystery solved.

There was Kathleen, red apron and too-tight T-shirt up around her neck and jeans unzipped, lying on a box marked Lay's. The irony of that was not lost on him.

A man in navy blue pants and a white-and-blue striped shirt stood over the clerk. Race didn't need to see any more to know what was going on. He'd like to tell Kathleen that he didn't care to see her secret sex life exposed, that he was really only interested in seeing that portion of the tapes that pertained to his investigation. But he didn't have time to explain it all to her. He needed those tapes. Now.

Yeah, so he was stretching the law just a bit, but a woman's life was at stake.

He'd view the footage alone, copy only those parts that he needed, and return them to the clerk before her shift was over.

Race ejected the CD from the computer's drive and pulled two more days' worth of videos out of the stack just in case. He didn't know why Kathleen didn't erase those portions of the tapes with her illicit activities on them—probably figured that as long as there wasn't a robbery on her shift, no one would bother taking the time to review the CDs.

The countdown in his head had reached ten seconds, so he crouched down behind the desk and waited for the security camera to finish its examination of the stockroom. Then he stood, pulled two one-dollar bills out of his pocket to pay for his soda, and escaped out the back door with the confiscated CDs.

SNEAKING out of the house was easy. Josie had done it a number of times when she couldn't sleep and just wanted to go down to the beach and think. And it wasn't like she was forbidden from going outside. This was her home, after all. It wasn't a prison.

Tonight she stayed well away from the water's edge, certain that there was really no underwater city with a prince who snatched girls from the land, but not willing to bet her life on it. She couldn't imagine how sad Daddy would be without her, probably as sad as she was whenever she thought about her mother.

She looked down at the tube of lipstick in her hands, then out at the water. Just as Aimee had described in her story, the stars glittered down like millions of diamonds and the moon shined down, nearly as bright as the sun.

Josie closed her eyes and pictured her mother's face, the one that smiled out at her every morning and every evening from the framed picture beside her bed. If her mom was somewhere where she could see her, Josie hoped she knew how much Josie loved her and missed her.

She removed the cap of the lipstick and pressed her thumbs hard against the top. *I love you, Mommy.*

"Josie? Is that you? What are you doing?"

Josie gasped and opened her eyes, nearly dropping the cap into the soft sand at her feet. What was Gi's mom doing out here? She shook her head. It didn't matter. She had to finish the ritual. Otherwise, her mother wouldn't know that Josie was thinking of her. She hastily put the cap back on the tube, reached back her arm, and threw the lipstick toward the ocean with all her might.

It hit the surface of the water, making a small splash that could barely be heard over the sound of the waves lapping at the shore, and Josie was filled with a sense of peace. Now her mother knew.

"What was that?" Giselle's mother asked, looking from the water to Josie and back.

Josie remembered what Aimee had said, that people would think she was crazy if she told them why she was tossing lipstick in the water. But it had helped, just like Aimee had said it would. And she hadn't even had to say "I love you" five times. She'd have to tell Aimee that it worked just as well even if you only said it once.

"It was just a rock," Josie said, crossing her fingers behind her back. It wasn't like she was telling a lie exactly. She was only keeping a secret like she had promised she would. Wasn't that more important? Besides, she knew the difference between a real lie—one that could get people in trouble, like when Giselle had stolen a bottle of rum from Daddy's liquor cabinet and told Josie to say that Mrs. Jacobs had broken it but Josie had told her dad because she knew that wasn't right—and a white lie that wouldn't hurt anyone.

That's what this was. A white lie. It wouldn't hurt anyone.

AIMEE looked out over Sydney's famed harbor with the dramatic sail-like domes of the opera house and boats leaving white wake trails in the deep blue water.

"What a beautiful city," she murmured, her nose pressed up against the window of Nic's private plane. She assumed that she had ridden in this plane once before—on the trip from San Antonio to the island—but didn't remember anything of that earlier ride. This trip, on the other hand, was going to be quite memorable.

Riding in a luxurious Lear jet was nothing at all like traveling with the masses on a commercial airliner. She had plenty of legroom and, thanks to the well-stocked kitchen and bar, could have had anything from scrambled eggs and kippers to sushi and mimosas. She'd chosen, instead, to have a plain bagel, hoping the bread would help settle her stomach, which had been rumbling nervously ever since Josie had called her room in the middle of the night and whispered a thank-you for the bedtime story. Aimee's hopes rose, thinking that Josie had managed to alert the CIA as to where Aimee was, but those hopes were dashed when the girl shared her discovery that only one "I love you" worked just as well as five. Which meant that Josie hadn't pressed the transmitter long enough to activate it before she'd tossed it into the ocean. Which meant that no one knew where Aimee was, that help was *not* on the way, and that her chances of surviving this ordeal were even slimmer than they had been twelve hours ago.

She hadn't slept well after that. Wondering if this was to be one's last night on Earth would do that to a person, she supposed. Instead of sleeping, she'd spent the night thinking about her life and about the people in it. Her sisters and her parents. Daphne and Raine. Race Gardner, who had made her feel more alive than she'd felt in years. She liked that he was more than what he seemed, that there was an entirely different person beneath the one he chose to show to the rest of the world. And all her talk about wanting more than he could give her seemed so stupid right now, when every moment she remained alive was like a gift from God. What good would money do her if she died here at the hands of a ruthless arms dealer?

"You've been awfully quiet this morning," Nic remarked from the other side of the plane. He had been working on his laptop since they'd left the island and hadn't contributed much to the conversation, either.

"I'm not a morning person," Aimee said. It wasn't actually the truth, but she didn't want to share what had really been going on inside her head.

Nic shut the top of his laptop and leaned back in the leather chair where he was sitting. He crossed his legs at the ankle and Aimee noticed that he had chosen a pair of black socks with blue dots that exactly matched the blue stripe in his tie. The man certainly did have impeccable taste.

"So, are you ready to tell me about this plan of yours?" he asked.

Aimee considered him for a moment. She knew that this was her last chance to prove what a valuable asset she could be. Although he seemed to appreciate her on a personal level and was impressed that his daughter liked her, too, Aimee sensed that wasn't enough to make him keep her alive. The only thing left for her to do was to help him with his business. It was either do that or accept defeat, and Aimee wasn't quite ready for that yet.

"All right," she said, doing her best to keep her hand from shaking as she took a sip of coffee. "You say the purpose of this meeting is to get these guys to order your new weapon. What if you had inside information as to how much they were willing to pay? Wouldn't that help you to know that you weren't leaving any money on the table, so to speak?"

"Of course," Nic said with a shrug. "But that's why they determine the meeting place, so that I won't have an opportunity beforehand to install any audio or video surveillance equipment."

Aimee waved her hand dismissively. "You don't need that. Here's what we can do. First, you're going to need a second cell phone. Before you go into the meeting, you call me on cell phone number one. You turn the second phone off and put it in your pocket. When you sit down at your meeting, put the first phone facedown next to your things. I will then be able to hear what is being said in the meeting at all times.

"When you've presented your information and are ready to make a deal, you tell the men that you must leave within the hour to make another meeting. You tell them that you're going to the men's room and when you get back, you expect to close the deal.

"Then you leave and turn the second phone on and wait for my call. The men in the room will discuss what they are willing to offer and, when they come to an agreement, I will hang up the first call and will dial you on phone number two. You can then go back into the meeting armed with this information."

Nic's eyes narrowed as he contemplated her plan. "What if they don't speak English after I leave the room?"

Aimee allowed a slow, smug smile to lift the corners of her mouth. "Ah, I guess I never mentioned that I have an ear for languages, did I? It's a very useful talent in my field."

Nic eyed her assessingly. "And what if these men speak a dialect you don't know?"

Aimee shrugged, feigning nonchalence. "If nothing else, it can't hurt to try, right? Unless the terrorists discover that you're, in effect, bugging the meeting, you have nothing to lose."

Raising his eyebrows at her, Nic said, "That's easy for you to say. You won't be the one whose life is on the line if our plan is discovered."

Aimee raised her coffee cup to her lips, keeping her gaze steady on Nic. "Yes, because I'm certain that if you don't return from this meeting, your pilot has instructions to simply let me go, right?"

Nic smiled and shook his head. "I've never before met a woman like you."

"And you most likely never will again," Aimee said with a wink, pretending a confidence she didn't feel as the plane touched down on the tarmac.

In minutes, they had taxied to a large hangar and Nic's pilot expertly maneuvered the plane inside. After the engines had been shut down, Nic stood up and began putting items into a thin silver briefcase. He left his laptop lying on the table and Aimee couldn't stifle the spark of hope that he might leave it here with her. If he did, she could get on the Internet and contact Raine and Daphne and tell them where she was. She was certain they could convince the local police to come rescue her. And though she had no idea where the island was located, she had tried to pay attention to the terrain and hoped that would be enough to help the CIA pinpoint the location of Nic's hideaway.

Aimee bit back a sigh of relief. Soon, she might be back in Atlanta, having successfully completed both her mission at McConnell and the job for the CIA. And maybe ... maybe she'd give Race Gardner a call and see if he'd be willing to give her a second chance.

"I'm sorry to have to do this," Nic said, slipping one end of a pair of handcuffs around her left wrist and connecting the other end to the armrest of Aimee's chair, which was bolted to the floor of the airplane.

No problem, she thought. The police could get her out of these in no time.

The cockpit door opened and Nic's pilot stepped out. Aimee scowled. It was Bill—the same guy who had plunged the hypodermic into her arm back in San Antonio.

"Ms. Devlin," Bill said and nodded by way of greeting.

"Bill," Aimee acknowledged coldly, resisting the urge to rub her upper arm. That had really hurt.

"I need to borrow your cell phone," Nic said. Without hesitation, Bill pulled his phone from the clip at his belt and handed it to his boss. Nic tucked the phone into the pocket of his jacket and quickly explained to Bill the plan he and Aimee had devised. When he was done, he turned to Aimee and said, "Bill can get you anything you need. And he'll be the one to call me once you have the information."

Aimee swallowed the despair climbing up her throat. Was she never going to escape? She didn't know why, but she assumed Nic's pilot would leave at least momentarily—either to take a break or to go with Nic into town. She gnawed at her bottom lip to keep it from wavering. She couldn't give up now. Not yet.

"See you later," she said, leaning back in her seat and attempting to pull off an uncaring attitude that she did not feel.

Nic nodded sharply and picked up his briefcase before walking to the door of the plane. He stopped in the doorway and turned to look back at the pilot. "Don't let her touch the computer. And if she tries anything"—Nic paused, moving his gaze to Aimee's face as he finished—"kill her."

TWENTY

"THAT'S it. We're out of leads." Jake crossed the last name off the airline passenger list he'd been checking and threw the report onto the conference table with disgust. "We've checked everything. Passenger records, phone numbers, e-mail addresses, conference videotape, outbound flight plans, even security video from that damn convenience store. And what have we got? Nothing. The fucking buyer didn't make even one goddamn mistake. Not one."

While Jake ran an agitated hand through his hair, Race stared out the window at the cloud-studded sky. It would be dark soon. Aimee had been missing for nearly three full days now and hadn't made contact with Race, her family, or her business partners. And one by one, each of their leads had turned into dead ends. The security video from the mini-mart had indeed shown a woman who—as verified through computerized facial analysis—turned out to be the buyer. But all she'd purchased was a six-pack of soda and a fifty-dollar prepaid calling card. Hardly the sort of thing that would convince their superiors at the Agency to mount a full-scale investigation.

Aimee had disappeared and there was nothing more the

CIA would do than allow Race and Jake to continue quietly and methodically working the case. There would be no secret spy planes violating anyone's airspace in an attempt to obtain information, no team of Navy SEALS (or, as Race would prefer, Army Rangers) sent out to save her.

No, he and Jake were all Aimee had.

And he wasn't going to give up.

Ever.

Race stood up and stretched. He'd been hunched over the computer for so long that his shoulder muscles seemed permanently stooped. He did a couple of shoulder rolls to loosen his tight muscles. Then he walked to the front of the room, picked up a black marker, and said, "Let's go over this one more time."

He ignored his partner's groan as he drew a line from one end of the whiteboard mounted on the wall to the other. He put a dot at the beginning of the line and wrote "Tuesday" and then 11:53 P.M.

"The first evidence we have is the buyer purchasing the calling card. Rita's phone records show that the buyer called the next day." Race added another dot and made a note of the call. "So, most likely she spent the night in San Antonio. Probably near the convenience store, unless she went out of her way to purchase the calling card several miles from where she was staying. Do we have a list of hotels in a five-mile radius of the mini-mart that we can start checking?"

Jake stretched his legs out in front of his chair and slouched like a kid trying to hide in the back row of math class. "I've already got an analyst working on it," he said.

"Good. So, what's next?"

Wearily rubbing the back of his neck, Jake closed his eyes and answered, "Wednesday night, Rita goes to Jefferson's house and accesses the plans. We assume that she and the buyer arranged a drop at the convention center on Thursday morning at the conference Rita was already scheduled to attend. Our buyer doesn't register for the conference, so we don't have a payment to trace there. The convention center surveillance tapes show the buyer entering the building, taking the escalator to the top floor at the appointed time, and entering the ladies' room. She exits the bathroom looking pissed off and looks around for someone, but Rita has gone back into the auditorium at that point and Aimee has already left."

Race made a dot for Thursday and scribbled some notes on the whiteboard. "Okay, we know nothing about payment terms between Rita and the buyer. How was Rita expecting to get paid after she delivered the plans? Surely, she wasn't dumb enough to just trust that they'd pay her once they had what they wanted?"

Jake shrugged and raised his hands, palms up. "She's dead, so we'll never know. We've reviewed all bank accounts known to be hers, but we've found no unusually large deposits anytime in the last two years."

"It's possible that they paid cash in advance for the plans," Race suggested, resting one hip against the conference table.

"Yeah, but that won't help us," Jake said glumly. "I wish our society would just get rid of cash altogether."

"It'd sure make our jobs easier," Race agreed.

"Okay, so we can forget about the payment for now. What else happened on Thursday?" Jake asked.

"There was another call from the buyer to Rita, presumably to ask what the hell was going on. That's also the night the buyer first e-mailed Aimee, but not with any specific details about when they could meet or how much she was willing to pay for the plans. The next day, Rita discovered her information source had dried up, and the buyer arranged a meeting with Aimee."

"I assume the e-mail leads you were checking went nowhere?"

"Of course. The account information she provided was all bogus. And since Hotmail is free . . ." Race's voice trailed off.

"There's no credit card associated with the account," Jake finished for him with a sigh.

"Right. Okay, so now we're up to early evening on Friday. Aimee and the buyer meet. We've checked records from all the cab companies and car services in the area and none show a car taking an unscheduled stop in the industrial area of town where they let Aimee out."

"At least none that they'll admit to," Jake interjected.

"True. But without the vehicle number or license plate,

that's all we have to go on," Race said, refusing to let defeat get a toehold against him in this mental game of tug-of-war.

"So, now we're at the end of our story. There's a fire at Rita's apartment building on Friday night that we're certain is arson, but we have no witnesses to place the buyer at the scene. That little trick gets Rita outside and unprotected long enough for the buyer to grab her. The buyer kills her and—in one of her only stupid moves so far—goes out of her way to dump the body in Jefferson's pool."

"Yeah, she let her anger get the better of her there," Race said. Or maybe she just thought she was so good that she'd never get caught, so why hurry? Why not have some fun with the killing? Race narrowed his eyes at the darkening sky outside the conference room window. He'd taken human lives before, and he wasn't naïve enough not to think that sometimes there might have been a better way to handle a situation than to do so, but one thing he'd never done was enjoy it. It was a necessary part of their jobs at times, but not one that anyone he'd ever respected had relished.

Jake cleared his throat, interrupting Race's thoughts. "Then she goes to Aimee's apartment building and pulls the same trick," he said, continuing to go through the timeline Race had begun.

"Only this time she stages it to look like Aimee's the one sounding the alarm, as if she is deliberately attempting to lose her tail so she can escape and meet with the buyer. Her disguise is nearly perfect, her hair color and length an exact match to Aimee's. Only she doesn't know about Aimee's tattoo," Race added.

Jake shot him a mocking glance from under his lashes. "Or she knows about it, but she doesn't know that *you* know," he suggested.

Race thought about the first time he'd seen Aimee's tattoo, that surprising glimpse of Taz peeking out from the top of her gray panties. Suddenly, something occurred to him and he put a thumb to his temple as he thought about—of all things—Aimee's lingerie. On Thursday, when he'd come to her apartment in the middle of the night, she'd been wearing a green silky nightie. He remembered her flirting with him as she reached across him to get a robe, though neither of them had really wanted her to cover up. "How did she get the pajamas right?" he murmured.

"Huh?" Jake asked, looking at him as if suspecting it was time for Race to get a psych eval.

"Her pajamas," Race repeated, rummaging through a pile on the conference table and pulling out the video that had been taken the night of the fire at Aimee's apartment. He pushed the video into the VCR, pausing it when the buyer appeared. Then he turned to Jake. "How'd she know that Aimee would wear her red shorts and tank top that night?"

Jake frowned and studied the carpet between his booted feet. Hmm. So maybe Race wasn't going crazy after all. Maybe he was on to something. "She had to do something to make sure Aimee had no other choice. Maybe destroyed all her other pj's or . . . I don't know, put them all in the wash maybe?"

Nodding, Race narrowed his eyes. "That means she had to go to Aimee's apartment to check out her lingerie before going to find a similar outfit."

"So? We've already dusted Aimee's apartment for prints and found nothing unusual there," Jake said.

"I know. That's not where I was going with this. Our buyer, she seems to be the meticulous type, right?"

"Yeah," Jake answered with shrug.

"So, what if instead of trying to find a *similar* outfit, she chose something she knew she could buy? A popular brand that she knew was readily available?"

"Like what?"

Race shot his partner a knowing look. "Aw, come on. You know where women go to buy sexy underwear. You've seen the catalogs."

Jake laughed. "Well, yeah, but she couldn't have ordered this from a catalog. She wouldn't have even known about Aimee—much less what brand of underwear she prefers—before coming to San An— Oh, shit. I get it," he said, grabbing for his gun and his wallet as both he and Race headed for the door.

"Hurry," Race urged as the hit the concrete steps outside. "Most retail stores close at nine. We've got eighteen minutes."

Jake was already on his cell phone, calling information to

get the list of Victoria's Secret stores in the area. Race pressed the button on his keychain to unlock his car doors, wishing like hell that he were driving his Beemer tonight instead of this sedan.

Jake swore as he got off the phone. "There's more than one store in this city," he announced.

"Damn. Well, let's start with the one closest to Aimee's apartment," Race said, flooring the Honda as he pulled out of his parking space and into traffic.

"I'll call to see if they carry something like what Aimee was wearing," Jake said. When he found out that they did, Race pushed even harder on the accelerator, uncaring that they were speeding through the mostly deserted streets.

It didn't take long to get to the mall near Aimee's apartment, but even ten minutes was too long for Race. He slammed the car in park and didn't bother locking it as he and Jake raced into the shopping mall. He ignored the odd looks the store clerks gave him as he rushed past. He was too close to finding out where Aimee had been taken. He knew it.

Race made it to the store ahead of his partner and spotted the red pajamas on a rack in the front of the store. He grabbed the hanger and ran to the counter, wildly looking around for a salesclerk. When one did not magically appear, he yelled, "Hello?"

At the same time that Jake got to the counter, a stern-looking woman poked her head out from around the fitting room door. She looked at Race and Jake over the top of her eyeglasses and said, "I'll be with you in a moment."

But Race was done being patient. For days, he'd calmly, determinedly followed every clue down every fucking rabbit hole they could think of. He was done doing this by the book. So instead of waiting for the clerk to come out, he went in after her.

"I need to ask you some questions. Now," Race said as he entered the pink-and-white striped dressing room.

A woman standing in front of the mirrors gasped and put her hands over her breasts, even though she was wearing a light green bra. Race instinctively shielded his eyes. "I apologize for the intrusion, ma'am." Then he blindly reached out and grabbed the salesclerk's arm and said, "Come with me."

The woman hurumphed but had no choice but to do as Race ordered since he was nearly dragging her behind him. Once they were outside the dressing room, Race let the woman go, but not before blocking her exit with his own body. He held out the red pajamas and said, "I need you to tell me if someone purchased this item last Friday."

"I can't tell you that," the clerk protested.

And Race was tempted to go through his whole I'm-with-the-CIA-and-can-get-a-warrant-for-this-information, but he made the mistake of looking at those sexy red pajamas, saw Aimee smiling at him with that look of hers that told him she was about to say something that would shock and surprise him, and knew that he couldn't wait any longer. He was responsible for what had happened to her. He'd brought her in on this case and told her that he'd protect her, but he hadn't. Because of him, she was missing. And it pissed him off that she was gone, because . . . because he fucking missed her.

Yeah, so maybe he'd let this case get personal. So what. Life was personal.

Race slid his hand into his jacket and calmly—and very patiently, he might add—pulled out his gun and aimed it at a rack of white underwear adorned with feathers. "Give me the fucking information," he said.

The woman's eyes widened as she looked from Jake to Race and back again.

Jake, thank God, didn't let loose with a smartass comment. Instead, he put his palms up in front of his chest and said, "Don't do it, man."

With shaking hands, the woman typed in whatever was needed to get her computer to spew forth the requested data. A printer hidden beneath the counter whirred and she handed a piece of paper to Jake, who took it and glanced down at it hurriedly as if afraid to take his eyes off his partner.

"She paid cash," he groaned. Then he looked at the numbers again and added, "Holy shit. Two hundred and twenty-five dollars for pajamas? No wonder your girlfriend refuses to work for free, man. She's gonna need one hell of a sugar daddy to pay for crap like this."

Race had no idea if Jake was aware that he was dangerously close to shooting his partner. He guessed not.

"Thank you," he said, grabbing the report out of Jake's hand before shouting, "I'm sorry," to the woman still hiding in the dressing room.

"That sucks." Jake sounded glum as he ushered Race out into the mall. Then he punched Race on the shoulder and said, "But good crazy cop impression back there. Mel Gibson would be proud."

Race dragged himself to a wooden bench across from the lingerie shop. It had been a long time since he'd felt this close to defeat. He put his forehead in his hands, not realizing that he was still holding his gun until he felt the barrel of it touching his temple.

"We're so close," he muttered. "I can feel it." He reached out a hand, as if by doing so, he could grasp that . . . that *whatever* it was that he could almost touch.

Beside him, Jake was shaking his head. "Come on, man. Let me buy you a beer."

Race didn't get up. He didn't want a beer. He didn't want sleep. He just wanted Aimee back, safe and sound.

The bench creaked when Jake stood up. "I'll be back in a second. I've just gotta use the ATM. I didn't anticipate going out tonight so I'm a little short on cash."

Race pinched the bridge of his nose between his thumb and forefinger and listened to the echo of Jake's boots hitting the floor as he walked away.

"Good evening shoppers, the mall is now closed," a mechanical-sounding voice intoned.

With a sudden intake of breath, Race looked up, wide-eyed. That was it! The buyer would not have anticipated an additional two hundred and twenty-five dollar expense, on top of the hotel rooms, meals, calling cards, cabs, and whatever else she had spent during her time in San Antonio. What if, instead of paying for the expensive lingerie with the inevitable plastic everyone carried around these days, she figured she'd outwit anyone who might be looking for her by simply going to the nearest ATM to withdraw the necessary cash instead?

Race got up and walked to the ATM. It was nothing out of the ordinary, with the usual places to slide your card, get cash, take a receipt, and such. He saw a sticker on the bottom right hand of the machine and leaned in closer.

Jake shot him an annoyed look and asked, "What the hell are you doing? Don't you know you're supposed to stay five feet back when someone's using one of these things?"

Race waved a hand at his partner. "Our buyer used this machine to get the cash she needed to buy those pajamas," he said.

Jake grabbed his card and money from the ATM and took a step back, eyeing it assessingly. "It's possible," he conceded.

"I know she did." And he did know it, with more certainty than he'd ever felt about anything in his life.

"It's possible," Jake repeated, obviously not as convinced as Race was. "But there's nothing we can do about it tonight."

Race pulled out his cell phone and dialed an 800 number. "It says right there who to call if the machine's been damaged," he said, pointing to the sticker at the bottom right hand corner of the machine.

"But nothing's wrong with it," Jake protested. "All they have to do to figure that out is to run a remote diagnostic test on it."

As the phone on the other end of the started ringing, Race looked at the man who had been his partner for nearly five years. "You know that I'll do whatever I have to do to get Aimee back, don't you?"

"Of course. I know you care about this girl," Jake answered immediately, not really thinking about what Race had asked.

"Good." Race nodded and then, pushing his partner out of the way, he took aim at the ATM and fired a single shot near the locking mechanism, where he figured it would do the least harm.

And as Jake picked his jaw up off the floor and sputtered, "Jesus Christ, man. You can't do that," a woman on the other end of the phone picked up and Race said, "Yes, my name is Race Gardner. I'm in security and I'm sorry to tell you this, but one of your ATMs has been damaged. Yes, ma'am. I would suggest you send someone out right away."

IT had worked. Nic couldn't believe it. Aimee's plan had worked. The representatives from Rabin's group were not the same tough negotiators that al-Zwahiri had been. They had agreed to pay nearly twice what al-Zwahiri had said was his top offer. And instead of a 10 percent down payment, which was as much as al-Zwahiri would fund, they agreed to wire 25 percent to Nic's account in the Caymans this afternoon.

He couldn't seem to wipe the silly grin off his face.

After nearly two hours of negotiations, Nic had walked out of the hotel meeting room, saying that he had to leave soon and expected to hear their final offer when he came back from the men's room. The call from his pilot had come seven minutes later, just as Nic was beginning to worry that the plan had failed.

But it hadn't failed. It had succeeded beautifully, and Aimee had just saved his company from ruin.

Nic swung open the door of the plane and stepped inside, still with that idiotic grin on his face. Aimee was exactly where he had left her, of course. Bill was sitting at the table with his back to the door, playing solitaire.

"We did it!" Nic shouted, barely noticing the surprised looks on the faces of the others before he bent down and kissed Aimee full on the lips as he'd wanted to do ever since the first moment he'd seen her. Her lips were full and soft, exactly as he'd expected them to be. She pulled her head back at first, obviously as shocked as Nic himself by the impulsive gesture. Then she relaxed and began kissing him back. It was only when she slid her free hand into his hair that Nic belatedly realized that she was still handcuffed to the chair.

He laughed and rested his forehead against Aimee's. "You know, before you, I never had to handcuff a woman to keep her with me."

"You don't have to handcuff me, either," she said, somewhat breathlessly.

Nic had always considered himself a good judge of character. He had to be, in his line of business. His doubts about Aimee's character arose from her willingness to sell out her employer, but that was nothing he, himself, would not have done. Like him, she simply wanted a better life for herself. That didn't make her a bad person, just a determined one. Determination was something he could understand. He would never have made it out of the life he had been born into without it.

Never before had he met a woman who he thought might

understand him and the choices he had had to make. But he felt that Aimee might. And if she could, if she were that woman, perhaps he could find in her the peace that had eluded him all these years, the peace of knowing that he was loved despite the things he had done to survive.

Aimee slid her hand around his neck to cup his cheek. "Are you all right?" she asked. "Your eyes . . . you look troubled."

Nic blinked and stepped back, astonished that she had been able to read what he was feeling. "Yes, I'm fine," he said, pulling the mask back down to hide his pain from the rest of the world. He realized then that he had completely forgotten that they were not alone, but when he turned, he saw that Bill had discreetly gone up to the cockpit and closed the door.

"I bought this to celebrate our success," Nic said, holding aloft the bottle of champagne he'd bought on the way back to the hangar. He set the bottle down on the table next to his laptop and then went over to close the door of the plane before fishing the key to the handcuffs out of his pocket.

Aimee stood up once he had released her and immediately excused herself to go to the restroom. Nic sheepishly watched her walk down the hall toward the back of the plane. He hadn't even considered that she might need to relieve herself when he'd locked her up earlier.

Nic pressed the intercom button on the wall near the cupboard that held glassware. "All right, Bill. Let's get back to the island," he said.

"You got it, boss," his pilot answered.

"Would you like a glass of champagne? I'm certain that one glass wouldn't impact your ability to pilot us safely home."

Bill chuckled. "No, one glass wouldn't hurt. But then, what's the point of having just one glass? I think I'll save my celebrating for tonight."

"Very well," Nic said, making a mental note to have a case of champagne sent to Bill's bungalow this evening. He flipped the intercom off as the plane's engines purred to life. Taking two champagne flutes out of the cupboard, Nic reflected on the decision he'd unconsciously made that afternoon. All he'd had to do was to make one phone call and Aimee would have been gone when he got back from his meeting. He wouldn't even have had to be specific. A mere "Take care of her" from him would have been enough. There would be no messy scenes for him to deal with, no reminders of her. She simply would have disappeared without a trace.

Only, he couldn't do it. Instead, he had been eager to see her again, to share this victory with her.

Nic expertly removed the wire cage from around the champagne cork and then eased the cork out of the bottle with a smoky pop. He filled both glasses with bubbly wine and then sat down and waited impatiently for Aimee to return.

After several more long moments, she emerged from the lavatory. Nic watched her walk toward him, her silky brown hair down around her shoulders. She wore a red and black patterned skirt topped with a black blouse that gave tantalizing glimpses of her skin when she turned just the right way. She was beautiful in a non-threatening sort of way. Some women were so attractive that they came off as cold and unapproachable, but not Aimee. She had a quiet beauty that drew others near.

Nic stood up and reached for her. She took his hand and allowed him to pull her close. Nic held her for a moment, breathing in the clean scent of her hair mixed with the light trace of her perfume. Then he handed her a glass of champagne and, holding his own glass aloft, smiled down at her and said, "To you."

Aimee looked up at him, her eyes solemn. "No, not just to me," she amended with a smile. "To us."

TWENTY-ONE

THE next day, Aimee was released from captivity. It was as if her willingness to help Nic with his deal had wiped away any doubts he may have had about her, and the door between the guest wing and the main house was not locked again.

After pleading exhaustion and spending the next twenty-four hours after they'd arrived back on the island alone in her room, Aimee emerged with renewed determination to somehow contact Race. She sought out Josie with the hopes that the girl would give her an excuse to go out and scout around the island, and Josie did not disappoint.

They walked along the beach, passing several houses similar to Nic's, only smaller. Aimee had discovered the morning before that a concrete path ran behind the houses and up to the airstrip. That path separated the oceanfront homes from a tangled jungle, and it appeared that this beach had been cleared to make way for the houses, because after they passed the last house, the vegetation encroached to within a few yards of the water's edge.

"Maybe we can get Captain Jack to take us into town tomorrow after my studies are done," Josie suggested, bending down to pick up an interesting-looking shell.

"We'll have to ask your father," Aimee said, hope once again rising in her chest. Maybe that was it—maybe Josie would be her ticket out of here. Perhaps Aimee could find a way to contact Race once they were in town. She didn't want to seem too eager to get off the island, but a shopping trip into town was certainly not so out of the ordinary, especially since all she had to wear were Diana's castoffs.

"Where is this Captain Jack person?" Aimee asked, much more interested in the boat itself than the captain.

"He lives over there," Josie answered, waving toward one of the houses on the opposite side of the small bay.

"Oh. And where is the boat?"

Josie gestured toward a dock jutting out into the water on the far side of the bubble-shaped bay. "It's usually there. He had to take Giselle's father into town today, so he's gone now. They should be back soon."

"So what else is on the island?" Aimee asked after they'd walked a ways farther down the beach. She hoped her questions were coming off as merely normal curiosity, rather than the information gathering they really were.

"Nothing except for some empty guest cottages," Josie answered. "There's just us. It gets kind of boring sometimes. Giselle and I go to Longport a lot, but Daddy doesn't like for Captain Jack to bring us home after dark, so most of the time, we don't get to go during the week. Sometimes, if Colin lets us out of our studies earlier, then we can go." Josie shrugged and bent down to pick up another shell.

"Do you ever go into Townsville on the mainland?"

"Sometimes. Mostly when Daddy has business and doesn't want Giselle and me around, so he sends us there with Mrs. Jacobs or Giselle's mom," Josie said.

Aimee tilted her head to one side. "What do you mean, when he doesn't want you around?"

Josie tossed the shell she'd just picked up into the sea. "Daddy has guests come to the island sometimes and he sends us away. We get to fly on the plane, which is neat, and we stay in hotels. I'd like to do that more often. Townsville is fun."

"Hmm," Aimee said. Interesting. So that's how Nic had managed to keep his business a secret from his daughter for so long. He got Josie out of the way whenever something big was going on.

The sun dipped below the horizon and Aimee turned back toward the house. They'd walked farther than she'd thought, nearly to the tip of land that jutted out into the bay and protected this harbor from the open ocean. From here, she could see that there was another small island a little to the north. "What's on that island?" she asked, pointing to the forested tip of one of the other island's rocky hills.

"Nothing that I know of. We went there a few years ago, and my dad and Mr. Simonds spent a long time walking around, but it's just the same as this place, only without the houses."

Aimee narrowed her eyes and squinted at the strip of land, but didn't see anything out of the ordinary. It looked exactly like what it was—a deserted island. "Well, we'd better get back so we can get ready for dinner," she said.

Their discussion of American clothing and hairstyles lasted until they got back to the house, where Nic was waiting for them. He sat on the veranda, watching as they approached, his expression unreadable. Aimee hoped she had not committed a blunder by asking Josie to come out with her. She hadn't seen the harm in taking the girl outside.

"Hi, Daddy," Josie said, bounding up the wide steps to land in her father's lap. For the first time since she'd met him, Nic looked disheveled. He was wearing trousers and a starched shirt, but he had untucked his shirt and rolled up his sleeves and had discarded his socks and shoes.

"Hi, baby," Nic said, dropping a kiss on his daughter's head. Josie, Aimee was beginning to realize, was Nic's one weakness. It was obvious that he loved his daughter and she softened him, made him human. "Did you two have a nice walk?" he asked, patting the seat next to him to indicate that Aimee should sit.

"Yes," Josie said.

Aimee sat down and took off her sandals to shake out the sand. "It's very peaceful here," she added.

"That is as I intended," Nic said.

Aimee laughed as she pushed her hair out of her eyes when

a sudden breeze blew several strands across her face. "And does life always cooperate with your intentions?" she asked.

Nic looked at her over the top of Josie's head. "Yes," he answered simply.

"Lucky you," Aimee muttered.

"Can I invite Giselle over for dinner?" Josie asked, completely uninterested in the adults' conversation.

"I don't see why not," Nic said, letting her off his lap with a squeeze of her shoulder. She ran into the house, eager to call her best friend, and Nic leaned his head back on the wicker sofa and closed his eyes. "I'm glad to see them getting along again," he said, with his eyes still closed.

Aimee was surprised that Nic wanted to talk about his daughter with her, but figured she had nothing to lose by hearing what he had to say. "Do they fight a lot?"

"They've been driving everyone mad with their arguing. One minute, they're the best of friends and the next, they say they'll never speak to each other again."

"If it's any consolation, I think that's typical of girls that age. Everything in their lives right now is so emotional. Every crisis seems as if it's going to be the end of their worlds."

"That's nice to hear. Perhaps they'll outgrow it."

Aimee thought of her relationship with her sisters, how their petty bickering as teens had been quickly forgotten once they reached adulthood. "They will," she assured him.

"I had Mrs. Jacobs move your things upstairs to the bedroom across from Josie's this afternoon," Nic said, without raising his head from the back of the couch.

"Oh?" Aimee said.

Nic lifted his head and wearily rubbed the back of his neck, sighing as if he'd had a difficult afternoon. "Yes. I know we haven't discussed your future, but after yesterday, I was wondering . . ." Nic hesitated and Aimee twisted around so that she was facing him.

"Wondering what?" she asked.

"Well, I wonder if you might consider working for me. I seem to spend an inordinate amount of time on things that really don't require my expertise. Making travel arrangements and creating presentations and such. If you're really as good an assistant as you say you are, I would like to hire you." He named a salary that was easily four times what a typical executive assistant earned, then added, "Tax free, of course."

Aimee knew her mouth was hanging open, but she was so stunned, she couldn't help herself. Nic Sabre was offering her a job? What a strange turn of events. "Um, of course I'll take it. You do realize that's an enormous amount of money for making travel arrangements and such?"

Nic laughed shortly. "The job will be a bit more involved than that."

Slowly, Aimee nodded. "Yes, I'm certain of that. When would you like me to start?"

"Tomorrow, if possible. I have a party scheduled for less than two weeks from now. The people attending are very important to the success of my new venture. It's critical that it come off without a hitch. I fear that I've not done a particularly capable job and I could use your assistance."

"All right. I'm happy to help. Especially for such a generous sum of money."

"Good. I've taken the liberty of ordering some things for you, and we'll see about getting you installed in an office tomorrow. From now on, you'll have free run of the house and the island." Nic paused for a moment, then turned to look directly at her. "But be warned, the staff have instructions to alert me if you ask them to help you get off the island. The nearest inhabited island is over fifteen miles away and, in case you've not read up on Australia, you'll note that the waters around here are quite full of sharks."

Aimee stifled a shudder at the thought of drowning or, even worse, being eaten by sharks. She'd seen *Jaws* enough times to have a vivid picture of what that would be like. "Don't worry, Nic," she said, laying a hand over his. "I'm not going anywhere."

HE insisted on making his move before another night passed.

Race had arrived in the city of Longport at midnight after over forty hours of being cooped up on airplanes. During the long trip, he and Jake had pored over maps of the area where Diana Simonds and her employer, suspected arms dealer Nic

Sabre lived. They had also made arrangements for their open-ended stay, planned their approach, and, occasionally, they had even slept.

Getting access to the ATM records back at the mall in San Antonio had been just the break Race had been praying for. A 250-dollar withdrawal five minutes prior to the purchase of the red pajamas had been traced to an account registered to one Diana Simonds. The address on the account had, of course, been bogus. But once they finally had a name to put with the buyer's face, they were able to obtain all sorts of information about who this Diana was and who she associated with. The name Nic Sabre had popped up too many times to be considered coincidence and once they'd traced Sabre to a private island in Australia, finding out that Diana also lived on the island had been easy.

Their intel on Sabre had been interesting. The guy had seemed to appear out of nowhere a dozen or so years ago. The CIA suspected he was an arms dealer, and they knew he associated with some real players, but they didn't have enough evidence to bring him down. Race was convinced that Sabre was the one interested in buying McConnell's plans and that Diana Simonds was merely his henchman. And during the long flight from Texas, he'd had plenty of time to wonder exactly what Sabre intended to do with those plans.

They'd arrived in Australia fully rested and prepared for whatever was going to happen next. Their contact in Townsville had been particularly efficient, and Race was impressed by the woman's attention to detail. In the trunk of their rental car, they'd found directions to a seaside motel, keys and a photo of the powerboat she'd arranged for their use, scuba gear, knives, and two Glock 9mm pistols.

The motel was perfect, a low-rent place with doors at the front that opened directly onto the beach and bathrooms in the back with low windows opening onto an alley. Race had learned early on in his military career that your chances of a safe escape grew exponentially if you had more than one entrance and exit point. Yes, it meant that you also had to guard both from attack, but it was worth the extra trouble to have a second means of egress.

The motel also owned its own marina where the powerboat

had been moored. It was this boat that was now taking them closer to where Aimee was being held.

Race stood at the bow, aiming a searchlight into the darkness to spot the markers that would lead them safely out into the South Pacific. The island where Sabre lived rose out of the ocean with a steep rocky shore. According to their map, there was a protected bay through a narrow inlet that Race was certain was well monitored. It would be easy to trap them inside the bay were they foolish enough to attempt to enter there, so, instead, their plan was to moor well away from the opposite side of the island, where it was less likely that they would be spotted. Race had already checked and rechecked the dry suit and scuba gear that would enable him to swim to the island. He'd packed a waterproof bag with hiking boots, a surveillance detection device, a knife, and his gun.

He was ready—no, more than ready—to take on whoever had captured Aimee.

"There it is," he said, spying the island in the distance. He turned to Jake and gestured toward the dark landmass rising up ahead of them. Jake immediately slowed the boat to quiet the engine. They had all the equipment to go with their cover story that they were simply fishermen getting an early start on the day's catch, but hoped not to be questioned at all.

Jake killed the engine at the spot they had earlier determined they would anchor and Race got to work putting on his gear.

"If I need you to come closer to shore, I'll give you three short bursts from my flashlight," Race said quietly, smearing greasepaint on his face and neck so that he wouldn't be as visible when he surfaced. They both knew that the only reasons he'd need to give the signal was if either he was bringing Aimee back or if he were injured and couldn't swim back out to the boat.

Jake leaned back against the side of the boat and crossed his arms over his chest. "We're agreed that your primary mission is not to extricate the subject, aren't we?"

"She's not a subject. And her name is Aimee," Race said, pulling up the zipper of his dry suit.

"This is about more than just you and some woman you've got the hots for," Jake said bluntly. "Something big is going on down here, but we can't stop this guy until we know what the threat is. If *Aimee*"—Jake emphasized her name, as if to prove a point—"is in a position to help, we need to keep her there to gather more evidence."

"If she's in danger, I'm rolling her up," Race insisted.

"Of course she's in danger, for God's sake. That's not the issue." Jake pushed a frustrated hand through his brownish blond hair. "You have to weigh the risk of one woman losing her life versus those that may be saved. If you can't, I'm scrapping this operation right now and we'll figure some other way onto this damn island." Unlike Race, Jake wasn't a trained diver, leaving Race as the only one who could complete this mission as they'd planned.

Race made the final adjustments to his scuba gear before turning to give his partner a cold look. "Has anyone ever told you you're a heartless bastard?" he asked.

Jake returned Race's cold look. "Yeah, every woman I've ever met," he said, his tone clearly telling Race he couldn't care less.

Without another word, Race turned his back on the other man and slipped into the dark water. The bitch of it was, he knew Jake was right. And despite his protests and his own personal feelings, he knew what was most important was to find out more about what was going on on that island.

Race surfaced a few hundred feet offshore to find the best extrication point. There were several spots where the foliage grew right up to the water's edge, which would make it easier for Race to remain hidden in case there were live patrols or surveillance cameras monitoring the perimeter of the island. He went down again, swimming, and then finally crawling the last several yards in an attempt to remain underwater for as long as possible. Finally, with slow, measured movements, he crept out of the sea.

Once onshore, he inched farther into the forest, listening carefully in case someone saw him and raised an alarm. Not hearing anything, he proceeded to strip off his dry suit. Finally, he pulled on his boots, tucked his pistol into the waistband of his pants within easy reach, and palmed his knife.

Now he was ready to hunt his prey.

TWENTY-TWO

AIMEE awoke from a sound sleep with a start, not knowing what it was that had awakened her. Her brain, still fuzzy from sleep, wondered if Daphne was up. Daff was waking up more and more in the middle of the night lately, tiptoeing around the house in an attempt not to wake Aimee, but unable to completely muffle the sounds of her footsteps on the creaky hardwood floors.

When she heard the sound of the ocean lapping against the beach below, she opened her eyes and realized she was not in Atlanta anymore. She reached up and rubbed her aching forehead, thinking it must have been a headache that had woken her.

That is, until a large, very strong hand was clamped over her mouth.

Aimee instinctively struggled to free herself, but stilled when a man's voice whispered her name in her ear. He didn't take his hand away, but turned her face to him. Aimee hated the feminine response, but she immediately started crying with relief when she found herself staring into Race's soft gray eyes. Race was here. Everything was going to be all right. He smiled, a quick flash of white against the dark of his face, and Aimee suddenly realized that had she not heard his voice, she would not have recognized the man crouched at her bedside.

"Is this room under surveillance?" he whispered, and Aimee shook her head, unable to do anything more than lie there and take in the sight of him.

He wore brown and tan camouflage pants that clung to his muscled thighs and a brown T-shirt that showed off his flat stomach and broad chest. Aimee couldn't stop staring. Her mild-mannered CPA was gone, and a warrior was crouching in his place.

She slid her arms around Race's back and pressed herself close. His shirt was damp and he smelled of soap and sweat and man, and he was just about the most welcome sight Aimee had ever seen.

Race took his hand from her mouth and buried it in her hair, holding her tightly to him. Aimee wished they could stay like this forever. For the first time in days, she felt safe.

"Are you all right? Did they hurt you?" Race whispered, his hands moving up and down her back as if preferring to check her out for himself. Then, without waiting for an answer, he kissed her, long and hard, their lips and teeth and tongues crashing and swirling together like a violent storm headed out to sea.

When he lifted his head, they were both breathing hard. Aimee had to take several deep breaths before answering, "I'm fine, although until this afternoon, I wasn't certain I was going to make it. I'm not sure double my usual hourly rate is enough for this job. Do you think it's too late to ask for a raise?" she asked, being flip to hide her embarrassing relief at seeing Race here.

She turned and missed seeing Race close his eyes, his face twisted in agony. "Don't joke about it," he said, reaching out to catch hold of her upper arm.

"Why?" Aimee asked, puzzled.

For the first time since he'd joined the CIA, Race was tempted to put his own desires ahead of those of his country. Let them find another way to figure out what was going on here. Better yet, let someone else sacrifice someone they cared about. He couldn't do it anymore.

But then, who will? If not you, who?

Race scowled, wishing for just one moment that he had never been born with a fucking conscience.

"I'm going to be okay," Aimee said softly.

Race clenched his teeth to keep from giving in to his desire to grab her up in his arms and drag her away from here. "Do you feel that your life is in immediate danger?" he asked, not answering her earlier question.

"I'm sleeping fifty feet away from an arms dealer," Aimee said. "Of course my life is in immediate danger. But I'm being paid to do a job and I'm not leaving until my mission is accomplished."

Race flinched but refused to look away. "What do you know about him? Do you know what he's doing with McConnell's plans?"

"His name is Nic Sabre and he's got a twelve-year-old daughter named Josie. He's moving into weapons manufacturing, but he wouldn't tell me what makes this new weapon so different or specifically what he needed the plans for."

"Did he tell you where the weapons are being manufactured? Or anything at all that might help us?"

Aimee was already shaking her head. "Not really. He mentioned that they'll start shipping the new weapon by the end of the year, but that's it. He had a meeting yesterday morning— or make that two days ago, I guess, since it's after midnight— but I didn't get the names of his contacts or which organization they were with."

"Nothing else?"

"No. I was held as a virtual prisoner the first few days I was here. I'm certain Nic was trying to decide whether or not to kill me."

"How did you convince him not to?" Race asked.

Aimee looked at him from under her eyelashes. "I charmed his socks off."

"I have no doubt about that," Race said, resisting the urge to crush her to him again. God, how he wanted to just grab her and throw her over his shoulder and get her the hell out of here.

"Besides that, I gave him an idea about how to bug his

meeting, which came off very well. He even offered me a job."

Race winced. That made it even more difficult to justify taking her out. If Aimee was working with Nic Sabre, that meant she had a chance of getting access to information about this new weapon. Without more specific intelligence, the CIA couldn't act. Hell, they didn't even know what the threat might be . . . or if there was any threat at all.

"Race, I can't leave. You know that," Aimee whispered, laying her head on his chest and making his heart constrict painfully.

He tightened his arms around her back, holding her so close that he could feel her chest rising and falling with each breath. Despite everything, he was tempted to ignore her—and his conscience—and take her with him when he left this damn island.

"Do you think that Nic Sabre presents a threat to the United States?" he asked, praying that she would say no. If she did, he would have her out of this place within the hour.

Aimee remained still, her nose pressed into his chest, her breath warm and moist through the thin fabric of his T-shirt.

Please say no, he willed her silently as the seconds ticked by.

Finally, she raised her head, the expression in her eyes troubled. "Yes," she answered. "He's so driven to become rich that he will stop at nothing to get what he wants. I don't know what Nic is planning, but I have no doubt that it's something terrible."

Race wanted to shake her, to ask her if she was so fucking stupid that she didn't know she should have lied. All she'd had to do was say that one word: *No*.

She dropped her hands from around his neck and pulled away from him. Then she closed her eyes and took a deep breath in and let it out again. "Look, you can't take me off the island. It's that whole 'good of the many versus the good of the one' principle. Although in our case, it's the good of the two being sacrificed," she said, attempting another lame joke.

"I'm sorry, Aimee. I —"

She surprised him by leaning forward and placing a finger across his lips. "Don't," she said. "This is the right decision and we both know it." Her expression softened and she shook her head slightly. "I'm sorry I left you that last night in San

Antonio. If I hadn't, none of this would have happened. It would appear that you and I are destined to remain apart."

Race grabbed her by the front of her short silky nightshirt and tugged so hard that she nearly toppled over onto his lap. "Fuck that. We are not destined to be apart, Aimee. We're going to get the evidence we need to roll this guy up and then you're mine. Do you hear me?"

Without giving her a chance to respond, he shoved his hands in her hair and kissed her possessively. She pushed him back until he was sitting on the floor and then straddled him with one knee on each side of his hips. When she rubbed against him, hot and catlike, Race feared he would explode. This was so wrong, so risky. Yet he couldn't stop. He had never felt such a strong desire to possess to a woman, to mark her as his. It was an urge so primal, he was driven by it, like a lion to the hunt.

He slid his hands up under her nightgown and put his hands in front of her breasts, just far enough away that her nipples barely brushed his palms as she moved. She tried to press closer but Race pulled back, teasing her until he was lying on the floor with her sprawled on top of him. She writhed against him with a breathy moan in his ear and Race felt his hips pulse in response.

Her breasts filled his hands but it wasn't enough. He needed more.

He trailed one hand down across her stomach, hoping she was ready. Every second he lingered here brought them closer to danger, but Race was beyond caring. He pushed her panties down her legs, then slid one finger into her heat and, oh yes, she was wet and ready, her body closing in around his finger, her hips greedily pressing down, taking more.

Race rolled them over, cursing his laced-up boots and the clothes that were in his way. He couldn't wait. He needed her. Now. He freed himself from his briefs and buried himself in her. She wrapped her legs around his waist and met each of his desperate thrusts, her heels pressing into his back.

That exquisite friction grew inside him, building and building, and he knew he couldn't wait any longer. He'd have to take care of Aimee when he was finished. He couldn't stop this driving need.

"Oh, yes," she whispered, and stiffened under him, her hips pushing into his as if trying to lose her entire self in him. The muscles inside her convulsed around him and Race thrust into her one last time, fighting the urge to roar as the force of his orgasm pounded through him.

When his senses finally returned from that black orgasm-induced void, Race opened his eyes and looked down at Aimee. She had smears of greasepaint on her face and on her nightgown, which should have alarmed him—how was she going to explain those black smears away?—but didn't. Instead, he was filled with primitive pride at having claimed her for his own.

Jesus, he was turning into a Neanderthal. Somehow, though, he couldn't seem to manage to work up any real concern about it. He dropped a kiss on Aimee's forehead and she opened her eyes and smiled up at him. He would have been happy to stay like that forever, their bodies joined, their hearts beating in unison. But he had to go, and they both knew it.

With Herculean effort, Race pushed himself off of Aimee and tucked in his various body parts and clothing before zipping back up again. He had never hated his job before, but in this moment, he loathed it with a hot passion equaling what he felt for Aimee.

He reached down, holding out a hand to help her up off the floor. She took it, her hand pale and small in his. She stood close, invading his personal space, which Race didn't mind at all. He liked her there, so close that he could count her eyelashes or the slight smattering of freckles across the bridge of her nose.

"I have to go," he said, raising one hand to tuck a lock of hair behind her ear.

"I know," she said.

"I'm staying at the Harborside Motel in Longport under the name Horace Gibson. I also have my cell phone." He gave her the number and told her to memorize it, then asked, "Have you got it?"

Aimee nodded silently, her eyes so solemn and sad that Race had to force himself to breathe around the tightness in his chest. He had to remind himself of the sacrifices others made to keep the world safe, soldiers leaving spouses and children, giving their lives to protect freedom around the globe. But it was small comfort, this noble objective, when he knew it might mean he'd never see Aimee again.

"We're setting up surveillance at the marina. If Sabre's boat shows up, we'll know within minutes. If you want us to make contact, leave a stripe on the second piling nearest the exit."

"Don't worry about me. I'm going to be all right," Aimee said, squeezing his arm reassuringly.

Race kissed her lightly on the forehead and then, after one final look back into the bedroom, he disappeared into the predawn darkness, wishing that her words could ease the ache that had settled deep into the pit of his stomach.

THE morning after Race's nocturnal visit, Aimee awakened early and hurried into the shower to erase all traces of greasepaint and sweaty man from her body. She hadn't dared take a shower right after he had left, afraid she'd wake Nic and arouse his suspicions. Her nightgown presented a bit more of a problem. She was cautious enough to believe that Mrs. Jacobs and the sparse housekeeping staff probably knew everything that went on around this house and a greasepaint-stained nightgown showing up in the laundry would cause some raised eyebrows. But if Aimee washed it herself and left it hanging to dry, would the woman who came to clean notice it and mention it to the head housekeeper? That, too, would seem odd. Why wouldn't Aimee just put the thing in the hamper rather than washing it out herself?

No, it seemed her best course of action would be to hide the thing, maybe under the rug in her room, Aimee thought. She couldn't imagine the cleaning people being *that* thorough, no matter how much Nic paid them. Hopefully, she'd be long gone by the time they got around to doing some spring-cleaning.

Aimee cursed both herself and Race for not thinking about this last night, but then, they'd had other things on their minds. Or rather, they weren't thinking at all. They were letting their feelings run the show. She refused to regret it, though. She had needed Race's strength to complete this mission, wasn't certain she could continue facing Nic Sabre with her false air of bravado without knowing that what she was doing was of vital importance. Race made that easy to believe. He seemed so sure of things, so assured that what he was doing was right, that his confidence had filled her, made her believe, too. It wasn't that she was prone to moral ambiguities, but the constant fear of taking a misstep that would cost her her life was interfering with the brash, I'll-do-anything-for-money role she tried to play. And she couldn't afford to let that mask slip, not even for a split second. If she did, she'd be dead.

As she stepped out of the shower, her mind was already moving ahead. Today she'd begin working for Nic. He'd mentioned the party that was critical to his new venture. Even if Nic tried to keep things from her, there were certain things he'd have to tell her . . . things like who would be attending this party. Somehow, even if she couldn't get off the island, she'd find a way to get this information to Race.

Seeing him had bolstered not only her confidence, but her courage. Now she would let nothing stop her from succeeding.

TWENTY-THREE

NIC thwarted her at every turn.

Her first task was to finalize a menu.

"How many attendees are we expecting?" she asked.

"A small group. Between thirty and thirty-five," Nic answered.

"What nationality? Are there certain food taboos I should plan for? Kosher food only, no beef?" she asked, her pencil poised to take notes.

"Just be certain there is a variety," Nic said.

"Well, could I get a guest list?" Aimee asked. "That might aid in my selections."

Nic looked up from the laptop on his desk as Aimee stood in the doorway, balancing a blank notepad in one hand. She strove for a "Come on, I'm not asking for anything that unusual" look.

"My guests are accustomed to eating in the finest restaurants in the world," Nic answered smoothly. "I'm certain their palates will be compatible with whatever you choose."

Aimee nodded, unwilling to pursue this further. She took her pad and pencil and went back down the hallway to the office

Nic had set up for her. He'd left an empty room between them. Aimee wasn't certain if it was a closet or a storage room or what, but the door was closed and locked. She suspected it was merely a way to ensure that she couldn't overhear his conversations. He may have been willing to ask for her help, but it was obvious that he didn't trust her completely.

She sat down at her desk and looked at the cookbooks Mrs. Jacobs had brought her that morning. Aimee was hopeful that Nic had a computer on order for her. If she could get access to the Internet, she could communicate with Race. Even if Nic installed spyware on the computer to track what she was doing, Aimee's partner Raine had taught her a few tricks to bypass the traps without getting caught.

For now, though, she had no way to contact him . . . and no reason to do so. She hardly thought the CIA could move on her tip that Nic was having a small party in two weeks. That was about as useful as telling them he had a hangnail on his right thumb.

Tapping the end of a pencil against her teeth, Aimee set about planning the menu. She hadn't been lying to Nic about her organizational skills. She had the ability to look at a problem, think it through from its smallest detail through the finished result, and manage people to do their part and do it well. As silly as it sounded, she often used visualization to accomplish the task, so she closed her eyes and imagined the living room filled with people. Some would be drinking and others would not. Because Nic wouldn't hand over the guest list, she didn't know if the party was to include spouses or merely be a business function, which made her job more difficult. If it were to be more slanted toward the social, she'd choose food that could be loaded onto plates and taken off somewhere to be eaten in smaller groups. If, instead, it was to be a business occasion, Nic would most likely want to keep people in the same room. The food would be less of the focus than the goal of making new contacts.

Since it was clear that Nic was unwilling to share anything more than just the number of attendees with her, Aimee decided to assume that this was to be a networking opportunity as opposed to a social occasion. Thus, her vision became more clearly focused on men and a few women, most with a drink in their hand, chatting with one another. Having to balance both a drink and a plate while walking or standing would be awkward, so Aimee would choose hors d'oeuvres that could be eaten in one bite and would not necessitate plating. That helped her to narrow her choices.

As she flipped through the first cookbook Mrs. Jacobs had supplied, she wrote down the name and page number of anything that looked interesting, keeping in mind that she was trying for a mix of dishes that would satisfy even the most picky eater.

By lunchtime, she was starving, her mouth watering at every tantalizing recipe she encountered. Before, when she had been kept in the guest wing, Mrs. Jacobs had brought her meals. Aimee wasn't certain if that was the typical protocol, or if Nic actually took a break for lunch. She had picked up the house phone and was about to ring the housekeeper, when Nic appeared in her doorway.

"Are you hungry?" he asked.

She hung up the receiver. "Starving. I was just calling Mrs. Jacobs to see what the normal routine for lunch was. Looking through these cookbooks all morning has made me famished. I was tempted to eat the last three pages of this one," Aimee said wryly, gesturing at the open cookbook on her desk.

"No need to resort to that," Nic said with a slight smile. "We'll have lunch in the dining room."

"Will Josie be joining us?" Aimee asked, pushing back her chair.

"No, not today. She's doing her studies over at Giselle's house and they'll eat over there."

Aimee suppressed a look of surprise when, instead of backing out of her office, Nic came toward her. He picked up her pad from atop the desk and walked over to what Aimee had assumed to be a closet. When he opened the doors, she saw that a small safe had been installed. Nic put the pad of paper in the safe, looked back toward her desk as if contemplating whether or not to add the cookbooks as well, and then shut the door. He spun the tumbler as he took an envelope out of his breast pocket and handed it to her.

"This contains the combination of the safe. Memorize it

and give it back to me after lunch. Every time you leave your office, and I mean *every* time, even if you're just going to use the restroom, I expect you to lock up your work."

"But that was just a bunch of menu selections," Aimee protested as Nic ushered her out into the hall.

Nic shrugged. "I don't care. I know it may seem silly, but I don't like to leave things lying around, no matter how unimportant they may seem. The staff here is as loyal as they come, but that doesn't mean someone couldn't get to them. I've always found it amazing the things people will do for what is, to me, a very small amount of money."

Aimee swallowed and gnawed on the inside of her bottom lip. "Okay," was all she said.

They entered the dining room, which was as lavishly set for lunch as it had been that first night Aimee had been asked to join Nic for dinner. There were two places set with gleaming silver and glittering crystal and fresh flowers in the middle of the table.

"I could get used to this," Aimee muttered as Nic held out her chair for her.

He chuckled as he took his own seat. They kept their conversation light as they were served French onion soup and a watercress and mandarin orange salad with toasted almonds, mostly with Aimee regaling Nic with stories from her fictitious childhood. She used the same cover story she had for years—orphaned at a young age, raised on a farm in the Midwest by an elderly grandfather who had since died, no siblings. Family complicated things, made you vulnerable. Besides, with family, you had to remember their cover stories as well as your own. And, sometimes, keeping the truth separate from the fiction was simply too difficult. Someone asked you a question about the sister who was supposed to be a clerk in an insurance agency somewhere and you couldn't remember the name of the agency and your cover was blown.

No, it was much better to be all alone in the world when going undercover.

"What about you?" Aimee asked, taking a sip of water from the goblet in front of her. "Where did you grow up?"

Nic's hesitation was so slight that Aimee would have missed it if she hadn't been paying attention. "Oh, all over.

My father was an engineer who worked on large projects such as building dams in developing countries. We never lived anywhere more than a few years."

"That must have been interesting," Aimee said, spearing a segment of orange from her plate.

"No," Nic said. "It wasn't."

Aimee decided not to be coy about this because her alter ego, the one running this show, wouldn't do so. She leaned over and put a hand on Nic's forearm. He turned to look at her, his eyebrows raised. "It's okay if you don't want to talk about it. Just tell me that it's a sore subject and I won't bring it up again." She paused for a moment, looking down at the spotless white tablecloth before raising her eyes to meet his again and saying gently, "We all have wells of pain inside of us that we'd rather not expose to the world."

It was total bullshit, of course. Yes, being the plain older sister to a couple of gorgeous siblings had been difficult, but it wasn't this great open wound that festered all the time. It bugged her sometimes that the world valued beauty so much more than brains—so much so that her sisters were millionaires a dozen times over because of how they looked in a bikini, while Aimee had never broken the six-figure income barrier ridding the world of bad guys. That is, until she'd met Nic Sabre. Now, with what he was paying her in addition to what the CIA had agreed to pay her, Aimee was finally going to make a damn good living. She supposed that if she were standing on the absolute moral high ground, when this was all over she'd give the money Nic was paying her to the U.S. government to offset their costs, but . . . Nah, there was no way she was going to do that.

"Thank you," Nic said softly.

Aimee squeezed his arm, then let go. "Let's see. What are some other things we can talk about? What do you do in your spare time? When were you born? What's your sign?" she teased, picking up her soup spoon.

"I'm a Scorpio. I celebrate my birthday on November 17. And I have had so little spare time in my life that I am uncertain what I'd do if I were to suddenly find myself with time on my hands. What about you?"

"I'm a Leo. Probably no surprise there. And I find hobbies

highly overrated. I mean, if you can't make money at something, why bother doing it?" Aimee lifted one shoulder as if completely perplexed by those who spent hours gluing together tiny pieces of model ships or knitting socks. In truth, she really did struggle with this, even knowing that the purpose of a hobby was simply to enjoy it. Sex was probably the only thing she did for the sole purpose of enjoyment. Everything else came with a price tag.

Nic laughed. "Ah, you are a woman after my own heart."

Great. Nice to know she had so much in common with an arms dealer. Aimee repressed a shudder. When this was all over, maybe she'd consider taking up cross-stitch or something.

They finished lunch with some meaningless banter and, when they returned to her office, Aimee was delighted to find that a computer had been installed during her absence. She tried to hide her elation, but couldn't help running her hand over the keyboard of the gleaming new machine.

"This is great," she said with a grin. "Now we can e-mail each other."

"No, we can't," Nic said, dashing her hopes. "Your machine doesn't have Internet access."

"Oh. And we're not on a network?" Aimee asked, disappointed.

"No. I'm afraid if you want to speak with me, you'll have to use the phone or come down the hall." Nic favored her with an indulgent smile, which Aimee returned. She'd find some way to use this to her advantage. She just wasn't sure how just yet.

The ensuing days passed in much the same manner, with Aimee attempting to coax things out of Nic in such a way as to not arouse his suspicions and Nic giving her the least amount of information possible in order to do her job. They had dinner together each evening, mostly just she and Nic and Josie, but sometimes with the Simondses as well. Diana treated her with barely veiled hostility that Aimee countered with a graciousness that would have made the queen proud. And Aimee became a master at listening at doors. Once again, her ability to remain unnoticed for long periods of time aided in this task.

There was one incident where she was almost caught, having been lurking in the hallway outside Nic's office when he and Luke Simonds were sequestered inside. They were amazingly quiet, which Aimee took to mean they were discussing something important, so she had pressed her ear to the door in order to hear what they were saying. Mrs. Jacobs had come to check on one of the recipes Aimee had flagged because her grocer was having a difficult time finding one of the key ingredients. Fortunately, Aimee had seen the woman's shadow just before she rounded the corner and had straightened from her crouch near Nic's door and ducked back into her own office just before the other woman would have caught her snooping.

She kept notes about the information she'd overheard, writing them on Post-its and storing them in a plastic bag she'd pocketed after she and Josie had asked Mrs. Jacobs to provide them with a picnic lunch over the weekend. Aimee had pinned the bag to the back of the drapes in her office using a safety pin she had also procured from the housekeeper on the pretense that she'd lost a button on her borrowed shorts. All she had to do now was to hope that no one caught her standing on her chair to add notes to her makeshift file.

The day before the party was to be held, Aimee's nerves were stretched to the breaking point. Before, when she'd been this jittery, she'd grabbed her keys and taken off in her convertible, letting the wind and the pounding music invade her head and calm her down. But here, she was trapped. The closest things to cars on the island were the golf carts used to ferry people and deliveries from the airstrip to the houses. Aimee didn't think taking one of those out for a spin would help clear her head.

On top of the stress of staying in this role for so long was the fact that Aimee felt she finally had some concrete information to share with Race. Her covert snooping had paid off that morning. For nearly two weeks, she'd watched and listened, noting Nic's patterns and routines. He arrived at his office at 8:00 A.M. sharp, as if driven by some internal time clock. At 8:05, Mrs. Jacobs arrived with a pot of coffee. Nic did not believe in eating at his desk, so he would already have had breakfast in the breakfast room. He did, however, drink several cups of coffee in the morning while working. And by 10:00, he was ready for a bathroom break. Aimee knew this because she watched him walk past her office every morning, a copy of the front section of the *London Times* tucked under his arm. She had no idea why men did that. Reading in the bathroom seemed more than a little disgusting to her, aside from the fact that, like most women, her bathroom breaks didn't last long enough to read one article, much less the entire front section.

Nonetheless, she was grateful for Nic's schedule. Because, today, she was going to try to exploit it.

TWENTY-FOUR

"WHY does your mom hate Aimee?" Josie asked, looking up from her French book. She and Giselle were studying in Gi's room, Giselle flopped out on her bed, while Josie sat at her best friend's desk.

"I don't know," Giselle answered, blowing a big pink bubble with her gum and popping it with her fingers before stuffing the wad back in her mouth.

"You haven't overheard anything?"

Giselle shrugged as if to say she didn't care enough to listen, which made Josie more than a little irritated. Typical Giselle. If it didn't concern her, she didn't care.

Well, it mattered to Josie. She wanted everyone to love Aimee as much as she did, and if they didn't, she wanted to know why so she could fix it. She could tell that her dad was really beginning to like Aimee. Every time Aimee walked into a room, Daddy would watch her with a little smile on his face, as if he had a secret that nobody else knew.

But Josie knew. She'd never seen her dad like that. And it wasn't like he hadn't brought women home before, because he had. Some, Josie had even liked. Since she didn't remember her mother, it wasn't like she was comparing them to some standard they couldn't meet. To be honest, Josie wanted a new mom. She'd realized the night that she first got her period that having a dad—even one as great as Daddy—wasn't enough. He didn't know about woman stuff, at least not like another woman would.

Aimee, she decided, would make the perfect mom. She talked to Josie like a real person, not like some of her dad's girlfriends, who treated her like a dog or a baby or something. And she didn't get embarrassed when Josie asked her questions. On a picnic they'd had a few days ago, Josie asked her about sex, because it was something Giselle talked about all the time, like she knew something Josie didn't.

It turned out that Giselle didn't know anything, either.

For some reason, knowing that Gi was just bluffing with all her talk of what went where and how it all worked was comforting. Sometimes, Gi liked to act all superior and, without having another source of information to rely on—and she *certainly* was not going to ask her father about something as embarrassing as sex—Josie hadn't been able to tell if her friend was just making stuff up.

But Aimee had become Josie's secret weapon. Not like Josie *wanted* to argue with Giselle or anything, she just got sick of always being treated like the dumb one in their relationship.

"Do you think maybe that your mom has a crush on my dad, and that's why she doesn't like Aimee?" Josie asked, voicing the suspicion that had occurred to her in the middle of the night last night.

Giselle jerked up on the bed and gasped as if Josie had hit her. "What are you talking about, Josie Sabre? My mom loves my dad and nobody else. How could you even think such a thing?"

In hindsight, Josie could see where maybe she might have been better off keeping her mouth shut about that. "I'm sorry," she apologized, immediately wishing she could take the words back.

Giselle sent her a look of such venom that Josie recoiled. Then she said the worst thing that she could think of to say. "I think you're just jealous because I have a mom and you don't."

Josie flinched as Giselle's arrow found its mark right in the center of her heart. She tried to take a breath but it felt as if her throat had closed up. What she had said may have been thoughtless, but she hadn't meant to hurt Giselle by saying it. She was truly just looking for a reason why Mrs. Simonds seemed to dislike Aimee and she knew that women liked her father, so that had seemed like it might be why.

But Gi's comment was meant to cause injury. And that it did.

Josie rose from the chair in Giselle's room and solemnly picked up her French book and put it into her backpack along with her notebook and her favorite green pen. She looked around the room to make sure she hadn't left anything behind, and then, with a seriousness that came from deep within her, she walked to the door leading out onto the veranda and paused for just a second before turning to face the girl who had been her best friend for her entire life.

"I don't want to be friends with you anymore," Josie said.

Then, without looking back, she took her backpack and her wounded heart and walked away, vowing that she'd never let herself be hurt by Giselle Simonds again.

"I'M sorry to interrupt, but I wonder if now would be a good time for me to use your computer to search the Internet for translations for these recipes?" Aimee said, poking her head into Nic's office at three minutes to ten in the morning. She'd mentioned her concern a few days ago, that if people had religious or cultural objections to certain ingredients in the dishes she'd chosen, it might help if she could provide a description of each hors d'oeuvre on a notecard. Nic had agreed this would be a good idea without giving it much thought. It was only when Aimee said breezily, "Oh, great. I'll need access to the Internet, then, to translate them into other languages. No use telling someone who objects to alcohol consumption that we're serving scallops in a white wine cream sauce if they can't understand what the card says." And when Nic had protested that he thought she had an ear for languages, Aimee had told him she did—but that her spelling wasn't worth a damn.

She supposed that Nic could have told her to forget the idea then, but he didn't. Instead, he muttered that he was going to be busy for the next few days but to remind him about it again. Which was exactly what she was doing.

Nic glanced up at her and then at the computer lying unused on his desk. With a shrug, he waved a hand at the chair across from his desk, and said, "Sure. Go ahead."

Aimee had suspected he wouldn't let the laptop out of his office, a decision for which she was grateful. She didn't want to leave his office, not when he had papers strewn about his desk that she wanted to get a look at. Now all she could do was pray that Mother Nature did her part to make this plan a success.

She sat down and put the laptop across her knees. When she opened the lid, she found it at a login screen. "What should I use for the user ID and password?" she asked.

"Guest and lors2963," Nic answered.

Aimee guessed that by this afternoon, the password would be changed. She had to hand it to him, Nic was pretty thorough. When she logged on, she found the only program that had been permitted for this user was Word and Internet Explorer. *Score two for Nic,* she thought. Even if she did surf to her webmail account, she didn't have anything to send. Her notes were in her office and she was by no means technically proficient enough to crack Nic's security and access his files to send as attachments, especially not with him sitting two feet away from her. Plus, of course, she was certain that he was tracking her every keystroke.

With all of the new technology, spying was getting more and more difficult every day.

Aimee typed the first menu item into the translation program's search engine and then asked, "Do you have a disk? If I have to write down all these kooky letters, I know I'll get them wrong. None of them make any sense to me, and I know that putting a line to the left rather than to the right will change the meaning of the entire phrase. I'll be telling people we're having goat testicles instead of fois gras. Although I'm guessing that some of our guests might not object to either one," she joked.

Nic nodded absently and pulled a disk from his top drawer. Aimee opened a blank Word document and cut and pasted the phrase the translation program had served up. She repeated this process several times, working fairly slowly to stall for time.

By 10:28, she was starting to perspire.

By 10:34, she was beginning to think this wouldn't work after all.

And by 10:42, she knew it was over. She couldn't stall much longer and she only had three more translations to run through.

Damn him, why did he have to be so freaking cautious all the time?

"I am never going to speak to Giselle again," Josie suddenly said from the doorway, her voice watery, yet determined. She hefted the backpack she was carrying onto her father's desk, where it spewed forth several textbooks and a notebook. Then she crossed her thin arms over her chest. "I would like to have Mr. Howe teach classes to me here from now on and Giselle can get her own tutor," she announced. And finally, as if she'd been holding back a great reservoir of emotion, she burst into tears and ran from the room.

Nic looked at Aimee and she looked back.

"Poor kid," Aimee said, truly feeling for Josie. Being her age was hard, with all those hormones and emotions you just didn't understand or have the skills to cope with yet.

But she didn't make a move to go after the girl. Instead, she remained seated, her fingers crossed that Nic would race after his daughter, leaving Aimee to check out the documents on his desk. Instead, the bastard paused long enough to scoop everything up and hurriedly shove it in the safe. Aimee wanted to scream. Wouldn't he *ever* make a mistake?

Trying not to let him know how utterly disgusted she was with his thoroughness, Aimee said, "Good luck," as he hurried out the door. Then, alone in the empty room, she sighed. When was she ever going to get a break?

She knew that whining wasn't going to help, though, so she quickly finished her translation task, popped the disk out of the computer, and stood to go.

And that's when she noticed it. Just the slightest edge of a piece of paper peeking out from under Josie's things like a rebellious teen sticking out just the tip of her tongue. Nic had finally bungled something.

Aimee didn't waste any time. She lifted Josie's backpack from the edge of the desk and smoothly stuffed everything, including the errant paper, inside. Then she left Nic's office, closing the door behind her. She went into her own office but left the door open, knowing that if she closed it, Nic would wonder why she had done so.

She propped Josie's backpack up against the drawers at the side of her desk and quickly rifled through it to find the paper that had been trapped beneath Josie's history book. Aimee read through the list of names written neatly on the page. Several names had lines drawn through them. Aimee counted the ones that hadn't been scratched off. Thirty-two.

Was this the guest list for tomorrow evening's party? She could only assume so.

Now what was she to do? She didn't have a copy machine, so couldn't duplicate the sheet. And taking it would be too risky. If Nic discovered the list was missing, he'd no doubt assume she'd taken it. Then he'd tear the house apart looking for it. No, she was going to have to copy down the names and then put the list back in Josie's backpack for her to find.

She still had no idea how she was to get this information to Race, but as she began writing, she became more determined than ever to make contact with Race and end this job, once and for all.

"I'M going back in," Race said as Jake pulled open the door of his motel room to let Race in. Normally, patience was his strong suit. He'd once waited almost six months for contact from one of his defectors-in-place, a high-ranking official in a terrorist network who had funneled Race vital information about upcoming attacks before going dormant for nearly half a year. Every day for six months, Race checked the dead drop where they had arranged for the man to contact him should he be ready to leave the country. Finally, the man had contacted Race, saying he had been in the hospital after a severe auto accident and was now prepared to leave.

Not once had Race been willing to blow the man's cover by going after him, even though he possessed enough information to identify Race and, most likely, to get him killed. Instead, he'd patiently waited for the man to get in touch with him, as he'd been trained to do. But now he was willing to ignore that training, to cast aside all that had been drummed into him because he couldn't bear the thought that Aimee was in danger.

Jake pulled Race inside and closed his door with a barely controlled click. "We wait for her to contact us," he said. "What if she's turned? You've seen this guy's file. Nic Sabre is rich and handsome and he plays in the circles your girl wants to play in—jetting off to Monaco in his private jet, racking up ten-thousand-dollar tabs at the local clothing boutiques. He is definitely her type."

Race took a deep breath and forced himself to calm down. One word from his partner and Race would be pulled off this case. Hell, he thought, rubbing his forehead, that might even be the best thing for all concerned. But the thought of leaving Aimee in anyone's hands but his own made Race want to pound his fist into something.

"Aimee's not the type to fall for a guy like that," Race insisted.

"Then you don't have anything to worry about," Jake said.

"I'm worried that she's been injured or is being held captive on the island, not that she's so besotted with a gunrunner that she's lost her ability to reason."

"Look, Race, we had to go in and make the initial contact to let Devlin know that we were here. It was a risk, but one we had no choice but to take. But it's only been two weeks. We can't take the chance of blowing her cover—or ours—so soon. We have to give it some time."

Race dropped down in the chair next to the wobbly desk in Jake's room. "I know. Sorry, I'm just getting tense with every day that passes with no word from her. Anything could happen out there and we have no way of knowing what's going on. I wish our own investigation would turn up something, but all I keep winding up with are a bunch of dead ends." Race was doing his best to find out what Nic Sabre was up to by tracing his money trail, but whenever he seemed to be getting close to something, the leads would vanish. "Maybe if we had more agents on the case . . ." Race said, voicing his wishful thinking aloud.

"Yeah, one day we'll work for a government that has unlimited resources," Jake said dryly. It was a common complaint: If only we had more people, or if only we had enough equipment for every job. Unfortunately, like every organization, the CIA had to make do with what it could afford. Their boss had taken the preliminary intel on this case seriously enough to assign two agents to it, and had even expanded their budget when Aimee got involved, but without knowing the seriousness of the threat Nic Sabre presented, there was no way he'd approve a request to turn this into a major op.

For now, all they could do was sit around, track down all the leads they could find, and wait . . . even if it meant that Race had to physically restrain himself from taking their boat and getting Aimee the hell off that island.

TWENTY-FIVE

"DID you take something off my desk?" Nic asked, making Aimee jump. She had been playing around with Microsoft Publisher, trying to find just the right format for the index cards that were to be placed in front of each dish at tomorrow evening's party, and her mind had been focused so intently on the task that he'd startled her.

"Pardon me?" she said, squinting up at him in bafflement.

Nic's eyes had that flat look in them they always got when he was angry. He seemed surprised that she was able to read him, but she found it astonishingly easy to do so. "I said, did you take something off my desk? I'm missing something that was there this morning before Josie came home."

Aimee shook her head. "No, I didn't take anything. Even if I'd wanted to, you put everything in the safe. Remember?"

"Of course I remember," Nic said coldly. "I'm having Mrs. Jacobs search your things. If it turns out you're lying . . ." He left the remainder of the sentence unsaid.

Aimee sighed. "Haven't we been through this already, Nic? I understand that you don't trust me—that you don't trust anyone, except perhaps your daughter—but I'm not stupid enough to risk my life for . . . for I don't even know what."

She waved her hands in the air. "What is this mysterious missing item? And what exactly would I do with it if I did have it? Is it worth the amount of money you're paying me? Is it worth my life?"

Nic frowned and licked his lips, crossing his arms over his chest. "I don't know. You tell me."

It was obvious that what she'd said had made him think. To a man like Nic, the only reason to steal information was to use it to make money. The guest list that she'd copied was of no monetary value to anyone. Even the CIA wouldn't pay for the information, although Race and his partner might find it useful in their investigation.

Aimee rolled her eyes heavenward, as if disgusted by his accusation. "Go ahead and search my room. Search here, too. But do you mind if I continue working while you do so? I'd really like to get these cards done before the morning."

Nic continued scowling at her as she turned her attention back to her monitor, treating his threats as if they were mere blustering. Aimee knew they were not, but she suspected that Nic found her refusal to show her fear intriguing. At least she hoped he did.

Without another word, he turned and stomped off down the hallway. She expected to hear his footsteps stop at his office, but they did not, the sound instead fading as he continued down the hall. Aimee swallowed and closed her eyes, silently praying that Josie would find the missing list in her backpack soon. If she didn't . . . if Nic had someone search Aimee's office and they found her hidden stash of notes pinned to the drapes or if Mrs. Jacobs found the greasepaint-smeared nightgown under Aimee's rug . . .

As Nic had done earlier, she let the thought go unfinished.

RAUL Sanchez.

Umar Amin.

Marcelo Mastrioanni.

Josie read off the names written in her father's neat handwriting on a sheet of blue-lined paper. She didn't recognize any of them and had no idea what the list was for. Obviously, it wasn't something meant for her and she had no idea how it had gotten stuck in her backpack. She set it on her nightstand, right in front of the picture of her mom. She'd bring it down and give it to her dad at dinner. It didn't look like anything urgent.

Listlessly, she looked down at her history book. Usually she didn't mind studying. It wasn't like she had a lot of other things to do, and sometimes it was even interesting. Today, though, she couldn't keep her brain from replaying Giselle's comment over and over in her head.

"You're just jealous because I have a mom and you don't."

How could Gi say something like that? It wasn't even close to the truth. Yes, Josie wanted her own mother back, but she had never once been jealous of Giselle because she had a mom.

Giselle didn't understand anything.

Josie sighed. Unfortunately, neither did her dad. When she'd told him what had happened, he hadn't agreed to let Mr. Howe come to their house and make Gi find a tutor of her own. Instead, he'd said that, while Giselle's comment was hurtful, she probably didn't mean for it to come across that way.

He didn't know anything. Giselle had meant to hurt her, Josie knew it. And the thought of having to face her again, to be forced to actually *talk* to her again, made Josie want to throw up.

She needed to talk to Aimee about this. Aimee would know just what to say to make her feel better. But Daddy had told her that she wasn't to bother Aimee when she was working, so Josie would just have to wait until Aimee was finished. Maybe she'd let Josie talk to her while she was getting ready for dinner again. Josie was fascinated with the process of putting on makeup, how a few pots of eye shadow and some liner could transform you from plain to beautiful. It was amazing. Almost like magic.

Until then, however, she'd better get back to studying.

With another sigh, she looked back down at her history book, only to glance up expectantly when she heard noises coming from across the hall in Aimee's room. Maybe Aimee had finished up early.

Pushing her history book aside, Josie hopped down off her bed and raced across the hall, only to stop in the doorway of Aimee's room when she found Mrs. Jacobs on her hands and knees, starting to roll up one corner of the rug beneath Aimee's bed, as if she were searching for something.

"What are you doing?" Josie asked.

Mrs. Jacobs turned to look at her, a startled expression on her face. "Oh, Josie. I didn't realize you were home."

Josie didn't know what to say to that. Obviously, she was home, and besides, that didn't answer her question.

"Uh, I'm just, um, making sure that Leticia did a good job cleaning Ms. Devlin's room," Mrs. Jacobs said, letting the rug fall back into place.

Josie rocked back on her heels. Okay, *whatever*. That didn't make any sense at all. Since when did Leticia start cleaning under the rugs? Josie knew that was the sort of chore that was reserved for the once yearly top-to-bottom cleaning Mrs. Jacobs supervised. Josie had the same feeling she'd had the day she'd first discovered Aimee in the guest wing—something was going on here that nobody would tell her about.

Just like her dad patting her on the head and telling her that Giselle hadn't meant to be mean, Josie felt that everyone around here treated her like some stupid child. She knew that Giselle was being a bitch, she knew that Mrs. Simonds didn't like Aimee, and she knew that Mrs. Jacobs wasn't telling the truth. Suddenly, she realized that Aimee was the only one she trusted not to treat her like a dumb kid. Her tenuous renewal in her faith in her father snapped.

Furious, she spun around and stomped back to her room. As she flung herself on the bed, the piece of paper on her nightstand fluttered to the floor. Josie glared at it. She was sick and tired of everyone keeping secrets from her. Just like those names on that sheet of paper. There was nobody on that list that she knew, and she'd be willing to bet that if she asked Daddy who they were, he'd give her some stupid answer that didn't make any sense but that he just expected her to believe.

Well, she was tired of being treated this way. If they were all going to lie to her when she asked stuff, she was going to start finding out things for herself.

Reaching down, Josie picked up the sheet of paper. She opened her notebook and neatly copied down the names of the people on the list. She knew that if her dad found that piece of paper, he'd take it from her and she wasn't going to risk it.

From now on, he would have to treat her like a grown-up. She would not accept anything less.

AIMEE was putting on mascara when Nic knocked on her bedroom door and called her name. She glanced from the robe hanging on the back of the bathroom door to her body, clad in matching dark blue panties and bra, and decided not to put on the robe. If sex appeal could save her life, she had no qualms about using it.

She pulled the door open just a crack and glanced out, making certain that Nic was alone before opening the door wider.

"Come in," she said, breezily gesturing around the room. "It should be safe. Mrs. Jacobs even checked my underwear drawer."

Nic came in and closed the door, having the grace to look sheepish. "I'm sorry. Josie found the missing document in her backpack. It must have gotten mixed in with her things when she tossed her pack down on my desk."

Aimee placed a hand on her hip and tried to raise one eyebrow, but doubted the move was successful. "Well, well, well. A man who apologizes when he's wrong. Somebody contact the press."

Nic's eyebrow-raising was carried off with a bit more savoir faire. "There's no need for sarcasm. I said I was sorry."

Aimee dropped the hand from her hip. "Sorry, it's just a bit difficult to deal with these constant threats on my life."

Nic seemed weary as he walked across the room and took a seat on the chair next to her bed. He ran a hand through his hair and let out a heavy sigh before saying, "Tell me about it. I can't remember a time when I didn't fear for my life."

Aimee blinked, surprised that Nic had admitted such a thing. Then, because she knew it would be appreciated, she sat down on the edge of the bed and put a hand on Nic's knee. "I know you said you don't want to talk about your childhood, but I'm here if you change your mind."

Nic reached out and took her hand in his, his fingers cool and dry on hers. He gripped her tightly, as if attempting to convey his hurt and pain to her without saying a word. Then he raised her hand to his lips and kissed each of her knuckles in turn. His lips were firm and warm and he watched her with his dark eyes as he turned her hand over and placed a kiss right in the center of her palm.

Aimee swallowed. Uh-oh. It looked as if her plan to use her sex appeal was working just a little too well.

"Thank you," Nic murmured, sliding his hands up her arms to rest beneath her elbows. He was sitting on the edge of the chair, his torso touching her knees.

Geez, what was she going to do if he wanted to have sex with her? The thought of it made her shudder with distaste. She wasn't naïve enough to think that this wasn't going to become an issue. She'd caught the smoldering looks Nic sent her way when she came down to dinner, dressed in the lovely designer gowns that had appeared in her closet, as if out of nowhere. No, she knew that if she were here on the island long enough, she would have to sleep with Nic. There would be no way she could avoid it, no excuse she could give him that would explain why she'd been so flirtatious with him if she had no intention of following through on her implied promise.

Nic leaned in closer, his lips nearly close enough to brush hers. "You seem nervous," he said.

"Two hours ago, you were threatening to kill me and now it appears that you're going to kiss me instead. I think I have a right to be nervous," Aimee said wryly.

She expected Nic to smile, but he didn't, looking at her solemnly instead. "Can I make a proposition?" he asked.

"Uh, certainly," Aimee said, terrified of what exactly that proposition might be.

"If I promise not to threaten you ever again, would you allow me to kiss you?"

Aimee touched the tip of her tongue to her bottom lip in a gesture she didn't mean to be provocative. She was merely stalling for time, but Nic groaned and leaned forward that remaining fraction of an inch and captured her mouth with his own.

Nic was a masterful kisser. He stroked her tongue with his languorously, then lightly nipped her with his teeth. Aimee had to shut off the voice in her head that protested this intrusion. If she could just make this purely physical, keep her soul, her spirit, and her heart out of it, perhaps she could give Nic the response he was looking for.

It's just sex, she told herself, knowing that in order to survive, she had to take morality out of the equation and let pure physical sensation take over.

Then she hit upon an idea. She would simply pretend that Nic was Race. Nic sucked her tongue into his mouth and Aimee moaned, trying to make herself believe that it was Race's lips on hers. But it was impossible. Race was pure, raw passion. Their lovemaking had a tinge of desperation, as if they couldn't wait to strip off everything between them and be joined. Nic was too smooth, too slow, too finessed.

When Nic drew back, his eyes were like the darkest chocolate. "You know I want you," he said.

Aimee drew in a deep shuddering breath and pushed both hands into her hair, smoothing it behind her ears. "I . . . You may find this difficult to believe, but I do not give of myself very easily."

Nic smiled tenderly and took both of her hands in his. "I believe you. Would you at least consider making love with me, then? When the time is right?"

Aimee lowered her gaze, knowing if she didn't that Nic would read the lie in her eyes. "Yes. I'd like that. When the time is right."

Nic squeezed her hands, and Aimee knew instinctively that her refusal to sleep with him had pleased him. *Freaking men,* she thought with disgust. *They want to have sex with you, but if you give in too easily, they think you're a slut. Like what does that make them?* Of course, she didn't say what she was thinking. Nic would probably have had her dumped, bleeding, in the shark-infested ocean before dinner if she had.

He dropped a light kiss on her forehead before scooting back in his chair and letting go of her hands. "I'm looking forward to it," he said with a smooth smile. Then his face took on a more serious expression. "By the way, I didn't come up here just to try to seduce you."

Aimee was suddenly feeling a bit too underdressed, so she slid off the bed and padded to the bathroom, where she took the terry cloth robe off its hook and belted it around her waist.

It was lined inside with a satiny cloth that caressed her skin. As Aimee put her hands in the pockets, she noted that they were lined with the same material. She'd give it to Nic, he sure did know about the finer things in life.

"Oh?" she asked, coming back to perch on the edge of her bed.

"No, although it was certainly my most pleasurable reason." Nic grinned at her and Aimee was struck again by how handsome he was. He should have considered a career in Hollywood . . . although from what she'd heard about actors, he was probably safer as an arms dealer.

Aimee smiled back at him, wondering what he was going to ask her to do. She might have to sleep with him, but she wasn't killing anyone. She'd damn well take her chances with the sharks if that was what he wanted her to do.

"Could you take Josie and Giselle into Longport tomorrow?" he asked.

Her jaw nearly dropped to the floor. He was going to let her off the island? She tried not to show her delight as she answered, "Yes, of course. But why?"

"Josie enjoys going into town and if Giselle goes, too, they'll be forced to spend time together. Perhaps they'll make up."

Aimee wasn't so sure. She had heard about what Giselle had said to Josie, and she'd be willing to bet that it would be a while before Josie could either forgive or forget Giselle's mean-spirited dig. But she would have been an idiot to say so. "That's a fabulous plan," she said instead, biting the inside of her cheek to contain her glee. "If you don't mind, I could even take the cards I designed today down to a copy shop and get them printed out on heavy paper stock. I was worried about how I was going to get them to stand up."

Nic shrugged as if to say he couldn't care less. "There's a self-service copy shop just off of Anderson Street, about two blocks from the marina. I've used them before when I've needed things copied and bound. I have an account there."

"Great, then I can kill two birds with one stone," Aimee said, then added, "Getting the girls back on even footing *and* taking care of some business," just in case her statement needed clarification.

"Yes. Now, I'll let myself out and allow you to finish dressing for dinner," Nic said, standing up and walking toward the door. Aimee started for the bathroom, but stopped when Nic turned in the doorway to say, "Oh, and Aimee?"

"Yes?" she asked, gritting her teeth. If he told her one more time that he'd kill her if she slipped up, she might actually kill *him*.

"There's a boutique just off the beach called Roxanne's. I also have an account there. Feel free to buy yourself some things and . . ." He paused.

"And?" Aimee prompted.

"And buy something fabulous to wear tomorrow evening. I can't wait to show you off," he said, and then, with an enigmatic smile, he was gone.

TWENTY-SIX

AIMEE forced herself not to look around nervously as she popped the disk into her computer and opened her desktop publishing program. She was supposed to meet Josie and Giselle out at the dock in half an hour. Fortunately, she was prepared—or very nearly so—to leave.

With a surreptitious glance out into the hallway, she hurriedly pushed her chair over to the curtains and fumbled with the safety pin holding her bag of hidden treasurers. Her hands trembled and her fingers were clammy.

So much for nerves of steel.

Finally, the bag came loose. Aimee rolled her chair back into place and sat down. Raine had taken both her and Daphne over and over how to bypass a system's keystroke logger, knowing that it might one day come in handy to know how to do such a thing.

"You have no idea," Aimee muttered, silently thanking her partner. Bringing the notes themselves was too risky. She had nowhere to hide them, unless she wanted to stake her life on the old "down the panties" trick again. Since her relationship with Nic had progressed to the touchy-feely stage, she wasn't willing to chance it. All he'd have to do would be to pull her to him and hear the telltale crinkling of paper to know something was amiss. And stuffing them in her purse didn't seem very smart, either. For all she knew, Nic was using this supposed outing as a trap. It made sense. He fooled her into believing he trusted her with his daughter and she got cocky and—wham!—the noose jerked tight around her neck.

No, she had to be smarter than that.

Once the spyware was disabled, Aimee opened a blank word processing document. She kept her Publisher file open so she could instantly close her Word document and make it seem that she was working on the index cards if someone suddenly came into her office. With the notes in her lap, she started typing, trying to keep her eyes on the hallway and on her computer screen all at once, which made her dizzy. Of course, it could have been the fear that was making her lightheaded. She couldn't be sure.

She entered all of the notes that she'd taken over the last two weeks. Anything she'd seen or overheard that seemed to be important, she'd jotted down on Post-its and hidden in her plastic bag. With shaking hands, Aimee finished typing the last name on Nic's guest list and shoved the handful of yellow sticky notes back into the Ziploc bag just as she heard Nic's voice from outside.

Oh, shit! What was she going to do with these?

Quickly, she closed and saved the Word document so Nic wouldn't be able to see it on her screen when he came in. Then, looking around desperately for a hiding place, she stood up, stuck her index finger under the rim of a heavy oil painting on the wall across from her desk, and slipped the bag beneath the frame. The picture made a slight banging noise as it came back to rest against the wall and Aimee cringed.

If Nic had heard that, what was she going to do? Bang the wall and say, "Mice"?

Right. Like he'd believe that.

She twisted back toward the door as Nic walked in. "Good morning," he said.

"Good morning," Aimee said back, sticking her sweaty palms into the back pockets of the white denim shorts she was wearing.

"You and the girls leaving soon?" he asked.

"Yes." She glanced at her watch as if she wasn't perfectly aware of the seconds ticking by. "In about three minutes. I was just finishing up some things."

"Ah. Well, I'll leave you to it, then. Have a good time."

Nic waved and continued down the hall to his own office. Aimee immediately jerked her hands out of her pockets and sat back down. She clicked on the seventh page of her Publisher document and opened a new text box. Then she selected *insert text file* and grabbed the Word file from her desktop. She highlighted the text that appeared and changed the font color to white.

Next, she clicked on the text box and resized it until it was just the tiniest dot on her document, nearly invisible when she deselected the box. Then, finally, she moved another object on top of the tiny text box, making it completely disappear.

With only another minute until she was supposed to meet Josie and Giselle at the boat, Aimee reactivated the keyboard logger before closing Publisher and moving her document onto her disk. As a last measure, she went back into her Word document, deleted the notes she'd typed earlier (knowing that the keyboard logger would only log the fact that she'd typed *delete* and not record the actual text she'd deleted as well), and then typed some meaningless notes to herself just in case anyone opened the document while she was gone, then saved and closed the file.

Quickly, she shut her computer down, grabbed the disk from the disk drive, and shoved it into her purse.

Houston, we have liftoff, she thought triumphantly as she turned toward the door.

And felt her heart drop to her toes when she saw Diana Simonds standing in the doorway, watching her every move.

"So, what's on the disk?" Diana asked, her voice dripping with forced nonchalance.

"Just some recipe cards I designed for the party tonight," Aimee answered, slipping the strap of her purse over her shoulder.

"Could I take a look at it?"

Aimee let out an exaggerated sigh. "Diana, I don't have time for this. I'm supposed to be meeting the girls at the boat in—" She looked at her watch again as if she didn't know exactly what time it was. "One minute ago."

"This won't take long. I just want to take a quick look."

Aimee debated her options. She could refuse, which would just make Diana even more suspicious. She could make a scene and drag Nic into the matter, which would only make it seem that she was trying to hide something. Or, she could give the disk to Diana and take her chances. Diana would have to know exactly where to look—and what to look for—in order to find the hidden text box.

"Be my guest," Aimee said, pulling the disk out of her purse and holding it out to Diana.

Diana didn't say anything as she took the disk and rebooted Aimee's computer, but the silence between them spoke volumes. They did not like each other. Diana had made it clear that she didn't trust Aimee or her motives when it came to Nic and Josie. Aimee couldn't really fault her for that, since she *was* here to spy on Nic. But Diana's open hostility did make Aimee's job more difficult.

Diana slipped the disk into the drive and looked up at Aimee with a sly smile that said "gotcha." Aimee leaned against the doorjamb and twisted one hand around to look at her fingernails. She was overdue for a manicure. Perhaps she'd take the girls in to get manis and pedis. That was always something she'd enjoyed doing, even at their age.

Aimee studied the nails on her other hand, refusing to watch what Diana was doing. Feigning disinterest seemed to be the best course of action, although it wasn't easy to keep her attention focused on her cuticles when Diana held Aimee's life in her hands.

After what sounded like an awful lot of mouse-clicking, Diana finally blew out a frustrated breath and popped the disk out of the drive.

"All right, this looks clean. But remember, one of these days, you *will* slip up . . . and when you do, I'll be there to catch you," Diana warned, shoving the disk under Aimee's nose.

Aimee resisted the urge to say, "Ooh, I'm scared," because that seemed like something Josie might say. Instead, she merely gave Diana a mysterious smile and a shrug that Aimee knew would piss her off. Then she put the disk back in her purse and walked down the hall, waving good-bye to Nic as she passed the open door of his office.

It wasn't until she was outside, with the warm breeze teasing the ends of her hair and blowing strands of it into her eyes, that Aimee let out a deep shuddering breath. Damn, that had been close.

Now, to get off this cursed island and get this information to Race. Her stomach did a little leap at the thought of seeing him again. She had tried remembering what he'd looked like when they first met, the real Race hidden beneath those thick glasses and the boring suits he wore. But she couldn't stop seeing him as he'd been the night he came onto the island. It was like trying to believe that Clark Kent was a mild-mannered milquetoast after you already knew he was Superman.

"You're late," Giselle complained as Aimee hopped onto the boat that would take them into Longport.

Aimee, who normally got along with most kids, had taken an instant dislike to Giselle Simonds. Whether it was the girl's biting comments or the whiny tone in her voice that did it, Aimee was constantly tempted to slap a piece of duct tape across the blonde's mouth. She was going to have a hard time encouraging Josie to make peace with Giselle when she couldn't stand the girl herself.

"Yes, I am," Aimee said, refusing to explain herself to some snotty teen. She turned to Josie and gave her a genuine smile. "Hey, Josie. You ready to go?"

Josie smiled back. "Yes, I'm ready."

Aimee nodded at Captain Jack, who climbed upstairs to the cockpit and started the boat's engines. It was a luxurious setup—a main cabin with a full kitchen, dining, and living room, plus three bedrooms and two baths. When she'd asked him about it, Nic said they'd never overnighted on the boat, but that if she was interested in doing so, perhaps that would be something Josie would enjoy, too. Aimee had filed that information away, thinking it might be a useful excuse to get Nic and Josie off the island sometime.

"What do you two want to do while we're in town?" Aimee asked as the boat got under way.

"I need to go to the library," Josie said without sparing a glance at Giselle.

"The library?" Giselle said, wrinkling her nose as if Josie had suggested something distasteful.

Josie responded to Aimee, as if it had been she and not Giselle who had commented. "I have a report due on French customs at the end of the month and, unlike *some* people, I don't like to wait until the last minute to do my homework. I need to go to the library to do some research. Then, I thought we could go shopping. I'd like to buy some lipstick," Josie said, looking up at Aimee with her big dark eyes.

Aimee knew exactly what Josie was getting at and she nodded. "Yes, I think we could do that. I have to go take care of some business at the copy shop first. How about we meet back at the marina at noon? We can go to lunch and then do some shopping. If we have time, maybe we could get our nails done."

Giselle rolled her eyes as if that was the most lame plan ever. "Whatever. I'm going to go to the arcade and see who's there. I don't want to get my stupid nails done."

Despite her dislike of the girl, Aimee didn't feel right just letting her wander around by herself. "I think you two need to stay together," she said.

Giselle just looked at her and then looked away, but Josie nodded.

Aimee and Josie spent the rest of the trip playing checkers while Giselle sulked on the couch. Aimee offered to let Giselle play the winner, but the teen just smacked her gum at Aimee and shook her head.

Aimee tried to recall if she and her sisters had ever been such brats and was willing to concede that they'd had their days. As Giselle continued to smack her gum, Aimee wondered how her parents had managed to not lock herself and her sisters in the closet and refuse to let them out until they were adults.

During the last fifteen minutes of their trip, Aimee was too antsy to sit still, so she and Josie went outside and stood at the back of the boat. Aimee's sense of anticipation grew as they got closer to land. If she wanted to, she could escape. Nic had taken her credit cards and her identification, but if she went to

Race and refused to go back, he'd have no choice but to help her return to America.

But could she do that? She knew the information she had on the disk might be useful, but it was hardly the sort of thing that would crack this case open. She hadn't seen the actual plans for the new weapon, nor did she know where it was being manufactured or who Nic's customers were. All she had were snippets of data—figures and technical expressions she didn't understand—and the guest list for this evening's party. She hoped this would help the CIA piece together a picture of what Nic was up to, but she knew that it wasn't enough and she refused to put Race in the position of having to choose between her safety and the threat to national security. She had a job to do and she was in this game until the end, no matter how tempting it was to walk away.

Her resolve didn't waver as they approached the island, a haven for tourists looking to get away from the more populated city of Townsville. The terrain rose sharply out of the water, but leveled off about twenty feet above sea level. A metal gangplank linked the marina to the mainland. Just beyond the top of the walkway was a heavily trafficked two-lane road that was lined on the non-waterfront side by a row of shops. A restaurant with an open deck was perched above the marina and Aimee shivered as she wondered if Race was there now, watching them come in.

"That's the ice cream shop Gi—" Josie stopped and grimaced, then began again. "The ice cream shop *I* like."

Aimee followed Josie's outstretched hand to see a glass-fronted shop with a giant ice-cream cone painted on the front just across from the chain-link gate leading into the marina. "Why don't we meet there at noon and decide where to go for lunch?" Aimee suggested as Captain Jack expertly piloted the boat into a slip that she assumed was reserved for Nic.

"Okay," Josie agreed, slipping her backpack.

"You coming?" Aimee asked when Giselle remained slouched on the sofa even after the captain turned off the engines.

"I suppose," Giselle muttered, seeming put out.

Aimee rolled her eyes. What a pain in the butt this kid was. "We'll be back at four," she told the captain. The party this evening was to begin at seven. Josie had adamantly refused to spend the night with Giselle, opting to stay at Mrs. Jacobs's house instead. Nic had already had her pack her things and told her he expected her to be out of the house no later than 5:30.

On the return trip, they would be joined by a handful of locals that Mrs. Jacobs had hired to help with serving and cleanup. Captain Jack would be taking them all back when the party was over, since the guesthouses would be filled with partygoers.

Aimee let Josie and Giselle walk in front of her toward the marina's exit as she rummaged in her purse for the lipstick she'd brought down from her bathroom. As she approached the second piling from the exit, she paused for just a second. In one smooth movement, she slashed a bright pink line across the wood and then brought the lipstick to her lips.

As the metal gate slammed shut behind her, Aimee dared a glance back. The bright mark against the piling glowed like a magical crystal with mythical powers. Now all she could do was hope that Race would see it and come to her.

TWENTY-SEVEN

"SHE'S here," was all Race said before hanging up on his partner. It was his shift to watch the monitor that beamed images from the camera they'd placed at the marina and he had clearly seen Aimee pause to mark the signal for them to meet. After two weeks of nearly crawling out of his skin waiting to talk to her again, Race stared at the screen, watching her as if trying to memorize her every move.

For a moment, she looked up, directly into the camera, and Race reached out and touched her soft lips. She turned and spoke to two girls, who both nodded and then set off up the gangplank. Aimee hesitated for a moment, as if waiting for something, then followed the girls.

Race was tying the laces on his boots when Jake tapped on the motel room door. He grabbed his keys from off the top of the dresser before opening the door. "I'm on it," he said, not giving his partner time to volunteer to tail Aimee. No way was he going to let Jake take over now.

"Be careful," Jake shouted after him as he headed across the yellowed lawn and toward the street.

Race waved a hand to let his partner know he got the message, then sprinted down the sidewalk in pursuit of Aimee.

* * *

"I don't want to go to the library," Giselle said as soon as Aimee had turned down a side street and left her and Josie alone.

Josie tightened the left strap of her backpack and refused to look at her former best friend as she stubbornly kept walking down the street toward the off-white building that housed the city's public computers. There was no way she was going to let Giselle win this battle, no matter how much of a fit she threw.

"I don't want to go there," Giselle repeated, stopping in the middle of the sidewalk.

Josie shrugged and kept walking. "Then don't."

"But we have to stay together. You heard what Aimee said."

"I don't care. I told her I was going to the library and that's where I'll be. If you decide to go somewhere else, that's up to you." By the end of her speech, Josie was nearly shouting.

She didn't know what Giselle had to say to that, because she reached the library entrance and went in before Giselle could speak. "So there," she muttered under her breath, knowing it was childish but unable to stop herself.

She opened the second set of glass doors and walked through the sensors, taking a deep breath as she stepped into the main room of the library. Josie loved the library, the way it was so quiet, so orderly. She even loved the way it smelled like old paper and cleanser. She almost never left without a giant armload of books, but today, instead of heading toward the stacks, she went upstairs where the computers were located.

Shrugging off her backpack, Josie sat down and took out her notebook. She flipped to the page where she had written down the list of names she'd found in her bag last night. Looking at the first name, she chewed on her bottom lip. Maybe she shouldn't do this. She knew her father was a good man. He couldn't be such a great dad if he wasn't, right? And this list, it could be a list of anything. Even if these were bad people, that didn't mean her father was one of them. Maybe it meant the opposite—that he was a cop or something. Hmm. Yes, maybe that was it. That would explain his frequent trips and the way he was so secretive about his job. Perhaps he was an undercover spy.

Josie laughed and shook her head at herself. That was silly. Mr. Howe often told her that she had quite an imagination, and she was letting it run away with her now. She'd most likely find out that the people on this list were the CEOs of companies or politicians. That made a lot more sense.

She scooted her chair closer to the computer and opened the Internet browser, pointing it to www.google.com. Then she typed in the first name on her list, using quotations to make sure the search engine looked up the whole phrase.

The results were returned almost instantaneously. Josie clicked the first link, which took her to a story from the *London Times* dated less than two weeks ago. "Guerrilla Group Storms Presidential Palace," read the headline. She skimmed the article. This Raul Sanchez was the leader of some group determined to overthrow the democratic government in his country. The group had broken into the president's home and assassinated him, then went through the house and rounded up the man's family. According to a maid who had been hiding in a closet, the guerrillas brought the family together and then killed them, one by one, leaving the president's wife for last. The mother was forced to watch her five children being tortured and shot. When the rebels got to the last child, a six-year-old girl, and started raping her, the mother grabbed the gun of the man holding her and had tried to kill herself, but failed. Instead, she lay there bleeding, watching as the soldiers raped her little girl to death.

Josie hadn't realized that she'd started crying until she came to the end of the article. No. This monster, this Raul Sanchez, couldn't be someone her father associated with. He just couldn't be.

She wiped her eyes and clicked the back button on the browser. Scrolling down, she looked for another reference to the man, one that didn't associate him with the guerrilla group. But she couldn't find one.

Josie moved on to the second name on the list, hoping with everything in her that her search would turn up nothing. She closed her eyes as she clicked "Search."

She breathed a sigh of relief when she opened her eyes to see that Umar Amin was the owner of an art gallery in New Mexico. *See,* she told herself, *this is silly. You just got the wrong Raul Sanchez on the first search.* After all, it wasn't like everyone the world could be found on Google.

Moving her finger down the page, Josie entered the next name on the list and then frowned when she saw multiple references to this man and a drug cartel in Bogotá, Colombia. She entered the next name and then the next and the next. Finally, she sat back, staring at the computer screen as if transfixed.

Drug dealers, guerrilla leaders, dictators, and thieves. Those were the people on her father's list.

With trembling fingers, Josie did one last search, typing "Nic Sabre" into the blank box.

There wasn't much. Only one article from the *New York Times*. But it said that her father was a "suspected arms dealer."

Josie tried to refute the evidence, tried to think of some reason why her dad would have a list of these people. The thought that he was secretly a spy for the government, that he knew these awful people because he was pretending to be one of them in order to catch them, gripped her. She wanted to believe this so badly, needed to believe that the arms dealer stuff was just her father's cover and not what he really did for a living. It just . . . it just couldn't be. If this were true, how could she ever trust her father again? How could she trust anything or anyone ever again?

AIMEE looked up from the printer when the door to the copy shop jingled open. Her heart seemed to stop, then started again at triple its normal pace when Race walked in. He breezed past her and she closed her eyes for a moment and inhaled his familiar scent. He stopped at the copy machine next to hers and slipped something in the document feeder.

"Can you talk?" he said quietly.

"Yes, but they know Nic here, so we've got to be careful," Aimee answered.

Race nodded and pulled his wallet out of the back pocket of his jeans. Aimee's document continued to print as he took out a credit card and fed it into the slot. When the green light came on, he pressed the start button to begin his copy job.

Aimee watched him out of the corner of her eyes. He had

on blue jeans and worn tan boots and a burgundy T-shirt, and she couldn't help thinking that he was just about the most handsome man she'd ever seen.

"How are you?" he asked, the question loaded with much more than its usual empty meaning.

Aimee took a deep breath, her chest suddenly tight with the urge to be comforted. The temptation to turn and bury her face in Race's shirt and let him hold her and tell her it was going to be all right was so strong that she had to grip the edge of the printer to stop herself from doing just that.

She had to swallow several times before she was able to form an answer. "I'm okay," she said. "Unless letting me off the island is just another test, Nic seems to have gained some measure of trust in me. I'm here with Josie and her friend, Giselle. Nic's hosting a cocktail party this evening and I believe I saw the guest list, although I won't be certain of that until I meet everyone tonight."

"He's letting you attend?" Race asked, sounding surprised.

Aimee nodded, not sure she really wanted to tell her lover that Nic had asked her to sleep with him. Then, because she wasn't sure she could handle his response—what if he encouraged her to have sex with Nic to get information out of the other man? Or if he was disgusted at the idea and then found out later that she'd had to do exactly that in order to stay alive?—she decided it would be best to keep her own counsel on the matter. "I've proven to be very effective as Nic's administrative assistant. I organized the party and I believe Nic is seeing how useful it is to have someone around to take care of the details."

"Then you don't want my help to get you out?" Race asked.

He was giving her a chance to escape, but, as much as she might want to be done with this case, she couldn't do it. Squaring her shoulders with resolve, Aimee replied, "No. I'm in this until it's over."

Race started to reach out a hand out to her, but stopped when he realized what he was about to do. Being near her but unable to touch her was agony. "Have you learned anything that might help us?" he asked, attempting to shove his personal feelings aside for the good of this case.

Aimee's job had finished printing, so she took the sheets of heavy card stock off the printer and tapped their edges to get them into a neat stack. Then, with a glance at the copy center employee running a large job behind the counter, Aimee slid the disk with her document on it over to Race.

"Page seven," she said cryptically.

Race smoothly palmed the disk and slipped it into his back pocket. Then, because he knew if he continued standing so close to her for one more second, he'd throw caution and procedure and thirteen years of training out the window, he shot her one final look full of desire and longing and pain, grabbed his credit card out of the copy machine, and turned toward the door.

Aimee refused to watch him go, although it felt as if he were taking her very soul with him. Instead, she forced herself to turn around, to take one step and then another toward the paper cutter on the counter a few feet away.

And, because her eyes were clouded with tears, she missed seeing the girl standing outside on the sidewalk, watching the man who held Aimee's heart in his hands glance back toward the copy shop one more time before walking away.

TWENTY-EIGHT

"I saw Aimee with a man today," Giselle announced as she entered her mother's bedroom and flopped down on the bed.

Diana pulled the black eyeliner away from her eye and straightened to look at her daughter. "Pardon me?"

"I saw Aimee with a man today," Giselle repeated, slower this time, as if her mother was a bit mentally impaired.

"What do you mean by 'with'?" Diana asked, narrowing her eyes. If Giselle meant *with* with, maybe she could convince Nic to get rid of the other woman for good. Diana didn't trust Aimee Devlin, and her being here jeopardized them all. But for some reason, Nic was smitten. Aimee had somehow managed to make him think that she was like them, but Diana sensed that something wasn't right with the other woman. Something about Aimee set off tiny alarm bells in Diana's brain, and she knew better than to discount that feeling. It had saved her life on more than one occasion.

"They were in the copy shop together," Giselle answered, throwing a bucket of ice water on Diana's hopes.

"Oh," she said disappointedly, turning back to the mirror to finish her makeup.

"She gave him a disk. I saw her hand it to him. And when

he left, he kept looking back at her, as if they knew each other and he didn't want to go."

The eyeliner fell from Diana's nerveless hand into the sink with a clatter. "You saw her hand him a disk?"

Giselle smugly crossed her arms over her chest. "Yes. He put it into his back pocket."

"You're sure? You're not just making this up to upset Josie?"

Her daughter shot her a disgusted look. "Of course I'm not making it up, Mother."

Diana held her palms up in the air. "Okay, I'm sorry. I just had to make sure. What else did you see?"

"Nothing. That's it. I went to find Aimee to tell her that Josie refused to go to the arcade with me and she was there at the copy place talking to this guy. They looked kind of funny, you know, like when you like a guy and you want to talk to him, but he makes you kind of nervous?"

"Um-hmm," Diana answered. Yes, she knew that feeling well. She felt it every time Nic Sabre was around.

"That's how Aimee looked. Nervous. They talked for a little while and she gave him the disk and then he left."

"Did either of them see you?" Diana asked.

Giselle shook her head, her soft blond curls dusting the tops of her shoulders. "No. I kind of stepped back into a doorway when the man came out of the shop. I . . . I don't know why I did that. It just seemed like I shouldn't let him see me."

"That's good," Diana said, pacing the floor, her brow wrinkling as she thought. What was she going to do with this information? She looked at her watch. It was 6:30. Half an hour until the party was to start. If she was going to confront Aimee about this, she'd better hurry.

"Would you get my dress out of the closet?" she asked, hurrying back into the bathroom to finish putting on her makeup. By the time Giselle returned with her knee-length cocktail dress, Diana was done with her makeup and was brushing out her hair.

"Thank you, honey," she said, taking the hanger from her daughter. "You were right to tell me about this," she added.

Giselle smiled up at her, looking like an angel with her blue eyes and blond hair. "I don't like Aimee being here, either.

Since she's been here, Josie seems . . . I don't know. Different, I guess."

Diana slipped on her dress and turned around so Giselle could zip her up while she slid on her shoes. Then she turned around, patted her daughter's shoulder, and said, "Well, you won't have to worry about it much longer. I intend to get rid of Aimee Devlin if it's the last thing I do."

"YOU look lovely," Nic said as Aimee stepped off the last stair and onto the main floor of the house. He had watched her descent, his dark eyes gleaming appreciatively.

Aimee had spared no expense on this dress, especially since it was going on Nic's tab. It was a floor-length, sleeveless red number, made of a fabric that clung to her in all the right places. When she turned to show him the back, Nic's eyes widened because there was no back. Instead, the dress scooped down to the base of her spine, her tattoo covered by a wide red bow.

"Very nice," Nic murmured, putting a hand on the bare skin at the small of her back.

"Ah, just the people I wanted to see," Diana Simonds said, wafting out of the living room with a martini in her hand.

"Diana," Aimee said coolly, wishing that she, too, had a drink.

"What can we do for you?" Nic asked, sounding distracted as his fingers lightly trailed up Aimee's spine.

Aimee shivered and sent Nic a flirtatious glance from under her lashes. If she was going to do battle with Diana once again, she wanted Nic firmly on her side.

"Where is the disk you took into town with you today?" Diana asked bluntly, mercilessly spearing the olive in the bottom of her glass.

"Excuse me?" Aimee asked, feigning confusion. Damn. How had Diana found out about the disk?

"The disk. You know, the one you had in your purse this morning. Where is it?"

Aimee squinted, as if trying to retrace her steps. She couldn't lie and say she'd brought it back, because she didn't have any other disks in her desk. It had been like pulling Milk

Duds off of dentures trying to get the one she had from Nic. "I must have left it at the copy shop," she said. "Now that you mention it, I don't remember taking it out of the disk drive when I was done with my print job. How stupid of me." She shook her head as if annoyed at herself.

"Giselle says she saw you hand the disk to a man. Perhaps you'd like to tell us what exactly was on that disk?"

The tinkling laugh Aimee gave was worthy of an Oscar. Inwardly, her knees were shaking, but outwardly, she gave the impression of being completely unaffected by the bomb Diana had just dropped. "That's ridiculous. There was nothing on that disk except for a bunch of notecards. I certainly wouldn't have given it to anyone. Even if it had 'fallen into the wrong hands' "—Aimee put two fingers of each hand in the air to mime quotation marks—"it's not like it contained any vital information. It was just a bunch of translations of the items on tonight's menu."

Diana stepped closer, her eyes hard and deadly. "You're a liar."

Aimee gasped, as if shocked at the accusation. Too bad it was the truth. "Look, I don't know what game your daughter is playing or why, but I swear, I did not give that disk to anyone." She turned to Nic, laying a hand on his arm. "This is all some silly story Giselle is making up to discredit me. I think she's jealous because Josie likes me and she's used to having Josie all to herself."

Nic nodded. That was certainly a plausible conclusion. Giselle *was* the type to make up stories in order to get what she wanted.

"If she left the disk at the copy shop, why don't you give them a call, Nic? It should still be there, right? It's not like the place gets a lot of business."

Aimee blinked and clenched her teeth. Geez, Diana was tenacious. "Well, it's possible that someone might have taken it after I left," she said, trying to give a reason why the disk wasn't there in anticipation of the phone call she was certain Nic would make for Diana's benefit.

Nic looked from Diana to Aimee and back again before slowly nodding. "All right. I will call. But if the disk is there, do you promise to stop this witch hunt? I can't tell you how tedious it is to have you two at each other's throats all the time."

A vein in Diana's forehead throbbed and it looked as if she were clenching her teeth as tightly as Aimee was, but she managed to say, "Yes. If the disk is there, I will put aside my doubts and do my best to be pleasant from now on."

Nic turned to Aimee, who dipped her chin in acquiescence. She knew that, while the absence of a disk wouldn't prove her guilty, it would reopen a tiny gap of doubt about her in Nic's mind.

Well, there was nothing she could do about it now. She hadn't had the money to buy a second disk to copy the file onto and had thought about asking Josie for some cash before they left the boat, but hadn't wanted to try to explain to the girl why she had no money. Then she had weighed the risk of putting a pack of disks on Nic's account and decided that the chances of anyone actually realizing she had returned without the disk were less than him seeing this charge show up on his account. She could have asked Race to buy a disk and make a copy of the file, but that, too, had seemed riskier than just giving the disk to him. The longer they were together, the greater their chances of being seen. So, she had taken a gamble and lost.

As they walked down the hall toward Nic's office, Aimee hoped she would not have to pay for the mistake with her life.

"THIS guy associates with some real scumbags," Jake said, aiming the parabolic dish toward the well-lit house a thousand feet away. The listening device looked like a satellite dish, only it had a microphone sticking out from the center like the pistil of a lily. The device allowed them to overhear and record the noise from the party. Later, a sound specialist would isolate specific voices and conversations and tell them if the intelligence they had gathered would be of any use in their investigation. Even now, they could pick out certain voices and words, although most sounds jumbled together, making it difficult to follow what any one person was saying.

Race adjusted the headphones over his ears, increasing the volume in his right ear. He kept the sound low in his left ear so he could still hear what was going on around them. Their boat was anchored just outside the entrance to the harbor of Sabre's island, as far away as they could get and still be able to pick up an audio signal from the party going on onshore. Both he and Jake knew it was only a matter of time before they were spotted. There was no way a man with Nic Sabre's reputation would neglect his security on a night like this.

After seeing what they all assumed was the guest list for this evening's party, they had received approval from the Agency to conduct audio surveillance on the island. Sabre's guest list read like a who's who of the criminal world—drug traffickers, terrorists, dictators, and guerrilla leaders. Of course, who else would an arms dealer throw a party for?

Race scowled as he picked out the sound of Aimee's laughter from the cacophony of voices coming over his headphones. He wished he could see her, but they'd already figured out that the long-range binoculars they'd brought were useless. The party was being held inside the house, away from prying eyes. But, fortunately, not away from prying ears.

"That's the third mention I've heard of the LoRS bomb Aimee referred to in her notes," Race said.

Jake nodded shortly and fiddled with the volume on his own headset. "Hopefully we'll get some information on it tomorrow."

They'd sent Aimee's notes to the analyst supporting their mission this afternoon. Almost immediately, she'd sent back dossiers on the people attending the party, with a note that some of the other information they'd sent would take a bit more time to research. They were particularly interested in what the analyst uncovered about the LoRS bomb. Race suspected it was the new weapon Sabre intended to manufacture.

"Damn, it looks like our party's over," Jake said, yanking his headphones off as he jerked his chin in the direction of an approaching motorboat, its engine buzzing like an angry mosquito.

Without another word, they scrambled to dismantle and stow their surveillance gear. Not many fishermen used listening devices to detect underwater sea life.

As the larger boat pulled up beside them, Race cracked open a beer. The bottle was raised halfway to his lips when a bright light was shined into his face, blinding him. Race played along, putting up a hand to shield his eyes and protesting, "Hey, turn that off. Are you trying to blind me?"

"Who are you?" a man asked, not lowering the light.

"What the hell is it to you?" Jake said, sounding even more pissed off than his partner.

"This is private property. You need to leave."

The man switched off the light and Race blinked, trying to get his vision back. It was easy playing the part of an indignant fisherman. They were well within public property and these assholes had no right chasing them off. "We're just fishing, and I'm certain we're not trespassing," he said.

"Look," a very large, dark-skinned man said, stepping close to the railing of the other boat. "We can do this the easy way or the hard way. It's my job to keep trespassers off this property and I intend to do it. You can either go peacefully or . . ." The man shrugged and let his voice trail off. When two more six-and-a-half-foot mutants stepped out of the shadows and joined the man at the railing, Race figured he'd made his point.

"We were told this is a great place to catch snapper," Jake said, refusing to give up too easily.

"Yeah, well, find another spot," one of the mutants said, pounding one fist into his palm menacingly.

"Come on. Let's go," Race said to Jake in order to give the impression that he was afraid to fight. He didn't know if he'd ever run into these goons again, but if he did, he wanted them to think that he was the kind of guy who backed down from confrontation. The truth was, he and Jake could take these guys if necessary. But for the moment, it wouldn't do their case any good to do so, so they backed off.

Mumbling like the weak kid who had just got sand kicked in his face by the playground bully, Jake reeled in the line he'd dropped earlier as a cover. Only, when he did, there was a sudden tug and the *zzzz* sound of his line being taken by a fish.

"I got one," Jake said, and Race nearly laughed at the surprised look on his partner's face.

One of the thugs pulled out a vicious-looking hunting knife, its silver blade playfully catching the light of the moon. With one swift movement, he cut Jake's line and said, "Get the fuck out of here."

Jake seemed genuinely angry now. "You asshole. I had a fish

on the line," he said, getting right up to the side of the boat, as if readying himself to board the larger craft.

The goon laughed and grabbed the front of Jake's shirt, sticking the tip of his knife right between Race's partner's eyes. Race's hand went to his own weapon, a Glock 9mm pistol that would blow a nice-sized hole in the other man's forehead. Race noticed that Jake, too, had a grip on his gun, and relaxed. This confrontation was all for show.

"All right, all right. There's no need for violence. We're leaving," Jake said, his voice shaking.

Race slowly reached out and turned the key in the ignition to make their boat's engine sputter to life. Keeping one hand on his gun, he held the other up as if in surrender. "Yeah, we're outta here," he said, easing the transmission into gear.

Sabre's thug held on to the front of Jake's shirt until he either had to let go or risk pulling his arm out of his socket. He chose to let go, leaving Jake indignantly smoothing the front of his stretched out T-shirt.

When they were out of earshot, Jake turned to him with a wide grin on his face. "Good job," he said.

But Race, who was looking back at the jerks standing on their boat watching he and Jake leave, had the sudden urge to turn around and engage their enemy. He had spent the first half of his life getting pushed around by bullies like that.

TWENTY-NINE

"ISOLATING a specific voice can be a tedious process, but the results are worth it. Here's how I did it . . ."

Race rubbed his forehead, attempting to control his impatience as the sound technician told them much more than they needed to know about his job. Never before had he felt such a keen desire for a case to be completed. This waiting was driving him insane.

"Did you find out any information about the LoRS bomb?" Race interrupted the lengthy speech the audio tech had launched into. "What it does? Where it's being manufactured? Anything?"

The man didn't seem surprised to have been interrupted. Race figured it probably happened all the time. "Well, not really. I mean, it was mentioned specifically several times on the tape, but not with any details that seemed relevant. Of course, you can judge that for yourself. I've e-mailed the transcript to you both."

Race looked over at his partner, who looked as glum as Race felt. "All right, thanks," he said, reaching out to end the telephone call, only to stop when the technician continued.

"There *was* one thing I thought was odd," the man said.

"Yes?"

"A date was mentioned several times by different people. Let me see. Yes, here it is," the technician said, and after what sounded to be the rustling of some papers, he named a date two weeks hence.

"That's it?" Jake asked. "Just a date? Nothing else?"

"I'm afraid so."

"So, we don't know the significance of this date—what might happen or where?" Race clarified, just to make sure he understood.

"Nope. That's all we got," the technician answered.

Race scowled at Jake as he hung up the phone. "We've got nothing," they said in unison.

THERE was a subtle shift in Nic's attitude after the night of the cocktail party. Aimee couldn't quite put her finger on exactly what it was, but even though she couldn't identify it, she was grateful for the change. If she were forced to explain it, she'd probably say it was a slight easing of tension, as if he still wasn't ready to trust her completely, but had taken that first step to at least believing that one day he might.

Aimee guessed it had started the moment he called the copy service and was told that, yes, they had found a disk that a customer had left in one of the computers. When they scanned the contents of the disk, they found Aimee's file.

She had been relieved—and grateful—for Race's foresight. She had no idea why he had thought to bring the disk back, but it had been a brilliant way to cover her tracks and she appreciated it. For the past week, Diana had remained true to her promise to lay off of Aimee, but Aimee did not for one second believe that Diana was giving up completely. She was too convinced that something about Aimee was not as it seemed.

Fortunately, Nic didn't appear to share Diana's concerns, and, while he didn't go so far as to give Aimee the combination to his safe, he did stop shutting his laptop and sweeping documents off his desk the moment she came into his office. Aimee had tried several times to get him to leave her alone in his office so she could photograph some of these documents, but, so far, he hadn't relaxed enough for that.

As she had every morning, Aimee quietly padded down the hall toward her and Nic's offices, hoping that today would be the day she caught him off guard. She had taken to not wearing shoes—one of the joys of working in a home office—so she made almost no sound as she walked. As she approached Nic's office, she heard him talking and strained to hear what was being said.

"Yes, tomorrow night is the big night," Nic said.

Apparently, he was on the telephone, because he paused for a moment and then said, "And you're certain you can have it delivered to me by then?"

There was another burst of silence and Aimee slowed her steps. What was happening tomorrow night? Did it have something to do with the new weapon? This was so frustrating, being so close to the information Race needed, but unable to obtain it. Over and over in her mind, she'd considered different plans to break into Nic's office and try to steal his documents. The thing was, she was no safecracker. That wasn't exactly a skill they taught you at Quantico. And since Nic never left his office without securing his files and his computer in the safe, then locking the door itself, that left her with no options except to wait and hope that he would relax his guard just long enough for her to take advantage of his lapse.

"See that it is," Nic said, his voice clearly full of warning that if the person on the other end of the line didn't come through as promised, there would be dire consequences. Then there was a soft beep as Nic ended the call.

Aimee paused for as long as she dared, then began walking again. "Good morning," she said, stopping to poke her head into Nic's office and give him a wave of greeting.

Nic smiled at her and leaned back in his chair, looking more relaxed than Aimee had ever seen him. "Good morning. Did you sleep well?"

"Yes, fabulously well. How could I not after the dinner we had last night? If your chef doesn't stop making such delicious meals, I fear I'm going gain twenty pounds before another month has passed."

Nic stood up and gestured for her to come in and take a seat. "Then you wouldn't mind remaining here for another month?" he asked, coming to lean on the edge of his desk, his long legs crossed at the ankle. Today, he was wearing ecru linen trousers and a light blue silk shirt—the sort of look only a man with Nic's absolute self-confidence could pull off.

Aimee smoothed her brightly colored pants across her knees as she sat down in front of him. "Mind? Heavens, no. I adore it here," she lied, crossing her legs.

Nodding, Nic's expression turned more serious. "I adore having you here," he said softly.

Swallowing her reluctance, Aimee reached out a hand and laid it on top of Nic's knee. "I'm glad. I've grown very fond of you . . . and of Josie." The latter, at least, was true, although Josie had been spending quite a lot of time in her room lately. Aimee figured her latest fight with Giselle was affecting Josie more than she'd like to admit, but whenever she asked Josie if she wanted to talk, the girl just shook her head, her large dark eyes filling with tears. Still, Josie was an easy child to like. They'd taken to walking the beach every night before dinner and Aimee's heart had constricted when the girl had tentatively taken her hand, obviously seeking comfort. Thinking back to her own early teen years, Aimee remembered the push/pull way she had felt about her own parents. On the one hand, they drove her crazy with their rules and overprotective warnings—since she was the oldest, they had no experience with letting one of their babies grow up—and most of the time, she just wanted them to go away and let her act like the adult she thought she was becoming. On the other hand, there were plenty of times she longed to climb into bed with them again as she had as a child and feel her mother's arms around her and be comforted.

"She's become quite attached to you, too," Nic said, interrupting Aimee's thoughts. She didn't want to think about what would happen to Josie when Nic was caught. If she let herself care too much, she would lose focus on her mission, a mission with repercussions far beyond the life of one lonely twelve-year-old.

"So, do you have a list of things you like me to do today?" Aimee asked, turning the conversation to business because it hurt her to think about Josie.

"Has anyone ever told you you're quite the taskmaster?" Nic asked with a slight smile playing about his lips.

"Well, you're not just paying me to sit around looking pretty," Aimee teased with a wink.

Nic leaned forward, his dark eyes intent. Slowly, he ran his fingertips down her arms, making her shiver. "You'd be worth twice as much as I pay you if I were."

Aimee forced herself to laugh, all the while wondering if Race Gardner was the only man who valued her for her brains more than for her looks. It struck her then how much she missed Race, missed the feel of his strong arms around her, missed that he cared enough about her to not want her to take this job, no matter how much it paid. She had to admit, if only to herself, that his "I can do dangerous stuff because I'm a guy but you can't because you're not" attitude was actually kind of cute. As long as he never actually tried to stop her from doing something she needed to do, they'd get along just fine.

"Actually, I do have quite a lot of things to do today that I'd like your help with, but I'll give you a few moments to get settled in first," Nic said, uncrossing his ankles and getting up from his desk.

Aimee stood up and walked to the door of Nic's office, surprised when he followed her out into the hallway. They walked toward her office a few feet away, which Aimee unlocked with her security code.

"I'll see you in about fifteen minutes," Nic said, continuing to walk down the hall.

Aimee held her breath, refusing to look back toward Nic's office. He had finally done it—had neglected to lock his office or even to put his files away while he was in the restroom. Aimee's pulse was racing and her throat closed up as if she'd just swallowed an apple whole. Hurriedly, she flipped on her computer to make it seem as if she'd been working all along and grabbed her gold pen from out of her purse. She had to be quick. If she were lucky, she'd have ten minutes alone in Nic's office. If she wasn't . . . he'd catch her in the act of photographing his documents and this charade would be all over.

AIMEE had just clicked the pen closed and stepped away from Nic's desk, when he appeared in the doorway and announced, "I've got a big surprise for you."

Oh, God. Had he been lurking out in the hallway, listening to her snapping away? Even worse, had he actually seen her looking through the viewfinder? She had hardly even looked at what she was photographing, knowing that time was of the essence. She didn't have the luxury of sorting through things to select the most critical documents. Instead, she'd just snapped photos of everything she could and hoped that Race would find some of it to be useful. Of course, if Nic killed her before she could get the pictures to Race, it really wouldn't matter.

"Oh?" Aimee asked, attempting not to let the fear she was feeling show in her eyes. She backed up a step, until she was trapped against the wall. For some reason, she felt safer that way.

"Yes, but I can't tell you what it is."

Aimee laughed shakily. "Well, it wouldn't be a surprise if you did, right?" she asked.

Nic stepped forward and tapped her lightly on the nose with his index finger. "Exactly. Let's just say it's something I think you'll be very pleased with."

"And when are you planning to reveal this surprise?"

"Tomorrow evening. Be prepared to be dazzled," Nic said with a glaringly white-toothed smile. "Now, let's get down to work. Where's your notepad?"

Aimee shook her head, realizing just then that she had forgotten to bring one. "I must need more coffee. I completely forgot it," she said, walking toward Nic to go to her office and get a pad.

But as she passed, Nic grabbed her arm in a firm grip. Aimee swallowed a gasp of surprise. Had he just been playing cat and mouse with her earlier? Did he suspect what she was up to?

"That's all right," he said, gently pushing her toward the chair in front of his desk. "You can use mine."

THIRTY

JOSIE buried her toes in the warm sand as the sun began to set, its rays tinting the clouds with neon pink. The deep sadness that had filled her ever since that day at the library was beginning to ebb. As awful as the truth had seemed at first, she had, like most people do when faced with such situations, begun to tell herself that it really wasn't that bad. And a small part of her still clung to the hope that it was all a lie—that her father was an undercover cop who only threw parties for those bad people in order to catch them. She was too afraid of finding out this wasn't the case to ask. What would she do if she asked her father about it, only to have him confirm her worst fears?

"Hey, how was your day?" Aimee asked, sitting down next to her on the beach.

Josie had to dig her heels into the sand to resist flinging herself into Aimee's arms. Aimee had become Josie's lifeline to normalcy these past weeks, perhaps because, unlike everyone else Josie knew, Aimee was not part of her father's past.

"Fine," Josie answered, turning her head to look at the older woman. Aimee's hair was down around her shoulders in a silky brown curtain. Unlike Josie's hair, which curled every which way it wanted, Aimee's hair was perfectly straight. Aimee wore a light amount of makeup and had on a pair of colorful pajama-like pants with a white tank top. She looked elegant and confident and Josie wished she could be just like her when she grew up.

"Can I ask you a question?" she said after they'd sat in silence for a while, listening to the sound of the waves lapping against the beach.

"Of course," Aimee answered.

"What do you do when you think that someone you know has done something wrong?"

"If it's something that's going to put them or someone else in danger, you need to tell their parents," Aimee responded carefully, wondering what this was all about.

"No, what I mean is, are you supposed to stop loving them?"

Aimee reached a hand out to squeeze Josie's. She assumed this was Josie's way of trying to make peace with how she felt about Giselle, who said and did some pretty mean things, but was still the only best friend Josie had ever had. "Just because someone does bad things, it doesn't make them a bad person," she said. Wasn't that the current parenting psychobabble? Your kid may do bratty things, but that doesn't make him a brat, right? Right. "Besides, when you love someone, you just love them. No matter what. It's not like you really have a choice," Aimee added.

Josie nodded slowly, her expression serious. "I never thought of it that way, but you're right. I can't just pick and choose who I love, can I?"

Aimee figured Josie didn't expect an answer, so she remained silent. They sat together on the beach for a long time, not saying anything, just watching the sun slide into the sea. Finally, Josie turned to her, and the heavy mood that had surrounded the girl seemed at last to have lifted.

When Josie threw her arms around Aimee's shoulders and hugged her tightly with a whispered "Thank you," Aimee instinctively hugged her back. She squeezed her eyes shut, trying not to think about what was going to happen to Josie when her father was arrested. Nic was all that Josie had. How could he have put himself in this position? And how could Aimee destroy the father without also destroying his innocent daughter?

AIMEE used Josie as a way to get Nic to let her go back into town the next day. It had been easy to plant the idea in Josie's head—what bored twelve-year-old wouldn't jump at the chance to do something outside of her normal routine? On the walk back home after their talk the night before, Aimee had said, "It's been a while since we went into town. You should see if your father will let you go tomorrow. It's a Saturday, you don't have classes, and it might be nice to do something fun."

"Will you come with me?" Josie had asked, adding, "I don't want to ask Giselle."

So, their little talk obviously hadn't sunk in, Aimee thought, grateful for Josie's stubbornness. "Of course. I'd be happy to."

Nic hadn't raised any objections, asking only that they be home before dark. Aimee did her best to seem excited at the thought of discovering what Nic's big surprise was, but the truth was, she didn't really like surprises, not when they came from weapons dealers.

As she stepped onto the boat that would take them into Longport, she heard a voice behind her and cringed.

"Wait a minute. I want to come, too," Giselle yelled, her sandaled feet slapping the wooden planks of the dock as she ran toward them.

Aimee expected Josie to protest, but she didn't. She didn't exactly give Giselle a warm welcome, but neither did she tell her that she didn't want the other girl to come. Aimee knew it was probably too much to hope that the girls would entertain each other, leaving her free to meet with Race for longer than just the second or two that it would take to hand over the pen with the photos on it.

She rubbed at the dull ache in her chest that had started at the thought of seeing Race again but being unable to hold him, to touch him, to have his comforting arms wrapped around her. It struck her suddenly that she was lonely, not just since coming to the island, but for much longer than that. Even before leaving the FBI, her life had had a sort of temporary quality, as if she couldn't really begin to live until . . . until whatever it was that she was waiting for finally happened. Aside from her friendship with her partners, Daphne and Raine, Aimee hadn't had a relationship with anyone, male or female, that lasted longer than a few years. She supposed that in the back of her mind, she was always waiting for the right time. Only, it was never the right time.

She'd had an active dating life back in Atlanta, but she'd fended off anything long-term by telling herself she didn't have the energy to devote to a relationship because she was so busy getting Partners In Crime off the ground so she could gain some measure of financial security. Before that, she'd been too busy taking extra courses and adding to her workload so she'd be prepared when she got out of the FBI to start up her own business. And before that, she'd filled her time with her studies, determined to graduate at the top of her high school and college classes so she could get any job she wanted.

But it had all been a bunch of excuses, designed to keep her from letting anyone get too close. What was she waiting for? Even worse, what the hell was she so afraid of? That she'd bring home a man she'd given her heart to and, like the boys in high school, they'd drop her the minute they met her dazzling sisters? Because of that silly hang-up, she was denying herself the chance of having a real relationship?

Was that the truth behind her "I want to be rewarded for my brains" attitude? Because hiding behind money made her a coward. And using it to push a good man like Race away made her an idiot.

"I am not lying. She's got a boyfriend here in town," Giselle said intently as the metal gate leading to the marina clanged closed behind her and Josie. Aimee had told them to go on ahead, that she needed to use the bathroom and run some errands and that she'd meet them back at the ice cream shop in an hour. Giselle had barely waited until they were out of earshot before dropping her bomb on Josie, who accused the girl she used to consider her best friend of being a liar.

"Well, I don't believe you," Josie said. She wanted Aimee

and her father to end up together, had already started imagining what it would be like to call Aimee "Mom." If Aimee had a boyfriend . . . No, Josie couldn't stand one more disappointment right now.

"I can prove it. Let's follow her. I'll bet you she ends up meeting with him."

"Yeah, right. So if she talks to any guy, you'll say it's her boyfriend. I know you, Giselle. You're just trying to hurt me."

Giselle stopped in the middle of the sidewalk and put her hands on her hips, affronted. "That is not true. I'm telling you, Aimee's got a boyfriend and she's going to meet with him today. If you don't want to believe me, then fine, think whatever you want."

Josie had to admit, Giselle seemed convinced that she was telling the truth. "What does he look like?" she asked tentatively.

"He's shorter than your dad, but taller than mine. He's kind of big—not fat or anything, but, you know, *big*." Giselle shrugged, taking her hands off her hips. "He has brown hair. I didn't get close enough to see what color his eyes were, but I know I'll recognize him if I see him again."

As she had when faced with information about her father that she didn't want to know, Josie felt conflicted. Was it better to follow Aimee and find out that she *did* have a boyfriend, or would not knowing be better?

"I'm going to follow her whether you want to or not," Giselle said, flipping her hair over her shoulder as she started across the street.

And Josie, who couldn't seem to make up her mind, let Giselle make the decision for her. Reluctantly, she followed Giselle, crossing the street and entering an alley that ran between two buildings. They hid behind a big green Dumpster, peering out from behind it like they'd seen in the movies. Josie had worn a sweater for the boat ride, but standing in the alley with the sun beating down on her made her start to sweat, so she took it off and hoped they wouldn't have to wait long for Aimee to appear.

Five minutes later, there was still no sign of Aimee.

"This is boring," Josie protested, unable to believe they were wasting a day in town hiding behind some stinky trash bin.

"Shh," Giselle hissed. "Here she comes."

Josie pushed Giselle out of the way and poked her head out from around the Dumpster just enough so she could see across the street. Aimee had just stepped off the gangplank and onto the sidewalk. She turned to the right and seemed to be looking at something, then suddenly twisted her head to look in Josie's direction. Josie leaped back, knocking into Giselle and sending the other girl sprawling onto the pavement.

"Ow. What did you do that for?" Giselle asked, rubbing her scraped palms together.

"Sorry," Josie muttered, holding out a hand to help Giselle up. "Aimee almost saw me."

"Well, be careful. We can't get caught," Giselle scolded.

"I know that," Josie said with a scowl. What, did Gi think she was stupid? Josie decided then that she'd had enough of Giselle trying to boss her around. If Giselle wanted to follow Aimee with her, that was fine, but Josie was done letting Giselle take the lead. "Come on," she said, peering out around the Dumpster to make sure Aimee was gone before creeping out of the alley.

Aimee was ahead of them by about a block, walking quickly toward a bluish gray two-story building. A large sign with the same bluish gray lettering proclaimed it to be the Harborside Motel.

When Aimee walked inside the office, Josie gestured to Giselle and said, "Hurry." Then she ran toward the motel as fast as she could, her sneakers sliding on the loose gravel. She could hear Giselle behind her, doing her best to run in the impractical sandals she was wearing. Josie leaped the curb and sprinted across the scraggly yard toward the motel. Panting, she hugged the side of the building, the concrete giving off the heat it had absorbed from the morning sun.

Giselle slumped down in the grass beside her, out of breath, her orange crocheted purse bright against the brown lawn.

Josie chanced a peek around the corner to see if Aimee had come out of the office. This was one of those motels where all the rooms opened up to the outside, instead of the sort of places where Josie and her dad usually stayed when they went on vacation, where all the rooms were accessed by central hallways. That was good, because that meant that they'd be able to see if Aimee went into somebody's room without having to follow her inside the building.

"Here she comes," Josie warned as Aimee hurried out of the motel's office.

Next to her, Giselle unzipped her purse and seemed to be rummaging around for something. She pulled out one of those small yellow and black disposable cameras and then crawled over to the side of the building to look out over the parking lot. Crouching down, she put the camera to her eye and Josie heard a click as Giselle zeroed in on Aimee's retreating figure.

Aimee walked purposefully toward a room on the first floor. Before she could knock, the door was flung open and Josie got a brief glimpse of a man's face before he stepped back and pulled Aimee inside. Then the door was closed again, as if the building had just swallowed Aimee up.

Josie slumped back against the side of the motel, feeling as if someone had punched her in the stomach and forced all of the air out of her lungs.

Aimee couldn't have a boyfriend. Didn't she know that Josie's dad liked her? Josie blinked. Maybe that was it. Maybe Aimee didn't know that her father liked her. Maybe that's why she was seeing this other man.

Yes, that had to be it. If Aimee knew that Daddy wanted her, she'd dump this other guy who lived in this yucky motel. Her dad had money and a really nice house and he was really handsome. All Josie had to do now was make sure her dad told Aimee how he felt. That would solve everything.

THIRTY-ONE

"I don't want you to return to that island. Please, let me arrange for you to go back to the States," Race said when he finally managed to lift his mouth off of Aimee's. They stood together without any space between their bodies, his hands buried in her hair and hers wrapped around his waist.

Aimee pulled him even tighter to her. "I can't leave now. Something is happening. I can tell it from the increased number of phone calls and hushed meetings Nic's been having. If I'm not on the inside, Nic could get away with whatever it is he's planning."

"But the risk of you getting caught increases every day you're there," Race said, dropping his hands to his sides and stepping away from her.

"Do you have another plan?" Aimee asked. Without Race's arms around her, she felt the emptiness that had welled up inside her on the boat ride washing over her again, so she wrapped her arms around herself, trying to quell the feeling. But it didn't work.

"I could go in and take over surveillance," Race said.

Aimee shot him an incredulous look. "Right. Like that's as effective as having someone on the inside?"

Race shrugged and raked his fingers through his hair. Then he began pacing, as if he'd been storing up energy waiting around that had to somehow find an outlet. Aimee was afraid the motel owners were going to have to replace the carpet after this was all over, because it seemed that Race was about to wear a hole in it from walking back and forth, back and forth, from the door to the foot of the bed and back.

"The night of the cocktail party, I heard several interesting things," Aimee said, sitting down on the edge of the bed. "First, the twenty-eighth of July came up several times. One man said he'd see Nic again on that date. Another asked if everything was set for the twenty-eighth. I asked Nic if there was something going on on that date, but he just sort of smiled and patted my head and wouldn't give me any specifics. I was afraid to press him on it. I've been on the lookout for anything with that date on it but haven't had much luck."

Race stopped his pacing and sat down in the chair across from Aimee. "Yeah, we were listening in that night from a fishing boat until Sabre's goons came and chased us off. We heard the same date, so we know something's up."

"But not what," Aimee said with a sigh.

"Or where," Race added glumly.

"I can't believe this. We barely know anything more than we did a month ago." Aimee stood up, taking her turn trying to wear a hole in the carpet.

"I know. It's like we're missing something that's right under our nose," Race said.

"But what? I mean, I pay attention to who's coming on and off the island and I haven't seen anything suspicious. Nic never goes anywhere—he spends all day, every day in his office, either on the phone or in closed-door meetings with Luke Simonds. If he's getting ready to demo his new weapon, why isn't he meeting with engineers and manufacturing specialists? How can he be preparing to launch this without ever visiting the plant? I just don't get it."

Race stood up and took her in his arms again to stop her from pacing. "I don't get it, either. We've been busy chasing down every lead we can get, but I can't stop worrying about you. Jake's nearly had to handcuff me here to keep me from going in and taking you out of this situation."

Aimee had to blink rapidly to hold back the tears that sprang to her eyes. It was nice to have someone care enough that they wanted to keep you out of danger. She didn't know anyone else—except maybe her mother—who felt that way about her. Still, she felt she had to make a point for women everywhere by saying, "So, it's okay for you to put yourself in the line of danger, but not for me to do so?"

Race cupped her chin in his hand and raised her gaze to his. "I'm not going to apologize for caring about you."

Aimee reached out her tongue and licked her bottom lip. "Okay," she said.

With a smile, Race leaned down and kissed her again, more tenderly than the passionately anguished kiss they'd shared when she first entered his room. When he raised his mouth from hers, they were both breathing hard. Aimee almost didn't care that his partner was in the other room, downloading the pictures she'd brought, and expected to return at any second. She needed to feel close to Race again, was afraid that the longer they were apart, the easier it would be for him to forget her.

"Do you remember back in San Antonio, when I said you couldn't give me what I want?" she asked, nearly whispering.

Race nodded.

"What if I . . ." She hesitated, chewing on the inside of her cheek. "What if I said I'd like to reconsider? You know, when this is all over and we're not so busy trying to save the world."

She felt his chest rise and fall against hers, slowly, as if it pained him to do so. "I'd say yes. Can't you tell that I've already fallen in l—"

An abrupt knock sounded on the connecting door between Race and Jake's rooms. Race sighed and said, "Come in," but refused to let Aimee pull away from him.

Jake stepped into the room and raised his eyebrows at them. "I'd tell you to get a room, but it appears that you already have one," he drawled.

Aimee turned so that Race's arm was draped over her shoulders and refused to rise to his partner's bait. "Was there anything useful there?" she asked, waving toward the pen.

"I don't know. We're going to need to spend some time

looking through the photos to see if there's anything of significance there," Jake said.

Race frowned, wondering why his partner sounded so vague. Surely, even after a cursory look at the pictures, he'd know if Aimee had turned up anything valuable.

"Here's your pen back. It's ready to use again if you get the opportunity." Jake handed the gold pen to Aimee and then crossed his arms over his chest, as if to say he wasn't going anywhere.

Aimee looked at her watch then, seeming surprised to discover that nearly an hour had passed. "Well, I'd better be going. The girls are probably waiting for me."

Race's grip on her tightened. God, he didn't want to let her go.

"Is there anything else you'd like to tell us?" Jake asked, leaning back against the wall of Race's motel room. "Anything you might be forgetting?"

Aimee closed her eyes and seemed to consider the question, then opened them again and shook her head. "No, nothing that I can think of. I told Race that Nic has some surprise planned for this evening, but I don't think it has anything to do with his new weapon. I got the impression it was something personal."

"Yeah, I'll bet," Jake muttered under his breath.

Aimee glared at the man. "What do you mean by that?"

"What's your problem, Haven?" Race asked, dropping his arm from around Aimee's shoulders and taking a step toward his partner.

Jake held out his hands, as if in surrender. "Hey, no need to get defensive. Sabre just seems to have the hots for her, that's all."

"Well, isn't that the point?" Aimee asked with a shrug. "If he didn't 'have the hots' for me, as you say, I'd already be dead. And then where would this investigation be?"

Jack backed away, like a lion that had engaged another hunter, only to discover that he was in the weaker position. "All right, all right. I said I was sorry."

"Actually, you didn't," Aimee said, resisting the urge to add "you asshole." Then she grabbed Race's hand and dragged him to the door, mostly because she feared he might plant a fist in his partner's face if she didn't get them away from each other. Standing up on her tiptoes, she gave Race a light kiss on the mouth, gently touching his face as she did.

She finally had to force herself to let him go. She stepped back, stopping with a hand on the doorknob. "When this is over, you and I . . . we'll start all over, okay?" she asked softly.

Race's gaze was steady on her as he answered, "There's nothing that would stop me from seeing you again. You can bet your life on it."

A few seconds after Aimee left, quietly closing the door behind her, Race turned to his partner, his features set like a figure carved from ice. "Would you like to tell me what the hell that was all about?" he asked, clenching his fists to hold in his anger.

"No," Jake said, turning and walking toward the connecting door.

Race knew if he took one step forward, he'd end up doing something he'd regret. He wasn't certain whether his fist would connect with the wall or with his partner's nose, but either choice was a bad one.

Jake paused in the doorway, turning his head to throw back over his shoulder, "I won't tell you, but I will show you." Then he disappeared into his own room, leaving Race staring at the empty air.

It took Race several deep breaths and two glasses of water to feel calm enough to follow Jake into the other room. "All right, what's going on here?" he asked.

Jake pushed his chair away from the small wooden desk where his laptop was perched and waved at the screen. "See for yourself."

Race walked over and tilted the screen up so he could see what looked to be a photo of papers on top of a desk. "This is one that Aimee took?"

"Yes. You can zoom in on any part of it just by clicking on what you want to see. That's what I was doing—just randomly clicking on different parts of the photos to, uh, give

you two some time alone together. That's when I saw this."
He pointed to a spot on the screen. Race leaned in and
squinted, then clicked the mouse where Jake's finger was to
enlarge the document.

It looked to be a receipt of some sort. He clicked again to
make that section even larger. Yes, that's what it was. A receipt from Robertson's jewelry here in Longport, dated three
days ago. It was for a canary yellow diamond ring flanked by
white diamonds. Three and a half carats in all. Forty-five
thousand dollars—more than Race had paid for his BMW last
year. The platinum band was to be engraved, the delivery date
today. And the words to be written inside the band?

To Aimee, with all my heart. Nic.

That was Sabre's big surprise. Tonight, he was going to ask
Aimee to be his wife.

THIRTY-TWO

"DADDY, can I talk to you for a minute?" Josie asked, poking her head inside her father's office. His door had been open and she had waited until he was off the phone to interrupt him.

As he always did when she dropped by, her father closed the top of his laptop before scooping all of his papers up off his desk and putting them in his safe. Josie was tempted to tell him not to bother, but found that she couldn't. Perhaps they were both better off keeping their secrets to themselves.

"Come on in." He waved at her as he sat back down behind his desk.

Now that she was here, she felt kind of nervous about what she was about to ask. Lacing her fingers together, she sat down and tried to think of the best way to say what she'd come to say.

"I thought you wanted to talk," her father said with a chuckle after the silence had gone on a little too long. "Did you have a good time in town? You're back earlier than I expected."

"We did everything we wanted to do," Josie said with a shrug. The truth was, she'd been too preoccupied thinking about what to do about Aimee to enjoy herself and had been glad when Aimee suggested they go home early. Even Giselle had agreed to leave, and Giselle never wanted to come back home before they absolutely had to.

Her father got up and walked around his desk, coming to sit next to her in one of his guest chairs. "What is it? Is something wrong?" he asked, laying an arm across her shoulders.

"Not exactly," Josie said, then just decided to say it. "I want you to marry Aimee. I don't think she knows how much you like her and if you ask her to marry you, then she will."

Nic gaped at his daughter. How in the world had she known? He had been putting off talking to her for days, not knowing how she might react. Would she be angry, thinking that he meant for Aimee to take the place of her mother? Or jealous that she was no longer the only woman in her father's life? Would she worry that he and Aimee might consider having other children, thus displacing her role as an only child?

Surprisingly, Nic had actually found himself wondering what it would be like to have another child. He hadn't thought he could love anyone except his daughter—had never felt the sort of connection with another human being that he felt with Josie—but as his feelings for Aimee grew, he began to hope that perhaps he could feel that way for another child. He couldn't imagine how it would be to have a house filled with people who loved him and whom he loved back. Maybe when that happened, Nicky Rodriguez would truly be dead for good.

Nic had to swallow around a lump that had formed in his throat.

Oh, how he loved this child. She had saved him from a life so filled with despair that Nic couldn't even imagine living without her.

"Daddy, are you crying?" Josie asked, sounding frightened.

Nic wiped the tears from his eyes with the back of one hand before enfolding his daughter in a tight embrace. "Only because I'm so happy," he said. "I hope you know how much I love you."

"I do, Daddy," Josie said, then hesitated before asking, "But what about Aimee?"

With another squeeze, Nic laughed, his heart lighter than it had ever been. "Yes, Josie, I will ask Aimee to marry me. Is tonight soon enough, or shall I go do it right now?"

Josie seemed to ponder the question, and Nic didn't want

to tell her that he had only been kidding. "I think you should wait until tonight," she decided. "You have to be all dressed up and get down on one knee, like in the movies. It wouldn't be the same if you just walked into her office and asked her."

Nic nodded, trying to keep the smile from his face. "I think you're right. I'll do it tonight after dinner. How about if you make an excuse about being tired right after dessert so that I can take care of it? I think this is something I should probably do alone."

He felt Josie's shoulders rise and fall as she took a deep breath and turned her dark eyes to his. "Okay, but do you promise to come tell me what she says? I'll never be able to sleep if you don't."

Nic placed a kiss on his daughter's forehead and gave her one final hug before saying, "I'll let you know her answer before you go to bed tonight."

Then they smiled at each other, pleased for their own reasons that their little family was about to get bigger.

"IF she says yes, we have to pull out," Jake said, cutting the engine on their boat. Sabre's island loomed ahead, its rocky northeast coast exposed to the constant pounding of the surf.

Race didn't bother to answer, instead tugging up the zipper of his dry suit.

"If she says yes, we won't be able to trust any of her information. Sabre could have turned her. She had to have seen that receipt when she was taking those photos. If she knew he was going to pop the question, why didn't she take you up on your offer to get her the hell out of there today?"

"Because she didn't know, that's why," Race said, refusing to believe that Aimee had been playing him that afternoon.

"Look, man, it's always been about the money to her. You and I both know that. Here she is, getting ready to be given a rock half the size of Texas. There's no way she'd turn that down. Especially not for you, a government employee. She knows how little money we make. She was there, too."

"If she's turned, why did she bring those photos to us today? Tell me that."

Jake shrugged nonchalantly. Yeah, it was easy for him not

to care. He didn't have his heart in a vise over this case. "I don't know. Guilt? She's been taking the government's money and figured she'd at least deliver something in return? You looked at what we got—it's not like she was handing over the keys to Sabre's kingdom. Maybe she thought she'd throw you a bone before she disappeared. She had to know we'd discredit any information she delivered after this."

"She hasn't turned," Race insisted. And yet, he'd been the one to suggest they risk another trip out to the island tonight. He told himself it was because he was going to take Aimee out if she turned Nic down, whether she wanted to be rolled up or not. If she even hesitated, he'd pull her out. There was a part of him that was deeply relieved that she would soon be out of danger, even though, as she had said earlier, they had a better chance of gaining real intelligence with her on the inside. Still, with what she'd delivered today, they had a few more leads, slim as they might be.

Race finished putting on his equipment and clipped his waterproof bag to his belt. Then he sat down on the edge of the boat and prepared to enter the murky water.

"Good luck," his partner said, his expression full of concern. "Don't . . . don't do anything stupid out there."

Race nodded sharply, then said, "I'll be back before dawn." And then, with a splash, he was gone.

JOSIE had been acting strangely all night, avoiding her father's eyes, giggling at nothing, having trouble remaining in her seat while the seemingly endless array of courses were trotted out. Aimee would have said something, but this was such a welcome change from the girl's earlier moodiness that she didn't want to do anything that might throw her back into that darker place. Instead, she just enjoyed the lighthearted mood, trying not to dread Nic's surprise. Whatever it was, she knew she had to do her best to seem delighted. Perhaps he was planning a vacation or . . . or . . . She couldn't even imagine what else it might be.

Although, actually, she could imagine some other surprises that she might not find as appealing, ones that she would find difficult to feign happiness about.

Almost immediately after she'd taken her last bite of crème brûlée, Josie covered her mouth during an exaggerated yawn and said, "Boy, am I tired. I'm going to go up and go to bed." Then she leaped up off her chair and gave her father a hug and a good-night kiss. To Aimee's surprise, when she was done, she hurried over to Aimee and did the same to her. That's when Aimee knew that her intuition was correct.

Damn. Nic was going to ask her to marry him. What was she going to say? She couldn't say no, which seemed to leave her only one other option. But that was unthinkable. She couldn't think of another way to stay on the island, though. If she told Nic she wouldn't marry him—whatever her excuse— he would be suspicious, at the very least. At the most, he'd decide he no longer needed her, and they both knew what the consequences would be if that happened.

Aimee shivered and tried to keep her food down. Tonight she was going to become a gunrunner's fiancée.

RACE froze as one of Sabre's thugs passed by, so close that he could have reached out and slit the man's throat if he'd wanted to. When Race saw that it was the jerk who had cut Jake's line the night of the cocktail party, he was tempted to do just that. But he resisted. It was one of those "just because you can, doesn't mean you should" scenarios.

The man walked by, making enough racket to alert anyone else who might have been in the vicinity.

Amateur, Race thought scornfully, although he supposed it was just as well that Nic Sabre's security force wasn't as efficient as his electronic security system. Not that it would have stopped Race from coming, but it definitely would have made his job more difficult.

Race waited until the man was gone before unfolding himself from the ground. Sabre's house was still about a quarter of a mile away, but the ground was already flattening out, making the going much easier than the first part of his journey. When he was a kid, chubby geek that he was, he'd never imagined that the skills he'd used to evade playground bullies would serve him so well later in life. Climbing, hiding, pretending to be invisible, running damn fast despite the extra weight he'd carried—all abilities he'd honed at a young age just to keep from being tortured. He'd used those same skills as an adult to save his own life.

When he got to within twenty yards of the house, Race dropped to the ground and slowly crawled through the dense beach grass toward the wraparound porch. On his earlier trip to the island, he'd discovered that, while Sabre's security was good, it was not foolproof. There were several blind spots where his cameras couldn't see and where the motion detectors mounted at intervals around the house missed. Race planned to slip into one of those "dead" pockets and gain entry to the house from there, but stopped when he heard the sound of someone walking toward him.

Race froze, his breathing slowing as the murmur of voices approached.

They passed by him, so close that Race could smell the woman's perfume mixed with the spicy scent of the man's aftershave. Race peered at them through the thick blades of golden grass, waving gently in the night breeze.

She looked beautiful, more beautiful than he had ever seen her look. Her hair was pinned up at the back of her head, with hundreds of flirty curls bobbing as she walked. She wore a nearly translucent dress the color of waves as they crested in the sea. Her tanned arms and legs were bare and she had taken off her shoes, hooking the straps around her index finger as she walked toward the surf, laughing.

Race watched in frustrated anguish as the man holding her arm stopped and dropped to his knee in the sand, his dark hair parted by silvery moonlight. The man spoke softly, too softly for Race to hear what was being said over the relentless lap of water against the beach. But he didn't have to hear the words to understand.

The man took the woman's hand, slid the glittering ring on her finger, and stood up.

The woman embraced him.

And then, with the moon's blessing, they kissed.

AIMEE stood in the middle of Nic's bedroom, fighting the urge to panic or throw up or both. His room was more spacious than hers, the bed larger, the wood darker. Her gaze shot from one thing to another to another, as if trying to find something that would get her out of this jam. But she already knew that she was going to have to sleep with Nic. There was no way out of this.

Nervously, she smoothed her sweaty palms down the sides of her dress. This would have been so much easier had Nic not broken off the embrace that had started down on the beach in order to go say good night to Josie. As long as Aimee remained in character, she could play along with this charade, but the moment her true self—and her true feelings—bubbled back to her consciousness, the thought of what she was about to do made her feel sick.

Aimee crossed her arms around her middle, trying to quell the roiling of her stomach. *It's just sex,* she reminded herself, but that didn't help. Never before had she been forced to do something like this, but, try as she might, she couldn't think of a way out.

Visions of leaping off the balcony and racing to Nic's boat to save herself came to mind, but she wouldn't even know how the start the thing, much less pilot it to safety. Besides, with the twenty-eighth just two days from now, she couldn't abandon this mission, no matter what the personal cost. Too many lives depended on her success.

No, she had to go through with this.

Unfolding her arms from her around her waist, Aimee forced herself to relax. Raising her hands, she slid the pins out of her hair and watched her reflection in the glass of one of the French doors leading outside. Then she nearly screamed with surprise when Race's face appeared on the other side of the window.

She was filled with a conflicting sense of relief mixed with disbelief. He wouldn't take this sort of risk just to save her, would he?

Aimee rushed to the door and unlocked it, shoving it open to let the cool night air wash over her.

"What are you doing here?" she whispered, with a look behind her to make sure Nic hadn't come back from Josie's room.

"Aimee, don't do this," Race said, clasping her hands roughly between his.

"Do we have enough evidence to stop Nic? Were the pictures I brought you enough?" Aimee asked, desperately hoping that Race would say yes.

A muscle twitched in Race's jaw. "It doesn't matter. I can't let you go through with this."

Aimee felt like dropping to the ground and howling out her anguish, but she forced herself to remain standing as she gently pulled her hands out of Race's grasp. "Do you remember when we first talked about what someone could do with the McConnell propulsion system plans? Didn't you tell me that with bombers that can make it around the globe in less than two hours, we may end up with global chaos? Is that really a risk you're willing to take just to save my virtue?"

"We don't know that's what Sabre's planning. Besides, it's unlikely that an attack would make it past our defenses," Race protested, although they both knew how weak his argument was.

"Perhaps, but it is a possibility, right? And Nic doesn't care about right or wrong. He only cares about money. What if I am our only chance to stop him?"

"You know that I could take you off this island right now," Race said softly.

Aimee squeezed her eyes shut, wishing with every fiber of her being that she could pretend to be helpless and let him do just that. Then, as much to convince herself as to convince him, she said, "But what happens when the next 9/11 occurs and we find out that we could have prevented it if I had stayed and found out what Nic was planning? Can you live with that on your conscience? Because I don't think that I could."

Race paused for a moment, then rubbed his aching temples, knowing they were out of choices. "I'm so sorry for getting you into this," he said softly.

Aimee reached out a hand and squeezed Race's fingers. "This is not your fault. I agreed to do this job, and I will do whatever is necessary to complete it successfully."

Race closed his eyes and gripped Aimee's hand so tightly that she winced. When he opened his eyes again, she saw the torment in their gray depths. They both knew what had to be done, no matter how much of a toll it took on them personally. Tenderly, Race brushed a lock of hair behind her ear. Then he lowered his mouth to hers and gave her a light, fleeting kiss. "I love you," he whispered, giving her fingers one final, painful squeeze.

Aimee raised his hand to her lips and pressed a fierce kiss into his palm. "I love you, too," she said. Then she dropped his hand and turned away, saying quietly, "Now please go. I can't bear the thought of you watching this."

THIRTY-THREE

"NOT you again. I thought we warned you that this was private property and you aren't welcome here. Obviously, you don't listen too well."

Jake had watched the other boat approach and did his best to pretend to be just another fisherman, but his disguise had obviously not worked. It wasn't like he had a lot to work with here—a few fishing poles, a baseball cap or two, a couple of lifejackets. He'd pulled the baseball cap low over his forehead and pretended to be asleep, but they'd approached anyway, coming around the side of the island too fast for him get the anchor up, start the engine, and get away.

"Look, I don't know what you're talking about. You said to stay away from the other side of the island and I did. What's the problem?"

"The problem," goon number three said, poking his gorilla-sized index finger into the center of Jake's chest, "is that we told you we didn't want to see you around here again. Cap-eesh?"

Jake rolled his eyes. "What are you, the Australian mafia?"

That earned him a swift punch in the gut that he hadn't seen coming. Jake doubled over, holding his stomach and fighting the urge to retch. Damn, that hurt. It had been a while since he'd been in a barroom brawl, and he was obviously out of practice.

Before he could catch his breath, goon number two was on him, landing a head-ringing punch on Jake's cheek. Jake fell backward, landing on his ass on the floor of the boat. He'd stowed his Glock in the dry storage area in the cockpit and hadn't wanted to arouse the thugs' suspicions by diving for it when he'd seen them coming, so he was unarmed and outmanned. As he lunged for the center of the boat where his gun was safely stored, he avoided a punch from goon number one, but got blindsided by a kick from goon number three. Then goon number two hit him from behind, sending him sprawling on the deck.

As they took turns kicking him in the ribs, Jake did his best to protect his head and wished like hell that real fight scenes were like the movies, where one good guy could kick the shit out of three bad guys with a cast on one arm and a gorgeous babe on the other.

He passed out thinking of James Bond.

WHERE the hell was the fucking boat?

Race checked the GPS locator on his watch again. He was at the exact coordinates where they'd anchored the boat a few hours earlier, but there wasn't a watercraft in sight. Race spun around in the water, squinting to see if perhaps the anchor had somehow come loose and the boat had drifted. But wouldn't Jake have noticed if that was the case?

It occurred to him then that Jake may have fallen asleep, but Race immediately dismissed the thought. Jake may be a cynical womanizer, but where the job was concerned, he was the best there was. Something must have happened. Jake would never have left him stranded out here if something hadn't gone terribly wrong. Now Race's only course of action was to get back to town and find out what had happened to his partner.

Race looked at his watch again, making sure he was heading west as he began to swim. At first, his mind protested, as it always did when the mission seemed too long, too hard, too daunting to complete. It had been one of the greatest joys in Race's life to discover that his physical limitations were all in his mind. He'd been recruited for the CIA during his senior year of college, but the job they offered had more to do with desks and sums than danger and spying. But Race had wanted something more, so he joined the Army instead and applied to be a Ranger. It was during this grueling physical training that Race discovered who and what he really was.

He wasn't just some geeky kid whose highest aspiration was to ace the accounting exams. He had a mental and physical toughness that he'd never even imagined. It was during his training that Race had learned that more than half the challenge of survival was in convincing yourself that you could stay alive despite all the evidence to the contrary.

So, he didn't think about the dangers—the currents, the sharks, the cold, his own physical stamina. Instead, he simply told himself that he would do what must be done. Then he turned his thoughts to Aimee, put his body on autopilot, and just kept putting one arm in front of the other as he headed toward the distant shore.

AIMEE inched the hot water up another notch, until it was nearly scalding her skin. No amount of scrubbing had erased the feel of Nic's hands on her body and the burning sting of hot water was no more successful. Aimee turned the water back down to a non-lethal temperature and stood with her back to the spray, her head buried in her hands as she sobbed silently, her tears running through her fingers and down her arms, dripping off her elbows to mingle with the water flowing into the drain. She wished her misery was as easy to wash away, but it clawed at her heart like a ravenous bird scratching for food.

She loved Race but had slept with Nic, and the thought of what she'd had to do made her feel as if she'd lost a part of her soul last night. If it hadn't been for the way she felt about Race, having sex with Nic would have been easy. After all, he was not a selfish lover and he knew his way around a woman's body. But giving herself to another when she knew her heart belonged to Race was like the deepest betrayal, even though they both knew she'd had no choice.

If she were able to take the emotion out of it, she could handle it. To trade sex with Nic for the chance to foil his evil plot was a no-brainer. Millions of lives could be at stake, a faked orgasm or two hardly seemed a great sacrifice.

It was the look in Race's eyes last night before he'd kissed her that was making her heart feel as if it had been torn from her body and was being wrung out before her own eyes.

"Aimee?"

She heard Josie calling to her above the sound of the shower splashing on the champagne-colored marble in the bath and knew she couldn't stay in here forever. Already, her skin was pruney from being wet for so long. Taking a deep, shuddering breath, Aimee wiped her eyes with the palms of her hands and turned off the water. She stepped out of the shower and wrapped a freshly laundered robe around herself, belting it tightly at her waist. Pushing her wet hair out of her face, she opened the bathroom door, releasing a cloud of steam.

"Hey, Josie. What's up?" she asked, feigning a lightheartedness she didn't feel.

Josie threw her arms around Aimee and hugged her tightly. "I'm so glad you're going to be my mom," she mumbled into the cloth at Aimee's chest.

Aimee swallowed and felt the familiar welling of tears behind her eyes. Oh, God, she hated this. Poor Josie. All the kid wanted was a mother to love her and what she was going to get was heartbreak instead.

She couldn't stop the tears from falling as she hugged Josie back. "Oh, honey. I don't know what to say." Her voice caught on a hiccup as she closed her eyes and tried to quash the guilt and regret and sense of responsibility warring within her.

"Why are you two crying? This is supposed to be a happy occasion," Nic said from the doorway of Aimee's room, sounding amused.

Aimee drew in a shuddering breath and blinked the tears from her eyes. She knew she had bruises under her eyes from lack of sleep and an abundance of crying, but there was nothing she could do about it until she could get to her makeup.

"Good morning," she said to Nic, tightening the already snug belt at her waist as Josie released her and crossed the room to kiss her father.

She had a difficult time meeting Nic's eyes, not because she was embarrassed, but because she feared her loathing of them both might show if she were to look at him right now. Fortunately, Nic interpreted her eye contact avoidance as maidenly shyness—snort!—and came over to give her a tender kiss on the forehead with a whispered, "You are everything I ever wanted in a woman . . . and more."

Aimee had to bite her tongue to not respond by saying, "Yeah, well, you're everything I ever wanted in a man . . . and less." Okay, so yes, money was important to her, but not wealth at the expense of countless innocent lives. How could Nic sleep at night, knowing what heinous crimes his weapons were used to commit?

Of course, she said none of this, murmuring instead, "I'm sorry, I'm running a bit late this morning."

"That's all right. You had a late night," Nic said with a smile and a wink that made Aimee want to gag.

"Can we go into town again today?" Josie asked, interrupting their private moment.

Nic squeezed Aimee's shoulder and stepped back, smoothing his trousers over his thighs. "No, I'm afraid not. Aimee and I have a lot to do today. Plus, Giselle's mother took the boat into town this morning. She had some errands to run and won't be back until this afternoon. Why don't you go see if Giselle wants to play?"

Josie looked down at the carpet and shrugged—teen-speak for "I don't want to, and I don't want to talk about it, either"—and said, "Yeah, maybe."

Nic laughed and ruffled Josie's hair. He was catching on to this new language. "Okay, then don't. But Aimee and I are going to be very busy both today and tomorrow. I have an idea, why don't we all fly to Port Douglas the day after tomorrow? You girls can go shopping, we'll eat out at fancy restaurants and stay in a nice hotel. How does that sound?"

Josie smiled at Aimee and Aimee forced herself to pretend

that they were a normal family, going off on a spur-of-the-moment vacation. "That sounds wonderful," she said, hoping her grin didn't look as forced as it felt.

RACE'S shoulder bumped the piling again as the wake from another boat entering the marina sent waves lapping against the rocky shore. He'd swam all the way from Sabre's island to Longport, but didn't have the strength left to pull himself out of the water and onto the pier, so instead he just let himself float freely while he regained his strength. It had taken over seven hours, but he'd made it. Exhausted but triumphant, Race's mental toughness spurred him on. He had a mission to complete and he couldn't do so while bobbing around in the water like a piece of driftwood. Spying an empty slip, Race kicked determinedly toward it. Once there, he grabbed onto a warm metal cleat to steady himself and began removing his scuba gear, placing each piece on the pier. Then, with an almost superhuman effort, he pulled himself out of the harbor.

Race rolled over onto his back and stared up at the cloud-studded early-morning sky, vowing that he'd get moving again in just a minute. When he woke, he felt a change around him, even before opening his eyes. The marina seemed busier, noisier. Race was sweating inside his dry suit and his mouth felt like someone had stuffed it full of dry rocks.

He unzipped the black neoprene and sat up, cursing his shaking fingers. As soon as he got this damn thing off, he was going to get some food and water and a hot shower. Maybe even all three at once.

Race peeled off his dry suit and snagged a light blue wheeled cart from a few slips over. Boaters used these carts to haul things to and from their boats and, while he technically wasn't supposed to take it out of the marina, Race really didn't give a damn about following any rules right now. He wasn't going to leave thousands of dollars of scuba equipment just lying on the dock and he no longer had a boat to lock it in, so he'd have to take it back up to his motel room and bring the cart back later. It wasn't like he had any intention of stealing the damn thing.

Once he got everything loaded into the cart, Race rummaged around in his waterproof bag for his boots. He'd worn shorts and a T-shirt under his dry suit and they were wrinkled and sweat-stained, but he wasn't exactly here for the Miss Universe tryouts.

With a determined effort, Race dragged the cart up the gangplank on unsteady legs. He kept telling himself that he just needed to get some fuel into his body and then he'd be all right. If he told himself that enough times, perhaps he'd even start to believe it. What he really needed was a twenty-hour nap, but that wasn't going to happen—not with Aimee still trapped on Sabre's island and the twenty-eighth only one day away.

They *had* to find out what was happening, and fast.

Race unlocked the door to his motel room and cautiously looked around before determining that it was safe. Without knowing what had happened to Jake, he couldn't be certain that their base of operations hadn't been discovered, but all was quiet.

He grabbed a bottled water out of the mini fridge and gulped it down, then pulled out another. Ripping open a packet of peanut-butter cheese crackers, Race wolfed them down one after another, stopping only to wash down the sticky mixture with more water. In less than five minutes, he had stripped, showered, changed, and eaten. Shaving took another minute, and dumping his scuba gear into the tub added thirty more seconds. Seven minutes from the time he'd returned, Race was ready to find out what had happened to his partner.

First, he did the obvious and called Jake's cell phone.

And was astonished when his partner answered on the first ring.

"Where the hell are you?" Race asked.

Jake sounded as if his teeth were clenched when he answered, " 'Ospital."

"Which one?"

Jake gave him his room number and the name of a small medical center a few blocks away. Race hung up after saying he'd be right there. He returned the cart to the marina and then hailed a cab, deciding it would be best to conserve his energy. The day had just begun.

* * *

"**WHAT** happened?" Race asked as he slipped into Jake's room. His partner looked like shit, with a mother of a black eye that was nearly swollen shut, a couple of nasty-looking cuts on his arms, and bruising around his jaw. And that was just what Race could see.

"Sabre's goons," Jake answered, sounding more than a little groggy. That's when Race noticed the wires on Jake's teeth. No wonder it sounded like he was clenching his teeth—the bastards had broken his partner's jaw.

"You're sure it was them?" Race asked, moving across the room to sit down in the chair at Jake's bedside.

"I never forget a pretty face," Jake joked. At least his sarcasm was still intact.

"I'll get our contact in Townsville to arrange for the local cops to guard your room," Race said, already flipping open his cell phone to make the call.

"Don't bother," Jake said, holding out a hand to stop Race, then wincing when he realized that even that slight a movement hurt like hell. Where were those morphine drips people talked about? Jake wouldn't object to a little mind-altering experience right about now.

"Why not?" Race asked with a frown.

"Plane's on its way for us," Jake ground out between bursts of pain.

"Let me get a nurse."

Jake inclined his head toward a contraption on his lap with a red button in the center. "I just called for one," he said.

Race sat back down. "Why is there a plane coming for us? Our mission is not complete."

"Aimee Devlin's been turned. She had to have been the one to have alerted Sabre's goons that I was out there. They didn't see us on that side of the island before."

"No way," Race said, shaking his head. "She'd never do that. Besides, if she had told them, why wouldn't they have just waited for me to return and attacked us both?"

"Maybe she figured you'd drown. How should I know?" Jake said irritably. "Doesn't matter anyway, because the boss agrees with me. He knows Aimee's just in this for the money and Sabre's offered her a hell of a lot more than what we could ever pay her. Besides, she told the bastard she'd marry him, didn't she?"

"What was she supposed to say?" Race all but shouted, getting up to stomp around the room. "If she'd said no, he'd have killed her."

"Did you make contact with her last night?" Jake asked.

"Yeah," Race answered glumly.

"And did she ask you to get her out of there?"

"No. Because our job is not finished. She's not going to risk the life of innocent—"

"Spare me the speech," Jake interrupted. "This woman is no saint and we both know it. She works for the highest bidder, and Sabre just outbid us. If she really said yes to him just to save her life, she would have taken your offer to help her escape last night. Hell, she probably planted that jewelry store receipt in the photos she gave us to get us out to the island." Jake paused, the words hanging in the air between them.

"That's ridiculous. She didn't know I'd be on the island last night."

"Really, you don't think she suspected you'd come to do that whole white knight rescue thing when you found out Sabre was going to propose?" Jake would have raised his eyebrows, but it hurt too much to even think about doing so.

Race scowled at the linoleum floor. He couldn't have misjudged Aimee, not this much. Yes, he knew money was important to her, but she had told him that she loved him.

Yeah, but look at all that Sabre has to offer, that doubting voice inside him said. The guy could be a fricking *GQ* model. Not to mention the bottomless bank accounts, limitless credit cards, the private plane, the freaking private *island*.

"Shit," Race said.

"I know," Jake agreed glumly.

"I still don't think—"

Jake's phone rang just then, and, with some difficulty, he flipped it open and said, "Haven," into the mouthpiece. After a terse, "Yeah . . . Yeah . . . Right," he ended the call.

"What is it?" Race asked after Jake pushed the red button in his lap two more times, refusing to meet Race's eyes.

Finally, Jake looked up, his green eyes clouded with a

mixture of pain and disgust. "Ten million dollars was just wired from a known drug dealer into Nic Sabre's account in the Cayman Islands."

Race shrugged. "Yeah, so what? We know he's a weapons dealer and that these guys are frequent customers."

Jake shook his head sadly. "Right, but the money was then transferred out of Nic's account and moved to a bank in Switzerland. Wanna guess who the account holder is?"

Race bowed his head and closed his eyes. "No," he whispered.

"Yes," Jake argued. "The account belongs to none other than Aimee Devlin. And we've been ordered off this case."

THIRTY-FOUR

DIANA Simonds sat alone in her office and looked over the photos her daughter had taken the day before. Here was the proof she needed to convince Nic to get rid of Aimee. In one shot, it was clear that the person opening the motel room door to her was a man, and the flash of white teeth said he knew her and was happy to see her.

There was no way Aimee could explain this away. She had no reason to be going into a motel room with a man.

Diana had finally caught the other woman in a lie.

And she should be feeling victorious, but she didn't. She knew that Nic cared for the woman, even though she couldn't understand why. Aimee *was* good with Josie, though. Diana had never seen the girl so happy. And she'd been around long enough to know, because killing Josie's mother had been Diana's first job for Nicky Rodriquez.

It had been a test, of course. Nicky thought she wouldn't be able to do it, but all she had needed to know was why Nicky wanted her killed. He had hesitated to tell her, and Diana got the impression that Nicky Rodriquez didn't reveal his feelings to very many people. That was fine with her. She didn't, either. For instance, she had never once told Nic that she was in love with him. Despite the fact that she and Luke had only been married for three years and she was already pregnant with their first child, she had fallen for Nicky, hard, the first time they met. But Nic had made it clear that he didn't welcome emotional attachments, and Diana didn't want to wind up like the one woman Nicky had proclaimed to love—taken, alone and frightened, out into the desert and shot, her body buried where it would never be found.

And the reason for Solana's demise? Nicky had found her weeping in the corner one day, complaining that the colicky baby wouldn't be quiet.

Solana was at her wit's end, unable to cope with the constant crying. That's when she made her fatal mistake. She'd threatened to take the baby back to her village, where her mother and sisters lived. She'd told Nicky that she was an orphan, but the truth was, she had run away from home. Now she wanted to take their baby and go back to her family, just for a little while.

That's when Nicky knew Solana had to die. Eventually, she would discover what he did for a living and would stop loving him. And then she would try to take Josie from him. Without a family, she would have nowhere to run, no support system to help her take his daughter from him. But with a family . . . No, it was too risky.

So, the order was given, and Diana followed through, and never once had Nic mentioned that he missed Solana.

But Diana suspected that he felt differently about Aimee. He was older now, more aware of what it truly meant to be betrayed. And she suspected that he really cared for Aimee.

Yes, Nic would be devastated when she showed him these pictures, but Diana had no choice. She couldn't risk letting Aimee get even closer to Nic, not when the ultimate outcome of this could be their lives. Diana ran the edge of one of the photos across her lips. Perhaps she should wait, though. The LoRS bomb demonstration was tomorrow, and that would be an enormous success for Nic. Maybe she ought to just let him have his moment in the sun. After all, what did waiting another day matter?

Diana tapped the pictures on her desk, arranging them into a neat stack. She was about to put them away, when she heard the sound of raised voices. Ah, Josie and Giselle were at it again.

She got up and walked down the hall to referee the fight, but discovered the girls weren't fighting after all. She held back to eavesdrop on their animated conversation.

"He asked her to marry him," Josie squealed.

"Ohmigod, really?" Giselle asked, then lowered her voice. "But what about that other man?"

"Forget about him. Aimee was only seeing him because my dad hadn't proposed yet. I'm sure of it."

Stunned, Diana backed up a couple of steps. What? No. Nic couldn't have proposed. She knew he had feelings for the other woman, but . . . No. She couldn't even think of what this meant for them all.

Hurriedly, she raced back down the hall and grabbed the photos off of her desk and headed to Nic's house to put an end to this charade.

She rapped on Nic's office door, hoping that he was not at the manufacturing plant. Rationally, she knew this probably should wait until the day after tomorrow, but for once, she wasn't feeling very rational. She could accept that Nicky had fallen for another woman, but not that he'd actually propose to one that Diana had made clear she didn't trust.

Well, this is what he deserved for not listening to her.

She knocked on the door again.

"Nic's in a meeting until noon. Would you like me to have him call you?" Aimee asked coolly, watching Diana from the doorway of her office.

"Mind your own business," Diana snapped.

"All right," Aimee answered, going back into her office and closing the door with a controlled click.

Nic flung open the door just then, a scowl on his face. His expression softened when he saw that it was her. "Oh, Diana. What do you want? I just sent Luke and our head of engineering back to the island. Were you looking for your husband?"

"No." Diana pushed past Nic and sat down in one of the chairs across from his desk, flinging the pictures down on top of the spreadsheets and plans strewn about. "I was looking for you. You need to see these." She paused, and then said, "And you might want to close the door."

* * *

RACE wasn't a big one for vapid platitudes. He hated those stupid supposedly motivational sayings that people spouted. And those posters companies put up on the walls showing majestic mountains or the pyramids or whatever with some pithy saying, like, "If we all pull together, just think of what we can achieve." Yeah, right. *And love conquers all and we should all just be friends, too,* he always thought.

But for some reason, as he trudged back to the motel, Race couldn't stop picturing a ceramic plaque his mother had hanging over their sink when he was growing up. "Faith is believing in something despite all evidence to the contrary," it read.

That's how he felt about Aimee. Despite all the evidence he'd been given, he believed in her. He knew, without a doubt, that she would never sell out her country—not for flashy jewelry or any amount of money. He had faith and he was not going to give up on her.

He let himself into his room and locked the door behind him. Jake had given him a copy of the photos Aimee had sent and Race wanted to spend a little more time with them, looking for any other clues as to what might be going on tomorrow. That was the key to getting Aimee out of this mess. Once he had the evidence required to arrest Sabre, he could get her off that island so she could explain why she'd had to do the things she'd done.

Race booted up his computer and spent several hours clicking over every inch of each picture, trying to make some sense of it all. There were spreadsheets—ordinary-looking cash flow statements that showed a large amount of cash outlay for capital spending, but without any hint of where the building or improvements might be located. The technical plans had already been forwarded to Langley for analysis. Also in the photos were several bank statements, which Race assumed was how the CIA was able to trace the funds coming into and out of Sabre's accounts. There were also what looked to be several packing lists.

Race studied those, hoping to find something useful. One of the packing lists was from a company called Mel's Air Service and included the usual household goods like paper towels, five pounds of steak, fresh flowers, and a case of expensive wine. Another was dated a few days later and included numerous cleaning products. From the looks of it, this latest delivery could have kept the Sabre household germ-free for years.

"Who needs a hundred gallons of Lysol?" Race muttered under his breath, moving to the next photo.

This one contained much the same sorts of things as the last picture. Assorted spreadsheets, the corner of a blueprint, and a report from Josie Sabre's tutor on her progress.

"Bright kid," Race said. Like him, she had all A's in math and science.

He'd clicked the mouse to move on to the next photo, when he stopped, suddenly struck by a thought. Wait a minute. Who *did* need a hundred gallons of Lysol?

Even a house as big as Sabre's couldn't use more than a gallon a week. Who would stock up on nearly two years' worth of cleaning supplies? Nobody. Unless that hundred gallons was going to a manufacturing plant, which would need to be cleaned every single day. Then, one hundred gallons of Lysol might only last for a few weeks.

Race powered down his computer and then slid it into the spot he'd rigged in the ceiling for safekeeping. Then, without looking back, he exited his motel room, muttering under his breath, "Look out, Sabre. Here I come."

SOMETHING wasn't right.

Josie couldn't put her finger what was wrong, but conversation between Daddy and Aimee, which had been light and easy this morning, was strained and awkward now. She tried to eat her dinner, but it was impossible to force food down past the tightness in her throat.

When her father tossed down his own fork with a clatter, Josie knew something was really wrong. Daddy never forgot his manners.

"I'm going to retire early," he said, barely looking at Aimee as he gave Josie a good-night kiss.

"What's wrong?" Josie whispered once her father had left the room.

Aimee seemed concerned, too. She was watching the doorway with a frown, her forehead wrinkling. Then she cleared her throat and put down her silverware. "I think your dad's just tired. Maybe he needs that vacation to Port Douglas even more than he thinks."

Josie wasn't sure that was it. Things had seemed weird ever since she'd gotten back from Giselle's house this afternoon. Was it . . . Could it possibly be that Giselle had told her mother about the man they'd seen? What if Mrs. Simonds had talked to Daddy about it? Maybe Daddy was worried that other man might still want Aimee, even though he had proposed and she had accepted.

Josie's eyes narrowed. It seemed to her that once Aimee had agreed to marry Daddy, the other man would just go away and let them be happy. But maybe Daddy was scared that Aimee would leave them.

Josie knew *she* was scared that Aimee might leave them.

She had to do something, had to tell this other man that Aimee was theirs and that he should just go away now. If he left and Aimee never talked to him again, she wouldn't be tempted to leave.

Yes, that was exactly what she'd do. She'd sneak into town as soon as Captain Jack went on another trip. And she wouldn't tell anyone about it—not even Giselle, who might tell on her just for spite—because this was something she had to do and she couldn't risk having someone tell her she couldn't go.

THIRTY-FIVE

FOR once, Nic wished the day had not dawned so glaringly bright and sunny. Although it would have interfered with his plans, he was more in the mood for a vicious thunderstorm, the sort where lightning struck the earth and made buildings shake and the rain pelted glass like millions of tiny poison darts. Instead, the sun rose and smiled down upon them, calm and unwavering, despite the turmoil roiling around down below.

Today, Nic was going to kill the only woman he had ever really loved. Her betrayal with another man gnawed at him like the soul of the rat he'd killed so long ago. Funny to have thought of his old life twice now in such a short time span, when he'd gone without thinking of life on the trash heap for so many years. Nic had almost come to feel as if that past belonged to someone else, but this morning, it had hit him like a hard slap in the face.

Why wasn't he good enough to love? His parents had thrown him away, left him at the dump when he was four years old as if he were a sack of rotting potatoes instead of a human being. And now Aimee, for all her pretense of caring for him, couldn't wait to be with another man.

Nic felt the black emptiness in his soul as it reached out

and tried to drag him under, but he refused to go. He would not allow this to defeat him.

But, oh, how he wished Aimee could have loved him.

Standing at the French doors leading from his office to the veranda, Nic nearly doubled over with the pain of his heartbreak. It was then that he realized he had to give Aimee another chance. Perhaps this man meant nothing to her. Perhaps she had only gone to him out of loneliness and now that she and Nic were to be married, she would be true to Nic, and only Nic, for the rest of her life.

Nic took a deep breath and straightened his shoulders. Yes, he would give Aimee one final chance. After all, she had not known how he felt about her when she had gone to meet that other man.

There was a light tap on his office door before Aimee tentatively called out, "Nic? It's ten o'clock."

He had told her to come to him at ten, vowing that he would make his decision by then. And he had. The rest was up to her.

Nic strode to the door and pulled it open to find Aimee standing outside. Today, she wore a wraparound skirt patterned with emerald green and the deepest turquoise with a matching green sleeveless tank. For once, she was wearing sandals—flimsy leather ones with turquoise beads running along the top.

"You look beautiful," Nic said, reaching out to pull her to him.

She looked up at him with surprise, her light brown eyes confused. "Thank you. You seem to be feeling better this morning."

Nic smoothed her silky hair away from her face, running his hands down her cheeks to her chin, touching her, memorizing her. "I'm very hopeful about today," he answered cryptically, then changed this subject. "Did Josie get off to Mrs. Jacobs's house?" he asked.

"Yes. I sent her there almost two hours ago, as you asked me to."

"Good. Then we're ready to begin." Nic grabbed her hand tightly and pulled her toward the closet where his safe was located.

"Begin what?" Aimee asked, hesitating at first before following him.

Nic threw open the closet doors and, with his free hand, unlocked the safe. Then he pressed a button and the front section containing his laptop and his files swung out, revealing a dark, empty space. Nic pushed Aimee toward the opening and felt her shudder as cool, damp air washed over her.

"Go," Nic ordered.

Aimee turned to him with narrowed eyes. "What's going on here?" she asked in her usual forthright manner.

"We're going on a little trip," Nic answered, his hand on the small of her back, pushing her toward the abyss.

She clutched the edge of the safe, stopping her forward progress. "Nic, tell me what this is all about," she said, her voice trembling with only the slightest hint of fear.

"The girls saw you go into a motel room with a man," Nic answered. "They got pictures, so please don't insult me by trying to deny it. Now move." He reached beyond her to flip on a light switch, revealing a set of metal stairs leading downward. He pried Aimee's fingers from the safe and moved them to the handrail. Then, with one final nudge, he pushed the button that would automatically close the safe door and stepped in behind her.

STOWING away on the boat had been remarkably easy. She had been on her way to Mrs. Jacobs's house when she saw the three men who worked for her dad heading toward the boat this morning and knew that she had to go with them into town. She couldn't stand another night like last night, with Daddy looking all sad and not talking to her and Aimee. She just had to talk to that other man, to make him see that Aimee didn't ever want to see him again now that she was engaged to Josie's father.

She had run to Mrs. Jacobs's house and told the housekeeper she'd be at Giselle's, then raced back to follow the men down the pier, pretending to be looking for fish in the water below. Surreptitiously, she had looked back toward the houses on the beach, hoping that no one was watching. When Captain Jack went up to the cockpit to start the engines, the three men went inside and Josie jumped onto the boat. There was a storage bin at the back of the boat that doubled as a seat. When they took the boat out for the day, Mrs. Jacobs often used that bin to store extra towels, their swimsuits, and inflatable rafts. It was plenty big for Josie to lie down in, although she did have to scrunch her knees a bit to fit all the way in.

After about five minutes, she began to wish that she'd brought a pillow, because the fiberglass under her head wasn't exactly comfortable. And after about fifteen minutes, she realized that this was going to be a really boring ride because there was nothing for her to do except trace a tiny crack in the lid of the bin and listen to the hum of the engines below her. She wished the men who worked for her dad would come outside so she could at least listen to what they were saying, but they remained inside for the entire journey.

Josie shifted positions and sighed. She should have brought a book or a snack or something.

By the time Captain Jack finally cut the engines, Josie was nearly ready to scream with boredom. Hurriedly, she pulled herself into a crouching position and pushed open the lid of the storage bin, only to let it slam back down when she saw her father's employees heading straight for her.

Screwing her eyes shut, she prayed they hadn't seen her. She waited another moment for their footsteps to pass, then lifted the lid again when they didn't.

The men had gone back inside the boat and stood with their backs toward her. Without waiting for another chance, Josie pushed up the lid and jumped out, nearly yelping with surprise when she realized her left foot had gone to sleep. Knowing she had to hurry, she limped off the boat, hunching over so she wouldn't look like herself if the men or Captain Jack happened to see her.

As fast as she could with her tingling foot, Josie raced out of the marina and up the gangplank, heading toward the Harborside Motel. She didn't know the room number where the man was staying, but she did remember where the room was, about halfway down the first floor.

Her feet were hot inside her sneakers, the pavement heated by the sun. Josie was glad she'd worn shorts and a T-shirt today. Jeans would have been too warm.

She stood panting at the man's door, her hands on her knees as she tried to catch her breath. Just as she was about to knock, the door was jerked open from inside and a large man stepped out, nearly knocking Josie over. She gave a little scream of surprise mixed with fright as he reached out with one strong hand to keep her from falling.

"I'm sorry. I wasn't expecting anyone to be out here," the man said.

Josie squared her shoulders and told herself not to be scared. "I need to talk to you," she said with a confidence she didn't feel.

The man looked surprised. "Me? You need to talk to me?"

"Yes." Josie nodded. "It's about Aimee."

Blinking, the man looked from her to the road behind her, as if expecting to see that she'd been followed. Josie looked back, too, but, of course, nobody was there. "What about her?" he asked, leaning against the wall of the motel and crossing his arms.

"She doesn't want to see you again. Ever. She's engaged to my dad now and she loves him."

"Did she send you here to tell me this?" the man asked with a hard look that made Josie swallow.

"N-no," Jose stuttered.

"Don't you think she should be able to make that choice for herself, then?" he asked, his voice softening.

"She did, and she chose my dad," Josie said stubbornly, then added, "My dad and me."

The man shook his head as if confused. "How did you even know about me?"

"My friend Giselle and I followed her the other day, and she came here."

"Oh, shit," he said, raising a hand to his forehead as if he were in pain.

"That's not a nice word," Josie said.

"Sorry, I—" The man looked up and broke off what he was saying. Then said, "Oh, shit," again, grabbed her, and dragged her into his motel room.

Before Josie could scream, the man put his hand over her mouth and yanked her across the room. Josie resisted with all her might, kicking and flailing with her arms and legs and trying to bite the man, but he held on too tightly for her to get in a good blow. He pulled open the closet door, jerked a blanket down from off the shelf, and shoved her inside, tossing the blanket over her.

"Stay in there and keep quiet, do you hear me? No matter what happens next, do not come out," he ordered, just before slamming the door in her face.

Josie struggled to untangle herself from the blanket and get up off the closet floor. No way was she going to—

"All right, asshole, open up," someone shouted with a loud bang on the metal motel room door.

Josie gasped and backed up into the corner, covering her head with the blanket. Suddenly, coming here didn't seem like such a good idea anymore.

There was another bang and then a crash, then a noise from behind her through the back wall of the closet with a muffled, "Thought you could get out the back way, huh," followed by a loud thunk that sounded like somebody's boots hitting the floor. Josie sat shivering, wondering what to do. Should she run out of here and try to escape? Or just stay put as the man had told her to?

She winced when she heard a loud thud and another crash from out in the room. There was no way she was going out there.

"Mr. Sabre doesn't like other men encroaching on his property," Josie heard someone say. She frowned when she recognized the voice of one of the men on the boat. But what were Daddy's employees doing here?

Slowly, she lowered the blanket from her eyes. Had Daddy sent these men to hurt Aimee's friend? But that wasn't right. Hadn't he always taught her that you were supposed to talk things out, not hit?

"Look, I'm not causing anyone any trouble," Aimee's friend said.

Josie inched toward the closet door to peer out from between the slats. The man had blood on his face and was holding his hands out in front of him. His eyes darted from one of her father's men to the other and then to the next, as if trying to decide if he could take all three of them.

"Yeah, well, we'll be the judge of that," one of Daddy's

men said, nodding to the others, who jumped forward to grab Aimee's friend's arms. The man ducked and almost made it to the door, but was tackled by one of her father's employees. Josie winced as the men fought, her jaw aching from clenching it. She felt like a coward, huddling in here while these men hurt Aimee's friend, but she was too frightened to move. What if they hit her like they were hitting him? Two weeks ago, she would never believe that anyone would hurt her, but now she wasn't so sure. She didn't know what to believe anymore.

She thought about Aimee saying that people who did bad things weren't necessarily bad people, but suddenly, she realized that it was a lie. Aimee had just been saying that to protect her. Her father . . . these men . . . the guerrillas who had murdered that family in front of their mother's eyes . . . they weren't just good people doing bad things. They were bad people.

Aimee's friend groaned and collapsed in a heap in the middle of his bed as Josie struggled not to cry. She watched as her father's henchmen shoved the man into a chair and tied him up. Then one of Daddy's employees stood on the bed and reached up, fiddling with something. When he jumped down, he grinned at Aimee's friend and said, "It's been a blast, but we've got to run."

The other two men laughed and gave each other high fives, as if this were some kind of game. Josie felt light-headed, like she was about to faint. How could they treat another person like this, as if he meant nothing? Yes, she had wanted Aimee's friend out of their lives, too, but not like this.

She sat in the closet long after the men were gone, mourning for the man out there, for her father, and for herself. Because she knew that, from this moment on, her life would never be the same.

THIRTY-SIX

AIMEE'S steps faltered as they reached the end of the darkened corridor. Nic refused to divulge where they were or where he was taking her, but after he'd told her that he'd seen her with Race, she knew what the end result was going to be. She closed her eyes, wishing she had let Race take her off the island when she'd had a chance because she had a feeling that she was not going to come out of this one alive.

They had been walking for about fifteen minutes in this chilly, metal hallway when they finally came to a door. Aimee's bare toes were cold, her arms covered with goose bumps. She walked with her hands wrapped around her middle, trying to stifle her shivers and reminding herself that she was not afraid.

It wasn't working.

Nic reached up from behind her and pressed a set of numbers on a keypad mounted on the wall. When a green light glowed, he nodded toward the door and said, "Open it."

With trembling hands, Aimee pushed it open, blinking from the light that met her eyes. Nic pushed her out of the corridor and into a cavern, well lit by bright fluorescent lights. A loud hum echoed off the walls and when Aimee saw the speedboat lashed to a dock, she realized that the noise was coming from the boat's engine.

Luke and Diana Simonds stood in the boat, Diana scowling at Aimee as Nic forced her to walk toward the dock.

What were they going to do? Kill her and drop her body in the ocean?

Her sandals flip-flopped on the planks of the dock as Nic herded her onto the boat, holding out a hand to help her get onboard. He hopped on after her, reaching out to untie the lines securing them to the dock after sitting her down in one of the back seats.

Aimee considered her options. She could jump in the water and . . . And get wet? That's about all that plan would accomplish. And that was all she could come up with. Her only option, then, was to sit tight and wait for another opportunity to escape. So that's what she did.

Diana Simonds expertly piloted the boat through a winding channel that led them out to the open ocean. She opened the throttle once they were clear of the island, heading toward another spot of green about a mile away. It was the island that Josie had told Aimee was uninhabited, the one where she said they'd picnicked on a few years past.

The boat slowed as they approached the island, as if Diana were looking for something. She found it, a tree bent at an unnatural angle that marked the entrance of another underground cave. This was why Aimee had never seen Nic go to the weapons manufacturing plant—because he had traveled to and from the island on a path that could not be seen from the house.

"Welcome to Sabre Systems," a young woman said, grabbing the line that Luke Simonds tossed to her.

"Thank you, Deborah," Nic said, leaping easily up out of the boat and onto the dock. He held out a hand to Aimee, which she reluctantly took. Then he guided her, gently but firmly, toward a set of metal doors set in the side of a rock wall. Nic put his hands on a fingerprint reader and leaned in to what Aimee assumed was a retinal scanner. The door slid open almost immediately, and Nic grinned at her. "The security system here is a little more advanced than the one at home."

"Yes, I can see that," Aimee muttered. She wouldn't be cracking this system using an ordinary mirror and a wild-ass guess.

Luke and Diana followed them silently down a hallway lit by buzzing flourescent lights. People in white lab coats rushed about, several of them pausing to greet Nic deferentially, but Nic only nodded in acknowledgment and kept on walking.

They turned a corner and Nic finally stopped at a large door, going through the fingerprint/eye scan routine again. This time, when the green indicator light flashed, he stepped back, pulled open the heavy door, and motioned for Luke, Diana, and Aimee to precede him into the room.

Aimee looked longingly behind her, hoping to find some means of escape, but Nic stepped forward, blocking her route. He put a hand in the small of her back and leaned forward. His breath was warm in her ear when he said, "Come on. I have something I want you to see."

She figured it wouldn't matter if she told him she'd really rather just go now, so, instead, she stepped across the threshold, surprised to find that she was in a large conference room filled with people. Some she recognized from the cocktail party and others she had only seen in newspapers, usually in stories about crime, violence, and death.

The room was blindingly white, with a white U-shaped conference table surrounded by black leather chairs. There were three empty seats at the front left side of the U, presumably having been saved for Aimee, Diana, and Luke.

Nic pulled her behind him to the front of the room, ensconcing her in the chair between Luke and Diana. She folded her hands primly in her lap and crossed her legs, but couldn't stop the shiver that ran through her body.

She did not have a good feeling about this.

Nic straightened his tie as he walked to the center of the room. Aimee had to admit that he had a commanding presence. Everyone, male and female alike, watched him, waiting with hushed anticipation for what he would say or do next. He walked to a large table draped with a bloodred cloth and stood in front of it, and Aimee realized he had chosen his black suit and crimson-flecked tie for the most dramatic affect.

"Welcome to the new headquarters of Sabre Systems," Nic

said to the assembled group, his voice demanding their attention. "As you all know, today marks the beginning of a new direction for Sabre. No longer will you turn to me to simply broker your arms deals. Now you can order the ultimate weapon, direct from Sabre Systems."

With a dramatic whoosh, he yanked the red drape off of the table to reveal a large, black, cone-shaped object.

"This," Nic said, then paused before continuing, "is the LoRS bomb—a long-range missile that can be launched from anywhere in the world and programmed to destroy a specific target. The bomb has been built with the latest stealth technology that allows it to evade detection, but the real innovation is how the missile itself travels. With the aid of a revolutionary propulsion system"—Nic gave Aimee a nod as if to thank her for her part in his scheme—"the LoRS bomb is equipped with a rocket that allows it to exit the Earth's atmosphere. Once the missile reaches an altitude of ninety-three miles above the Earth's surface, it can circle the globe in under ninety minutes. Even if your target discovered the impending attack, which is highly unlikely because of the cloaking mechanisms of the bomb, it would be too late to launch a defense. Furthermore, there's no way to trace it. You will be able to destroy any building at any time with impunity."

The crowd gave a collective gasp before a low hum of whispering began.

Aimee swallowed her own gasp of horror. This was even worse than she and Race had imagined. What would become of civilization if one government—or one person—could launch an attack against another without warning, provocation, or repercussion? It would be the end of the world as they knew it.

Nic held up his hand to stop the chatter. "For today's demonstration, I've chosen two targets. The first is purely professional." Nic flipped a switch and the walls around them instantly changed to television screens, each showing the same clear view of the Washington Monument in Washington, D.C., the gray obelisk mirrored in the reflection pool below. "Because of the distance required for the bomb to travel from here to the United States, we won't see the results of our first launch until the end of today's presentation. But I'm certain you all don't mind waiting," Nic said with a mocking smile, eliciting a round of low laughter from the crowd.

"What about the second target?" Diana asked, her gaze focused intently on Aimee and not on Nic.

Aimee clenched her fingers even tighter, knowing she was not going to like Nic's answer.

Nic casually leaned back against the bomb and crossed his arms over his chest, his gaze also locked on Aimee. "I believe that's up to my fiancée," he said, then raised his chin in the direction of the television screens.

Aimee tore her gaze away from Nic's remorseless dark eyes and looked up at the screens.

"No," she breathed, standing up and walking to the screen as if in a trance.

The camera was focused on a bloodied man's boot, lashed to a chair with a coarse, thick rope. The camera inched upward, revealing bruised shins, knees, a torso. Aimee reached out, touching the scraped and bloodied hands tied to the arms of the chair. She knew those hands, had felt them touch her, caress her, cradle her comfortingly.

"Race," she whispered, just before the camera moved up to show the man's injured face, proving her to be horribly, terribly correct.

She felt Nic's hot breath on her neck, but didn't move her hand, left it resting on Race's on the TV screen. "You know," Nic whispered, lifting her hair off the nape of her neck, "I really loved you."

Aimee watched Race straining against the ropes holding him, as if he could see Nic touching her. She felt Nic's hot breath on her skin, but still, she didn't turn around. She knew now where Nic would send his second bomb and would give anything, even her own life, to save Race.

Turning, Aimee took Nic's hands in her own and eyed him steadily, never more sure of herself than she was at this moment. "If you spare his life, I will devote mine to you. You and Josie will never know that I once cared for this man."

Nic reached down and kissed her softly. "Every time I kiss you, I will know," he said.

"No," Aimee said, squeezing her eyes shut and feeling the

tears drip down her face. "Please don't kill him. I'll do anything you ask."

"Really? Would you . . . love me?"

Aimee opened her eyes, trying to hide the truth that Race was the only man she would ever love, and knowing she'd failed when Nic dropped his hands and released her.

He shook his head sadly and whispered, "I could have given you the world."

Aimee knew it was no use to lie any longer. "I don't want any part of the world you envision."

"Pity," Nic said. Then, turning on his heel, he strode back to the table and hit another button. This time, the television screens showed an ordinary-looking trawler sitting in a bay. Aimee recognized Nic's house behind the fishing boat. Suddenly, there was a flash of light and a dull black object launched itself off of the boat's deck. The trawler rocked back and forth for a moment before settling back on the glassy surface of the harbor.

"Ah, and now let's watch the end of this emotional drama, shall we?" Nic said almost gaily, flipping the view on the screens back to the motel room.

Race's bruised and swollen face filled the screen. Aimee screamed in anguish and ran to the door, trying to get out, to save him, to stop this horror. But the door was locked and no amount of pounding and tugging would get it to open.

Through her sobs, Aimee barely heard Nic's order to Luke and Diana to make her stop, but she did feel the slap across the face Diana gave her after Luke pulled her away from the door and held her with her hands behind her back, forcing her to watch the drama unfolding on the screen.

The camera panned out again to show Race struggling against his bonds. Suddenly, he seemed to still, his attention drawn to something on his right.

A closet door opened and a dark head cautiously poked out, looking around the room, as if fearful of what might be found. Slowly, the door swung open and Josie Sabre stepped out, looking right into the camera with her large, dark eyes, the expression in them unreadable, just like her father's.

THIRTY-SEVEN

"JOSIE," Nic roared, sounding as if the word had been ripped from the very bottom of his soul.

"No," Aimee whispered, with a growing sense of shock. Not Josie, too. She struggled to free herself from Luke's grasp, which had loosened upon seeing Josie in the room with Race.

"Where's Giselle?" Luke asked frantically, shaking his wife's arm when she seemed too stunned to answer.

"She's home. Oh, God. Please let her be home," Diana prayed.

Aimee raced to the front of the silent conference room and grabbed Nic's arm. "Stop it," she ordered frantically. "Make it turn back."

Nic turned to her, his eyes filled with such pain as Aimee had never seen before. "I can't. We were behind schedule and had to focus all of our efforts on the propulsion system. We had no time to perfect a recall mechanism."

Aimee fisted her hands in her hair and dropped to her knees. *No, no.* This couldn't be happening. What was Josie doing with Race?

She looked up in time to see Josie sit down on the bed across from Race. If only she would untie him, they could both escape. Instead, Josie just sat there, unmoving, until the screen went black.

NIC ran to the nearest television screen and ripped at it with his bare hands, his terrible moans making Aimee clap her hands over her ears to try to drown out the sound.

"I killed her," he kept repeating, gouging at the screen as if it were his own eyes that he'd like to tear out.

"Stop it, Nic," Diana ordered, trying to get him to calm down, but Nic had become a madman, picking up chairs and hurling them at the buzzing, blank screens. His potential clients had all stood up and moved away from the spectacle, as if Nic had somehow become infected with a highly contagious disease.

"Nic, please," Luke said, holding down the back of another chair when Nic attempted to pick it up.

With a mad roar, Nic punched his longtime business partner, laying him out cold on the tile floor. Diana instinctively launched herself at Nic. She had to stop him.

Only, Nic saw her coming and grabbed her left arm, twisting it painfully behind her back. "Give me your knife," he hissed in her ear.

"I don't have it," she lied.

"Give it to me," he screamed, jerking her arm up until she feared it would snap.

"All right," she said, then reached down to pull the wicked-looking knife out of the ankle holster she always kept it in. It would be ironic, wouldn't it, if he killed her with her own weapon? And for what? She'd had no part in his daughter's death or in his betrayal by that bitch Aimee. No, it had been she, all along, who had cautioned Nic against getting involved. Look where that had gotten her.

Well, she wasn't going to just give in without a fight.

Twisting around, she made to plunge the knife into Nic's gut . . . only he was too fast for her. But instead of taking the knife from her and killing her, he put his hands over hers and helped her drive the blade so far into his body that the tip came out his back.

Shocked, Diana let go of the knife and took a step backward

while Nic staggered toward her. He started to fall and, belatedly, she held out her arms to stop his forward motion, but it was too late. He fell to his side on the floor, his blood pooling on the white surface.

It only took Diana a moment to regain her wits. She lunged for her husband, who had a gun strapped to his chest under his suit jacket. She pulled it out and held it in front of her, her legs shoulder-width apart, aiming it directly at Aimee's forehead.

"This is all your fault," she accused.

Aimee slowly stood up, her heart so heavy that it almost wasn't worth the effort to move or speak. Never before had she thought that she had nothing to live for, but she felt that way now. With Race gone, all she could see was years of darkness ahead of her, with only work to fill the abyss. What did it matter anymore? What did any of it matter?

"This is your fault," Aimee said wearily. "And your husband's fault, and Nic's fault. All you care about is money. You don't care about the world you live in, or the world your children will inherit. There's no amount of money that could justify what you're doing here. You disgust me."

With that, Aimee finally felt a sense of peace that she'd never felt before. Since she'd been a little girl, she'd struggled for a sense of self-worth. It was what had driven her to do more, to achieve more, to earn more, because she never felt that just being *her* was enough. Suddenly, she realized that it was enough, though. What she did made a difference in the world, whether the world acknowledged that or not. She didn't have to earn as much money as a supermodel or have an appreciative audience or an enormous bank account to prove her worth.

She had worth because she was a good person, because she was a caring friend and a hard worker and a good daughter and a loving sister. Nothing else really mattered.

Aimee stared at Diana, her gaze hard and level. She knew that Diana was going to kill her. Or that she was going to try.

Diana squeezed the trigger just as Aimee dove under the conference table like a batter heading for home plate. She scrambled down the length of the table, her gaze intent on the goal. Diana shot at her again and missed as Aimee reached for the hilt of the knife sticking out of Nic's side. He groaned as she pulled the knife out, but he didn't move.

Aimee tried to dodge another bullet, but felt a searing pain rip into her upper thigh. Damn. The bitch had shot her.

She crab-walked sideways, grabbing the still-unconscious Luke Simonds by the hair and dragging him so that he was nearly on top of her.

Aimee put the knife to Luke's neck and peered out from under the table to find Diana aiming the gun at her husband's head. "Fire again and I'll kill him," Aimee said.

Diana began to lower the gun, then raised it again when the conference door suddenly blasted open with a cloud of smoke that filled the room.

"Everyone drop your weapons. This is the police."

Aimee's grip loosened on the knife. The police? What were they doing here? How had they found the island?

"Aimee? Where the hell are you?"

The knife clattered to the floor when Aimee heard a voice she never thought she'd hear again. "Race? Is that you?"

But before he could answer, there was an explosion and Aimee felt as if a train had run into her chest. She was knocked backward and lay there with Luke Simonds's body draped over her, his blood mingling with hers as his wife was wrestled to the ground.

THIRTY-EIGHT

RACE crouched next to the stretcher in the plane carrying Aimee and the rest of the wounded to the hospital in Townsville. Although her wounds weren't as serious as Nic Sabre's or Luke Simonds's, Race had forced the medic to attend to her first. He hadn't had to put a gun to the EMT's head, but the look in his eyes had told her that he would do so if she didn't do as he ordered.

Those bastards could bleed to death for all he cared.

Slowly.

One fucking drip at a time.

Race gently reached out to hold Aimee's hand, being careful not to jar her injured shoulder. Diana Simonds had been so intent on revenge that she'd shot Aimee through her own husband's body.

Some devoted wife she was.

Aimee's eyes blinked open and she winced from the pain in her shoulder and her thigh. Damn. Getting shot hurt.

"Hey, how are you doing?" Race asked.

Aimee licked her dry lips. "You mean aside from the extra holes in my body that I didn't have this morning?"

Race smoothed the hair away from her face. "Yeah, aside from that," he said tenderly.

"I'm okay. How about you?" She reached up to touch him, but the movement hurt like hell, so she let her arm drop back to the stretcher.

"I'm fine. Just a little banged up."

They were quiet for a time, just drinking in the fact that they'd both survived this ordeal. Then Aimee asked, "What happened? I thought you and Josie . . ." She swallowed and blinked rapidly to hold back the tears, unable to say the words aloud.

"I'm sorry, but that's what we needed Sabre to think, to give us time to launch our counterattack. If he knew that I had escaped from his thugs, he might have altered his plans. That's why I let his goons take me, why I had to hide Josie from them so they wouldn't tell Sabre to stop the demonstration. You see, I found out yesterday the location of Sabre's manufacturing plant."

"How?" Aimee asked.

Race stood up and started pacing, as if the airplane was too small to contain his energy. "In the photos you took, there were bills of lading from a delivery service in Longport. One of the deliveries was for a large amount of cleaning supplies, which didn't make sense if it were just going to Sabre's home, so I asked the guy who runs the service if it was delivered someplace else. I thought I'd hit another dead end when the guy said no, but then he told me something odd."

"What?"

"Well, he said he'd seen the boxes he'd delivered being loaded onto a cart and, when he took off from the airstrip, he saw a boat coming out of nowhere, loaded with those same boxes. He said when you were up in the air, you could see everything for miles. So I asked if he knew where the supplies ended up and he said the boat had headed toward a supposedly uninhabited island and disappeared. He'd flown around for a while, just to make sure the boat hadn't sank, and saw it returning to Sabre's island about half an hour later. He thought it was strange, but nothing that he should report to the authorities."

"Ah, so you called in reinforcements."

"Yes. That's when we discovered the weapons plant. We've been following Sabre's people since yesterday."

"So what about the bomb? Was it intercepted?"

"Yes. We stopped both bombs that Sabre launched," Race said, then flashed her a quick grin. "Although it wouldn't have been such a tragedy to see the Harborside Motel blown to smithereens."

Aimee gave a weak laugh and held out her hand so that Race would take it and stop pacing. He was making her feel guilty for just lying there. "Okay, so what's the rest of the story? How did you get to the island so quickly? Where's Josie?"

"I didn't get to the island so quickly. Not really. We put the film on an hour delay, so what you were seeing happened sixty minutes before it aired. Sabre's goons came to rough me up while Josie—who came to tell me that you belonged to her and her dad now, by the way—hid in the closet. She came out and, after wrestling with her conscience for a few minutes, did the right thing and untied me."

"Good girl," Aimee muttered, squeezing Race's fingers.

"Yes. But it really didn't matter. The rest of my team was waiting for me at the airport. I didn't show at the appointed time and they were already on their way back to get me. That's why we didn't get there in time to stop the launch completely. But we were prepared for an attack in any event."

"And Josie?"

Race's forehead wrinkled and he sighed, obviously troubled. "Well, as you can imagine, this has been really hard on her. She knows what her father has done and she knows how wrong it is, but . . ." Race shrugged. "He's her father."

"Is Nic going to make it?" Aimee asked softly, her heart aching for Josie no matter what the answer might be.

Race glanced away, then looked back at her and said, "It doesn't look good."

"What's going to happen to Josie and Giselle?" Aimee whispered, wishing the girls' parents hadn't put their children in this predicament.

"The child welfare people will try to find out if the girls have other family we don't know about—grandparents or aunts and uncles. If not . . ." Race made a helpless gesture with his hands and they both sighed.

Aimee felt a sudden wave of weariness wash over her. She was so tired—both in mind and in spirit—her soul hurting for the two innocents caught up in the web of their parents' deceit.

"What about us?" she said after a while, opening her eyes again to fix on Race's face. "Do we still have a chance?"

Race's fingers tightened convulsively on hers. "What do you think?" he asked.

Aimee smiled up at him weakly. "I think I love you," she said.

Race leaned down and pressed a feather-light kiss on her lips, one Aimee would have liked to deepen if it didn't hurt so damn much to make the slightest movement. "I think I love you, too," he said.

She let out a deep breath, relieved and exhausted and hopeful, all at the same time. She finally allowed her eyes to close again and her mind to start drifting into unconsciousness. And just before she fell completely asleep, she heard Race whisper, "But just because I love you, that doesn't mean I'm going to let you keep Sabre's ten million dollars."

THIRTY-NINE

Six months later

"AIMEE, Aunt Lauren is here," Josie Sabre shouted up the staircase, like any healthy American teenager would do.

Aimee sighed and covered the mouthpiece of her phone. The problem with having a home office was that sometimes it was too much home and not enough office. Of course, this was like closing the barn door after the horses were already out, or whatever that stupid saying was. The man on the other end of the line was already chuckling.

"Don't worry, I have kids, too," American Trust Bank's president Keith Melman said.

Aimee chuckled, surprised that after only a few short months, she was getting used to having someone assume that Josie was her child. Even more strange, she liked it. It felt so right somehow, just as it had felt right to go through the process of becoming Josie's adoptive mom when they discovered that all the family Josie had had died in the wars between feuding drug lords a decade ago. They had managed to uncover a grandmother in Giselle's family tree, and the woman was delighted to take in the granddaughter she never knew she'd had. Aimee was glad for that—she had never felt the connection with Giselle that she had for Josie, but wouldn't have felt right just throwing the poor kid to the wolves.

She was saddened for a moment, thinking of the tragedy of these girls' lives. Giselle's parents had gone to prison, with Diana Simonds serving two concurrent life sentences for murders traced back to her once the police had her in custody and ran her fingerprints through their system. Luke had fared better, would probably only serve five years of a ten-year sentence for money laundering and tax evasion.

Josie hadn't been so lucky with her one remaining parent. Nic had died in the CIA's custody without ever regaining consciousness. Race had brought them the news the day after Aimee was released from the hospital. She had worried that Josie might blame Race or Aimee for her father's death, but she hadn't. Instead, after a long bout of crying for the father she had lost, she had tentatively taken Aimee's hand and said, "I know my father did some very bad things. But is it okay if I still love him for being my daddy?"

Aimee still teared up, remembering how eagerly Josie had accepted her embrace.

Blinking back tears, Aimee cleared her throat, dabbed at her nose with a tissue, and forced her mind away from her sad memories.

"As I was saying, Mr. Melman, I think my colleague Daphne Donovan would be the perfect fit for your case. She's an ace investigator—can find anyone, anywhere, anytime." A skill Daff had proven by turning up not only Nic Sabre's true identity, but the whereabouts of both Josie's and Giselle's extended families. "She's finishing up a case up in Manhattan right now, but we can have her down in Florida by next week."

"That's great. I'm sure she'll welcome the warmer weather this time of year," the bank president said.

Aimee wasn't quite so certain of that. She suspected that Daff would have moved to the North Pole and lived out her life in frozen misery if she and Raine would let her. But she didn't say that, of course. "I'll give her your contact information. You can expect her in your offices on Monday at nine o'clock," she said before hanging up.

Now, on to her sister. Aimee stretched and stood up, burying her sock-clad feet in the throw rug. The creaky hardwood floors groaned as she made her way out of her office and down the stairs to the kitchen, where, in usual form, Lauren was delighting Josie with tales of her latest exotic photo shoot.

"—and it was so cold that they had to keep spraying me down with warm water so the photos wouldn't show me with goose bumps all over my skin," Lauren said.

Aimee padded into the kitchen and dropped a kiss on her sister's cheek. "Ah, the hardships a supermodel must endure," she teased.

Josie giggled.

"You done for the day? Hi, Lauren," Race said, poking his head into the kitchen. He waved to Lauren, barely sparing her a glance before his gaze landed on Aimee.

Aimee tried not to laugh. Lauren always seemed a little put out that Race wasn't wowed by her beauty like every other man she met. Not in a bad, jealous sort of way. More like momentarily nonplussed at the strangeness of it all.

"Hi, Race," Lauren said back.

Race clicked the mechanical pencil he was holding and turned his gaze to Josie. "Hey, did you finish your math homework yet? I'd be happy to quiz you on the properties of triangles again if you want."

"Thanks, Race, but I think I've got it now. Last night's study session really helped."

"You two are such math geeks," Aimee said, rolling her eyes even though she was secretly delighted at how well Race and Josie got along.

"You're just saying that because you can't tell the difference between an acute triangle and an obtuse one," Race answered with a disdainful sniff and a wink on Josie's direction.

Josie giggled.

"I'll give you obtuse," Aimee growled, grabbing Race by the front of his shirt and pushing him back toward their bedroom, where he had just finished changing after a grueling day of pretending to be a mild-mannered accountant. Aimee waggled her eyebrows at him. "Hey Clark, wanna play superheroes again?"

Race played along, letting her back him up until they reached the bedroom, where he tugged the door closed and then switched roles completely, grabbing her wrists and pushing her up against the wall. "Okay, so are you going to tell me what happened to that ten million dollars or do I have to force it out of you?"

"I told you, you're never going to find it," Aimee all but purred, rubbing her knee along the outside of Race's leg.

"I wouldn't bet on that. You know I'm damn good at tracking down leads," Race said, trailing a line of kisses down her neck and making her shiver.

"Ah, yes. But I'm damn good at covering my tracks," Aimee said. She nudged Race's feet apart and pressed her hips against his. "Besides, I've told you, that money belongs to Josie, and I'm not giving it back. It came from thieves and terrorists and it's the least I could have done for her."

"Hmm, maybe you're right," Race said, sounding distracted as she rubbed against him a little more.

"Anyway," Aimee said, tugging her hands out of Race's grasp and winding them around his neck, where she buried her fingers in his hair. "Your hard-on is jabbing me in the stomach, and I think it would be better if we continued this discussion once we're undressed."

Race kissed her then, long and fierce and full of promise. When he lifted his head, they were both breathing hard. He reached down and put an arm beneath her knees and lifted her as if she weighed no more than an underfed supermodel. Then he tossed her on the bed, grinned, and said, "I couldn't agree more."

Turn the page for a special preview of
Jacey Ford's next novel

DEAD HEAT

Coming soon from Berkley Sensation!

"I thought I'd find you here."

Daphne Donovan didn't bother looking up from her eighty-five-cent cup of coffee as the man slid his stocky frame into the booth across from her. Outwardly she appeared calm and unruffled—uncaring, even—despite the thought that ran through her head: *I'm so busted.* She raised the porcelain cup to her lips, ignoring the heat coming through the too-hot cup and burning her fingertips as she pretended to take a sip.

"I was just following up a final lead before my meeting with the client," Daphne lied without so much as a blink or a flicker of her eyes to give her away.

"What sort of lead?" her brother, ex-NYPD cop and current *New York Times* bestseller Brooks Madison, asked, resting one arm along the top of the booth.

Despite his Ivy League name, Brooks looked more like

a thug than a member of the Republican Party and he was currently leveling his best "Don't give me any shit" look directly at her. It took a lot to intimidate her, however. Certainly one dirty look from the guy she'd hero-worshipped since the day her mother had dragged her reluctantly into the Madison household when she was twelve wasn't enough to do it. Maybe it would have worked if Brooks hadn't always been so nice to her, letting her tag along with him even if it meant he'd had to endure the ridicule of his friends. Daff had often thought Brooks treated her like a three-legged dog—a creature to be mildly pitied despite the fact you sometimes had the urge to tie tin cans to its tail just to see it hop around. But maybe that's just what it felt like to be a little sister. Since she'd been an only child until dear old Mom dropped her off at Brooks's dad's house and then, two months later, pulled the Disappearing Woman act, Daff didn't know if the way she felt about the man she thought of as her brother was normal or not.

Probably not, since nothing in her life had ever been normal.

Daff took a sip of scalding coffee, careful not to let the man across from her know that it was burning her throat as she swallowed. "Yeah, I followed Dean down here yesterday and saw him walk into that electronics store over there," she said, indicating a storefront across the street with her chin. The windows were brightly painted with red hearts and yellow flowers announcing the upcoming Valentine's Day sale. Daff suspected that on February fifteenth, the hearts and flowers would be replaced with cherry trees and stovepipe hats for an upcoming Presidents' Day sale.

"Convenient," Brooks muttered under his breath as the waitress who had brought Daff's coffee sidled up to the table and gave Brooks the once-over about three times.

"What can I get you?" the waitress asked.

Brooks looked across at Daphne and said, "You eaten?" with a quirk of one brow.

Daphne swallowed and curled her fingers around her cup of coffee, fighting a sudden wave of nausea. She couldn't eat here. Just the thought of it made her gag.

Brooks sighed and looked so sad for a moment that Daphne lowered her head to hide the sudden sheen of tears welling up in her eyes. God, she hated that. She was disgusted with both having her brother feel sorry for her and the tears that never seemed far from the surface these days.

"I'll just have coffee," Brooks said, and the waitress disappeared after giving him a disappointed nod.

Desperate not to talk about what was really on both of their minds, Daphne squeezed her cup tighter and blurted, "Dean bought a cheap clock radio. Nothing fancy. Didn't even have a CD player or anything."

Her brother reached out and laid a hand on her arm. "You shouldn't have followed him down here," he said quietly.

Daff clenched her teeth and blinked rapidly to stop the tears from falling into her coffee. "I'm being paid to find out what he did with my client's money. I can't do that if I don't run down my leads."

"I could have checked this one out for you," Brooks said.

Daphne lifted her head to look out the window beyond

her brother's shoulder. The sidewalk outside was filled with the usual array of busy New Yorkers, their eyes straight ahead, hurrying past without looking either right or left. The world was gray, the air filled with a heavy wet dust that seemed to color the people walking past. The occasional car or bus sped by, but traffic seemed lighter, horns honked almost timidly on this stretch of roadway. Beyond the street stretched the gaping hole of the World Trade Center redevelopment site. Progress was slow. From day to day, it was difficult to tell that anything had changed. Yet Daff remembered what it had looked like on September 11, 2001. She remembered the devastation, the heat, the stench. She remembered being overwhelmed by the sheer massiveness of the tragedy. And as one day passed into the next as they searched the rubble, futilely looking for survivors, she remembered thinking that nothing in her world would ever be right again.

"Please tell me you haven't been coming here every day again," Brooks said, sliding back along the booth so that he, too, could see the massive construction site. "You promised me that you had stopped."

Daphne took a swallow of her finally cooled coffee as the waitress arrived with a fresh cup for Brooks. She didn't waste a lot of time placing the cup in front of Daff's brother before disappearing again. The two cups of coffee they'd ordered wouldn't net her more than a buck or two in tips, so why bother?

"I told you, I just came down here to check out what Dean was doing at that electronics shop. I kinda figured him for a high-end-stereo kind of guy and thought maybe he'd be cracking open his secret piggy bank for a new

Bang & Olufsen sound system. Turns out he just needed an alarm clock. And since I'm supposed to be meeting with my client on Water Street in"—Daff paused to glance at her watch, even though she knew exactly what time it was—"forty-three minutes, it didn't make sense to hoof it back to the Upper East Side." This, of course, was a complete lie. Well, maybe not a *complete* lie, because she *was* meeting with her client on Water Street in forty-three minutes. And she *had* followed Joshua Dean to an electronics store yesterday where, as she'd discovered half an hour later after slipping a twenty to the sales guy who had waited on Dean, he'd purchased a plain Jane alarm clock and nothing else. So what if the electronics store was in Greenwich Village and not downtown? And so what if, yes, okay, she *had* been making time in her day to come down to Ground Zero? It was her life. She could spend it however she liked.

For the first few days that she'd been back in Manhattan, she'd been able to stay away. Then, like an alcoholic promising herself that she could stop after just one scotch, she had taken that first sip. Now, six months later, she was addicted again. Her day wasn't complete without a stop at the site of one of the country's greatest tragedies.

A tragedy Daphne could have stopped ... if only she'd been better at her job.

Continue reading for a special preview of
Vickie Taylor's novel

CARVED IN STONE

Also coming soon from Berkley Sensation!

Nothing reminded Nathan Cross he wasn't human so much as an attractive woman watching his every move from across a crowded room. She wasn't a regular at the Chicago Museum of Fine Art's patrons' gala; if she'd attended before, he would've remembered. A woman like her made an impression on a man.

Even a man who wasn't really a man.

She had hair the color of sunshine, as light as his was dark, and she wore it rolled up in an old-fashioned chignon that lent her an air of classic elegance, yet appeared perfectly contemporary, thanks to the tendrils she'd left free to spiral around her face in spindly whorls. Her gown added to the impression of modern sophistication, flowing over her slender body like liquid emeralds, offering just enough shimmer to catch the eye without being gaudy, cut low enough to tantalize without being risqué.

But it was the slit rising above one knee, exposing a stiletto heel secured to her ankle by a single delicate strap, and her long, shapely calf that had Nathan's blood simmering as he waited for her next step . . . and his next glimpse.

Clenching his fist around the fragile stem of his wineglass so tightly he was lucky it didn't shatter, he turned his back on her.

Curse his unholy nature, making him burn for something he couldn't have. He wasn't looking for a woman tonight—any night.

Nathan had only come for the art.

In art, in the muted pastels and dark dashes of oil, the raw emotion, he celebrated mankind's greatest joys, suffered the depths of its despair.

In art, he experienced humanity.

And if art were a cold mistress, she was at least a faithful one. Nathan had been born, lived, and died fourteen times, and through it all she'd remained his constant. Brought him peace in a way no woman could.

In art, he found his solace. Found his soul.

Refusing to spare the temptress in green another thought, he focused on the twelfth century tapestry displayed in front of him. He was reading the placard detailing the history of the hanging—as if he wasn't intimately familiar with its origins—when the scent of rosemary wafted past on a puff of conditioned air. His unnaturally sharp senses identified the fragrance as uniquely hers among the other women's heavier florals and musks and the zesty men's colognes perfuming the gallery.

Helpless to stop himself, he continued to stare at the placard, concentrating more on the shiny surface of the Plexiglas mounting than the writing beneath, until his vision blurred. The glass caught the reflection of the crystal chandelier overhead. Hundreds of individual bulbs coalesced into a single brilliant source, a midnight sun.

The sun bore a channel through time and space. Nathan swayed as his senses left his body, following the light, spilling into the tunnel of Second Sight, a kind of self-hypnosis that allowed him to see things his human eyes could not.

Within seconds the woman's image appeared in his mind's eye. He watched as she glided across the room behind him, wending her way through the gallery with frequent smiles and interludes of small talk among clusters of patrons, stopping a uniformed server for a fresh flute of champagne. She appeared to wander in no particular direction, and yet every click of her heels on the marble floor drew her inexorably closer.

To him.

Tall and lanky, she moved with cultured grace. The emerald pendant bobbing in the hollow of her throat competed with eyes the same color for brilliance—and lost. She would have been the picture of female perfection except for one detail: Above her unflawed eyes, her left eyebrow arched at a slightly higher angle than the right, giving her face a gentle, crooked look he found endearing.

In women, as in art, it was the tiny imperfection that made a good work a masterpiece.

"Magnificent, isn't it?"

Her voice at his shoulder was curiously rough, in opposition to the smooth sophistication of the rest of her. The husky timbre swept the spurious Second Sight image of her from his mind. With some difficulty, he resisted the temptation to turn his head and take a look at the real thing. Instead he studied *Le Combat de Rouen*, the medieval tapestry on loan from Museé de Cluny that he'd come to see tonight. It had been a long time since he'd laid eyes on the pictorial record of the birth of his people.

"It's amazing how clearly the artist portrays the triumph of Christianity over paganism," the woman in green continued.

Nathan rolled the stem of his wineglass between his fingers. "Is that what it portrays?"

"The symbolism is obvious. The dragon is the embodiment of the pagan belief in magic and mythical creatures. The priest kneeling in the middle is using prayer to slay the dragon. Christianity slays paganism."

"Those don't look like prayers tearing that dragon apart with their beaks and fangs and claws to me." He didn't need to look at the tapestry to imagine the beasts doing battle with the dragon. He could hear the roars, taste the blood. He hadn't been there himself, but his forefathers had passed down the memory.

They'd made sure none of his kind ever forgot.

He didn't point out to the woman that the priest knelt in a faint, but visible, pagan circle, that some of the beasts had human faces, or that around the edges of the battle scene, only figures of women and children looked on from the streets of Rouen. The men were notably absent.

The woman rolled her shoulders subtly. "One might assume that the priest used prayer to call upon the beast to do his bidding."

"One might assume that," he allowed. *If one didn't know better.*

Romanus had deceived the villagers of Rouen. Used their own magic to trick them. Their own religion to curse them.

Thanks to the bastard priest's treachery, Nathan and those like him were damned to forever carry a monster inside them, slumbering, but always ready to Awaken.

Always hungry.

Oblivious to the rage rising within him, the woman stared at him with cool green eyes. "The detail is incredible. There's not another work from this period with a range of color like this."

He calmed himself with a deep breath. Romanus was long dead and Nathan was too intrigued by a woman who recognized range of color in a medieval tapestry to ruin this night over something that had happened more than a thousand years ago.

"There is one," he said, aware of the danger of getting drawn into a conversation with her, but not able to stop himself.

"I can't imagine where."

He realized he was staring—and not at the tapestry—but he couldn't bring himself to look away from her. "Tibet."

"Doesn't count." Her eyes were as bright as her smile. "The Easterners had an unfair advantage. Silk thread."

"Unfair or not, they set a standard for color and pattern that the West wouldn't match for another two centuries."

"Three, at least."

"Perhaps."

She raised her glass in salute. "You know your hangings."

"As do you." A fact that honed a fine edge on his already-sharp awareness of her. Too many women cared only for their own beauty these days. Realizing she wasn't one of *them* had desire cracking and snapping like a whip low in his belly.

His breath deepened and the gossamer bouquet of rosemary surrounding her enveloped him, invaded him. Beneath it, his predator's senses caught another, headier scent: feminine awareness. She was interested in him.

He wheeled and strode toward the next exhibit, a gleaming broadsword with a gilded handle, before he completely gave in to this idiocy and asked her name.

Unfortunately, she followed.

She stopped too close behind his shoulder. Invaded his space. His peace of mind.

"Are you a collector or a dealer?" she asked.

"Neither." Although he sold the odd piece from time to time to make ends meet.

"You must be quite a patron of the arts to go all the way to Tibet to visit museums and look at tapestry. Do you travel a lot?"

"When it suits." He didn't bother to correct her assumption that he'd been to the museum in Tibet. The weaving he'd had in mind had hung in a great maharajah's hall; Nathan had been present when the prince unveiled the masterpiece he'd consigned specially for his maharani. But that had been many lifetimes ago. Literally.

"And does it suit often?"

"Often enough."

She frowned, a shallow furrow forming above the bridge of her impertinent nose. "Are you always so forthcoming with information?"

"Do you always ask so many questions?" Her curiosity put a chill on the heat her interest had stoked in him.

Why had a woman like her—educated, poised, socially at ease—singled out a man like him from among the wealthy, erudite snobs milling about to grace with her attention tonight? His body language had stated clearly enough that he wasn't looking for company.

"Just trying to make conversation," she said.

"I'm not much of a conversationalist."

"No kidding."

The flirtatious sheen melted from her green eyes, leaving challenge blazing in its place and confirming his suspicions. She had an agenda. He just didn't know what it was.

Or what to do about it. Especially since he found the fiery reality of the warrior unmasked even more attractive than the façade of civility she'd worn before.

Temptation raked him with her razored claws. His kind were born with two undeniable compulsions: to protect humans from evil and to procreate.

At that moment, he didn't see anyone in need of protecting.

He clasped his hands around the stem of his glass to give them something to do other than twist in the curls that fell around her face in sunny ringlets. While he stood staring at her, the woman huffed out a breath. The furrow between her brows disappeared and her smile returned, somewhat chagrined. She wrinkled her nose ingenuously, and his body tightened like hardening clay.

She shifted her drink to her left hand and extended her right. "Well, now that we've had our first fight, I suppose I should introduce myself. I'm Rachel Vandermere."

Nathan left the delicate fingers untouched, not trusting himself to lay a hand on her. He'd always had a passion for beautiful things, and she was certainly a work of art with her golden hair and bejeweled eyes. But more than beauty drew him to her. There was something familiar about her. Something he recognized on an instinctual level, the way he'd recognized that she—unlike him—wasn't here just for the art, or interested in him simply for his knowledge of ancient hangings.

He felt a connection with her deep inside, weak but palpable. A synchronous vibration, like two tuning forks singing the same key. He almost felt as if his mind could connect to hers if he reached out and tried, the way he could connect with others of his kind, but that was impossible.

There were none of his kind like her. No women, beautiful or otherwise.

The magic that made Nathan what he was passed only to male children. His people depended on human women to bear them sons, but female offspring possessed none of his race's unique characteristics and were considered inconsequential, while male children were highly prized, for producing a son in this life guaranteed rebirth into the next. As soon as a boy child was born and suckled first milk, males of his race left their human mates, taking their sons with them to be raised among the congregation and learn the ways of their people.

Ways no human would understand.

Nathan had lived, died, and lived again many times in this way, but no more. He would not mate in this lifetime. There would be no male child born to him, and the price for this refusal to contribute to the survival of his species would be that his essence would not reincarnate.

This life would be his last, and he would live it alone.

He dragged his shoulders back, feeling the full weight of the course he'd set for himself. Suicide of the soul.

The woman in green still held her hand out toward him.

I'm Rachel Vandermere.

It wasn't a name he'd soon forget. No matter how hard he tried.

Cutting his gaze away from her, he downed the last of his champagne in one gulp. "And I'm late for another engagement," he said, and stomped toward the exit.

THEY'RE EXPERTS IN CRIME—AND PASSION.

Dangerous Curves
by
Jacey Ford

THEY CAN BREACH THE SECURITY AT ANY BANK IN ATLANTA AND STILL BE DONE IN TIME FOR COCKTAILS.

Aimee, Daphne, and Raine are former FBI agents who have started their own security company: Partners in Crime. But when Raine's old boyfriend, Agent Calder Preston, has a job for the Partners, sparks—and bullets—begin to fly.

0-451-19685-2

Available wherever books are sold or at
www.penguin.com

BERKLEY SENSATION
COMING IN MARCH 2005

Mr. Impossible
by Loretta Chase
When a reckless rogue and a beautiful scholar set off to foil a kidnapping, tensions flare—and so does love.

0-425-20150-3

Ashes of Dreams
by Ruth Ryan Langan
In 1880s Kentucky, Amanda Jeffrey is a young widow, left to raise a family and run a farm alone. But when she enlists the help of an Irish immigrant, she finds her long-dormant passion is rising from the ashes.

0-425-20151-1

Total Rush
by Deirdre Martin
New from the bestselling author of *Fair Play*, a story of a new-age girl and a fireman. They couldn't be more different—or any more in love.

0-425-20111-1

For Pete's Sake
by Geri Buckley
Meet Pete. She's a modern-day Southern belle trying to hold her dysfunctional family together, while keeping her love life from falling apart.

0-425-20153-8

Available wherever books are sold or at
www.penguin.com

Penguin Group (USA) Inc. Online

What will you be reading tomorrow?

Tom Clancy, Patricia Cornwell, W.E.B. Griffin,
Nora Roberts, William Gibson, Robin Cook,
Brian Jacques, Catherine Coulter, Stephen King,
Dean Koontz, Ken Follett, Clive Cussler,
Eric Jerome Dickey, John Sandford,
Terry McMillan…

You'll find them all at
http://www.penguin.com

*Read excerpts and newsletters,
find tour schedules, and enter contests.*

Subscribe to Penguin Group (USA) Inc. Newsletters
and get an exclusive inside look
at exciting new titles and the authors you love
long before everyone else does.

PENGUIN GROUP (USA) INC. NEWS
http://www.penguin.com/news